PRAISE FOR
THE SKY WAS OURS

"*The Sky Was Ours* is an immersive fever dream of a novel, beautifully written and boldly imagined. It's a dark fairy tale with a gripping human pulse; attuned to global crisis but also rooted deeply in the psyches of its characters, animated by their grief and most of all by their longing—longing for wonder, escape, transcendence, hope for our profit-rotted world; a longing that soars through these pages with an energy and tenderness utterly its own."

  —Leslie Jamison, *New York Times* bestselling author of
The Empathy Exams

"A fascinating account of, among other things, how the American default to individual action undermines the collective force we must gather to deal with our perilous moment. A very American Icarus!"

  —Bill McKibben, author of *The End of Nature*

"Humane, cinematic, and unstinting in wonder, Fassler's debut—a captivating tale of freedom and disenchantment—asks nothing less than what it might mean to live an uncompromised life in a terribly compromised world. It is a beautiful achievement."   —Hermione Hoby, author of *Virtue*

"With energy and insight, *The Sky Was Ours* probes the twin dreams of human flight and freedom from fossil fuels, following a trio of loners as they strive to bring a new world into existence. In rich, evocative prose, Fassler evokes a sky-wide canvas of emotions: exhilaration, love, greed, grief, and the yearning for transcendence. Bittersweet, life-affirming, and unforgettable."

  —Kyle McCarthy, author of *Everyone
Knows How Much I Love You*

PENGUIN BOOKS

THE SKY WAS OURS

Joe Fassler is a writer and editor based in Denver, Colorado. He is an MFA graduate of the Iowa Writers' Workshop, and his fiction has appeared in *The Boston Review* and *Electric Literature*. In 2013, Fassler started *The Atlantic*'s "By Heart" series, in which he interviewed authors—including Stephen King, Elizabeth Gilbert, Amy Tan, Khaled Hosseini, Carmen Maria Machado, Viet Thanh Nguyen, and more—about the literature that shaped their lives and work. That led to editing *Light the Dark*, a book-length collection that included favorites from "By Heart" alongside new contributions. Fassler's nonfiction has appeared in *The New York Times*, *Wired*, *The Guardian*, *Bloomberg Businessweek*, and *The Best American Food Writing*. *The Sky Was Ours* is his first novel.

joefassler.net

Featuring a Reading Group Discussion Guide

THE

SKY

WAS

OURS

JOE
FASSLER

PENGUIN
BOOKS

PENGUIN BOOKS

An imprint of Penguin Random House LLC
penguinrandomhouse.com

"I Can't Help You," by Ryszard Krynicki, translated by Clare
Cavanagh, from *Magnetic Point*, copyright © 2017 by Ryszard
Krynicki. Translation copyright © 2017 by Clare Cavanagh.
Reprinted by permission of
New Directions Publishing Corp.

LIBRARY OF CONGRESS CATALOGING-IN-PUBLICATION DATA
Names: Fassler, Joe, author.
Title: The sky was ours / Joe Fassler.
Description: [New York] : Penguin Books, 2024.
Identifiers: LCCN 2023038439 (print) | LCCN 2023038440 (ebook) |
ISBN 9780143135685 (trade paperback) |
ISBN 9780525507390 (ebook)
Subjects: LCGFT: Novels.
Classification: LCC PS3606.A777 S59 2024 (print) |
LCC PS3606.A777 (ebook) | DDC 813/.6--dc23/eng/20231117
LC record available at https://lccn.loc.gov/2023038439
LC ebook record available at https://lccn.loc.gov/2023038440

Printed in the United States of America
1st Printing

Set in Haarlemmer MT Pro with Chronicle Display Condensed
Designed by Sabrina Bowers

For Rachel, and for Luke

I am learning to fly . . . no one is
teaching me.

—OCTAVIA E. BUTLER

Why, in the face of every warning,
have we been unable to act?

—CHARLES A. REICH

THE

SKY

WAS

OURS

PART
ONE

The maze was so hard to navigate that
even Daedalus struggled to find his way
back through it.

—OVID, *METAMORPHOSES*

The border between the unresolvable and
the unlivable is not marked; one often
crosses it without knowing it.

—YIYUN LI

ONE

If you lived upstate the summer I went missing, you definitely saw my picture on TV. The papers ran headlines like "Student Vanishes from Campus" and "Find Jane: Search for Classmate Turns Up Empty." It was the kind of sad bit you notice and forget, dark but not extraordinary. Ithaca is a college town built across a network of gorges, after all, and kids sometimes get swallowed. It's terrible, but it's simply what happens when you take thousands of drunk twenty-somethings, crank up the academic pressure, and make them live on top of a bunch of ravines.

After a few days of silence, the bodies usually turn up. The weird thing, in my case, was that after a month—more—I still hadn't been found.

❧

It started with a bad decision I made, once upon a time: to cast my lot with an intensive postgrad program in computer science. Partridge University—the few, the proud. It was a barely accredited private school on the north side of town, technically Cayuga Heights, where Ithaca's funky hippie vibe surrendered to corporate office parks and skittish white-tailed deer. The campus emerged from the woods off Triphammer Road, the original home of a seminary that had lost its financial way, and the buildings were cheap, with hallways that smelled like iron and dust. Sometimes I thought I could still sense them in the restless air, the previous tenants and their worries about god. When you left through the side door of Building D, you could catch a glimpse of Cayuga Lake in the distance—the water like the flat, blinding surface of a mirror in the sun.

Partridge was the last place on earth I would've ever imagined myself, but I was trying to be practical. I'd spent my undergraduate years laying track to become an English professor, my grand plan to sidestep the soul-deadening rhythms of office life and rush-hour traffic. Even this modest, book-sodden dream somehow escaped my reach. In the spring of senior year, eleven different PhD programs rejected me. The flimsy little envelopes that came weighed nothing and crackled with cellophane and seemed to have no idea how much they hurt.

So instead of wandering through the library searching for overlooked monographs, I subjected myself to two-hour coding sprints. Instead of lavishing a critic's care on sentences I loved, I was reading *Extreme Success: How U.S. Army Green Berets Lead and Win*, required reading for all incoming students. I was learning languages no human tongue could speak. It wasn't what I'd ever wanted for myself. But this was how it happened, I realized. You spent your childhood thinking you'd blaze your own trail, believing that the path ahead is up to you, only to grow up and find out it's the opposite. Life takes the wheel, shunting you into places you'd never willingly go. It happens subtly, right? The wide-open world becomes a road that becomes a tunnel, which then becomes a room, or seems to be, until the day you notice how much the walls have narrowed, and you realize you've been living in a cage.

I set my alarm for six-thirty every weekday. Enough time to sway in the shower with my eyes closed, holding on to the tendril-ends of a dream until the water ran cold. Dressed, ready, I'd light the day's first cigarette on the porch and check in with the trees: they were going to sleep for the year already, their leaves flaming up briefly before flittering down toward the gutters. Then I'd start the two-mile uphill walk to school. A travel mug of coffee in one hand and a first-generation iPod in the other, the kind with an Etch-A-Sketch screen. I can almost see myself as I was then, like a movie of someone else's life. My backpack freighted with textbooks, my ears muffled with headphones. Listening over and over again to the same Elliott Smith song, the one with the ambiguous line—*You can do what you want to, there's no one to stop you*—that was either a wish or a warning.

～

The computer science classes were a recalibration, a way to forget the aimless year I spent after college waiting tables in New York, banished from the only future I'd prepared for. They had the enthusiastic approval of my father, who'd always warned me that the real-world usefulness of my English major would quickly wilt and rot, a degree with the shelf life of bruised fruit. I'd always ignored him, tuning out his insistence that coding skills would be like basic literacy in the twenty-first century economy. Yes, we were in the first seasons of a new millennium—but wasn't everything basically the same? I only knew that the dot-com bubble had burst, that computers still felt like quaint little things, and that I was headed to grad school, a magical land where nothing really mattered except returning your library books.

Then I didn't get in.

To his credit, he didn't start in on me right away. I'd moved to Brooklyn and had worked at the restaurant six months when pamphlets started coming in the mail. Campus photos, glossy and well lit. Brick buildings sweatered in ivy. My name, printed neatly on the label. "Recent grad," one of them read, "your journey isn't over yet!"

At first the flood of mail was unnerving, inexplicable—like a sign from god, though no god you wanted to believe in. I threw them in the trash, fine stock and triple-folds and all, without ever looking too closely. But the volume only increased, as if a spigot had been turned on somewhere. Before long, it was enough to spook my roommates. What was happening? they asked. What was all this mail? I could only tell them that I didn't know.

Then my dad confessed. Casually, like he wasn't totally sure he *was* confessing. Had I received any interesting solicitations? he wondered. He'd put my name on some lists.

It was late morning on a Friday, and I was getting dressed for work, my flip phone sandwiched between my shoulder and my ear. I couldn't believe it, though I don't know why I hadn't seen it sooner.

"You shouldn't have done that," I said, my voice shaking a little. "Why wouldn't you ask me first?"

"I still don't see the harm in it," he said mildly, as if he were being perfectly reasonable while I was causing a scene.

"Because it's *my* name!" I said. "It's my address! It's my life!"

"What's wrong with a little more information?"

"Information I never asked for," I said. "I'm just going to keep getting this stuff forever?"

"I doubt it," he said. "You'll age out of their target demographic."

"What *problem* are you trying to solve?"

"No problem," he said. A pause. "I just want you to be happy."

"Well."

"*Are* you happy?"

"I'm figuring it out."

"And how long does that take?" he said. "Figuring it out?"

"How could I possibly know that?"

"You have to *try* things," he said. "You can't just expect the answers to arrive at your doorstep. The heavens opening. You've got to *try* first. If something doesn't work out, okay. Now you cross that off your list, and guess what—you got to know yourself a little better in the process."

Except my problem wasn't a lack of self-knowledge. I already knew what I wanted, and kind of always had. What I desired most was a certain cast of life, a way of being that's nothing like the way we're asked to be. It's a feeling I associate with being younger, when I could lose myself in books all Saturday, before I realized how miraculous it was that you could hallucinate vividly for hours simply by running your eyes over some words on paper, whole worlds born and falling away inside your mind. It didn't seem so unreasonable to try to preserve that feeling, to keep it sacred if you could—and maybe even take part in the alchemy yourself, one day, by authoring a printed incantation that might touch a lonely girl sitting tear-streaked on the floor, retreating to her bedroom after an argument with her father. Something about reading would make her feel better, as I'd felt better. Once you understood that magic was actually possible, that it was real, why would you ever need anything else?

In my quieter moments, I could admit that, maybe, my obsession with grad school wasn't really about grad school at all—that it was simply a back door, a way to professionalize and validate the experience I craved. Which was what? To give myself the time to simply *be*, to live, to think, to wander, and to read—and read, and read some more—and see what finally came of it one day. My problem wasn't that I didn't understand this. It was that the entire world had been designed to make the yearned-for life impossible, it was that other things were always intervening.

My father was right, I wasn't happy. But at first I saw no need to rush off into another life. What feels abundant, people squander, and I was rich in time—so young the word "someday" still had a sweet, palliative pull. Eventually, I'd impose a larger narrative on my days, but I didn't have to yet, and that was a relief. There were orders to take and plates to carry, paychecks waiting at the end. I let my mind fill up with ephemera—new menu items, every table's allergens, ingredients Chef had eighty-sixed. I tried to take pleasure in pouring a perfect glass of wine, that subtle turn of my wrist.

Entire seasons passed that way, short and vivid as pop songs. Except now and then, as I was getting dressed for work, I'd notice a certain slant to the light and hesitate, turning toward the window to peer at the sky, suddenly pained by how quickly the day was passing. Or I might catch a glimpse of my father's pamphlets—which had started to pile up unopened on my desk—and feel weirdly unmoored, as if an important errand had slipped my mind and remained undone too long.

Then, a specific morning. I'd stayed out late with the staff the night before, and I had a hangover, one that was intensified by the unbearable suspicion I'd made a fool of myself somehow, though the details were lost to the night. My body hurt, literally from my head down to my toes. A pair of too-cheap shoes was slowly destroying my feet—I hadn't realized it was the shoes yet, I just thought I was getting old—and I woke up every morning with a screaming pain in my arches that peaked as I got out of bed, relenting only slightly as I hobbled down the hall to the toilet.

I do wonder what would have happened—how it all might have been different—if I hadn't bought that pair of shoes. Because on that morning it was the pain that stopped me, the raw, physical insistence that something had to change. I would have done anything to avoid the train, the unending underground walkway at Bryant Park. As I pulled a shirt down over my head, my gaze fell across the stacks of brochures on my desk. A row of campus buildings somewhere, young people playing Frisbee in the sun.

I skipped work that day for the first time, pushing my phone away when the texts started to come in. I pulled the applications up on my laptop, delighted to find that most places accepted applications on a rolling basis. My FAFSA status was still current. There was nothing in the way. I could see it all unfold before me: I would ride the coming tech boom I'd been promised, transmute loan money into real money with hard skills, and, sustained by lucrative part-time contract work, I'd figure out the larger problem of my life.

I stayed up until five in the morning finishing, the kind of vigorous rush I hadn't mustered since college. It didn't last. I woke up the next day and regretted everything, slinking back into work with my eyes bleary and my absence unexcused. Doubt crept in; I wasn't sure anymore. I'd almost forgotten the whole thing entirely when the first acceptance letter came, a startling blue volt of pleasure. I learned something about myself then: I'd go anywhere, if only it meant I was wanted.

~

In the beginning, I went to class on time, did all the assigned reading, and completed endless sprints in Python, PHP, and C. From my seat in the front row, I took notes with an expensive mechanical pencil—one that made such fine, precise lines that I'd sometimes marvel at the beauty of my own handwriting, which I'd known my whole life, but had never seemed a model of elegance and order until then. My notebooks were so new and crisp that their pages sliced my fingers with surprising frequency, secret little cuts that opened like fish gills and stung more than they should. I tried not to mind. I was exploring a new theory about pain: if you acknowledged it, if you learned to live with it, it was only what it was.

The curriculum had been designed to possess you completely. It was a four-year degree crammed into eighteen months, an intensive schedule that meant class all day and assignments all night, and no time left for anything else. Not that I was tempted to socialize—my classmates, it's safe to say, were not my people. I was the only woman, for one thing. I felt more like a different species. They grouped outside the classroom doors, chattering in little cliques, and would fall silent each morning as I approached. To them I was more strange than anything, more unsettling than interesting, like the sight of a lone flamingo padding down the hall.

Still, there was something almost consoling about my first few months at Partridge. I'd winnowed my existence down to a manageable scope, for once, set free from the oppressive questions of what to do and how to be. I was busy. Coding had an obstinate logic I could learn. And I had plenty of money, at least superficially. At the start of every quarter, funds showed up in my account, like magic. The thrill of that was so wonderful it was easy to forget they were a mix of private and federally unsubsidized loans, every dime of which I'd have to pay back with interest. I felt rich enough to buy organic vegetables, decent wine, and a gym membership. I could even afford an ongoing misadventure that cost me hundreds of bucks in gas: a long-distance affair with Bruce, my poetry professor from college, my only concession to disorder.

Bruce and I met at motels, inns, and lodges in all the weird Catskills towns, places halfway between Ithaca and Manhattan, where he lived. He always paid for the room, which was fair, since I was in my twenties and he was in his forties, and since he had family money while I was piling up debt. I wondered what they made of us, the hotel clerks and concierges.

The glaring difference in our ages, no sign of travelers' luggage. If it was just a night or two, I could pack all my stuff in a tote.

Sometimes I missed school because of Bruce. But aside from that, I was a model student, if not a naturally gifted one. I worked hard. I went to class, finished my assignments, and fueled myself enough on food and rest to do it all again the next day. It was only at night that the composed face I showed to the world sometimes dissolved. I could lie for hours in the darkness watching the black blur of the ceiling fan. My sleep felt thin and cobwebby, a flimsy hammock I was always slipping through into wakefulness. I had an odd recurring dream where I'd start at my computer screen trying to code, except the markup had baffling hieroglyphics sprinkled through it—owls, scissors, strange glittering eyes. In life, and in sleep, I applied the full force of my brain to the problems I was given. And when I scraped by with Bs and As in the first few months, I dared to wish that I might pull it off—extreme success, or whatever getting better meant.

⤙

When my apartment started to feel too small, I'd gather my stuff and head for a coffee shop down the block, a vegan place called the Compassionate Cup. The food was terrible, the coffee scorched and cloying with soy milk, everything overpriced and self-hating. Something was very wrong with their scones, which had the dry, crumbly texture of sand. But it helped to get out of my own space for a while—abandon my desk for a quiet space with good light and a two-minute commute.

That was where I met Zena, the barista who poured the buckwheat waffles, who steamed the soy milk lattes. Zena was the opposite of the world on my laptop screen, the cold universe of numbers, of if/thens, of unyielding rules. She was bleached white hair with lavender streaks. She was a jeweled stud sparkling in one nostril. She was bright swag pins that clicked against each other on her pilot's jacket when she moved. Sometimes I'd look up from my work and catch her watching me from behind the counter, an amused expression on her face. She seemed to sense some inherent comedy in everything I did, as if she saw what I couldn't: the absurdity of a person trying so hard to be something they're not.

Zena was determined to be my friend, and came at me with a persistence I didn't understand. Even my bulky headphones weren't enough to dissuade her—she'd touch my shoulder, start talking through the music. When work was slow, she'd sometimes join me on my cigarette breaks. We'd lean up against the large plate-glass window together, smoking. She'd quit a few years back, she said, and had solemnly sworn never to spend another dollar on tobacco products. But her promise had a loophole: she could still bum smokes from other people, which meant she was always bumming them from me.

"You're going to kill yourself with these things," she said, the first time she lit one of my hand-rolled, unfiltered specials. "Damn. You smoke *how* many of these a day?"

Yet her eyes narrowed with pleasure as she inhaled, the cinder crackling, and I liked how much she liked it.

I probably shouldn't have given her my number. It could be the middle of the weekend, and I'd be elbow-deep in an assignment, when my phone would buzz, shimmying in a half circle on the table. Something was always going on. Cops had cleared the Jungle, a tent community that had existed peacefully by the railway tracks for years, seizing possessions and forcing people out. An Ithaca High student had complained of racial harassment, and instead of acting the district covered the incident up. There was a rally, there was a protest. Was I coming?

I wasn't sure. I had to work. I didn't think I could.

But I did feel, sometimes, like I had to do something. It was the middle of the Bush years, his two wars premised on maddening lies. There was this sense of decency slipping away, of something too obscene to be named—especially after the Abu Ghraib revelations, which had come out the year before. I forced myself to look at all the pictures in the paper, even though I didn't want to. Some vague sense of complicity, witnessing as asking for forgiveness. They haunted me for months, those pictures, coming back at the oddest times to disturb the day. I couldn't imagine anything worse than torture—to be at the mercy of someone who wanted to hurt you, who could do with your body whatever they wanted, extract from you whatever they wanted.

Zena raged constantly about the war.

"They're bombing *children*," she'd say. "Children."

And it was true. But I just felt frozen somehow, unsure where to put my anger. This sense of looming defeat, the battle already lost before it started. The systems that confined us were too powerful already, so mighty and coercive that people had already stopped fighting against them, had forgotten that they could. Me, too. I trudged dutifully every day to a school with an absurd name, to take classes I resented, paid for with money I didn't have, all in the name of pursuing a theoretically better future that might not really exist. Where did you start, when you were that far gone? There was so much I wanted to change about the world—god, how I wanted to change it—but I couldn't even fix myself.

"What can we actually do about any of it?" I asked her once, exasperated. "Like *actually* do?"

She took a drag, sizing me up.

"There are things," she said, mysteriously.

"Like what?"

She returned my stare with a hard, significant look, and I sensed it was an offer of some kind. She was willing to draw me into something darker and more complicated, if I wanted. But I was at Partridge to let go of what I wanted, and I let the moment pass.

Two

For the first time in my life, I didn't go home over winter break. I told my family I needed to stay at school to keep studying, a lie that felt true: the specialized language I'd learned, all laden with question marks and parentheses, was a cathedral I'd built stone by stone with my mind, and held together through sheer will, and I feared that if I took my attention away for even a second, the whole thing would fall down around me in a crash of mortar and rubble.

I spent much of the break lying on my bed, overwhelmed with relief that the term had ended, trying to guard my brain against anything that could push the code out. My tiny pine-box bedroom had no windows, and there was nothing to look at except a few old cobwebs on the ceiling, these dangling wisps of dirty silk. But that was enough, really: to watch them fluff and blow, animated by air from the heating grate.

It was a lonely time. I left my room on Christmas Day to buy some apples from the convenience store that never closed, a cave with the wooden floors of an old saloon. The streets were cold and deserted, and I remember feeling kinship with the few stray strangers who were out. As our eyes met and darted away again, recognition flitted between us: *You, too, are alone on a day like this.*

I called my brother a few times, trying to feel him in the long gaps of silence on the other end. I wanted to see Bruce, but he was busy with family stuff all through the holidays, locked into the encompassing choreography of life after divorce. He didn't seem to understand the power he had over me. How afraid I was that, without him, I'd slowly forget the person I'd been, back when my whole life still seemed to radiate with promise.

He finally agreed to meet me at the most inconvenient time, a random Wednesday night after the new semester had started. I'd checked into the hotel early and was at the little desk trying to work when I heard his keycard in the slot. The door opened, and there he was: standing with the snow still melting on the shoulders of his jacket, a smile on his exquisite, fine-boned face. He was achingly pretty, the way that only smaller men seem to manage, a feature he tried to hide halfway with his salt-and-auburn beard.

"Sorry I'm late," he said, grinning, because he was always late. He was carrying a bouquet, the same pale lilies he typically arrived with, picked up at some bodega on his way. Like everything in our relationship, the flowers were symbolic: a callback to the lily-heavy set design of Nirvana's *Unplugged in New York* concert, a record I'd adored since I was twelve. Early on, it astonished me to learn that Bruce had actually seen the show in person. This was a marvel that defied belief, like someone saying they'd flown to heaven in a plane. The explanation was mundane—in 1993, he'd been a youngish Manhattan native with the right connections and his ear to the ground. Still, the fact that he'd actually *been* there filled me with a reverence that mutated over time into envy and anger, a twist of feeling so forceful and complex it made my stomach hurt.

That night, we lay in bed eating an enormous pile of french fries on a white room-service platter, complete with a single-use glass bottle of Heinz ketchup. We'd smoked the joint Bruce had brought with him, and with the window open to let the smoke out, the room was way too cold. He'd pulled one of my textbooks off the desk, which was close enough that he could reach it from the bed, and started aimlessly flipping through it.

"*Look* at this," he said, shaking his head. "You're telling me you can actually read this?"

"You don't really read it," I said. "It's not language, really. It's more like . . . an operation. But, yeah."

I felt too high.

"There's so *much* of it," he said.

"So much of what?"

"So much punctuation. It's all punctuation!"

"They all have different functions," I said. "And intense names. *Delimiters, separators.*"

I lowered my voice robotically.

"*Terminators.*"

"God," he said, astounded, turning another page. "I can see why you hate it."

I shrugged. It was true. I'd procrastinate sometimes by writing Bruce emails—long, clever letters that spelled out the precise nature of my hatred. I detailed the absurdities of life at Partridge, which I mockingly called "Computer School," skewering my classmates' pretentiousness and tech baron aspirations. I wrote about the whole experience as if I were a castaway stranded on an unfamiliar island, reduced to drudgery and plagued by misfortune, but stubbornly determined to survive. Bruce mostly didn't respond to these dispatches, though he'd sometimes comment on a line or two to prove he'd read them. I think we both knew the emails were really for me.

"Ugh," he said, closing the book. "Wow. That made my *soul* hurt."

He was starting to irk me. The blunt dismissal of an entire field of science. Yes, I'd entrusted him with all my secret loathing, but I didn't want it mirrored back. It was for me, not for Bruce, to say what I despised.

He peered at me, earnest and stoned.

"Is there any poetry to it?" he asked.

"Poetry?"

"Yeah," he said. "Any beauty? Is there artfulness?"

He was almost pleading with me, really wanting to know. He wanted reassurance that I wasn't a totally lost cause, that I'd found some meaning in the thing I'd gone and done.

I thought about it for a second before I felt myself shut down.

"I guess I'd have to ask you," I said. "I'm not qualified to discuss poetry."

His face changed.

"Come on," he said.

"I'm not."

I couldn't help the iron in my tone.

"Janey," he said. "What?"

"What?" I shot back.

"You're mad?"

"No."

He sighed.

"So we're here again," he said. "With your not going back to school."

"I *am* back in school," I said, though it wasn't what he meant.

"I still don't see why you don't reapply," he said. "You should be back in school, and not for computer science."

"I guess eleven universities would disagree."

"That," he said. He laughed softly. "Come on—it happens! You gave up too easily. A lot of people don't get in the first time around."

"The verdict seemed pretty clear to me."

"Come on," he said again. "You would have gotten in."

"Well," I said, a black scrim sliding over my mood. Then I stopped. Something was off.

"*Would* have?"

I'd reflexively agreed with him, but the words hit on a delay, and I realized I had no idea what he was saying.

"What do you mean, would have?"

I turned and looked at him dead-on, assuming there'd be some simple explanation. Instead, Bruce's face went completely slack.

"Should have," he said, trying to recover. The cartilage bobbed once in this throat. "You *should* have gotten in."

"That's not what you said."

"It's what I meant."

This wasn't the reaction I'd expected. I'd seen enough, though. I knew what was happening, even if I didn't know why.

"You're lying," I said.

The look on his face as good as a confession. I sensed the presence of some dark truth hidden under his tongue like a stone.

It wasn't easy, but I pried it from him.

❧

Bruce's academic specialty was American poetry from 1950 to present, and he especially loved Kenneth Koch, John Ashbery, and the New York School's other clever men. Specifically, he wrote about what he called "lines of transmission"—subterranean forms of artistic influence that stemmed more from parties, fevered late-night conversations, and pillow talk than anything on the published page. "There *is* no art," he once claimed to me, absurdly. "There's only people, and what they owe each other."

I felt some curiosity about his intensely biographical approach to criticism, the way he scoured correspondence and personal archives for unpublished anecdotes. But I could also see he spent more time looking for evidence of friendships and trysts than he did analyzing poems, and the whole thing could seem like a highbrow kind of gossip.

Bruce's central scholarly accomplishment had been to demonstrate the ways Frank O'Hara's death and packed 1966 funeral had influenced a range of contemporaneous poems and paintings—the topic of the single slim book he'd written for an academic press. So he was an odd choice for my thesis committee, since I was writing about the language of trauma in *Moby-Dick*. But by then we were spending so much time together. In his campus office. In the mostly empty uptown studio he rented as a *second* office, the book-lined walls surrounding nothing but a desk, a coffeemaker, and a bed. We met in unfashionable cafés and bars, places where we could perch on the stools with our knees touching, or kiss with the taste of whiskey on our lips, and never be seen by anyone we knew. It was risky to have him on my committee, we both knew that. And yet I also wanted an official connection to him, a formal role others would recognize and accept—even if it was only a proxy for the bigger, deeper, more complicated thing, these lines of transmission between us.

I would need an ally, as it turned out. The problem was Professor Devin Flood, our department chair, who *had* to be on my committee since he was the faculty's only Melvillean. Flood was oddly distressed about my interest in creative writing, and he'd warned me repeatedly about taking too many "liberties" with my thesis. What he didn't get was that the paper's somewhat unorthodox style was a tribute to Charles Olson's *Call Me Ishmael*, a strange, hallucinatory book that Bruce had handed me early on, and which turned out to be everything. Olson had helped establish that there had been two *Moby-Dick*s: the one that Melville published, but also an earlier one that he abandoned almost completely when he started reading Shakespeare, a creative epiphany that sent wild, King

James–inflected English spilling from his pen. I argued that *Moby-Dick* is, functionally, a palimpsest, a formal quality that mirrors its depiction of trauma—trauma, this force that annihilates the self and rewrites a new, unstable identity on top of it, the new self reaching endlessly for the old self the way a myth reaches for truth.

At every turn, Flood was there, trying to rein me in. When I added more academic sources to appease him, he claimed they were the wrong ones. He dismissed Derrida as "vain and incomprehensible." Mostly, he insisted that I write in a style he called "plain scholar's English," and seemed offended when I asked if that wasn't an oxymoron. Sometimes as he lectured me my mind would go to a faraway place, and I would think only of telling Bruce about the exasperated way he tugged at his beard, as if to punish it for not being longer.

But if I was stubborn, Flood was more stubborn. Bruce forwarded me an email Flood had written the committee after our mid-year check-in:

> Our job here is to evaluate this work in terms of its scholarly merit. What we've asked young Jane to do is demonstrate her ability to perform according to the expectations of our discipline. While she may feel she's a poet, she has no credentials as a poet. And yet I see no evidence she can, or even wants to, produce work that conforms to the professional standards of our field. In that critical regard, this work is so far insufficient. And I think we would send Jane a dangerous message by signaling otherwise.

Bruce and I mostly laughed it off. The old goat. He was outnumbered and outgunned: My incredible adviser, Debra Singer—who wrote the definitive biography of Margaret Fuller, and edited the Norton Critical Edition of *The Morgesons*—was completely behind me. And I had Bruce. There was nothing to worry about.

But that night in the hotel, as I forced Bruce to tell me everything, it turned out I'd had plenty to worry about. He was too high to lie, and in a gravelly, penitent voice spilled the whole steaming cauldron of beans.

In the end, I'd asked Flood for a recommendation. Everyone said I had to. To not have one from my school's only Melville scholar—someone so distinguished, who'd been on my committee—would look weird. So I did it. Flood assured me he'd write a fair one. And I thought we'd worked it out between us, some kind of tentative truce.

But Flood, it turned out, hadn't been finished with me. He told people that I was bright, articulate, impressive, with all the makings of a promising young scholar. But, also, he said, I didn't have the maturity. He suggested schools take my candidacy seriously, and also that they not accept me—yet.

"Let her take a year or two in the real world," he wrote. "See if she comes back. Then we'll know she means it."

English department people, for all their radical politics, are bureaucrats at heart. They tend to love hierarchy, and abhor uncertainty and risk. In Bruce's view, one chiding letter had been enough.

As Bruce told me all this, I gradually fell silent. The pot had started to turn on us, and I felt sick. Bruce had the covers pulled up to his chin, a spooked look on his face, as if he'd just told a ghost story and had even scared himself. I stared at him in the glow of the bedside lamp. The TV was still on, muted, the screen throwing unsteady blue light across his face.

"Why didn't you *tell* me?" I said finally, my voice rising.

"I *am* telling you!"

"Yeah," I said. "Now!"

My legs kept shivering, the room so cold. I clutched at my knees to still them.

"How long have you *known*?" I said. I almost howled it.

He looked vacantly down the length of the bed.

"I don't know," he said, his tone all hollow, as if I'd really asked a much more complicated and profound question, something about god or death, the kind no one can answer, the kind that might have no answer.

"How long?"

"Janey."

"Tell me!"

He looked away.

"It was too late," he said. "It was already too late."

He was lying again. His words hung in the air like a fart.

"Why didn't you *do* something?"

"Me?" Bruce said, surprise edging into his voice for the first time. "What was *I* going to do?"

"To start with," I said, "maybe not let him write the completely fucked-up letter that ruined my life?"

"I didn't have a say. It was his letter."

"You could have stopped him—"

"What could *I* have done?" he said. "I mean, consider the position I'm in—"

I think I was crying then. I hid my face in my hands.

"Janey," he said. "Jane. Don't *be* like this."

I felt him place his hand on my shoulder in the darkness.

"You . . . should be happy!"

"*Happy?*" I said. The word burst out of me, an incredulous sob.

"Isn't it better to know you deserved it?"

⌘

I woke up feeling tired and scraped out, as if someone had drained the blood from me, victim of a vampire's kiss. I opened my eyes and saw the lilies on the table before anything else, the air still heavy with their smell. The last stubborn buds had opened, their starfish limbs spreading, undone by a night's soak in the ice bucket we'd used as a vase. I peered at them a second and then everything came crashing back—the betrayal of it, the outrage, the unbearable term I'd been forced to serve for the crime of being myself.

It was early, I could tell by the light. Bruce lay next to me, out cold. The thought of waking up with him sickened me. I only knew I had to leave as fast as possible, put as much physical distance between us as I could. As if the room had become the site of a nuclear meltdown, everything radioactive. The malignant, invisible power enough to make your cells go berserk, to split your skin with sores.

I pulled the sheets away in a subtle lift. I dressed, and gathered my things, moving with the briskness of a thief. And then I was in the hallway, my warm jacket on and my suitcase beside me, looking back at him. Or what I could see of him, given the cast of the room—a single bare foot sticking out past the edge of the blanket, the bony knob of his ankle.

I paused there for a second, wondering what to do. I wanted to shut the door, a gesture with some finality to it. But the electronic whir and thump of the lock might wake him, and that would make things harder. I lingered until his legs shifted drowsily, rustling the covers—for an awful moment I thought he might sit up and see me. But then he went still. My heart lurched, the decision made. I turned and ran down the corridor with the door still open, into a post-Bruce life.

❧

The cars in the lot all looked vaguely the same, their features hooded with fresh, erasing snow. So it took a minute to spot mine—the white '92 Saab Turbo I'd bought from a Craigslister in Hoboken before leaving New York. It stood out thanks to a piece of gear the previous owner hadn't removed: a kayak rack, two steel bars jutting crosswise from the roof. It was an odd feature for me, since I'd never even seen a kayak—but apparently it was a top-of-the-line model, and the guy had been very excited about it.

"Honestly, for the price you're paying," he'd said, "it's like you're buying the 'yak rack and getting the car for *free*."

This wasn't the selling point he thought it was. But I'd found the Saab to be punchy and basically dependable, despite its whacked-out alignment—it would drift toward the shoulder if you let it, like a ghost had taken the wheel. I'd even started to feel fondly toward the boat rack, this accessory I couldn't use and hadn't wanted. It came to be what gave the Saab its me-ness, somehow. We find ourselves in what we didn't choose.

I brushed the snow from the windows and mirrors, glancing back now and then at the inn, bracing myself for Bruce to come skidding out the door after me. He never did, and then I was driving, though I didn't even make it to the highway before I fell apart.

࿔

By the time Bruce called, I was still in a gas station parking lot, trying to collect myself. So he'd finally woken up. I let the phone ring out, shivering unanswered on the dash. My stomach ached as if I'd eaten something rotten, the rage and shame as searing as a stomach flu. The way they all clearly *knew* about it—saying nothing to me, thick as thieves—made me want to curl up, close my eyes, and power down, my mind blipping out for good.

He called again, and when my phone stopped ringing, I shut it off. The next time, he'd get my voice mail, and that was how he'd know it was over.

What was over, exactly? I didn't have a word for what Bruce and I had been, for the thing we'd shared between us. He wasn't my boyfriend. I'd never seriously entertained a future with him, I wasn't that naive. But I did believe we loved each other—love in the most basic sense of attendant mutual care. That was the standard, in our case. And by that standard, he'd failed.

I kept getting stuck on one thing in particular: the way he'd let me persist in my unknowing for so long. He'd hid the truth the way you hide things from a child, spelling out the bad words. You can't love someone and hold yourself apart from them like that. If love means anything, it's wanting to share a point of view.

For all our problems, I'd believed that Bruce and I were true companions. Like two people watching a play together in a theater, committed to an act of shared witnessing. If we disagreed later about what was good, or bad, or even about the central facts of what we saw, we knew at least we saw it together, from a common corner of the room. Our arms close enough to touch, drinking from the same glass of wine.

But lying—the serious kind—casts people in different relation. You're not seated together anymore. The lied-to person *becomes* the play, tossed up onto the set, an unconsenting actor. Because what can you be, with the truth hidden away, except a character trapped in a premise, living a make-believe life? You go cluelessly about your days, unaware you're on a stage, while the liar watches from the shadows, seeing everything you don't. He can get up and leave the theater, but you can only stay there in the dark. Wondering why he seems so far away. Squinting up now and then at the klieg lights you've mistaken for the sun.

❧

I ignored Bruce in the days that followed, no matter how many times he called. Switching the ringer off when my phone buzzed, a wasp's incessant drone. And yet everything else seemed up for grabs. My plans could shift several times an hour: I'd drop out of Partridge immediately. No, I'd stay, finish out the term, then quit. Or a leave of absence, to keep my options open? Or maybe it was too late for me already, and the best thing would be to stick with it after all. . . .

I couldn't decide if the revelation about Flood was good news or bad news, like one of those eye-tricking pictures that can be a vase or a pair of faces—the image flipping around while you stared at it, refusing to be one thing. Walking up the hill to school, I might feel a surge of gladness: there was finally someone else to blame for all my failures. I knew what had gone wrong, and I could fix it, and that was an indescribable relief. But just as easily I'd start dwelling on how unfair it was to be sabotaged, to have your future stolen from you by a petty husk of a man. When I thought about how much suffering Flood had caused me, and how much time I'd squandered thanks to his meddling, any brightness I'd felt would curdle into grief—a dark, volatile feeling that often simmered into rage.

The angry streaks came on without warning, thrilling, scary, teetering at the edge of my control. I wrestled with urges I'd never had before: to start screaming obscenely in the middle of class, to scratch long, ugly lines into parked cars with my house key, to attack lampposts and garbage bins as I passed them on the street. Thankfully those moods boiled over quickly, the way froth settles in a pot when you kill the heat. Then I'd settle back into my default mode—a numbed-up state of resignation, where it seemed impossible to feel anything ever again until the second I did.

I went about like that, stranded in the middle of a weird, shape-shifting cloud. But an objective fact loomed out of the mist: it was already mid-January, which meant it was too late to do anything right away. The fifteenth of the month had already come and gone, and with it the vast majority of application deadlines. So, by withholding the truth from me as long as he did, Bruce had unwittingly screwed me over one last time. If I was going to reapply to school, I'd have to wait another year.

The question was what to do in the meantime. Part of me was tempted to just drop out, return the loan money I hadn't spent yet, and spend a year gearing up to try the whole thing over again. But going home to live with my parents seemed out of the question—I wouldn't be able to think with my dad around, hovering, wheedling, lecturing, unable to hide his disappointment. That meant I'd need to find somewhere else to live, and *that* meant getting a job. I wasn't sure life at Partridge was inherently worse than a job. Learning for loan money was better than getting paid to pass the time.

As I mulled it over, I made a more unsettling discovery: my heart, it seemed, wasn't quite in it anymore. Don't get me wrong, I wanted to want to go back. But I couldn't locate the old fervor, the strident certainty I'd felt about where I was headed, where I belonged. If I could have snapped my fingers and suddenly become a second-year English PhD at a halfway decent school, I probably would have done it. But when I thought about everything I'd need to do to actually get there, I felt so ambivalent I'd sometimes literally sigh.

The truth was that I'd spent well over a year trying to convince myself to accept the message the world had sent me: that it was time to find a different path. It had been an excruciating process, but it had worked. I'd killed off the bright, blindered person I'd been, and replaced her with someone scrappier and more practical. In other words, I'd grown up quite a bit—and I could no longer see the institutions that had rejected me through the same starry eyes.

How good was the existence I'd longed for, in the end? To spend my days quibbling over obscure details in journals no one read, surrounded by arrogant bores? Sparring forever with people like Flood? If I was honest, material benefits had always been a huge part of the attraction: sabbaticals, a four-month summer break. In other words, I had dubious reasons for wanting to join their club—not to be there, but because they made it so easy to leave. In that sense, grad school had always been a proxy for the real goal underneath it all—relative freedom, a chance to set the terms of my life.

I absolutely still wanted to read, to write, to think. To *feel* things the way you can only when your hours aren't relentlessly structured, when your time is more or less your own. But I no longer believed that academic life was the only way to get there. Partridge sent its second-year students down to job fairs in New York, and we all knew the kind of money you could make coming out of the program. Six figures easy, if you were good. And I was starting to think that I was good.

I could feel myself changing, a divining rod in me turning the other way. Say I *did* go through with it—finish Partridge, do my best. The worst that could happen was that I'd apply again for PhDs toward the end—the timing worked out—with brand-new skills to set me apart, towering above the frauds who lorded over the so-called digital humanities with their self-taught HTML. Or I'd start a new career entirely, and that scenario had its own alluring logic. I could pay off my loans, with money like that. I could get ahead. I could shore up my family against the financial precarity that had always plagued us. When you rely on services the way we do, you're always one right-wing governor away from disaster. It would be so good not to worry anymore, for all of us.

I could always return to grad school, if I wanted. Make $15K a year as a TA for the better part of a decade, then cliff-dive into a shallow job market. Or . . . I could take advantage of the historical moment I was in. Because, no matter who I wanted to be, no matter what values I professed, I wanted freedom more than anything—and that meant making money. Supposedly you could get twenty days of paid vacation in a starting package, that wasn't nothing. It would require an intense term of servitude, but then I could be done with it.

I was taking a career unit that term, Partridge's way of orienting us toward our future. There was a shortage of people like us, we were told. The tech industry couldn't hire fast enough, with companies like Amazon bringing on hundreds, even thousands of coders every year. The professor had a comforting refrain: *Everyone in this room*, he liked to say, *can retire by fifty-five.*

～

When I got home from class, I'd do a couple push-ups to get the blood flowing. I'd slap my cheeks for that skin-awakening sting. Then I'd sit down at my desk, square my jaw, and get to work. I coded until night fell, ate at my desk, coded some more, and finally slept a little while, knowing in the morning I would do it all again.

For a few weeks, I was perfect. I chained myself to the desk, steadfast as a nun. I shipped my assignments early and skipped ahead, practicing until my fingertips went numb. My operations spat out the date. My operations spat out my name. My operations spat out a world clock with a drop-down, styled beautifully in CSS, that could give the current hour and minute for any major city on the earth.

Where are you, Zena texted, and before long her name stopped lighting up my phone. Bruce's texts and emails piled up unread. Finally, I wrote him: *I never want to see you again.* A single sentence. I was satisfied to know it was that simple. I felt a hard, glittering resolve at the center of me, something sharp and compressed as a diamond. It demanded my whole attention, the jewel I carried inside, and each day it grew stronger and more bright.

It might have gone on like that. I might have learned to lead and win. But on my path to future glory, something else started to happen. Sometimes, when I sat down to code, I found I simply couldn't do it.

It didn't matter how much work I had left, or how productive I'd been that day. The feeling was inexplicable, like when a car won't start. I'd sit there, sending brain signals down my limbs. *Lift, hands*, I'd think. *Fingers, you will type now.* But nothing would happen, some connection severed between my body and my will.

Stationed at my desk, my books open to the proper pages, my assignment waiting on the screen, I'd wait for something to change. But a person can only wait so long. As the minutes passed, my eyes might wander over to the row of paperbacks I kept on a shelf by the kitchen. If I felt stuck enough, I'd stand up—this wish my body obeyed—to go feel their familiar weights again, their pages soft from my thumbs. It could help me buckle down, to read a little while. But not always. Sometimes it would be one in the morning before I knew it, and I'd have read eighty pages of *The Secret History*, and my work wouldn't be started.

Luckily, I had a better motivator: rolling cigarettes. The ritual of it ordered my mind, somehow. I loved the way the phyllo-thin papers came free from the pack, with a rattle of tiny thunder; the pull of the shag and the burst of pencil-shaving smell; the filling and folding of the little sheet, which drew tight into a Doric column; and the quick glue-lick at the end, that kiss of chemical tang.

I'd take a walk to smoke and clear my head. Sometimes, as I climbed the long hill toward College Ave, inspiration would strike with such urgency that I'd break into a halting half-run, trying to get back while it lasted, fumbling madly with my keys at the front door like a person who has to pee. But at my desk, the eagerness would seep away again, and a dull lobotomized blankness would set in.

I'd force myself to sit there anyway, though even the smallest things became hours-long derailments. Since the junk doors in my apartment slid loose if I didn't lock them, sometimes the front door drifted open with an eerie, muted wail—a poltergeist energy in the room, urging me to abandon my station, which I often did.

I reminded myself that I was taking on thousands of dollars in debt to do this, that it was urgent, that it mattered. I *had* to get my act together. I had a BA already, and four years of loans I'd only deferred by taking out *more* loans. The whole thing amounted to a very expensive mulligan, and grabbing a sliver of the coming tech boom was the only way I'd ever dig myself out. But, while a certain kind of arm-twisting could help me get the job done—*You idiot. You lazy, godforsaken idiot. Just do it, that's all. Right now*—sometimes nothing helped. My brain felt broken, like I was missing some basic neural pathway everyone else had.

It got harder and harder to sit down at my desk, a feat I could only manage through an inspired combination of coaxing, nicotine, rituals, and magic. Even when I did succeed, the battle never stayed won. I'd be scowling at some ugly, half-finished code unit when I'd realize I was hungry. So I'd have a cigarette to ease my stomach, but that made me tired. So I'd have some coffee, which then made me nervous. So I'd go for a walk, which in turn made me hungry—and the cycle continued.

By the time I'd destroyed the kitchen preparing and devouring an elaborate lunch, my hands would be shaking, my stomach sour, my vision starting to blur. When all else failed, it was time for a nap. Naps were permitted, but only on my punishing, too-short couch—that way I never really enjoyed them.

I'd arrange my laptop so that my assignments stared me down the second I woke up. And I usually *did* feel ready to code when I opened my eyes again.

But first, a little coffee.

And so on.

I'd seethe as the end of the day inevitably came, faced with the hard fact of my wasted hours. When I pulled back the curtains to glare at the night, sometimes I could almost see my rage shoot in bright, broken forks through the sky.

That's when I first remember wanting to disappear. To lift my hands, and see the computer screen shine through them, and then not see any hands at all. To rise and glide down the stairs that way, out into the wintry air, there and not there. It was invisibility I thought I craved—some way of vanishing that was gentler than death.

～

I made it until mid-February, and then I missed my first assignment. Just didn't hand it in. By then, an hour's effort seemed to take me five. I did everything I could, even when it meant working through the night. I ran the coffeemaker overtime, water gurgling through the crushed beans well after midnight. I learned to take emergency hot/cold showers, the best way I knew to clear my head. I ran up the hill to class more days than not, having finished only at the last possible second.

That first missed assignment happened because I just couldn't *think* anymore. I couldn't shake this woozy, concussed feeling, a losing boxer in the last rounds of a match. So I set my clock for three and went to bed. There was a split second of darkness and then the alarm's blare woke me up. I sat up and realized it had been blaring a long time, that tomorrow had started without me.

I'd failed, finally, an odd relief. That morning there was leeway to linger in the shower, to drink my coffee at the little kitchen two-top I never used, to have a cigarette on the porch and look up at the naked trees. I didn't need to rush, for once, since I was already too late. As I walked up the hill to school, it occurred to me that I'd never missed a deadline before. Not in high school and not in college. It was something I would have said I wasn't capable of, except I apparently was.

Nothing happened when I got to class. No one looked at me funny. My professor didn't seem to realize anything had gone awry. It was almost as if the world didn't *care* whether I'd done my homework. I coasted on that unexpected feeling, a high that made me act strangely, like I was in love. As I walked home later, the sky seemed huge and impossibly blue. I took myself out to dinner that night, ate by candlelight with a magazine and a glass of wine.

But as I returned to the apartment I felt the weight of what I'd done. Instead of having one batch of assignments to finish, I now had two. And it was already nine at night, and my cheeks were flushed with drinking.

Things didn't spiral right away. I tried to recover, did my best. It was just that my best kept getting worse and worse. By early March, I'd fallen behind on half a dozen assignments— though I still told myself I'd get them all in, would work twice as hard to make up for lost time. I couldn't help noticing the way my professor sometimes peered at me a beat too long, biting his lip, before turning back to the whiteboard. *I'll be okay*, I tried to tell him telepathically. *I'm going to be all right.*

Except I wasn't really all right. I'd sit down at my desk and feel completely overwhelmed, not sure if I should finish the late assignments for salvaged credit or start in on the new ones. Something in me dashed about like a squirrel in traffic, every second an agony of indecision, scampering back and forth madly in front of an oncoming car.

You can't fail, I'd warn myself. *You simply can't. Not here, not now, not this far in. It can't happen. You can't LET it happen.*

And sometimes I'd hear a small voice say back: *But I am.*

I gritted my teeth. I chose a lane. I came right home from class and parked myself before the glowing screen, ready to battle as long as it took. Dark bruises grew under my eyes. It didn't matter. Outside of class, I barely saw a soul except my neighbors in the stairwell—two Dorito-stained math PhDs, both named Stephen, who came and went at odd hours of the night.

⌇

Winter dragged on, everything crushed under blankets of snow. My panic drained away—I almost missed it—replaced by an endless, enervating *weight*. I felt numb and over-ballasted, like a person trapped forever in a leaden X-ray vest. On bad days, I could barely lift my head. It took an epic force of will, on trips to the cigarette store, to look the cashier in the eye.

As rest became mandatory, class became optional. But even sleep, my usual cure-all, failed me. The hours spoiled by weird dreams. I'd forgotten crucial assignments. I begged phantom professors for forgiveness, their faces blurred and shadowy. I woke up wracked with guilt. Or I'd find myself back in the exam halls of my childhood, peering around as everyone else scribbled away in a storm of concentration. I'd look down again at my test booklets, all of them blank. Or filled instead with spooky handwriting, a scrawl that wasn't mine. Sometimes the pages were soaking wet, and the ink ran purple down my wrists, staining my hands.

❧

That quarter's finals were all on the same day, a Monday where you were shunted from room to room for eight hours. My plan had been to spend the weekend cramming, trying to make up for weeks of delinquency with the raw power of adrenaline and caffeine. On Friday night, I somehow reached the state I coveted: I'd eaten and slept and smoked enough, but not too much, and my head felt clear for the first time in days. I brewed a cup of steaming tea, notes and textbooks spread across my desk. If I spent every minute in a state of radiant concentration, there was a chance I'd pass.

But instead of working I found myself wandering over to my bookshelf again. For the first time since I left college, I took my old, worn copy of *Moby-Dick* from the shelf—the gorgeous Northwestern University Press edition, edited by Hershel Parker—and opened it. Every paragraph carved up in blue Bic pen, underlines and checkmarks and countless stars, my detailed notes scribbled in tiny script. They ached with surprising force, those small reminders of the person I'd been.

I put some water on to boil, threw a box of mac and cheese in, and settled back into the couch with my book. I turned the pages and felt myself flood with terrible longing—longing for what? To start over, sure. To come back new, unburdened by all my mistakes, ready to try again. To be someone who could still channel ideas and energy into endless blue ink. But most of all, it was a *feeling* I missed. A feeling you take for granted on certain days when you're younger, when you have nothing to do for an afternoon but find a sunbeam and claim it, and then read until your ears ring with the silence. Or in the hours I spent with my brother, Ian, listening to music, lying on the floor next to his chair, only sound coloring the time and the damp heat of his hand.

Where did it go, that feeling? And how could you get back to it again?

As I lay there wondering, I fell asleep.

When I opened my eyes, strange light flickered around the room. A nasty smell, like singed hair. The cigarette in my hand had burned down, an ashy cylinder that crumbled away as I sat up. Then I saw the stove was on fire. Or not the stove—I'd left the mac and cheese on, and the pot had changed into a writhing, three-foot column of orange-blue flame. I stood there, awestruck, the fear briefly numbed with wonder. Vivid blue tongues licked out of the inferno, so spectacular you almost wanted the end of the world to come.

～

Before I had time to do anything, I heard a sound in the hallway. My junk front door had drifted open again, as it inevitably did when I forgot to lock it, and footsteps were coming down the hall. It was the math PhD, Stephen—not heavyset Stephen with the permanent scowl, but thin Stephen, who failed to hide a wine-stain birthmark behind his patchy blond beard.

He stood there blinking in the light. And I saw myself as he saw me: a disheveled wreck in a fallen-open bathrobe, still clutching the burnt end of a cigarette. Then the fire alarm went off.

The alarm's electric throb shook me from the dream. The numbness fell away. I vaulted over the back of the couch and turned off the gas—choking down panic, the plastic knob sticky hot. Stephen was yelling something. I'd left a dirty soup pot in the sink, filled with brackish water. I hauled it out and threw the water on the fire, which hissed and sizzled in a scalding puff of steam. Then I turned the sink on, yanked the nozzle out on its plastic rope, and sprayed. Steam and smoke fogged everything.

By then Stephen was in my apartment, yelling at me over the noise.

"What the hell are you *doing*?"

"Open the windows!" I shouted back, training the sink-spray on the stove. The alarm was killing my ears.

Stephen walked gingerly across the room, like he might step on poop or something if he wasn't careful, and started tugging on the windows. There were clothes and stuff on the floor, it was true. But I was too stunned to care, shivery with adrenaline. When the fire was out, I started waving at the smoke detector with a broom, trying to make the piercing rhythm stop.

"Should I call the fire department?" Stephen shouted.

"Fuck that!" I shouted back. "Don't call anybody!"

"You were just standing there!" Stephen said, the disbelief raw in his voice. I ignored him and kept fanning. From the open windows, I felt cold outdoor air at my back. Then Big Stephen entered the doorway. He looked at us through the smoke and dropped into a runner's crouch, as if he'd just heard a gun go off.

"Gah—! What—?" he spluttered. "What's happening?"

"She almost burned the goddamn building down!"

The alarm stopped. I lowered the broom and tied the belt on my robe. My ears rang in the quiet.

"It was an accident," I said.

"Wow," Big Stephen said. He stood looming in the doorway. "Your ceiling is *fucked*."

"Just leave, please," I said.

"Don't we need to do anything?" the first Stephen said.

"Just go."

"Sure," he said. "Don't thank me or anything."

"Get out."

He crossed my living room again—turning slowly as he went, as if I were a wild animal he had to keep his eyes on—and walked out the door backward. I heard them talking in low voices as they ran down the stairs in a tumble of feet, and then they were gone.

I closed the door, locked it, and surveyed the damage through the silty air. Dark puddles of foul water pooled on the counter and across the floor. The metal stovetop was all charred with blast marks, as if a small rocket had launched from it. The cabinets were ruined, their lacquer blistered and blackened. The ceiling sported a smoky, expensive-looking stain.

I slumped against the wall and slid down, slowly, to the floor. Something about the wreckage helped me see my apartment with fresh eyes. Dirty dishes stacked in precarious mounds. Coffee cups I'd repurposed as ashtrays, overfilled and stinking with roach ends. Clothes and junk and worksheets everywhere. It was shocking, really, that I'd let myself live like this.

I felt it slip away. The perfect weekend I'd planned, the studying I'd do. My last, best chance to save the term. I'd promised to be my Best Self, but instead I'd destroyed my apartment. Disasters like this took time to fix. And money. And might involve matters of law. I felt like crying, but I was too scared I'd throw up.

I tried to clean up what I could, starting with the smoky water that lay in dark, depressing puddles across the kitchen floor, pooling where the linoleum dimpled. I used a ratty bath towel, since I didn't have a mop, wringing the foul stuff by hand into the sink. The scorched smell still lingered, even with a box fan pointed the wrong way out the window. A pile of finished worksheets I'd left out on the counter had gotten soaked, the pages all bogged together, beyond saving and signed over and over with my name. Each one conceding failure—Jane Hannah-Smith, Jane Hannah-Smith.

I worked quickly at first, trying to fix as much as possible before anyone showed up—the landlords, the Stephens, the cops. But it started to seem obvious no one was coming, any larger consequences deferred until morning. I kept cleaning anyway, as if a better-kept apartment would somehow purge me karmically, lessening the burden of my guilt. I filled three big trash bags and hauled them to the dumpster out back. I cleared the counters and wiped them down. But the longer I kept at it, the shabbier my apartment became. My efforts made the damage look worse by contrast, emphasizing the fire-scarred cabinets and smoke-fouled ceiling I could do nothing about.

I'd been up for hours. Exhaustion was starting to catch up with me, the apartment only half cleaned. I turned to look back at the disaster I'd made of the kitchen, the rag in my hand stinking with Lysol, and confirmed: Yes, it really was that bad. Like a photo of a crime scene. I closed my eyes. Dread rolled through me. I listened to the thudding of my heart and knew that I was finished.

I put the rag down. I pulled my suitcase out from my closet, unused since my final trip with Bruce. I threw a few clothes in, my toothbrush and toiletries. Almost out of habit, I gathered all my textbooks, notes, and handouts, too—not yet able to imagine going anywhere without them—and stuffed them into my backpack. I took everything with me out into the weird blue dawn.

I didn't know where I was going, exactly. Only this sensation like a UFO had fixed me in its tractor beam, and I had no choice but to obey.

I'd parked my car on a steep hill, one tire squashed against the curb, the e-brake on. I drove, and a light rain started to fall. Stopped at a light, I saw a robin pecking a flattened soda cup on the median, its bright chest the first harbinger of spring. It stabbed joylessly a few times with its beak, then cocked its head and seemed to think better of it, before bursting away in a sputter of wings. The snow had melted, I realized, and then the light turned, and I was gone.

THREE

I drove. I had no plan beyond flooring the gas pedal, a cigarette on my lip, the world smeared to a brown-green blur. Letting the miles melt away in a fuel-injected rush. I became a body in motion, and I stayed in motion to defer what felt intolerable—the questions of where to go, and how to be, and what should happen next.

I fought to stay awake. Stopped for coffee, stared hard at the road. But I'd been up through the night—my brain foggy, my wires frayed—and I started to nod off at the wheel, little stolen nips and jerks of sleep. It wasn't until I stumbled on a motor lodge, cheap enough to pay in cash, that I surrendered to my body. The room had two beds and stank powerfully of detergent. I shut the door behind me, flipped the bolt, and swelled with indescribable relief. The sun was still out—it didn't matter. I pulled the shades down, choking out the light. I crawled between the sheets.

For a brief, delicious minute, there was nothing but darkness and the cool touch of cloth. I dropped down, down, into a soft and woven place—a place with no sound, where nothing moved. It was such a simple thing I wanted, I thought, as my breath slowed. A certain stillness, that was all, and time to listen to the rising staircase cadence of my heart.

I slept for sixteen hours. Sleep that was epic, vigorous, like climbing a mountain or swimming the English Channel. The motel room was almost entirely dark, so waking up there wasn't that different from being asleep. I came to gradually, the borders fuzzy, lingering in the twilight that starts in a dream's last moments and ends as a day begins.

The truth filtered back slowly. Yes, my last-ditch cramming session had ended when I'd almost burned down my apartment. Yes, the fire had been tall and blue-hot, like the flame from a giant blowtorch. Yes, I'd driven off with the ceiling smoke-spoiled and the cabinets charred, to hide instead in a far-flung motel. But these facts struck me as neutral, like objects I could pick up and set aside. I examined them all and put them down when I was done with them. I felt new, wiped clean, what I imagine people feel emerging from a coma.

Morning waited behind the drawn shades, light pushing at the corners of the windows. I sat up in bed, let my feet down on the carpet. Out of habit, I expected to feel the usual things— the leaden weight, an acrid scorch-taste of remorse. Those first stirrings of panic, like a treadmill ramping up. But no. There was something else instead, as I crossed the room. A feeling rest alone couldn't explain. It hit more fully as I opened the curtains to let in the sun: a dawning gladness, lovely and delicate as a gilded egg.

∽

That feeling stayed with me even as I left the motel, driving out again into the world. Like I'd won somehow, no matter what had happened. Like I'd been trapped for so long in someone else's body, or maybe with the wrong brain in my own body— but now I was whole again, and finally living out a story that was mine. Nothing mattered except keeping that feeling going, I decided. I would do whatever it took to make it last.

The most important thing was not to cave, not to get cold feet and crawl back penitent to Partridge. I had to kill off any chance some future Jane might have a change of heart. I parked the car by a high, rusty bridge and ran to the edge, brown water thundering through the valley depths. Then I dumped my backpack. Months of worksheets and notes burst out in a soft white explosion. As I watched the pages flitter and whirl toward the river, I promised I'd never go back.

All I had to do was harden my will and not return to Ithaca for another day. My exams started at eight the next morning— and if I missed even the first one, a threshold would be crossed, dropping out would be the only option left. I wasn't sure what I'd do after that. Grab a few last things from my apartment, I supposed. Tell the landlords where to send the bill. Then I'd drive to my parents' house in Connecticut and admit defeat. It wouldn't be easy, but none of that mattered yet. The first thing was to take Partridge off the table forever, the only way my real life could finally actually start.

So I drove around some more. Fueled the gas tank, kept on driving. Took food from a pickup window, a burger in grease-proof wrappers and fries that stank of starch. When it started getting dark, I looked around for a new motel. It surprised me how often you'd stumble across them—on the outskirts of some towns, or scattered through the hills. I wasn't the only one looking for a bed in Nowhere, New York. Other cars parked in the lots, a sign of other people in the rooms. I wondered who they were.

～

In the morning, as my classmates took their sharpened pencils to the exam room, I got back into the car again. I drove, steeling myself against the image of my empty desk. I watched the minutes tick by, triumphant, each one making a different future more inevitable. Then, a welcome sight outside Elmira: a little shopping mall with a bookstore in it.

It was just a Borders, a middling corporate chain. But I flicked on my turn signal, pulling off Route 17 at the last second. It was Monday morning, finally, and the lot was mostly empty. I parked so close that the building's shadow fell across my hood. Then I was inside, my pulse ticking up as I walked through the glass double doors. Countless books on countless shelves, their many-colored spines like a rainbow put through a paper shredder.

I'd started to avoid bookstores. That year in New York, rejected from grad school, they felt too painful somehow—like returning to a hospital room where you'd had a limb amputated. Some places hurt too much to go back to, though I occasionally tried. Once, on a night off, I lingered at the back of a poetry reading. The lights felt too bright and everyone seemed to know each other already. It was a relief when the proceedings finally started. The poets stood up and down, their awards were named, and they read. As I felt the rhythm of their words, their pulse and buckle, I felt outclassed and ashamed: what vanity to think that I could have a life like this.

But as I walked inside that Monday morning, the grief-haunted feeling was gone. Instead I couldn't wait to give myself over, linger in the aisles awhile, see where my wandering took me. A clerk looked up from a display table and smiled as I walked by. For the first time in forever, I had all the time in the world.

Hours passed before I knew it. At some point in the afternoon, I glanced up and happened to see the time. How strange to think of everyone trapped in the same stuffy rooms all day, the nervy silence of exams. They'd be on the coding portion by then, cobbling up programs on the fly. I felt sorry for them. Or, no—they were doing what they wanted. But I was surer than ever about quitting Partridge, and I was sorry I'd talked myself into staying for so long.

I walked out to my car later, my mouth sour from coffee and biscotti. I'd bought a few things—Ishiguro's *Never Let Me Go*, freshly laid out on the new releases table. Also *What Color Is Your Parachute?*, a career self-help book my dad had bought for me before, but which I'd lost or misplaced in a Freudian way. It would help, I figured, when he saw me with the book—I'd use it as a prop, an olive branch, a gesture of good faith. Also a dark black journal, still wrapped in cellophane, that I planned to fill with striking observations.

It wasn't until I got back to the car that I realized I'd missed a call. My little black Razr was still sitting on the center console, its message light flashing. I sat down, tumbling my books into the passenger seat, and snapped it open.

Mom, the phone said. And she'd left a message.

The air thinned around me a little, the dizzy first signs of altitude sickness. I told myself there was nothing wrong. Moms called, it was what they did. But a low paranoia started to whir, the fantasy playing out darkly in my mind—the school had called her, so she'd called me.

Where's Jane? It's finals, she's still not here.

That was absurd, and I knew it. I was an adult. I could skip whatever I wanted to without anyone calling my parents. But I found myself considering a new, more plausible possibility: the apartment. Elite Rentals had forced me to list my parents on the lease as guarantors, since loan debt was my only form of income. In a situation where the kitchen had been left torched, the ceiling scarred, the tenant missing, would they get a call? They absolutely would.

The message light flashed, a steady reddish blip.

The gladness I'd felt—joyful, pyrrhic—started to seep away, the slow twist of water down a drain. My pulse bumped chaotically, a mouse in a watch box. There it was again: that old, familiar dread that creeped in as I sat down in front of the computer, offering myself to the blank screen.

I wasn't ready to go back.

FOUR

I was last seen at a bank in Trumansburg. The security cameras caught me wandering over to the counter, where I emptied my accounts: about two thousand bucks in loan money, plus three hundred more I'd set aside from the restaurant job. How did I want it? the teller asked. I loved that I could choose. He paid me out in three handfuls—first the spare change, then a few loose ones, and finally the Bible-thick stack of bigger bills. A lovely sum, thrilling to conjure all at once, and mine to spend until it was gone.

As the day wore on, I started eyeing the cheap motels I stumbled on now and then—the Firefly Lodge, the Blue Spruce Motor Manor. I got a room at the Pleasant Sleep Inn and tried to settle in with the Ishiguro. But I couldn't focus, not at first. My attention felt thin and splintery somehow, distracted by something in the corner of my vision. The room phone on the bedside table nagged at me, its curved grip shape cradled in black plastic. It sucked up brain force, the way it sat there waiting to be used.

I knew I should call my parents, a lingering insistence I couldn't quite tune out. But I'd never even listened to the voice mail from my mom. I'd turned my cell phone off instead, dreading the thought that she might try again—or, worse, that the tiny device might give me away somehow, its plastic antenna beaming signals out to towers in the distance. It helped me relax, to have my phone powered down and stuffed away in the glove box, out of sight. Except now and then, when I took a turn too hard, I'd hear it tumble around in there, the muted thump a little hit of guilt.

What was I so afraid of? One call could save my parents from so much. I could try explaining. I could tell them where I was. But the thing I was after felt delicate and fleeting, a bubble blown from a wand, and the slightest thing could puncture it. Besides, we often went long stretches without talking, with unreturned messages on both sides—it might be weeks before they started to worry. I sensed I was still in a beautiful grace period, that rare interval before freedom sours into consequences. If that was true, I needed it to last.

The impulse seized me in a rest stop parking lot. I took the Razr out of the glove box and broke its back, forcing it backward until it tore at the middle joints with a satisfying sound, like a crab cracker opening some freshly boiled crustacean's shell. I tossed the plastic carcass in the trash, glad to be done with it— the temptation finally out of reach, another boundary crossed.

I felt better with my phone gone, out of reach and profoundly on my own. That was why the room phone spoiled the mood, as I sat there trying to read in the motel: it breached the solitude I craved. I leaned against the headboard for a bit, wrestling with myself, the book in my lap. Then I stepped out of bed and looked around for the phone line. I followed the cord to the plastic jack, and I pulled it from the wall.

❧

I had until the money ran out. That was the deadline I set— and then I'd either go home, or call my parents and make some kind of case. It wouldn't be long. Cheap as they were, the motel stays ate through my funds. I could physically feel my reserves get lighter.

At night, I read. I loved the cool, coiled voice of Kathy H., her riddle of donors and carers, the whole thing a mad dream springing from a fissure in the world I knew. The rooms I stayed in usually had some kind of fan you could control, a unit below the window. With the speed cranked up all the way, any god-forgotten motor lodge could drape itself in a womb-like quiet, drowning out the sound of fights and sex and footsteps in the hall. Space and time were finally mine. I'd fall asleep with the lamp on, happy at last, the book on my chest the only companion I needed.

Sometimes the serenity I felt would roll away, and I glimpsed the darkness beneath it—the way a tide recedes to reveal the ocean floor, its crags trashed with litter and teeming with crawling things. Was I a terrible person, disappearing like that? Was something *wrong* with me? The shame could be overwhelming, little guilty heart attacks that made it hard to breathe. Anxiety, too, flickered here and there at the edge of everything; strange people lurk in motel parking lots, and I was so alone. And yet the despair I'd felt at Partridge, that all-out, merciless bleakness, was slowly ebbing away. *That* was what mattered: I finally felt like myself again, even if I had no idea what I was doing.

So I studied my road atlas and vowed to go farther, deeper. The dorsal fin of New York State, where all the nothing was. Barely any anything, far from the red-and-blue vasculature of America's freeways. Because there had to be more than that, right? More than fast-food chains lifting joyless beacons to the night, brake lights making the sky glow pink after a crash, the world churning on as it always did for no reason anyone could say. Something had to be out there, and I wanted to find it.

Once, I pulled the car into a field and sat on the hood to watch the spilled-salt stars.

Once, I saw steam rise from the bloody body of a shattered deer.

Once, a factory loomed up in the night like a great dark castle, the moon shining on its smoke-puffs like movie lighting, and the air for miles around smelled like corn.

The road cut through forest and pasture, past smashed-window warehouses and the hulking old wrecks of barns. The one-light towns were dust-blown and emptied out, as if everyone had fled some plague. Maybe it should have scared me, that derelict look. I took it as a sign I was getting closer to something, a place beyond the reach of what I knew. A forlorn majesty in all that abandonment, the things I hated relinquishing their hold.

The trees got taller, growing up to the very edge of everything, fenced out only by phone poles and the road.

❦

One night, I couldn't even find a motel. The sky a darkening abyss and no chance of a town. I pulled off on a roadside somewhere, not a single house in sight, and waited for the dreaded rush of headlights. They never came. Slowly, I lowered my seat and lay back. *If I can do this*, I thought. If I could make it through the night. It might change everything, allow me to explore a little longer. My money worth more as every second passed.

It scared me to let my guard down like that. At the mercy of whatever might be out there, the fish's ignorance of the world beyond its bowl. I slept with a can of pepper spray clutched in one hand. In the other, I kept my keys balled in a fist, a jagged bronze edge glinting out between my knuckles, ready to puncture a throat. I slept very little, and fitfully. But as I woke up with the sunrise in the morning, the sky a lurid glow, I felt victorious—a door had been unlocked to me, a threshold forever crossed.

It happened just a day or two later. I was shooting down some back road when I saw something: An ancient water tower, rising up over the hill. A single word flaked in dark paint across its broad powder-blue face.

LACK, it said.

Funny, I thought. What a name for a town. A non-place, a thing defined by its absence.

I found myself wanting to get closer, I'm not sure why. There was something about the tower I recognized—that quality that's both mythical and real, somehow, like the memory of a dream.

∽

Downtown Lack was just a crossing of two roads, four corners meeting around a single four-way stop. On the southeast side, an old gas station sat next to a mini-mart. Its flyspecked sign, the tallest man-made thing in sight, listed fuel prices by the gallon. The northeast quadrant was home to a squat, defunct building with chipped white paint, its porch conquered by vines. SAM'S GENERAL STORE, an old billboard read, next to a crude cartoon picture of a pig licking its lips, as if it just couldn't wait to eat itself. Across from Sam's, a shop that sold motorized sleds had closed for the season, or possibly for good. The fourth corner was empty, a grassy lot littered with take-out cups that quickly gave way to the forest.

I drove through, past a shuttered Methodist church, trying to get closer to the tower. Its chlorine-blue dome floated over the trees. A path looked like it went there, stretching along the edge of a nineteenth century cemetery. Or not a "path" so much as a set of parallel lines showing where, over time, tires had killed the grass.

I parked and got out, picking my way through the graves. Most of the stones were illegible, jutting like teeth from the earth, their inscriptions worn and splotched with lichen. I followed the tire tracks into the woods until I reached the tower.

It stood mounted on a fenced-off square of broken concrete, in a little clearing surrounded on all sides by trees. Where the pavement split, tall, feathered weeds reached for the light. A silver ladder started in the cement slab and ended near the clouds.

I stared up into the enormous undercarriage, struck by its bulk, by the chemical blue that failed to match the sky. I walked over to the fence, tempted to scale it and climb the forbidden ladder to steal a view from above. A loose wall of ivy had writhed its way into the chain links, and I noticed someone had twisted flowers in, too—little husks that hung there wilted and dead, their stems clearly knotted by hands. A whimsical adornment, this left-behind sign of human feeling. So others had been drawn there, like me. Some old, flattened beer cans—the kind you had to open with a church key—lay half buried in the leaves.

There was something about the place. This sense of height and scale. A quiet, dilapidated glory. Tender blue light filtered through the naked trees. I could really be alone here, I thought, my breath misting out in little wisps. I waited for five minutes, and I never heard a single passing car.

∽

For a little while, I had everything I wanted.

I'd backed the Saab twenty feet into the woods, where it sat obscured, within view of the tower's base. I couldn't imagine anyone looking for me there, and it wouldn't have been easy to spot me if they did. Still, I locked the doors at night, the windows cracked half an inch for air. I'd leave the keys hanging from the ignition. If anyone came, I was ready to peel out.

During the day, I'd walk through the woods toward the mini-mart. I'd cross the road and walk in through the smudged glass door, my presence announced by a dull electronic chime.

The aisles were stashed with all the standard stuff: candy, chips, snack mix, infinite variations on the theme of processed corn. Tragic pizza spun on a pan under a heat lamp, the pepperonis cupping little pools of grease. I drank a lot of milk, which seemed like the healthiest option. The full-fat kind was surprisingly filling—not to mention thick, cold, and, at eighty-nine cents a quart, unthinkably cheap.

Two attendants, both women, swapped off shifts. My presence barely seemed to register. The older one was always glued to her television, which hung near the checkout counter by the door. She usually lowered the volume as I came in, her clicker raised in the air, as if to keep the contents better to herself. She rang me up and made my change without looking at my face.

The other woman was quite a bit younger, though still much older than me, and gave off a very different vibe. She stood in silence at the counter, still as a doll, staring down the center aisle at nothing in particular. With her frowning, troubled expression, she seemed to be forever recalling something that disturbed her. As I came over with the stuff I'd picked out, she'd suddenly stand to her full height, as if she'd just remembered the character she was there to play. Like the first woman, she never really seemed to see me. If she understood I had an existence outside the mini-mart, it was nothing she wondered about.

Besides the two of them, it was rare to see another soul. And when I didn't want to risk an interaction, which was most of the time, the occasional strangers were easy enough to avoid. I could see their cars from the woods, sunlight glinting off an unfamiliar shape. All I had to do was wait five minutes, and they'd be gone.

I read for hours in the car. One afternoon, it was finally warm enough to keep the windows down, the earth fully settling into spring, the branches studded with buds. I'd been in

Lack a few days, with nothing to do but plow through a copy of *Middlemarch* I'd bought from a Salvation Army in Canton. It was a classic I'd never gotten to in college, one I was vaguely ashamed not to have read. I'd braced myself for a dry and hard-won slog, the kind of "difficult" book best read for bragging rights, and was delighted instead to encounter a *story*—one that was witty, and earthy, with gem-like insights that glittered on every page, lovely and cutting as precious stones. Dorothea and Casaubon tugged at me especially, I think, since I was somehow both of them at once: the young woman, brimming with promise and energy, whose hunger for fulfillment led her to make terrible mistakes; the failed scholar, anxious that his life's work had amounted to so little. I tore through, chapter after chapter, the last pinch of pages under my thumb thinning fast. I didn't want the book to end, didn't know what I'd do when it did. But I read on, and sipped a beer I'd bought from the mini-mart, which helped the time pass slower, too, and for a little while I was content with the illusion that all of this would last.

As I was reading, I heard something. I looked up slowly, let the book fold shut in my lap. There it was again: a swish in the grass nearby, the unmistakable sound of someone's feet near the car.

⌘

Slowly, as carefully as I could, I turned my head and looked. Through the branches I saw a man lingering by the tower's fence, not twenty feet away. He hadn't seen me, the Saab well hidden in a thicket of pine branches.

I noticed his clothes first. A set of pitiful rags—frayed pants woven from rugged beige cloth. Some kind of improvised fur moccasins covered his feet, tied at the ankles with ribbon. He was painfully thin. Black wavy hair spilled down his back. All the local men dressed the same, coveralls, camo, and plaid. This was different: he looked more like Robinson Crusoe, shipwrecked and transported here from the eighteenth century.

I barely dared to breathe. My blood loud in my ears. I was close enough to hear him murmuring to himself, some aimless two-note tune. The wrists that shot from his too-short cuffs were barely wider than a ruler. He wasn't a man, I realized, but a boy. Someone my age, maybe younger. Something about him was hard to place. His face, when I caught glimpses of it, was gentle and appealing, at odds with his desolate clothes. His skin was tan, some combination of his genes and the sun.

I just sat there, frozen, breathing silently through my nose, and as I watched him, only my eyes moved. Slowly, I realized what he was doing: stripping the fence clear, pulling away the dead plant husks that dried there, their buds wilted and brown. When he was done, he picked up a fistful of flowers he'd gathered, early spring wild ones with pale, ghostly blooms. I watched as he twisted them into the chain links, weaving their stems around the wire until each blossom stayed on its own, hanging there with the ivy.

He knotted dozens of new flowers that way—droopy white and purple petals, yellow starbursts in the center. Watching him, I felt like I'd been let in on a secret.

When he was through, he knelt for a minute on the ground. For a long, loaded moment, the tips of his fingers hung from the wire. He bent his head as if in prayer—or in tribute to something, or someone, I couldn't tell.

I wanted that, I realized, with a sudden pang of envy. Anything to make me feel that kind of reverence. It almost didn't matter what it was.

When he finally stood again, I saw the bicycle beside him—I hadn't noticed it through the branchy view. A heavy old cruiser, its unpainted metal the color of stone. He threw one leg over, knocking the kickstand away with a neat sweep of his foot, and rode off in a clicking of spokes.

He passed right by the car as he set off, but didn't see me— my hiding place did the trick. Then he was gone. I felt my body relax, the tension going out of me. I could breathe again, and my eyes closed helplessly as I slumped back in my seat, glutted with relief. I let my chin tilt upward, sucking hoarsely at the air.

It struck me only as my heart rate slowed: in another few seconds, he'd vanish forever. The thought was strange, panicky in a new way. A window closing. I opened my eyes. *Middlemarch* lay across my lap, nowhere near enough pages left. The beer getting warm in my hand.

Something came over me, then. I decided to follow him.

❧

I started the engine and eased the car out of the woods, branches scrabbling at the metal. By the time I reached the road, he was biking like hell in the distance.

The boy moved with furious power, standing now and then to pump harder with his fur-clad feet. I pulled out onto the road and trailed far behind him, keeping a large gap on the straightaways and gunning it to catch up when he took a turn.

He led me down a twisting course of country lanes, so far that I wondered dimly if I'd ever find the water tower again. The road got narrower and the forest got thicker, marked less and less often by ramshackle houses with tar-paper sheds. Then the asphalt turned to dirt. I turned a corner just in time to see him bike straight into the forest, disappearing through a gap between two trees.

I kept driving—not quite sure what to do, not wanting him to see me. The road veered on through the woods, and I followed for another minute or two before doubling back to where I'd lost him. Then I pulled off into the weeds and got out.

It surprised me to discover that the road also continued in the direction the bike had taken, though it didn't look like anyone had driven there for years.

I looked around, no sign of him. I thought about it. And I stepped into the woods.

❧

The dirt was strewn with rocks and roots and scraps of last year's leaves. It had once been wide enough that the trees on either side no longer touched overhead, a gap of sky where their limbs couldn't quite reach. But roads can die, like people do, and I knew that one wouldn't be found on any map.

I followed along for a while, just listening, no sound but the looping trill of a bird somewhere. I passed the carcass of a house set back in the forest, three walls left standing and the roof caved in, just a broken cup for rain and falling leaves. The windows smashed, trees growing through, the sun-facing side webbed with ivy. The boy was long gone; I didn't even know what I was doing. I thought I heard the low rush of water in the distance, but it was hard to tell.

I couldn't help notice how far away I'd gotten, how distanced from the safety of my car. A thought occurred to me, all glittery with nerves: Maybe the boy knew I was following him. Maybe he'd ducked into the woods to throw me off. It wasn't a place anyone would go, at least not on purpose. Maybe he'd lured me out there. Maybe he was lurking in the pines somewhere, and now he was watching *me*.

This last thought was too much to handle. I scanned the trees, my knees tensing up, my keys clutched in my fist. I remembered the little cylinder of pepper spray, sitting useless on the passenger seat.

I was about to turn and run back when I saw something: the

sloping lines of another house—there, fifty feet off, where the road ended.

I bit my lip. It really did seem like no one was around, that no one had been there in my lifetime. I told myself to relax, and I walked to the end of the road.

It was an old Victorian, the kind falling down all over the state: a glorious ruin that stood in a patch of knee-high grass, tall and gabled and dark. The shingles were weathered and warped like driftwood, like they'd been carried out to sea and tossed back. A porch wrapped around the first floor, and in places its roof had fallen through, the debris just left there, loose boards hanging over the rubble. A stone chimney pushed its open mouth toward the sky.

I stared up at the high, forgotten turrets. Clouds swept by behind them, and I sensed the brisk, revolving speed of the world.

No one could live there, I thought. *The place has been empty for years.*

As I turned to go back, something caught my eye. It was the color I noticed first, a whiteness so at odds with everything else. I bent to look and found a crumpled scrap of paper, half buried in the leaves. It had some markings on it. I picked it up and smoothed it out across my palm.

My first impression was of something arched and soaring. A bird in flight. No, it was much stranger than that: a careful drawing of a human figure wearing a set of mechanical wings. The face had been ripped away, but you could tell it was a man, his arms outstretched, his muscles flexed. The wings themselves were drawn with intense attention to detail, the lines clear and assured, all marked with notes and annotations. Almost like a patent illustration.

Wings. A serrated, bat-like span, this mix of man and bird.

I'd never seen anything like it. And as I traced my fingers over the paper, feeling the furrows the pencil had left, something happened to me. I'm not saying the heavens opened, or anything like that. It was only an instinct at first. A shiver beyond the reach of conscious thought.

❧

I walked up onto the porch, holding the drawing like an address I'd been given. Everywhere paint had chipped from the slats, scattering the deck with large broken flakes. I knocked, just to prove to myself the place was empty. One, two. I held my breath and listened, hard, for any sound beyond the hush of wind through the trees. My calves tensed, ready to run. But no one came.

The old place was abandoned. It had to be.

The drawing had been lying there for years.

I pushed through the door and went in.

All I know is I felt I had to do it. Sometimes life just calls out to you, and you either answer or you don't.

The room I stepped into was a barely controlled chaos. It was order and madness both, a river rushing up against the mouth of a dam.

It had been a living room, once. Beneath it all, I made out a couch, an old easy chair, a low-bellied coffee table. But everything—I mean everything—was covered with paper, pages stacked three, four, five feet high. Pages in all different shapes and sizes, yellowed in various shades of age. So many, even a constantly scribbling hand would need a lifetime to fill them all. And not just that. Everywhere, countless wooden pieces leaned in strange shapes—like half-finished oars, like bows without string. Even the walls were full, nearly papered with notes and odd clippings from old dailies, all tacked up with cheap tape, mad scratchings in the margins.

I looked closer and saw a series of pictures of what appeared to be a flying man. They seemed to be reproductions of nineteenth century lithographs, monochrome and dusky, but what they showed was clear: a bird-like human body, suspended in the air. There was even a portrait of a bearded, athletic-looking man standing on a mountain ridge, clad in an elaborately constructed set of wings.

"Fig 90," a printed caption read. "Last model with movable pinions, designed for motive power (without motor)." Next to that, someone had written a note in pencil, two words in all caps: "HUMAN FLIGHT."

I should have left. Instead, I stepped deeper into the house. In places, papers were stacked so high the rooms felt more like a maze of narrow corridors, claustrophobic with fruit boxes and milk crates. Taxidermied owls and falcons perched on wooden plinths, smelling like vinegar and watching me with marble eyes.

I pulled air through my nose, slowing my heart down. I knew I should go. I decided to finish a quick loop through the house, and then run as fast as I could to the car.

I stumbled through a kind of library, where rows of academic hardbacks waited on cinder-block shelves. A long wooden propeller dangled from the ceiling like a bad chandelier. Bat skeletons hung on poles in dusty bell jars, meshed in their own long finger bones.

At the end of the house, I found a kitchen—faded counters, cast-iron stove—and pushed out a screen door into the sunlight again. My heart kicked, as though I'd just come up for air, and I stood there for a second before I realized where I was: a hidden back meadow, mangy with tall plants and ringed by high trees. A few low-slung buildings sat planted in the reedy grass. Open-mouthed equipment sheds had been piled high with junk by an outhouse with a real crescent moon cut in the door. In the distance, the roof of a barn jutted up over the gently sloping hill.

I had to leave. I had to. But I was towed on by something like the urge to pull a scab—the way you flinch against the sting to see the wound underneath.

I kept going, almost stepping in what appeared to be a mound of horse poop. The barn was big and church-shaped, its white paint peeling to reveal an earlier red coat, a mottled effect like blood in milk. A few squarish windows were set into its flaking sidewalls. I peered in through the glass. The panes were misted with filth, but I could see strange shapes hanging in the gloom.

Would anyone have turned back then? I looked back across the meadow to make sure the coast was clear.

I found a small side door, and the old knob gave a nice, smooth turn.

The barn was huge and dark, this sense of cavernous stillness. At first I couldn't tell what I was seeing. Then my pupils spread, and light filtered into my brain.

The barn was filled with wings.

They dangled in pairs, wooden frames stretched with pale, tight-fitting cloth, with long, supporting veins beneath the fabric that formed bat-like ridges along each edge.

Pair after pair hung suspended in midair, semitransparent, each outline different, like leaves held to the light. Some hung only five feet off the floor. Others were high enough to jump and graze with one hand, and still others swayed in the upper reaches of the barn, as if they'd flown there themselves. When I moved around the room, I noticed this subtle crosshatch overhead—thin strands of rope secured them to the rafters.

I raised my hands to feel the cloth between my fingers.

A winged skeleton of naked wood lay unfinished on a squarish worktable in the center of the room, covered with fragrant shavings. It looked like the bat bones I'd seen in the house, skinny, tapering phalanges that hooked into a scapula-like frame.

I rushed around the room, wanting to linger but also desperate to go, committing all I could to memory. Every time I gathered my wits to run, some new discovery made me pause. Tall bundles of fibrous sticks were stacked in a corner. An old loom, strung like a harp with thread, sat in the middle of the floor. A manual Singer sewing machine, built into a piece of desk-like furniture, complete with a foot treadle. A cot against the wall. By the far window I found a desk freighted with sketches, hundreds of pages drawn on in blue drafting pencil, just like the fragment I'd found in the road. On sheet after annotated sheet, flying men spread their limbs in winged machines. I tried to read the notes scrawled in looping script—odd phrases like "airfoil, blackbird pattern," and "see 1894 glider warp," and "30 m² #00 muslin."

The portraits' faces were vague and indistinct, often left unfinished above the neck, but the wings themselves were rendered with exquisite care—so detailed and realistic that I half expected them to flap from the page. As I leafed through the drawings, marveling at their beauty and audacity, tracing the pencil lines with my fingers, I briefly lost all sense of time.

Then I heard something near the door.

I froze, suddenly cast in bronze. Someone was outside, so close there wasn't even time to hide. I was trapped.

Silently, I commanded myself to burst into a puff of fog. If not fog, flames.

But the body never obeys.

I could only stand there pitifully in the flesh as horse doors thundered open along the wall, like curtains parting across a stage.

FIVE

A man stepped into the barn.

It wasn't the boy I'd seen at the tower. This person was older, though it was hard to say how old—in his fifties, at the very least. His beard was gray and full, but his unruly mess of windswept hair had stayed stubbornly reddish gold. Thick glass disks hid his eyes.

He saw me and went stiff.

"Oh," he said.

He looked at me strangely for a second. Then he walked into the middle of the room to lay some sheets of paper on his worktable, totally unfazed, as if he'd expected to find me there all along.

I couldn't run without passing him, I saw that. I stood by the far wall, helplessly caught. The air seemed to cool twenty degrees, my hands shivering like the knobs of some machine.

"I'm sorry—" I started to say.

The man held up his hand.

"Shh," he said.

He stood there and peered at me through the glasses, cocking his head as if to listen for something far away.

"I'm sorry," I said, again, my pulse flogging my ears. "I shouldn't be here. I'll go—"

"Don't be sorry," he said. "Just feel what you're feeling."

It was an odd remark, so unexpected that for a second I forgot to be afraid.

"It's all right," he insisted. "It takes time, I know."

He was wearing an ancient flannel shirt—the cloth gone all frizzy, the colors running together. It was eerie, the way he spoke, like he was referencing some earlier conversation he remembered and I didn't. For a second it was so quiet I could hear every little thing: the way his breath wheezed in his nostrils, bugs whirring in the grass outside. The cry of some distant bird.

Then he started to limp toward me—he had a bad ankle that gave with every step, reducing his gait to a frightening lurch. The fear flooded back, a hand at my throat. He wasn't much taller than I was, but he was muscular, the thickened look of a person who did hard work with his body. I felt a scream coming on, this pressure building in my chest like a cough.

"What do you feel when you see them?" he said.

"See them?" I hated how I sounded, the words high and pleading.

"The wings!" he roared.

I backed away as he came closer, feeling behind myself for the wall. His nose had healed funny after a break, and the way the bridge curved made his face look like an ill-fitting mask. He was close enough to grab me.

"Please," I said. It came out as a whisper.

"You've felt it all your life, haven't you?" he said. "All your *life*. Me, too. What's your name, my sister?"

I stared at him, terrified and uncomprehending.

"Your *name*," he said again.

"Jane," I said, before I had the sense to lie.

"Jane!" he said brightly, like it was a wonderful bit of news. "Look up, Jane."

A sweet, fetid smell rolled off him, like a gone-off cantaloupe. The last thing I wanted to do was turn my gaze away from him, make myself vulnerable like that.

"Look up, my sister," he said, and there was a new note in his voice—something gentle, even affectionate, an old friend surprising me with a gift. Something in his tone convinced me, just a little. It seemed to matter less that I was so afraid.

His eyebrows lifted expectantly. He would wait until I did it.

I looked up. The wings hung over us in the rafters, posed mid-flight in a dozen frozen postures.

"We're going to fly, Jane," he said.

The words hit like icy water.

"You. Me. All of us. We're finally going to leave the ground on our own power, and everything will be as it should be. But you've always known this. Flight has always waited for us. It's what we're here to do."

His voice purred low in his throat, almost like he was talking to himself, and I suddenly found I wanted to lean in closer to hear him. *Flight, finally, always*—these were words I'd known forever. But I felt like I was hearing them for the first time, parts of a language I didn't yet understand, expressing things I never knew could be said.

"We're really going to do it, this time," the old man said. "We're going to correct the human body. Here, come with me."

I felt the universe shift just slightly. It was the strangest thing: like the earth had tilted on its axis toward the sun. The laws of physics began to subtly bend. Something was happening to me. His words rushed through my skull in a tide, crashing onto the bright shore of my mind.

To correct the human body.

As if lightning were about to strike us both, all the small hairs rose on my arms.

୬

I followed him over to the naked wood frame that lay across his worktable. Huge and skeletal, the bones curved with the taut power of a pulled-back bow.

"This," he said, "is everything I know. The work of my life. The *answer*. My god, we only need to fix the fabric to the wood—a day's work, less—and we'll be finished. Tomorrow, in the morning . . ."

His sentences picked up speed and intensity as he spoke. What he was implying seemed obvious, and impossible: That he was building a pair of wings to *fly* in. That the skeleton on the table would have the power to lift him, rising bird-like into the air. I peered over at him, trying to see past the thick, mirroring panes of his eyes.

"When you're finished," I repeated, gesturing down at the table, "you mean—you'll be able to . . ."

My mouth faltered at the word. *Fly*. It seemed too childlike to say, and somehow too profane.

The old man nodded.

"Yes," he said. "Yes—that's *exactly* what I'm telling you."

My brain churned with effort. What he was saying made no sense. Not that the idea was purely science-fictional, like time travel or werewolves. Birds, bugs, and planes flew every day. I'd just always assumed that people couldn't do it. Everyone did. But suddenly I wasn't sure why.

The man watched me, smiling, as if he'd already sequenced the exact progression of my thoughts, and was delighted to watch the emotions play as expected across my face. He shook his fists in a warm, celebratory gesture, his whole being bristling with energy.

"Oh, it's a *sign* you've come to us now," he said. "In the last hours—and not a minute sooner. My sister, you're right on time."

I wondered who he meant by *us*—if that meant there were others, or if it was simply the pronoun that best expressed the expansive cast of his thought. There was something almost embarrassing about how eager he was, the ardency in his voice.

"What about those?" I asked, deflecting him. I pointed to the ceiling, where the other winged shapes hung, looming over us in the darkness.

He nodded.

"Those," he said, "are different. They're my models, my studies, my works-in-progress. My failures. Incomplete solutions to the question. What I'm saying is—they don't *fly*. Not like this one will, once we're finished."

He gestured to the table. Then he seemed to think of something.

"Here," he said. "You should see this."

He limped over to the far wall. I kept my distance and started to relax a little, the jitters slowing in my knees. I could outrun him if I had to. He could barely walk.

He started to unlash a rope from a mounted iron tie, like freeing a boat from a dock. Overhead, a giant bat-like glider started to lower, the ropes whispering as they slid. I had to move out of the way to make room.

"This," he said, "is an exact replica of Otto Lilienthal's 1894 glider. You've never heard of Lilienthal, have you?"

I hadn't. The glider settled on the floor with a gentle creaking of wood.

"No one knows him, not anymore," he said. "But he was once the most famous man on earth. A great, strapping genius of a German. This was years before the Wright Brothers. You've heard of *them*."

"Of course," I said.

"They don't deserve the credit they get," he said. "Not a fraction. They stole wholesale from Lilienthal. Everything they knew about air pressure, wing design, the lifting proper-ties of curved surfaces—it all came directly from him. But the Wrights, they corrupted Lilienthal's vision. It was never about *planes*. What he wanted—what *we* want—was to fly, in the true sense, to use our arms like wings. To soar freely, powered only by our bodies. *That* was the dream. It was much too quickly forgotten."

He spoke so intensely, in such an outpouring of admiration and anger and longing, that I couldn't think of anything to say. The idea of this winged German seemed outrageous, and I sensed he was exaggerating.

"You see it, don't you?" he went on. "How, for a brief mo-ment, we were focused on the right thing. The only thing. *True flight*. Lilienthal inspired the world to think of the sky as ours, to dream that we could correct our bodies and *take* it. People forgot about him. They moved on with their war planes, with their TWA. But it could have been different. When he died in 1896, *millions* mourned in the streets."

He'd nearly talked himself out of breath, and fell silent for a second to recover, the air wheezing heavily in and out through his nose.

"How did he die?" I asked, trying to be polite.

"Lilienthal? He was killed in a glider wreck," he said.

"Ah," I said.

"He died at his peak," the man said. "At his absolute peak. In a machine he'd made, with movable wings. He'd captured the world's imagination with gliders like this one, fixed struc-tures that could carry him hundreds of feet in good wind. But he died trying to *fly*. He might have gone on to do it, too, if he'd survived—he was that far along. But now that's over. What we've built in the last months"—he gestured over to the worktable—"builds definitively on Lilienthal's advancements. On the whole forgotten history of flight."

His glasses flashed, two signaling mirrors.

"Gliding isn't enough," he said. "Planes are not *enough*. You see that, don't you? How free, unfettered flight would be everything? How it would liberate the human spirit? And we'll do it! Starting tomorrow. Our wings will break open the world as we know it and allow something new to be born—"

I heard something behind me and turned around. A thin form paused in the doorway, someone with long dark hair. It was the boy I'd seen at the tower, I realized. He lingered in the opening.

"Oh," the man said, breaking out of his monologue. "It's Ike. My boy! Come here, Ike."

❧

The boy stepped into the barn, giving me a wide berth as he walked across the floor. His hair hung like a veil over his face, a sullen method of concealment. He didn't look at me or speak.

"This is my son, Ike," the man said. "This is Jane, Ike. She's here to help us. I'm Barry, by the way," he told me.

The boy said nothing—he just stood there, way too thin. His ragged clothes, I realized, shared a look with the gliders overhead. They were cut from the same cloth.

"It occurs to me we should *show* her, Ike," the old man—Barry—said, speaking to the boy, but smiling at me. "Shouldn't we? So she can see it for herself!"

He'd reached a state of high animation, delighted with how the population of his barn had grown.

"Come on," he said. He grabbed one of the glider's wings and lifted it half off the floor. But the boy stayed still.

"Dad," he said.

"Come on!" Barry roared.

"Dad," the boy said again, softly. "Stop."

"What are you just *standing* there for?"

"Just don't," the boy said. "Please." He kept himself angled away from me, standing still with the quiet intensity of a person keeping vigil.

"Ohh," Barry groaned dismissively, waving him away. He turned to me. "He gets like this. Help me, won't you?"

For a second they were both looking at me, the glider between them.

"Help you how?" I said, trying to stall.

"Help me carry this outside!" he roared, shaking the glider with his hand. "I'm going to jump off the roof."

It was a startling declaration, despite everything he'd said. I could feel the high darkness of the barn, the roof sloping upward like the ceiling of a church.

"Jump . . . ?"

"Oh, forget it," he said. He lifted the glider himself and began to limp across the floor with it, the wings bucking in the rhythm of his lurch. The contraption was large and unwieldy, but I could tell how light it was by the nimble way he guided it through the barn's double doors. I couldn't see him anymore, then. There was a loud thump, and he shouted something back at us, yelling unintelligibly.

The boy, Ike, and I looked at each other. He seemed to be a few years younger than me, with the half-formed look of someone in their very early twenties, and his eyes were pretty—a sea-glass brown. But his face seemed stuck in a permanent wince, as if the whole situation were a source of chronic pain. It seemed wrong to be that young and look so sad already.

Then it dawned on me: the old man, Barry, was insane.

Of course he was gloriously strange, that was obvious. But he'd spoken with such torrential authority, and the gliders themselves were so compelling, that I hadn't thought to write him off completely as a kook. Yet Ike had tried to stop him. I could still hear his soft, exasperated voice: *Dad, stop, please.*

Maybe Barry was merely in the grips of some mania, compelled by the logic of madness. Maybe I'd provoked someone who needed no provoking, and now he was all stirred up and ready to jump from his roof.

"I—"

I stammered out some faltering thing.

But Ike just shook his head, a pained expression on his face, as if he couldn't believe what I'd done. Then he was moving. He backed out the double doors and was gone.

I followed, but by then he seemed to have vanished into the meadow. I rushed around the side of the barn, only to find Barry climbing a silver ladder that was bolted to the wall, the glider laid beneath him in the grass. He couldn't really bear weight on his left foot, so he made his way up with his arms more than his legs, grabbing the crossbars with both hands and pulling himself higher and higher in a series of quick one-legged hops. Then he pulled himself over the lip of the roof, his boots scraping on the shingles.

Before I could say something to stop him, the glider started rising, a hallucinatory upward slide into the air. I looked up, startled. Barry was standing on a cantilevered wooden platform that jutted from the roof, and was turning a crank that squealed as it wheeled around. He'd fixed the glider to some kind of rigged-up rope-and-pulley system—I could see the metal hook he'd fitted into one of the wooden ribs. The wind pulsed in the cloth as the winged shape lifted, causing the frame to twitch and shiver like a living thing.

The barn had to be more than two stories tall—it was hard to say how tall exactly, but it was clearly a dangerous height. Maybe he *was* crazy. Maybe his broken body was not a sign of some interior wildness—of course it wasn't—but the legacy of his falls. A slow, eerie sensation filled me. The feeling you get when you discover mold on a piece of bread you've already half eaten.

"Remember, this will be *gliding*, not flying," he called down to me. "Just a prelude—a promise!—of what's to come."

I felt sick.

"You're sure you want to do this?"

He laughed.

"My sister," he bellowed. "Of *course* I'm sure!"

Behind him, the sun had already started to set, the clouds purpling with the vivid colors of a bruise. He stooped and lifted the glider.

There was still no sign of Ike. *I can't stop him*, I remember realizing. Whatever was going to happen was going to happen.

I watched Barry guide the glider over his shoulders. Suddenly he was transformed. The man was gone, replaced by something winged and huge. Sunlight hit the fabric, turning the stretched cloth into two lit panes. His arms vanished in twin baths of light. He hobbled to the edge of the plank.

My knees tensed. I wanted to appeal to some higher authority, some minister of safety and sense, but of course no one was there.

The tips of Barry's boots stuck out over the ledge. He swayed gently, swooning to some slow, private music. The wings tilted subtly this way and that, as if tasting the direction of the wind. Then a breeze gusted, so strong it bent the grass. Before I could do anything, Barry took a step forward and jumped.

A rush of wind bucked in the glider's fan, and his body lurched upward. His shape started to float through the air, as smoothly as if he'd been mounted to a track. As the wings soared over me high above, I heard more than saw them pass—the wind made a tiny thunder in the grass, his body briefly blotting out the sun. It was spectacular. A human form parting the sky, suspended in midair. My pupils opened, and my brain felt every neuron fire—the world spreading out around me, everything so much bigger than I knew.

I turned in time to see Barry rushing toward the ground, far into the meadow, completing a right triangle's longest line. The glider lifted a few feet again at the end, so that, for a moment, I thought he might rise again toward the sky.

Instead, he dropped gently, staggering a few paces before falling to all fours in the grass.

The whole thing took five seconds, maybe less.

I ran toward where he knelt in the grass, gasping. The glider shielded his body like a strange white shell, moving subtly as he breathed. His head stuck out through a hole in the fabric, but the rest of him stayed hidden. He was all right.

"See?" he shouted. "You feel it, don't you?"

That was when I saw his eyes for the first time: two bolts of mad, dancing blue, like flames in a gas range. A sob built in my throat, taking me by surprise. I stammered something, who knows what.

"What you just saw," Barry said, his voice shaking, "a German did more than a century ago. He was on the brink of it, even then. But we've nearly finished what he started. Tomorrow, Jane, it's time!"

Across the meadow, Ike stalked toward us. Something flashed in the grass—Barry's glasses, thrown from his head, rested half folded in a mess of stalks. I snatched them up.

"Your glasses," I said.

"Go ahead," Barry said. "Put them on me. I can't see a thing."

It seemed so strange, considering his fierce blue gaze, that I was just a blur to him.

I put the glasses on for him again, guiding the wiry arms into the red-and-gray hair above his ears, and as I did it struck me how much had changed since that morning. I could never have imagined, as I woke up into the stale smell of my car, the way the meadow would look with Barry's glider fanning out over the grass, the old man peering up at me from the middle of his contraption. If a single day could shift like that, anything was possible—anything could happen under the neon clouds, the endless Day-Glo chamber of the sky.

"Help me, Ike," Barry said, and suddenly the boy was there, standing mutely just three feet from us.

As Ike lifted, I saw the undercarriage of the glider—Barry's arms were not outstretched, like I'd thought, but folded across his chest, embracing a wooden axis that held the machine together.

"Let's eat," Barry said. "A feast—we're going to need it. Because tomorrow, the real work starts. We'll want full bellies."

He looked at me.

"But first," he said, "there's something you should do."

"Me?" I said.

We brought the glider back into the barn, and then Barry led me over to the edge of the woods, past a fenced-off chicken coop I hadn't noticed, where hens waddled and scratched about in the dirt. A small wooden crate sat in the shadows. Something moved behind the slats: a nervous brown lump of fur, with eyes like black jewels. A pink nose twitched at the air.

"Goody," Barry said. "We're in luck."

"A rabbit," I said.

"The whole place is thick with them," Barry said. "As the land will be, once it's allowed to heal."

Something about the way he said *the land* made me think of the wheat fields on a cereal box, airbrushed and overwrought.

Ike bent down and opened the trap, pulling the creature out. He held it against his chest, and its dark eyes bulged with terror.

"When we finish the wings," Barry said, "everything's going to change. I mean *everything*—you need to hear this, Jane. What did you eat for dinner last night?"

I wasn't sure I'd *had* dinner last night—maybe a plastic tube of trail mix from the gas station.

"Whatever it was, I'll bet you bought if from the *store*. Didn't you?"

I nodded, even if the truth probably wasn't what Barry had in mind. The rabbit's black eyes glared back at me.

"Listen very carefully to me, now," Barry said. "When we finish the wings, the deliveries are going to stop coming. The stores are going to close. Maybe not tomorrow. Maybe not next month. But they will. People aren't going to waste their lives toiling anymore, not when they can fly. The whole extractive system will start to fail. And when it does, you need to be ready. The way me and Ike are ready."

We walked around the side of a junk-crammed shack, where a four-legged structure stood—tall and thin, like a lifeguard's chair. A traffic cone hung upside down on ropes from the center of it, the last six inches of the orange tip raggedly sawn off. The grass below was blackened with stains.

It was blood, I realized. Then I understood.

"Ike and I, we live off this land completely," Barry said. "We use no electricity. No fuel but good old wood. We pay no taxes, have no bills. And everything we eat, we grow and catch."

The rabbit's bulk struggled against Ike's embrace, its hide swelling and shrinking with panicked breath. Ike seemed to whisper something into the shallow dish of its ear, and then he stuffed it headfirst into the cone. The creature hung there, upside down, hissing silently at us. We heard its body struggling inside, a weak scraping of claws.

Barry picked something off a wooden stool and handed it to me. A hunting knife, the blade crested with teeth.

"Cut its throat," Barry said, "and we'll eat well tonight."

In the fading light, his glasses shone, twin moons.

I'd never killed anything before. I looked over at the boy, who turned away, as if the whole thing pained him—though I couldn't tell if he was shamed by his father, by the slaughter, or by me.

"This is the transaction," Barry said. "There is no life without death. It's always been that way. They just hide it from you."

The blade shook in my hand.

I could tell he was testing me. He wanted to see what I would do.

I looked into the rabbit's face, the gleaming pebbles of its eyes. I recognized its fear. There had always been a frightened rabbit inside me, too, huddled in a slaughter cone. I had just never known I could kill that part of myself.

Their eyes were on me, watching.

I cupped the small skull in my palm and drew the blade across its throat. Blood fell from the open neck in a long string of red drool.

"Moment of silence," Barry said, and while the animal drained we hung our heads.

"Thank you, rabbit," Barry finally said, after a while.

"Thank you, rabbit," the boy whispered. So I said it, too.

Eventually Ike pulled the body out, carrying the slain thing by its ankles as we walked toward the house.

❧

By then the afternoon was coming to an end—the sun would be down soon. The three of us stepped up onto the warped back porch, which groaned as if it might collapse under our weight, and I followed them inside.

Ike produced a weathered tin can, its mouth sawed open

and the lid still attached, with some holes punched in it. He dumped a twiggy bundle from the can, messy as a bird's nest, and unwrapped it to reveal a dully glowing ember. He stuck a twist of cloth against the coal, and when he pulled it away again it was on fire. I looked on, surprised, as he used the flaming wick to light a candle, then blew it out. Then he wrapped up the ember again. It all happened quickly as a magic trick, some pyrotechnic sleight-of-hand I couldn't fathom.

We were in the kitchen. I recognized the sink and counter, the round table flanked by chairs, the cast-iron stove. Barry carried the candle through a side door—its light bounced and fluttered as he limped down a set of stairs, before fading from view. While I stood there in stunned silence, Ike spread the rabbit out on the counter and started to saw vigorously at its neck, drawing the blade with a gruesome grinding sound across the spine.

My cheeks burned and my ears rang like I'd been slapped, but there was nothing to do except watch.

Barry emerged holding a heavy sack, and tumbled a few sprouted potatoes across the table. "Can you cook?" he said.

I shook my head.

"Well, that's another thing," Barry said. "There won't be any Howard Johnson's where we're going. Watch Ike."

I peered over Ike's shoulder while he attacked the corpse, until the head finally lolled free. Then he skinned the poor thing, a process like pulling a too-tight glove away from an alien hand. The wetness underneath sparkled in the candlelight and smelled like blood. Then he cut the rabbit open and reached into its belly. He pulled out handfuls of organs and bowels, which he flung into the sink in a glistening heap.

While he worked, something caught my eye. It was a mouse, nosing its way along the counter. I dug my nails into my arm. Did I say something? Before I could decide, Ike raised his arm, and with a casual backhanded thwack sent the mouse flying. I heard it splat against the floor and scurry off.

A sound built in my throat—a scream or laugh, I couldn't tell—and I had to suck my tongue to the roof of my mouth to choke it down.

Later, we walked out into the yard again, all laden with supplies. Ike carried the rabbit on a kind of pointed spit, the tin can dangling from a rope around his neck. Barry hauled a cast-iron pot of sliced potatoes, the eyes cut away. They'd handed me a gallon jug of fuzzy brown liquid. We laid our things down by a rock-ringed ash pit in the yard, stacked high with firewood, which lay between two tall, slingshot-shaped wooded stakes. Ike laid the spit across them, and the rabbit hung there, pink and headless on its skewer.

I truly didn't know if I'd be able to eat it. I'd gone hours without a cigarette, and by then I'd passed into a state beyond wanting, beyond disgust—I only knew that my stomach ached in my guts, a tired fist that couldn't come unclenched.

The firewood had already been prepared, a crisscross of logs that graduated into smaller branches, kindling twigs, and bark shavings. Ike shook out the contents of his can and unwrapped the coal again, blowing on it until it was orange and molten. Before long, he had flames leaping in the pit.

They pulled a few log stumps out of the shadows, and we sat to watch the fire lick the bottom of the hanging pot. When the carcass dripped hissing grease into the flames, Ike got up to turn the spit.

"Cider?" Barry asked, though he was already pouring me a mugful. I lifted the porcelain to my mouth and tasted, a prickle of cinnamon and sweet apples. I started to feel drunk on the first sip, my cheeks numb even before the juice had made its way down my throat.

The meal took a while to cook. As we waited, I watched cinders chase each other toward the sky. A bat twittered overhead, beaming silent radar out into the trees. I tried to remember how I'd ended up there, in the middle of a wild meadow with two homesteaders as the sun set, the sky a rumpled length of purple-orange silk.

When the food was ready, Ike tore the rabbit into three pieces, and we ate. The skin crackled on the tongue, the meat so sweet and tender I could almost feel each taste bud stand erect as I chewed and tore.

Then Barry began to speak.

When the wings were finished, he said, it would be different. We'd rove out down the country lanes, and visit all the run-down houses where people suffered through meager lives, and show them what we'd done. They'd see the wings, and their eyes would widen, and they'd know that things could never be the same.

I closed my eyes and listened, heat in my cheeks from the fire and their homemade booze. It was nice to let Barry's words flow in and out of my ears, until his voice just seemed like part of the landscape, cousin to the fire and the crickets and the wind. I reminded myself that what he said was crazy, of course. *He* was crazy. Anyone could see that.

But in some private, rubbed-raw corner of my heart, I was desperate to believe it.

Six

Barry fell silent after his monologue, then dropped his plate in the grass and stood, apparently finished. He limped away without a word, leaving me alone with Ike.

I watched him go, helpless and confused, unsure if he meant for me to follow. But Barry disappeared into the barn without looking back once. So then it was just the two of us. I looked at Ike across the fire, trying to think of what to say. But Ike barely stirred—he didn't seem to feel he owed me any conversation. He stared into the fire, barely blinking, this distant look on his face, his focus so insistent that I could glance over at him without feeling self-conscious. Flames clicked and snapped in the pit.

It was easy to see what I'd felt drawn to at the tower. There was something almost otherworldly about him. This quiet intensity. The way he pushed his hair away from his eyes, an absent brush of his hand. The right alignment to his boyish, pleasing features. He might even be handsome, I realized, if he'd only just relax—but his knitted brows and downcast gaze gave him a mournful expression, this plaintive look that overwhelmed his face. Something about him cried out to be comforted.

Across the meadow, Barry started up his work again, the scrape of his tools echoing softly over the grass. The sound somehow made the silence between us more awkward, and I wanted to fill it. But before I could say anything, Ike stood. He picked up Barry's cup and plate, nesting them inside his own. He bent down again for Barry's fork and returned with everything to the house.

I sat there stranded in the gathering darkness, holding my own dirty plate. Candlelight bobbed in the windows of the barn. I looked up at the house, its high angles looming in shadow, and felt like a stranger there again.

I set my plate down, arranging my cup and fork as neatly as I could on the stump. I knelt in the plants to wipe the grease from my hands. After that I got up and started walking away—slowly at first, then quicker, until I was running. I ran across the meadow, through the hip-high grass along the side of the house, and down the dirt road as it filled like a bowl with night. I didn't stop until I reached the end of the road, where the Saab sat parked in the roadside gully.

I banged inside, collapsing onto the front seat. The familiar, sealed-in quiet of the car.

"What the *fuck*," I whispered, laughing softly to myself.

I reached for a half cigarette I'd left on the dash and lit it, my fingers shaking. I took a drag, exhaled, and let my forehead rest against the steering wheel.

There had been wings in a barn. Strange men. Talk of a mythic German. I had killed and eaten a rabbit.

I felt giddy at first, drunk on the pleasing rush that follows an unexpected encounter, knowing I had a new story, a good one, one of the more bizarre episodes of my life. To fly—really? It was outrageous. I could almost feel myself workshopping a new bit, an anecdote for parties, reaching for the language that would tell it best.

But as I sat there, smoking, I sensed I couldn't dismiss Barry so easily. His craftsmanship had obvious worth, the confident rasp of his voice. What if they were on to something, way out there in the woods? Could that be true? I barely allowed myself to consider it, the idea was so absurd. And yet stranger things had happened before. Weren't the Wright Brothers originally just a pair of bicycle salesmen tooling around small-town Iowa, or Ohio, or wherever it was they were from? Surely they seemed crazy, too, until the day they didn't?

I drove, the cigarette crackling pleasantly with each pull. The whole idea bent my brain. Either Barry was right—and it was physically possible to fly like that, given the right design—or he wasn't, and he was simply in the grip of a pointless obsession, obstinate in the face of proof. But which one was it? It was strange and dislocating not to know.

The more time passed, the more embarrassed I started to feel. I remembered Ike's pained silence, the way he just barely endured the seconds as they passed. As if his father's claims physically drained him. That wasn't the way you treated a groundbreaking genius; it was how you survived a self-deluded bore. Ike wore the cost of Barry's passion on his face: it was a dangerous fantasy, grandiose at best, and I sensed the disappointing truth that lay beneath. For the first time since leaving Ithaca, I started to feel lonely. I wished I had someone with me, another person to remind me what was real.

⌇

I stayed in a motel that night, for the first time in a while. Another brokenhearted little operation, just twelve rooms set into a roadside slab. The neon VACANCY sign that buzzed in the lot threw a hot pink splash on the lawn. All I wanted was to sleep in a real bed, a door I could dead-bolt, a little time to think. And a shower. It would feel so good to be clean.

After all those nights in the Saab, my room felt lavish, palatial. There was a queen bed with a floral spread: pink poppies and carnivorous birds. The fake stucco walls had the frosted surface of a cake. I stripped off my clothes and showered for the first time in forever. The water was hard and smelled like sulfur, but the pressure was gorgeous, a hot, stinging rain. Grime fell away in brown cascades. I massaged an entire vial of free shampoo into my scalp, working out the tangles in my hair, slowly starting to feel human again.

Later, I got into bed with my book, but found myself reading the same sentence over and over. I couldn't tune in to Eliot's voice, not even after all those pages. My brain kept returning to Barry, to Ike, to the fine-grained light in their barn. When I closed my eyes, winged shapes floated through the darkness.

I glanced over at the phone, sitting there on the bedside table. I had this sudden urge to talk to someone, to hold a familiar voice up to my ear. What I'd seen was so strange, too much to process by myself. It got so that I could hardly breathe with the secret of it, a phantom sitting on my chest.

I reached out and touched the plastic handle. Of course I thought of my parents. Not because I actually wanted to call them—I couldn't. But because phones are inherently associated with parents. Every single phone in the universe is a reminder that, hey, there you are, not calling your parents.

That feeling gets especially acute when you've run away from your life without telling anyone why, or where you might be going, or whether or not you're dead.

What did they think had happened to me? Where did they think I'd gone?

Some things start to feel inevitable once you've imagined them. I would dial the ten-digit number etched into my memory. My parents would be home, and I'd treat them to the sound of their daughter's voice. I was not so far away after all. The whole thing could end in thirty seconds.

I picked up the receiver, listened to the dial tone, set it down again. Then I picked it up a second time, and called my brother instead.

Ian.

It always comes, the moment when I decide to talk about Ian. In every new friendship, every new relationship, though sometimes I'll wait for months or even years. Yes, I have a sibling. No, I won't elaborate. Until I do.

I used to suspect the worst of myself, that I omitted Ian from my story out of shame. But I came to realize that that wasn't it at all. I had learned to be ashamed for other people, for the way that they tended to be. I flinch away from talking about Ian because—almost invariably—people react like I'm telling them about a tragedy, like I'm dying from some terminal illness. They get sad and weird and uncomfortable. They think I'm telling them about loss, when I'm only telling them about life.

There is nothing inherently tragic about the way Ian is embodied. What *is* tragic—what's wrong—is only that the world makes things so much harder for him than they really have to be.

Ian lives at the Hearth at Pine Gables, a group home for adults with developmental disabilities. The campus sits on a few acres with a tennis court and a little lake where a patient white crane hunts for goldfish. Ian lives on what's called the Heroes Ward. Pine Gables has all kinds of residents with all kinds of challenges, and the heroes are what they call the ones who need the most support.

If my brother is a hero, he doesn't know it. He only knows his body as it's always been, and like all of us there are things he can and cannot do. He can't speak, and he can't walk. He needs to be pushed in a wheelchair, and lifted into the bath. But he can move his hands in a wandering way. He can smile, too, and his eyes are dark and bright as they dart from face to face. When he trains his attention on you, smiling like that, you feel something swell in you, like you've just grown a fifth chamber in your heart.

He loves to eat, sitting in his chair, a throne with jacked-up supports that keep him from falling over. He has trouble chewing and swallowing food, so his meals are pureed and spoon-fed to him. I've spent countless hours feeding him that way, an act as intimate as anything I can think of. Hand to mouth, our eyes meeting between bites. When there's time, I'll put on a record—because, more than anything, Ian loves music—and we'll listen together as he eats.

A change comes over Ian's face in the presence of music. You can feel his attention deepening. I've played him everything over the years, Mahler and Coltrane and Bowie and Nina Simone, old salsa records and Bach cello suites. Once I put on Kreisler's *Praeludium and Allegro*, and when I looked back I saw tears in his eyes. But he likes pop music, too, especially Top 40 stuff with bass lines you can feel. He'll shimmy in rhythm when he's happy, swaying side to side in his chair. His all-time favorite is "You Make My Dreams Come True" by Hall and Oates. Of all the music in the world, a three-minute Hall and Oates track does the most to get him rocking—his clock-pendulum dance, the amped-up wattage of his smile.

I missed him.

Before I knew what I was doing, I'd picked up the phone and was calling him at the Hearth. I knew the number by heart, all ten digits and the special PIN. I glanced at the bedside clock. The aides would be readying the floor for lights-out.

"Heroes Ward," someone said.

"Can you put me on with Ian, please?" I said. "It's his mother."

I can impersonate my mother's voice exactly, a superpower I've had since childhood. Almost no one can tell the difference.

There was some shuffling in the background, the high, crazed music of a cartoon, and then I heard his voice.

For years, I've called Ian just like that, to listen to his breath. I talk to him, and sing to him, and tell him I'm there. He knows it's me, I have no doubt about that. And as I listen to him breathing, I know he's there, too.

"Ian," I said. "It's me. It's Jane."

Breathing.

"I miss you," I said. "I'm very far away."

Off in the distance, I could hear the television.

"I'll come and see you soon," I said. "I don't know when, but *soon*. I promise. Okay?"

Breathing.

"Someday I'll tell you about all of this," I said. "When I come home. I hope you're feeling good. I hope you're doing well. And I miss you."

Breathing.

"You," I sang, softly, "you make my dreams come true."

The subtle sound of saliva on his tongue and teeth, a cluster of small bubbles popping. I knew that sound: it meant he'd smiled.

I had to hang up before he heard me crying.

I was so grateful to Ian for that, his gesture of recognition and delight. But as I sat there on the side of the bed, trying to collect myself, I somehow felt worse than I had before. The dank little room, cast in the glow of a ten-buck lamp. My clothes bunched in a heap by the heater, the wallpaper blotched with stains. What was I even doing? It all seemed so dirty and desperate and small.

I turned off the light, sinking the room into blackness, and shut my eyes. But the sheets felt scratchy and too hot, and my mind wouldn't slow down. I flopped around on the bed, itchy and restless, chasing comfort through a hundred different sleep positions, none of them good enough.

After a long time, I got up from bed and opened the curtains. The moon was out at last. Dark air seeped in through the open window, chilled and pollen-sweet.

I got dressed and went outside to look up at the stars. They glittered overhead, salt spilled across an endless black cloth. I stood there barefoot in the parking lot and remembered what was real: that we are just tiny, fragile creatures riding a huge orb through the night.

I fully felt the weirdness of that truth. The beauty, too.

When I went inside again, the sheets were cool.

I even got some sleep.

～

I woke up in the daylight. The distant sound of a radio rushed in through the open window, the curtains lifted and dancing. My bedsheets lay in a huddle on the floor—I'd thrashed them off in a dream.

It had rained all night. When I walked out to the parking lot, I found the asphalt all splattered with long, waterlogged worms. They lay there blind and marooned, like so many scraps of wet bootlace.

I felt a surge of pity, a nagging urge to pinch them one by one and fling them back into the grass. I could almost hear them struggling, a slow, wet slurp as they turned imperceptibly on their bellies. But I didn't want to dirty myself with their cool, fish-like flesh, and besides, there were so many of them.

I lit a cigarette and looked up at the sky—everywhere, a deep, unbroken blue—and felt the pull again, the familiar urge to disappear. To push my soul out through my mouth, leaving my body crumpled there on the pavement like a cast-off suit of clothes. And me, just a rising wisp of cloud.

I could have done it. Left. Moved on to the next town.

Instead, when I got behind the wheel, I found myself driving back to Barry's.

I was lonely, that was definitely part of it. They were the first people I'd been around in weeks, the first tentative human connections I'd made in so long. But there was a voyeuristic element, too. Was he really going to try *to fly*? It was a mad, implausible desire, and yet it also seemed impossible that Barry could be all bluster. I could still feel the white heat of his conviction, the future so certain he could reach out and grab it. He was either a genius or a fraud, but neither option felt quite right. The two possibilities pushed up against each other with the force of geologic plates, the resulting curiosity so intense it almost made me tremble.

I wanted to see what would happen, that was all. I just wanted to know.

I retraced my route back to the place where I'd pulled the Saab off the road. Except this time I nosed the car between the trees and onto the long dirt lane again, driving all the way down to where the house towered in its bed of seedy grass, all ramshackle elegance and dark, somber turrets. I got out and crept along the sidewall of the house, toward the meadow. Tall plants swept my legs and left stains on my jeans.

I walked all the way out and didn't see anyone. But as I approached the barn, I heard the scrape of a blade grating wood. I peered in through one of the side windows, listening. Overhead, Barry's failed gliders hung suspended in the air, taut and white. I say they were white. But they weren't, not really. The hemp cloth must have been a darker, more organic color. There was no bleach or powdered dye, anything that could render a color so unnatural. Still, when I think back, I remember his gliders, his wings, as white—I don't know why. I think of them as something brighter than they were.

I steeled myself and went in. Barry was bent over his worktable, tinkering with something.

"Hi," I said.

He looked up at me and froze like a startled deer. For a second, he was still.

Then a smile broke out on his face—the broad, unguarded smile of a person who's just been proven right.

"Hello, my sister!" he said.

Later, he'd say he always knew that I'd come back.

He never had even the shadow of a doubt.

⌖

The half-finished pair of wings lay naked across the worktable. The essential shape was there, but it was missing the long struts that splayed through it, holding the cloth together with the arched strength of a spider's legs.

"We've got to move quickly," Barry said, waving his hands over the network of wooden bones. "Every *second* matters. Because people are out there"—he gestured broadly with his hand—"and they're waiting for us. They've spent their *lives* waiting for us, and don't even know it."

His limbs quivered as he moved, his body like a toy too tightly wound.

"See these?" he said, pointing to the long, skeletal pieces. "They're willow rods—basket willow, not weeping. I've planted them by the river, coppices we cut back and harvest a few times a year. Enormously quick-growing. Feel it."

I touched the rod and pulled my hand away, surprised to find it tough and subtly pliant, bouncing back into shape like the cartilage in your ear.

"Strong, right?" Barry said. "But light. And hollow, like bird's bones. Willow rods are what Lilienthal used in his gliders, a technique overlooked completely by modern aviation. They grow naturally in the exact shape we need them to be, almost like a gift from Mother Earth. Like the world is just waiting for us to reach out and take what should be ours—the sky!"

I should have been embarrassed by such an unchecked outburst of emotion. It was such an absurd, overweening thing to say. But something seemed to happen as I watched him, that bearded man whose glasses flashed for emphasis as he spoke, whose knobby hands gestured with the intensity of an orchestra conductor. The air itself seemed to warp toward Barry as I listened, the way light bends toward a black hole.

"If we work hard enough," Barry said, "we can finish by nightfall."

His words thrilled me with their audacity. I wouldn't even have to wait very long to find out if he was full of shit.

The frame itself was held to the table by a sequence of metal clamps. Barry told me to hold it steady anyway, I think just to give me something to do. Then he attacked the wood with an ancient tool, an old drill he cranked by hand. The corkscrew gradually drew shavings from the wood, filling the air with piney scent as they drifted to the floor.

For what felt like an hour, I stood there clutching the frame, watching as the shavings peeled and fell. It was clearly hard physical work. Barry gritted his teeth, his lips pulled so far back with exertion that at times I could see the mottled pink of his gums, the missing tooth at the back of his jaw. I stood there, pushing down on the wood, trying to feel like I was helping.

My shoulder blades started to ache. Then my calves started to pulse with hurt, a dull glowing soreness that spread up through the notches of my spine.

Not only that, I needed a cigarette. I needed one so bad my elbows shook and my vision blurred. I didn't *want* to want a cigarette so much. But the need was there, glowing ever more brightly in my veins.

And yet I couldn't leave. It was clear Barry wanted and expected me to stay, and the simplest thing was to obey him. So I was stuck there, a semi-willing captive, trapped the way you get trapped in a bad conversation at a party. The minutes passed, and I started feeling foolish. I could have gone anywhere that morning, and I'd opted instead to toil in a too-warm barn.

Now and then, I'd glance longingly out the double doors toward the fresh world outside. In the distance hens milled about behind their chicken-wire fence, little daubs of brown paint. And I'd catch occasional glimpses of Ike as he passed back and forth across the meadow. He never came and said hello, or even looked my way. Instead, he haunted the property, grimacing and silent, pretending we weren't there—like Barry and I were some kind of persistent hallucination, unreal and better off ignored.

I must have watched him for an hour chopping firewood on the scarred tree stump he used for an altar, hacking logs in half, then in half again. There was something intentional and patient about his movements, as if he took pleasure in lining up the wood just so, savoring the moment before the blow. His ax-blows beat the morning's rhythm, each one an interminable clock tick as time oozed along. Then he was gone.

I wanted to leave, I realized. In the fantasy that played on repeat in my head, I just walked away, leaving Barry there, breaking off in a run the second he called my name. But I just couldn't force myself to do it, the thought of a sudden breach made worse by all that silence. By then I was so ravenous I thought I might faint. My gut started to make funny, humiliating noises, purring and growling like a pet ready to turn on its master. I hoped Barry didn't hear. But after one especially loud stomach gurgle, he briefly looked up at me. His glasses held the light, two moons.

"Hunger is energy, my sister," he said.

Then he threw himself back into his work, cranking away with his sad little drill.

I flushed, somehow mortified, insulted, and humbled all at

once. I hated that the inner workings of my digestive system were audible, that I couldn't hide the need I felt. But I tried to engage with the idea that hunger is energy. I tried to pretend the pain I felt was sustaining. Instead, I just felt sick. My legs ached secretly under my jeans. I was woozy and nauseous and ready to pass out.

I looked down at Barry, his forearms sweat-slick, bulging with effort as he turned the crank.

"Halfway through!" he announced.

"With this hole?" I asked feebly.

He nodded. "Then it's just eleven more to go."

The words burst from some deep part of me, this desperate, impatient part that didn't know what it was saying.

"Maybe there's a faster way to do it?"

Barry put the auger down and looked intently at me.

"This," he said, resting his hand on the tool, "is a manual bit. Why not use a power drill—that's what you're wondering, right?"

"I'm sorry," I said. "I'm not—"

"Electric drills wreck the grain, and fill the hole with backdraft," he said, talking over me, his voice steadily rising. "But it's not just that they're reckless and imprecise tools. It's so much more than that, my sister. What we are trying to build here is an approach we can *sustain*."

He loomed over me, a rank, prickling stench rolling off him, and I shrank back. For a second I thought he might actually grab me by the shoulders and shake me. I hadn't pegged Barry as a violent type. But the intensity in his voice was not the kind I wanted to hear from a male stranger, miles out in the woods, where I couldn't call for help.

"The power's going to go out one day, Jane," he said. "You see that, don't you? One way or another, the system's going to fail, and leave us all in the dark. Maybe it will be because we keep attacking the planet, unleashing a catastrophe that disrupts all the conveniences of so-called civilization. Or—and this is if we're lucky—it happens sooner, because of *us*."

He picked up the drill again, rattling it for emphasis as he spoke.

"When the system fails—and either way, it *will* fail—electric tools become no good. Just bad props, busted hunks of steel and plastic. They depend on the power of the old world—which is not power at all, but theft, deferred debt, suicide. See what I'm saying? We've got to be *ready*. We've got to be able to keep working in the darkness, the second the lights go out!"

He said all this in one great rush, a speech of such sudden intensity that I could only stare. His words flooded my brain somehow, though I wasn't quite sure what he wanted them to mean. Mostly I felt like crying, from the hunger and the strain and the rough way he'd raised his voice.

"Here," Barry said, before I had time to think. "Don't just stand there watching. *Do!*"

He opened a drawer under the worktable, pulled out another drill, and thrust it at me. It felt thick and clumsy in my hands.

"Do it," he said. "Right here."

He guided the tip of the corkscrew into the wood.

"Go. Hold it steady," he said, so I began to turn. My muscles clenched, and wood filings poured away from the frame like sand.

By the time I'd finished the first hole and had moved on to the second, my hair was plastered to my forehead, to my cheeks, my sweat-damp T-shirt clinging to my ribs. It was getting hotter as the day went on, and Barry stank—sometimes I'd catch a whiff of him so strong I had to turn my face. But when I started to feel like I couldn't go through with it, I'd look up into the upper reaches of the barn. The wings hanging from the rafters were things of otherworldly beauty, huge and intricate and light. Their strangeness, and the distance, started to play tricks with my sight, and in a delirious way they sometimes seemed like they were falling.

I looked away, through the double-wide doors again, letting the sight of the world outside restore my senses. The meadow was vividly green and lush, backed by a row of stern pines. And then, the strangest thing: a horse's head entered the frame.

I was sure I was hallucinating.

An enormous chestnut mare walked slowly past the doorway, like a vision in a dream.

"Excuse me," I said. "There's a horse."

Barry looked up, his eyes radiantly blue.

"Hm?" he said.

He slowly put on his glasses and looked outside.

"Oh," he said. "It's Friday. Here—let's go say hello."

I followed behind him, and felt this swell of gratitude—for a break from the monotony and the physical strain, and because what I'd seen was real.

After the darkness of the barn, the meadow felt almost painfully bright, electric with life and light.

"This is Friday," Barry said, patting the animal's haunch.

I ran my palm along the horse's ribs. Her muscles bristled at my touch.

"That's a nice name," I said.

"She comes and goes," Barry said. "She loves the grasses here. She probably escaped from a stable somewhere, because she'll let you ride her, and she'll take a bit. But we mostly let her do what she wants. No one ever really owns a horse."

The only horses I'd ever seen were the ones that clopped around Central Park pulling carriages, depressed-looking creatures that shared the road with taxis and were whisked off at night to box stalls so godforsaken they occasionally made the news. But this one was naked and gleaming, like the horses I'd loved in books from childhood.

"Come on," Barry said, and his voice was softer then, as if the animal's presence had somehow made him gentler. "Come with me."

I followed him at a distance around the side of the barn, to where an old iron spout jutted from the earth, above a metal bucket.

Barry pumped the handle, and the water gushed in, ounce after ounce. I was so thirsty that I couldn't bear to watch somehow, and glanced up at the woods. And there, at the edge of the forest, I saw something else.

A plane—or the skeleton of a plane.

It was like something from a history book—big and ancient-looking, with parallel wings held six feet apart by thin crisscrossing supports. The twin propellers had rusted still, the once-white muslin torn to rags by rain and time.

"Barry," I said, and pointed.

He looked up.

"Oh," he said, still pumping the handle. "That."

"What *is* it?"

"A model of the Wright Type B Flyer," he said. "The first commercially available aircraft the Wright brothers made. A steady, even-keeled machine. It's a masterpiece for what it is. You could fly across the state in that plane with enough gas and good weather. I powered mine off a lawn mower engine. I used to build them."

The water rushed into the bucket.

"I wanted to fly," he said, "since I was very young. And when a boy wants to fly, he thinks: planes. He's been *conditioned* to think in terms of planes. So when I came out here that was what I did, at first. I built planes and I flew them. I had quite a reputation with the locals, let me tell you. But I started to realize that flight could be something so much bigger and bolder than a plane. That was the last one I made. I left it there, and let the forest take it."

The bucket was full.

"You have to be careful with machines," Barry went on. "The things we make to serve us quickly become our masters. Choose *very* carefully what you want to be mastered by, Jane. Personally, I think of words from the philosopher Lao-tzu."

His eyes flashed at me, their Bunsen-blue.

"To paraphrase," he said, "the sharper the tools, the darker the times."

He offered me the bucket, and I drank, my forearms straining against the weight.

It was no city tap water, tepid and inert: this kind was stunningly cold, with a molten, metallic taste I found delicious. I pulled the lip of the bucket away, gasping, and drank deeply again before I set it down.

Barry lifted the bucket to his own mouth then, slurping greedily, raining droplets from his beard.

"There," he said. "Now, back to work."

Somehow, my hunger was gone. I felt refreshed and full, as if I'd had a meal, and I was ready to keep going.

❧

The barn door let the breeze in, and the pasture's sweet smell, and also the flies: thick black ones that scythed the air, worrying the quiet with their wings. I listened to them drone as I drilled, whisking them away with my hand when they landed with a sudden itch on my skin.

The frame was finished by late afternoon, and all we had to do then, Barry said, was attach the cloth. He'd taught Ike to make bolts of rough fabric by spinning fiber threads—which came from the flax they grew outside—on their loom. Once we'd sewn a skin around the skeleton we'd made, the wings would be complete.

"We're just *hours* away now," Barry said, his hands blistered and shivering.

Barry stationed me at their Singer sewing machine, the old iron model built into a wooden desk, pulled up close to the larger worktable. This was where I could actually be useful. He showed me how to pump the treadle, a kind of back-and-forth motion with my feet, like balancing on a board. Stitches juddered into the cloth as Barry helped to guide the wings under the needle. It was exacting, interminable work. I watched as lines of black thread made their way down the seams, ants filing in slow motion from a hole.

Night started to fall, and the barn filled up with twilight, a gathering darkness almost thick enough to cup in your hands. It would still be hours before we finished: a huge section of the wings still lay unsewn, the cloth loose as the hanging edge of a sheet.

I heard something at the door, and Ike stepped into the barn. He stood there in his moccasins and muslin rags, all frayed at the hems.

"Where have *you* been?" Barry said gruffly, barely looking up.

"Come eat," Ike said.

I was so hungry. I looked at Barry hopefully, but he didn't even answer.

"Dad," Ike said. "You need to eat."

I stopped sewing. The barn was very quiet.

"Fine," Barry said, and without another word started toward the door, the trochaic lurch of his limp.

Outside, Ike had a fire roaring in the pit. The three-log stumps were out, and in the unsteady light I saw a cup and bowl sitting on each one. He'd set out a portion for me, too, I realized, the first time he'd directly acknowledged my presence.

But when I looked over at him, ready to show some gratitude in my face, he only stared down at his food. We ate in silence. The metal bowl in my lap was filled with some kind of dark, bitter greens, a texture like cooked spinach, flavored with pungent chips of garlic. I flinched at the feral, foraged taste—later I'd learn to recognize the flavor of wild dandelion leaves—and washed it down with more of their hard cider. It wasn't much, and it was gone quickly. My stomach wanted more.

Ike stood, holding a large glass jug he had to manage with two hands, and refilled Barry's glass. He lugged the jug over and stood expectantly beside me, waiting for me to complete the ritual, too. So I held out my cup, and he refilled it. Then he sat down again and filled his own. I drank deeply, starting to feel the slow, unwinding sensation that kicks off a buzz. High above, the stars were out, a patient miracle of light.

Barry drained his glass.

"Cider," he said, sighing with satisfaction. "I'll take another, Ike."

Ike topped him off again.

"We do almost nothing to make this," Barry said, wiping his lips. "Cider just kind of happens. We press the apples and put them in the jug, seal the opening with a cheesecloth. Then, in a few weeks: cider."

He paused.

"Do you know why?"

He'd turned the full, disorienting beam of his attention toward me, and I sensed it was a test of some kind. I resented the ridiculous, pedantic question, the way he felt he could grill me. But I wanted to please him, too.

"Fermentation," I said, a word that came like magic to my lips.

"Well, of *course* it's fermentation," Barry said. "What I'm asking is *why*. Why does the cider ferment?"

I blushed in the darkness. Ike sat there looking at the ground, as if none of this was happening.

"I don't know," I said.

"Wild yeast," Barry said. "A fine, invisible layer that powders the world. There's yeast in the air. Yeast on our fingers. Yeast on the apple skins. Little single-celled creatures—fungi—and they get into the juice almost no matter what you do. It's a *feast* in there for them. They eat and eat, converting apple sugar into alcohol and bubbles. It's alchemy. They do it every time, and they do it all for free."

He held out his cup while he spoke, and Ike knew to hoist the jug and refill it.

"We don't hardly have to do anything—do we, Ike?"

Ike stayed silent. I wondered what Barry was driving at. It was strange and wonderful to think about all that invisible work, millions of unseen organisms transforming apple slush into something richer and more potent. An immaculate conception, straw into gold. At first I thought that was the larger point Barry was trying to make, something about nature's generative power and inexhaustible vitality. What Hopkins called, in a poem I loved, "the dearest freshness deep down things."

But he kept going.

"These little creatures," he said, "once they're bathed in sweet, rich juice—well, they won't stop. They *can't* stop. They don't know how to stop. They eat and eat and eat and eat, gobbling up sugar, reproducing, growing their population with unchecked speed. And as they do, the broth they swim in gets more and more polluted. Alcohol and CO_2—the stuff *we* want to drink, but they don't know that. It only takes a couple weeks to transform the world inside the glass. At a certain point, the yeast can no longer survive the waste it's made. Crash. Their whole, wriggling civilization dies off all at once."

Barry fell silent. The fire snaked and billowed and snapped. I looked into my cup, a small apocalypse in my hands.

"That's where we're headed, too," Barry said. "I know you know this. We're not so different from the little critters. Our jug's getting awfully full. My sister, there is going to be so much death. Can you imagine the misery? We're starting to see it already. Everything we love and rely on is dying, and we know it, but we aren't strong enough to stop."

At the time, I only dimly sensed his implication: that flight could chart us on a different course, stop us from being how we are. It would take time to make that link. But his words gave language to a dread I'd carried with me. The sense that we were hurtling toward a poorer, more wretched future, locked in more tightly by the day. We couldn't go on like this. Our reckless feast could only spoil the vat.

A time of great suffering is coming, we sensed it even then. And all because we are addicted to what we hate—to time clocks and oil rigs and screens. Clogged highways. Shopping. Obscene and pointless wars. We barely remember to be human. We no longer fight the forces that confine us, squeezing us into smaller and then smaller cages. We forget to look up at the fading stars.

SEVEN

It was late, and we were drunk, but we kept working. I sat at the sewing desk pedaling, while Barry and Ike pulled the wings back and forth under the needle. It was the first time Ike had joined us, a sudden shift—as if our momentum had pulled him in somehow, the task finally too serious to shirk. The three of us barely spoke, nothing but the revolving sound of the pedals and the stammering of the machine. The shush of cloth as it slid. Candles flickered on the sills.

We were close to finished, I could see that. What would happen when we did? I had no idea. It seemed impossible that Barry would strap the completed wings on, like he said he would, and take off into the skies. But I also struggled to believe—after so much work, and so much talk—that it would all just come to nothing. Either way, I needed to see it through. I'd always wonder, unless I put the question to rest.

Occasionally Ike would pause to refill our cups with cider. I welcomed it, grateful for the tangy sweetness on my tongue, a break from the monotony of work. I tried to catch his eye, but he never looked my way.

Some time passed before I noticed his hands.

He and Barry would guide the wings through the machine, the Singer planting its little line of thread. But there was something else, too: his long, slender fingers worked furtively at the cloth. He had the hands of a piano player, that same unnerving mix of elegance and strength.

I tried to watch without being too obvious about it. It was hard to tell at first, since I didn't want to stare. But once, when I glanced over again, I saw a flash of metal. All at once, it dawned on me. He was using something—a tool, a knife maybe—to tear open the stitches we'd sewn, hunching his shoulder like a shield so that his father couldn't see. I was dumbstruck, gawking openly at his face. Barry, who was deep in cider by then, seemed oblivious to the work Ike had undone, a looseness in the way he moved.

Then Ike looked directly at me for the first time. His solemn eyes held the candlelight, bright pinpricks in their depths. Something passed between us—I felt him will me into silence. I said nothing. He stood and refilled his father's glass.

All that cider, I realized, had been tactical. A way to blunt his father's speed. And it had worked. Barry had loosened up, slowly succumbing to exhaustion. He kept at it the way a sleepwalker might, hunched over the wings with his head slung to one side, his whole body drooping with fatigue. The rhythm seemed to lull him. His eyes would close and then jerk open, only to slowly close again. Within a few minutes, he'd stumbled back into his chair and had fallen asleep.

Ike stood.

"Dad," he said softly. But Barry was out, his shoulders rising and falling with his harsh and heavy breath. All his vigor had drained away, and he seemed to me to be an exhausted, beaten-down old man.

Ike backed off, a triumphant look in his eyes. Before I could say anything, he whisked out of the barn.

I went after him. Outside, night bugs whirred in the grass. The trees at the meadow's rim swayed under the stars. In the moonlight, I could see him stalking toward the house, his silhouette darker than the darkness.

"Wait," I called out.

He turned around and watched me coming. It was so dark I could barely see him through the blackness.

"Where are you going?" I stammered, not sure what else to say.

"Stop," he said briskly, barely hiding the anger in his voice. "Stop what you're doing."

"What?"

"You're *pushing* him," he said. "Don't."

"I—"

He cut me off.

"My dad," he said, "he's crazy—he—"

He shook his head.

"He's just going to get hurt."

He said that word—*hurt*—with startling, bitter force.

"Hurt?"

"Why do you think his leg is broken?" he demanded. "Why do you think his face is like that?"

I felt myself struggle with the obvious: that Barry had spent his life jumping from roofs, reaching for a mad dream in the sky. Not flying, falling. The many failures written across his body. I didn't want it to be true.

"You don't think—"

"No. I know."

The air ached with the crushing finality of it.

"Why did you come here?" Ike asked, his voice plaintive and accusing.

He didn't give me time to answer.

"You could help us, you know," he said. "He won't listen to me. But *you* could tell him. Make him stop this crazy, crazy—"

His voice choked off, his whole being tense at the thought of it.

"Or, if you can't do that," he said, "then just, please—don't come back. I mean it. Don't come here anymore."

We were both still for a minute, his face a hard-to-see shadow. His words hung between us, a threat and a plea. Then he turned away from me and walked quickly back to the house. From somewhere in the darkness, the screen door groaned and slammed.

~

That night, I pulled the Saab between the trees and slept in the woods. Or tried to. I lay there with the seat cranked back, and felt this subtle rocking motion, the same stitching rhythm I'd practiced for hours, as if the wings were still being worked on by a pair of phantom hands. Their shape kept floating up behind my eyelids, and I could feel myself being pulled toward the beginning of a dream. Then I'd remember how alone I was out there, and my eyes would fly open. It was so dark outside the car, the windshield a black void. I might as well have been floating through space.

I tried to tell myself no one would find me there, the pepper spray gripped in my hand. I told myself I was safe—no one was around—a story I was drunk and exhausted enough to half believe. But when I did manage to close my eyes for long enough, falling toward a place that bordered on sleep, this strange emotional cycle would begin. At first there was this restless, yearning feeling, the way I used to feel on nights before the first day of school. All the newness and possibility the morning would bring. I was still excited about the wings, I realized. A subterranean part of me believed everything Barry had told me. I was going to wake up in the daylight and watch a man fly from the roof of his barn.

But as my anticipation grew, I'd remember how impossible it was. No, I'd tell myself. I'd think of Ike, the expressive sorrow his features channeled, the plaintive twist of his mouth.

My dad, he's crazy—he—

Could someone really be so wrong, believe like that and be so wrong? Yes. Of course, I knew that. Still, the disappointment that flooded me at first would inevitably seep away, like blood cleansed in a river, and this wordless elation would start churning up again, restlessly turning, turning. Until I forced myself to remember Ike's face.

～

I woke up in the car, my jacket spread over me for a blanket. It was early—I could tell by the mild quality of the light. I ate a few handfuls of trail mix, then went for a walk in the forest. I'd learned how to pee outdoors.

Later, I sat on the hood smoking, trying to think what to do. I knew what I wanted: to return to the barn, finish the wings we'd started, and see what would happen next. I wanted to make sense of Barry's wild and passionate energy. There was something about his conviction that I loved. And the wings—they spoke to me somehow. I wanted to learn more about it, this curiosity I barely understood. Except that was exactly what Ike had warned me not to do. Had I encouraged someone in the grips of a delusion? Was he dangerously ill? Barry didn't seem crazy, at least not fully, at least not to me. But what if he was?

I weighed everything. I smoked too much and felt unwell. Eventually, I just gave up. Whatever would happen would happen. With no decision made, I started walking down the road toward the house.

Now and then, I peered up through the trees, hoping—and feeling silly for hoping—that I'd glimpse his shadow in the sky.

I heard them first. Voices raised, an argument. They were standing out in front of the barn. The wings were there, complete and glorious, leaning up against the outer wall. Barry was shouting something, gesturing emphatically in the air.

I froze, unsettled by the sight.

I shouldn't be here, I thought.

Then Barry saw me, roared my name. It was too late to run. I walked toward them, not sure what else to do.

"Thank god you're here," Barry said, his glasses flashing. "Ike's not being any help at all. Listen—I finished the work this morning."

He made an energetic gesture with his hands, like he was shaking the bars of a cage.

"We're ready, we're ready. Despite my loyal son's best efforts," he added, glancing darkly at Ike. Ike looked miserable.

"Don't let him do this," he said.

"My god, Ike!" Barry said. "There's nothing to be afraid of!"

"Just please," Ike said again, his dark eyes searching my face. "Don't let him."

Barry shrugged at me.

"Forget him," he said. "You're here now. I'm going to need your help. Come on."

With that, he hoisted the wings over his head and started limping with them around the side of the barn. He didn't look back once. He was that sure I'd follow.

"Please," Ike said. It was terrible to hear him beg. "You have to stop him."

"I—"

"He's going to break his head open."

"Jane!" Barry roared offstage.

"I'll talk to him," I said. But I had no idea what I was going to do.

Barry had brought the wings up with the rope and pulley, and they were floating overhead on their hook. He'd started to climb the silver ladder, a herky-jerky ascent.

"Come on," he said. "I'll need you up here with me."

"You're sure this is a good idea?" I said. I hated the meekness in my voice.

He stopped and looked down at me.

"What? Of course it's a good idea. It's a *beautiful* idea. The *best* idea."

"Ike said—"

"Ike," he said, "frankly does not know what he's doing. Come on."

He started to climb again. I looked behind me, desperate. Where was Ike?

Barry pulled himself onto the roof and crawled over to the platform. He bent down unsteadily toward me.

"Jane," he said softly. "I know it seems impossible. But I'm asking you—see for yourself. Give it a chance."

I said nothing.

"Just listen to yourself. You know why we're doing this. You want it as much as I do, don't you? You do. And there's no reason you can't have what you want. No physical reason. You've seen birds do it your whole life. I'm telling you, it's time."

Then Ike reappeared, rounding the corner of the barn. I looked up again—Barry had stood up on the platform, and was suddenly out of view. The wings creaked on the rope.

"He says he'll be fine," I said.

"Sure," Ike said. "He *says* that."

"Do you think there's any chance—"

"No," he said. "Never."

I hesitated for a second. Ike stuck his hands into his hair and moaned, shaking his head.

"Okay," I said. "Okay. I'll talk to him."

I climbed the ladder and pulled myself onto the roof. Barry stood there on the platform, beaming. We were really high up. My heart knocked in my chest.

"Barry—" I said.

"What?"

"I just don't know—"

He waved his hand dismissively.

"Enough," he said. "Enough, my sister. Let me show you how it works."

He started to explain the improvements in this new design, pointing to features on the wings that hung beside me, the language hard to parse and way over my head. Then he stepped into a harness that pulled up around his hips, hugging all the way up to his ribs. He showed me how to lace it behind him like a corset, ready to secure his body to the larger frame. I told myself it didn't matter, that I was only learning. I tried to think how I could make him stop.

"Now," he said. "Time for the good part."

I couldn't see Ike from where we were standing. I felt myself weaken, my will starting to dissolve. I wanted to trust him so badly, for the future he promised to be real.

"Go ahead," he said. "Bring them over."

The wings waited behind me, dangling from the hook. He made it sound so natural, like he was only asking for a glass of water. This was the moment of intervention, I sensed it. But my resolve had fallen away with the rest of the world—with the meadow, and Ike, and all the other things I barely remembered. The whole universe was just the two of us, up there on the roof.

"My sister," Barry said. "It's all right."

In the end, I brought the wings to Barry. I didn't know how to refuse him, I realized. Not when his eyes were so insistent and blue.

There was barely room for both of us on the platform, and I had to step carefully to avoid the drop, staying close to him. I tied his wrists in the way he showed me to. I knelt and tied his ankles to the frame.

"Thank you," Barry said gently. I'd been dismissed.

I took a couple steps back, and then—over Barry's winged shoulder—I saw Ike in the grass, hugging himself, shaking his head in disbelief. I felt so guilty, seeing him. But it was too late, I'd made my choice. For better or worse, the demonstration was ready to begin.

I watched from behind as Barry stood on the cantilevered platform, nothing below him but air. It was awe-inspiring, the way the wings' shape transformed him. He let the moment linger, swooning gently, swaying to some distant music only he could hear. I could almost feel the whole world bending to his wish.

The sky was by then such an electric blue that it was almost no blue at all, but a brightness that floods the mind through the eyes, and threatens to fill the skull.

I looked at Barry, the way the wings rose and fell in rhythm with his breath, his gaze fixed above us on the heavens. I looked at the wings, huge and shot through with light, the dark bony framework we'd made all illuminated. And I looked at Ike down below, all tense and wretched, the wind teasing in his rags. I wanted him to feel what I'd felt watching Barry soar downward in the Lilienthal glider, the audacious majesty of it that made you want to shout.

I looked down from the lofted platform, trying to gauge the danger of the fall.

"Ready!" Barry shouted, his voice softened by the wind.

"Barry—" I said.

But before I could stop him, he stepped to the end of the ledge and jumped.

EIGHT

A rush of air hit the cloth, the sound of an umbrella opening. The wings' wooden frame creaked and held—and for a second, Barry almost seemed to float.

The wings snapped once, powerful and agile, thrusting him forward in the air like a swimmer. For a brief moment between a few heartbeats, it was almost like he flew.

But as the wings drew back to pump a second time, gravity started to reclaim him. He sailed at a gentle angle toward the earth again, in the smooth, swift glide of a parachuter, and then he fell.

Just like that, it was over. He'd dropped abruptly out of sight, and I was pattering back down the ladder to the ground.

I ran toward him across the meadow, wildflowers whipping at my knees.

The height had knocked Barry's breath out, this terrible sound scraping from his throat as he twisted in the grass. He squirmed inside the thing he'd built, like a grub speared on a hook.

Ike had dropped to his knees beside him. He pulled on Barry's arms, his shoulders, as if freeing him from the wings might somehow save him. It seemed wrong to yank on him, with him all winded like that, so I tried to get between them while Barry's harsh croaks filled our ears.

We wrestled that way for a moment: Ike trying to pull Barry from the machine, me trying to pull Ike away from

Barry, Barry thrashing against both of us, hard enough to almost levitate through sheer will. All of it was useless, but the disappointment stung too badly to hold still.

By the time we had him standing up, Barry had his breath back. His eyes flashed brightly at us.

"I don't understand!" he roared, his voice hoarse with grief. "Every detail was in place—I'm sure of it—"

"Shh," Ike said. "Stop it. It's all right."

When we lifted the wings away, Ike tried to hug his father, but Barry fought him off, muttering to himself, and started limping madly toward the house. The screen door banged, and then Ike and I were alone.

I just stood there, still numb with the shock of the fall.

"What *happened*?" I croaked.

It had been so glorious, the way he'd briefly moved through the air. Before it had all gone wrong.

"It's always like this," Ike said. "I *told* you."

He shook his head.

"He works and works and works and works. Sometimes he doesn't sleep for days. And then he jumps, and he falls. He was lucky, this time. It's been so much worse. . . ."

I wasn't ready for the terrible dismay I felt smashing toward me. I don't know what I'd expected to happen—but I'd let a small part of myself hope for something extraordinary. I'd wanted to believe we were on the verge of something new and different, even if I couldn't say just what.

"He'll *kill* himself one of these days," Ike said. "He really will. So many twisted ankles. I think his whole left foot is smashed. His knees, just gone. He broke his collarbone once— you could see the broken bone under the skin. But he doesn't let me take him to a doctor. . . ."

There were tears in his eyes.

"He always thinks the next time will be different. Oh, this

time, this time, he'll *fly*. One year, he was so sure that we never even prepared for winter. As if we'd just go south, like birds. And when winter came, we almost *starved*. He was so proud, even then. I had to go banging on the doors of houses, begging strangers to help us. . . ."

He just sort of crumpled, the strength collapsing from his shoulders.

"He won't *stop*."

I felt a surge of pity for him. His skinny frame in home-made clothes, his mouth twitching all over the place, the way his eyes sought understanding in mine. The sadness I felt was at the edge of horror. To watch someone you loved hurl himself endlessly, unsuccessfully at the sky—

"I need to go check on him," he said suddenly. "Sometimes—after—he goes crazy. I mean, *really* crazy. He—" He stopped.

"Okay," he said, as if we'd agreed to something. Then he was running full-tilt toward the house.

❧

I lingered around outside awhile, alone. Had a cigarette—one, then another. After a while, I went inside the barn again, the tobacco stink still on my hands, to look at the wings again. The thorny fan shape of Barry's gliders hovered above the floor. I still remembered the wonder I'd felt when I first saw them. That feeling was still there, but it was tinged with something else—a leftover bite of a meal you loved that's since spoiled.

They were gone a long time. I started to feel like I had to do something—I couldn't just leave, not after that. Eventually I stalked up onto the back porch and stuck my head through the door. I didn't hear anyone inside, so I went in.

As I walked through the kitchen, I sensed the rabbit's severed head still lay out on the counter, though I couldn't actually bear to look. I walked quickly, so I wouldn't have to see the dark pebbles of its eyes. Then I was in the house again, surrounded by the stacked columns of boxes, decades of winged figures sketched out in Barry's hand. I'd forgotten the sheer bulk of it, the crowded intensity—the sense you might bump into the wrong thing and set off an avalanche.

What had it been like for Ike to grow up inside all that? Hemmed in by notebooks and sketches and carved, flightless beams—

"Hello," I called into the house, but no one came.

I wandered into the room they'd fashioned into a kind of library, hundreds of books on cinder-block shelves. I still wasn't sure I was welcome, cowed by the overwhelming scale of papery clutter. A bat skeleton watched me from its jar, its finger-bones long and pale as dry spaghetti and sharpened at the tips. I told myself that both of them—if for different reasons—would have wanted me to stay.

Almost without meaning to, I started to inspect their books, and soon curiosity overruled my shame. There's no pleasure like a stranger's bookshelf, and I brightened a little at all the strange titles, fingering their spines. They had whole rows of *Mother Earth News* and the *Farmers' Almanac*. I found a nineteenth century medical manual filled with morbid pictures, all eye pustules and amputations. There was an Audubon's *Birds of America* in elephant folio, and I marveled at the variety and brilliance of the species—incandescent fliers posed on stilt legs, chests puffed as if they were all holding their breath. Then I stumbled on a treasure: a book called *Progress in Flying Machines*.

Published in 1894, it included everything known about flight mechanics at the time. There were hundreds of illustrations of historical man-made wings, alien crafts forged by feverish, bird-mad minds—wryly noting the grotesque deaths of their creators, who invariably smashed to the ground, trapped in their own failed machines. These Steam Age would-be aviators reached for the sky in all kinds of desperate contraptions, from hot-air balloons to pedal-powered plane-like gliders and of course sets of bird-like human wings. As I read, I started to understand something: A hundred years earlier—not very long ago at all—the world had been gripped by a collective hysteria, this wild longing to lift the human body into the air. There had been others like Barry, too many to count.

I was mesmerized. I'd studied the nineteenth century in college, and they had never told us this.

There was even mention of Otto Lilienthal, the mad German Barry had told me about—so he really existed—who was evidently still alive at the time the book was published. The author described his gliding experiments, the way he soared for hundreds of feet off a constructed sand hill near Berlin. An accompanying picture jolted me with recognition: the shadow of a body in the air, held up by wings so much like Barry's.

He wasn't so alone after all, I realized. There was ancestry here, a long and troubled lineage. I was totally absorbed until a nearby sound shook me out of it—an uneven gait tramping somewhere down the stairs. Then Barry was in the library. He seemed totally unsurprised to find me in the house. Ike raced in after him.

"Jane—my sister!" he shouted. "I've just had the most wonderful *idea*!"

With his glasses off, his eyes were smaller than I'd remembered. They burned crazily, a lunatic blue.

"I was lying there, and then—god, it just came to me—I know exactly what went wrong. I know exactly what to do!"

He shook his fists with emotion.

"Come on—we don't have long! Back to work!"

He lurched past me toward the kitchen, and I heard the screen door slam. Through the window, we could see him staggering onward, pushing his way through the tall, tufted grass. The air almost seemed to pulse in his absence, the way the wake rocks you long after a speedboat passes.

Ike hung his head. He started to clear some papers from a battered armchair—its ancient leather splitting, the stuffing starting to escape. At first I thought he was looking for something, but he just wanted a place to sit. He slumped down in the chair.

"So," he said finally. "You see now what he's like."

He prodded a stack of Barry's drawings with his slippered foot.

"He'll go on like this for weeks," he said sadly.

It started to make sense, Ike's cold treatment of me. I'd stumbled into a fairly desperate situation, only to start recklessly spurring his father on. I was ashamed. I'd believed Barry so readily. I'd played right into his hands.

Not that I felt he was a total fraud, necessarily. The wings were too impressive for that. And what I'd just seen—it hadn't been a simple fall, but something much more interesting. A kind of doomed wrestling with the air. But I saw how dangerous it was, this obsession. How futile. I knew why it felt unbearable to Ike, a decades-long parade of hurt.

"I'm sorry," I said, and I meant it.

Ike winced, sinking deeper into the chair.

"It's not your fault," he said.

We were quiet for a little while. I sat down on the dusty floor, the book in my lap. I just wanted to make some space for him to talk.

"Where did you come from?" he asked me, finally.

I drew up straighter. I hadn't expected the focus to pivot back to me.

"I was just wandering around in the woods," I said, oddly flummoxed by the question. "That's all."

"But where are you *from*?" he said. "Do you live near here?"

"No," I said. "I live in New York. The city. Brooklyn."

I said this before realizing it was no longer true. My brain had leapt right over the months in Ithaca, that whole chapter stricken from the record. As far as what made me *me*, I was apparently still a recent college grad from New York.

Ike leaned forward with sudden, intense interest.

"New York *City*?" he said.

"Yes," I said.

"Do you know the Halibans?"

"Um," I said. I had to laugh. "So, it's a city of eight million people."

"So, no?" he said.

"No," I said.

"That's our family," Ike said. "I thought you might know them, maybe."

It was heartbreaking, how naive it was. Still, I was almost relieved to hear that he and Barry had other family, a link to the world beyond their homestead. Clearly, that fact was meaningful to Ike.

"Have you been there?" I said.

"No," he said. "I've never been anywhere."

It was a wretched admission, one that betrayed more sadness than he wanted to reveal.

"I hope someday," he added.

So we were both connected to New York by imagination and memory—a city where I no longer lived, and one he could hardly fathom.

"There's nowhere like New York. You should go," I said, quickly realizing how glib that was to say. It would be impossible for a million reasons. It felt cruel to even suggest it.

"Maybe I could take you. Sometime."

I'm not sure I literally meant it. I just wanted his situation not to sound so bad, wanted to pretend he wasn't as stranded as he was. But I watched something change in his face, then— his features slackening, as if something had occurred to him.

"I would go with you right now," he said.

The intense finality of it was startling.

"Except," he said. "I can't just *leave* him. My dad—without me around, he'd . . ."

He trailed off. His mind seemed to pivot to a second, parallel track.

"We need each other," he said. "I don't have anyone else."

I thought I knew what he was trying to express. It was a complicated guardianship. Ike was both protector and protected, a parent to Barry and his child. So, while he had every reason in the world to leave, there was more to it than that. I'd experienced that in my life, too. With Ian, but not only with Ian. A bond that's more than purely rational. A love beyond justification.

Ike stood. He went to the window. I waited for a long moment, just trying to be okay with all that stillness. With his back turned to me I could finally watch him, the sunlight beaming down on him from elsewhere. He slowly tucked his hair behind his ear, an absent, lingering gesture that took much longer than it had to, that made it seem like he was deep in thought.

He was so unlike Barry physically—leaner, and darker, and somehow more elegant, where Barry was muscular, ruddy, and fair. There was a certain intensity to both of them, like they were overacting slightly so even the people in the back rows could see, and a certain ineffable look they both had in their eyes. But that was where the resemblance ended. I found myself wondering about Ike's mother, whoever had birthed him. What she must have been like. If Barry had loved her the same fierce way he loved his wings, and what had changed in the absence that she left.

"Maybe you could help us," he said, and turned around. "Would you? Help me with him?"

He knelt down beside me on the floor, confronting me with the intense specifics of his face. I was so close I could have touched him, and at first his sudden nearness registered more than anything he said.

"He'll slow down," Ike said. "He has to. Like a crash. When he *knows* he can't do what he's always said he would do. When it seems pointless, broken, all of it. When he doubts everything. Himself. It never lasts long. But that's the only time I have a chance."

He almost didn't seem to blink.

"We could wait it out," he said. "He won't listen to me. But he might listen to you. To both of us."

I remembered how I'd first seen him at the tower, his whole body bent into a posture of reverence and wanting. I felt the same energy then, except now his prayer was aimed at me. His face was beautiful, and yet so strange, so warped with unmet need. He felt me hesitate.

"Please," he said. "Please help us."

"I—" I held the air in my lungs a second, a consequential breath.

I told him I would try. That I would stay with him and try. That part was easy, since I had nowhere else to go.

NINE

So I started living there. I didn't see it that way then. In my mind there were still clear boundaries between us—I was fascinated by Ike and Barry in an ethnographic way, but I certainly wasn't *one* of them. I owed them nothing. I could have left at any time. The whole thing was threaded together out of my curiosity and the brief, tenuous grace of kindness between strangers.

And yet something changed for Ike, after that. After ignoring me so long, he started taking pains to include me in everything—as if, by witnessing Barry's brief, violent plunge from the roof, I'd become indelibly tethered to them somehow, with all the privileges and responsibilities of membership in their club. I sensed a shift in the story he told himself as we lugged the cast iron from the pump together, sloshing with cooking water, joined by our grasp on a thin handle that pinched at your skin like wire—his future expanding to include me in its scope. He assumed we'd share in the weight, just as we'd share in the meal that followed. This binding presumption of kinship. It unnerved me a little, how fast his attachment came. But I liked that I'd earned my stripes with him—even if, as the minutes went by, I was less sure how to do what he'd asked of me, less sure what my continuing presence promised.

Ike started the fire, using the tin can I'd seen before, the one with the bundled-up coal inside. The white-orange ember flamed up when he blew on it.

"It just stays lit in there?" I said, amazed, gesturing at the can.

He shrugged.

"For the night," he said. "Until morning. Or all morning, until night. You just have to bed it with moss. Or fire mushrooms."

"*Fire* mushrooms?"

Certain mushrooms, he told me, burned so slowly that an ember could feed on them for hours without blazing up, a self-conserving fuel. I'd always thought of fire as a chaotic, destructive force, not something you could tame into consuming only what it needed. No one had told me you could keep small pieces of a fire and use them to seed the next one, a system that could go on forever as long as you took enough care.

The traps were empty, their gardens still spring-young and vulnerable to overharvest. So we took a few knobbly potatoes from a crate in the basement, and some salt from an ancient fifty-pound sack that sat up on bricks beside it. We boiled them, dumped the water, and roasted them again over the flame to season them up a bit, their skin puckered and crispy from a spoonful of rabbit fat. It made for a meager meal—enough to fill the belly a little while, not much more.

We ate in silence. Now and then I glanced across the fire at Ike, who sat bent over his food in a mannerless hunch. He raised the bowl close to his mouth, as if to whisper to his potatoes as he ate them. And I had offered to rescue him from this life. It was hard to imagine taking him and Barry with me the way he wanted, the way I'd recklessly promised: crossing the Triborough Bridge with Barry staring grimly out the window, and Ike in his homemade rags, peering up at the high-rises from the backseat.

Ike straightened on his stump, reminded of something.

"We should bring some to my dad," he said.

We'd set aside a few potatoes in the pot for Barry, but they looked too scanty on their own, so Ike pushed a few from his bowl into his father's. He didn't seem to question this, small as his own portion was, like an obligatory tithing to a god.

I trailed along as Ike carried the bowl over to the barn. Barry sat at his desk, his back to us. A candle fluttered by his elbow, and by its light I could see that he was drawing, his hand tracing long, graceful lines across a page.

"Dad," Ike said.

Overhead, the gliders drifted gently, stirred by a subtle breeze.

"We brought food," Ike said. "You should—"

"Shh," Barry whispered loudly. He lifted his hand, silencing us, and without turning around went on drawing.

He kept at it that way, with one admonishing hand raised, for so long that at first I thought he was asking us to listen, that there was something in the night he wanted us to hear. But in time he lowered his arm again. His elbow returned to the table, the unoccupied fist discharging some excess energy as he worked, clenching and unclenching in rhythm like a heart. By then he seemed to have forgotten we were there.

I looked at Ike, our offering rejected. He bit his lip, cradling the bowl of potatoes meekly in both hands. So this was devotion. It ran deep, the thing in Barry he wanted us to break.

⟿

The days that followed were impossible to fill, buckets with holes in the bottom. I'd wake up in the Saab, nosed deep enough into the woods that no one would see me if for some reason they went out along the hidden dirt road. Then I'd go for a walk, explore all morning if I wanted, the forest brushy and unmanicured, waving away deer flies with my cap. No matter how long I hiked, the daylight stretched to accommodate. It seemed like I could walk forever and still head to the meadow in time to join Ike for breakfast, the eggs he gathered from their chicken coop at dawn and cooked without fail as the sun came up. He stood and waved when he saw me coming, and I'd raise my hand to signal back.

Ike was busy almost every minute of the day, absorbed by the logistics that kept their compound running. He gave me a shovel, and we spent hours expanding his garden beds, breaking apart the earth until my hands were blistered and the fresh soil was ready for planting. He brought me inside their greenhouse, a long wooden frame tacked together with clear tarps that trapped the light and smelled inside like melting rain. Seedlings grew everywhere, sprouting gamely from rows of wooden planters and various pots and troughs. We transferred them into the worked-over dirt we'd made, sowing them at intervals we measured in thumb-lengths, and I learned to identify squash and broccoli, chard and collards, by the singular shapes of their leaves.

When Ike wasn't gardening, or fishing, or cooking, or sweeping the chicken coop, or chopping firewood, he was busy making linen. Barry had an endless appetite for cloth; the feeling seemed to be that they could never have enough. So Ike was almost always engaged in some aspect of making the material that covered the wings and his own body—a complex, multistep process that I never fully figured out, and which totally consumed him.

He showed me where they grew flax in a grove by the river, this year's plants already poking from the soil in forked shoots. Their drying sheds were filled with tall bound bales from other years. He'd untie the bales and scatter them in the grass to gather dew overnight, turning them again each morning, a slow ritual that gradually rotted the stiffness from the stalks. When they were ready, he'd break them down further with a crude smashing device that he pumped like a paper cutter, freeing the long, ropy tissues beneath. He processed those fibers further with a *hackle*, a small bed of nails he held in his lap, drawing the flax through in a series of rough motions, like brushing a horse's tail. The idea was to straighten and soften the fibers until they were ready to spin into thread. But to me, the long strands looked rough and rambly as corn silk, and it was hard to imagine the day they'd be soft enough to run through Ike's spinning wheel—let alone the finely woven loom, a prospect that seemed as far away as Barry's dreams of flight.

Through it all, Barry sat at his desk in the barn, drafting out new designs. He could be eerily quiet, so quiet it sometimes seemed he wasn't there at all—as if he were only a mythic figure Ike and I had invented, discussed in whispers the way children speak of ghosts. Except now and then he'd show himself. I'd happen to spot him limping across the meadow toward the house, occasionally swinging along on a pair of wooden crutches he kept around to hasten his travel, and all at once I'd be reminded of his strange intensity, the fury and desire channeled through his broken gait. When I passed the barn at a certain angle and glimpsed his shadow—hunched in fierce concentration at the desk, or stalking in circles around the worktable—the very air could seem to crackle with the vigor of his thought.

"What's he doing now, do you think?" I'd ask Ike from time to time, still curious in spite of everything.

He'd wave the question away, as if the answer couldn't be less relevant. He'd seen the cycle play out too many times for that.

"He's still in the thick of it," he'd say, reminding me that the fervency of Barry's efforts had no bearing on the final outcome. Inevitably, he'd fail again, and failure alone changed him: his elemental force would ebb away, and a different version of his personality would briefly surface, like the tiny islands that are visible only during certain phases of a tide. It was impossible for me to imagine that version of Barry, someone Ike described as weak, and penitent, and suggestible, someone who could actually be talked into things. But that was the person we needed to wait for if Ike was ever going to make his first, tentative foray into a different life.

Sometimes we talked about where we'd go later, once we convinced Barry to give up. Ike fantasized about a trip to New York, or to my parents' house in Connecticut, or to the ocean, which he'd never seen and asked endless questions about. But if I'm honest, I hoped all that would be a long time coming. It scared me, the idea of Barry *breaking* the way Ike said he would—not to mention what he might do before his madness crested. I couldn't handle a second reckless leap from the roof, steeled myself against the frantic memory of Ike begging him to stop.

Besides, I was starting to like my surroundings. A languid rhythm to the days. If only it could have stayed like that, I might have been totally content: happy to wander in and out of their lives, slinking off into the woods when I wanted to, returning to pal around with Ike and pitch in with his work. I'd never used my body like that before, and the sheer physicality of his routine worked a trick on me, like magic. By the time night fell, I felt fully worn out, my muscles swelled with blood, my brain numbed of worry. Was it April already? It must have been, how soon was May? Somewhere, in a world far away, Partridge students had finished the quarter and were on to the next one. I thought back in growing disbelief to the time I'd squandered there—squinting for hours at a computer screen, barely leaving my chair, convinced of the value in torturing myself. My days with Ike were different, no trace of the panic that had clutched at my throat like hands. The sun was heating up. I borrowed a fraying wide-brimmed hat to keep my skin from burning. I cut my jeans into shorts at the knee.

When the days ended, I struck out toward my car and forgot the two of them quickly. The night out there seemed huge and luxuriant, bugs creaking unseen in the grass. The meadow a cradle of silver light. No one would ever find me, I realized. Not until I was ready. Even better to be safe, with people I trusted nearby, an assurance that made deep sleep possible. Melatonin flooded me, the seductive pull of the darkness hormone. I'd stumble along the side of the house, and as I came out front the road sometimes surprised me with fireflies. Their green bulbs pulsing in Morse code: *Here I am, here I am, here I am.*

ᔕ

After his chores were done, Ike liked to pass time by the river, fishing. The rocky silt near the bank hid dozens of worms, and Ike would pinch them from the earth and spear their bodies on the tip of an old hook, thanking them softly for their sacrifice. The willow canes made great fishing poles, and they kept a few on hand for that purpose, already tied with line. I sat on a log with my feet in the water, minnows nipping at my toes, and watched him. The river rushed around his knees. The sun was good to his skin, his moccasins left by the shore.

He was painfully thin, not an ounce of fat on him. His handmade clothes hung off his bones, ragged and too loose, his chest hairless and flat as a child's. Not that he was frail—he just had nothing to spare. I liked the way he moved, the assurance in his limbs, the sense he'd done it all a million times before. I also liked the way he felt no need to fill the silence. We let the river do the talking. It was a full sound, both ends of the piano: a deep subterranean rush that broke, high and glassy, against the rocks.

In moments like that, I could feel almost perfectly content. Like I'd finally stumbled into the longed-for existence, simple and luminous, where the hours passed slowly and everything crystallized into scenes of painterly grace. And yet that sensation depended on a kind of willful numbness, because Ike, my guide and companion, was so clearly troubled, pained by everything that pleased me. Sure, he took some satisfaction in the water, in the sunshine, in the patient wait for fish. But it wasn't hard to see how his enjoyment was blunted by the sense he was *stuck* there, a prisoner held against his will, barred from the better life elsewhere that was quickly passing him by. So, while I felt at peace by the river with Ike, I also knew—when I really thought about it—that he was exiled from the very feeling he ushered me into. This unnerving duality lurked at the edges of our time together. His presence made a certain kind of carefree happiness possible for me, and, at the same time, threatened to derail it.

At one point, when I looked away from the river back at the barn, I saw Barry stalking across the meadow toward the outhouse, the slow and stubborn progress of his limp. It didn't seem possible that he would ever leave that place, especially for an outside world he clearly hated—a world I, too, had fled. And yet what seemed almost more implausible was the idea of Ike starting again somewhere else. He'd been so profoundly shaped by their isolation, by the hard work of survival, by the confines of their tormented bond. Could you ever really leave that? I found myself thinking about the years he'd missed out on, all the normal stuff, the playgrounds and birthday parties and sports meets after school, the gymnasium dances and smoke-filled cars, the feeling of your heart quickening when a certain person passed you in the hall. The kind of time you can't get back.

"Hey," I said, "how old are you?"

The question surprised me. It wasn't until the words came out that I realized I'd been wondering.

He shrugged.

"I don't know," he said. I heard an ambivalent bell-note in his tone, slightly defensive, but also like the answer might not matter much. He pulled the hook from the water and recast the line.

"How old are *you*?"

"I'm twenty-four," I said, trying to hide my astonishment. It had never occurred to me you could be free from that, the numbers and dates that defined you. He didn't even seem embarrassed. Like it was nothing not to know your own age, as natural as the way he tucked his hair behind his ear when he was deep in thought. That easiness, I envied it—and yet, the duality was there, too, another reminder of how shipwrecked he was, deprived even of access to the most basic details about his life.

"Hm," Ike said, a noise that suggested what I'd told him was moderately interesting, that he was filing it away. Then he turned his attention back to the water, the bait bobbing on the surface, tugging in a frenzy against the current. With a slow, delirious feeling my emotions shifted again: I realized I had no idea what day it was. I only knew that spring was veering toward summer. You could feel the sun turning up the wattage of its lamp, the air filled with the gently mind-bending smells of plants. What I'd told him, was it even true? My birthday was in May. I didn't think it had come yet, but couldn't say for sure. It was a lovely sensation, not knowing how long you'd been alive. I tried to let that feeling fill me as I watched Ike fish, the pleasant dislocation of being unmoored in time.

If we were lucky, we could catch a nice fat trout. Sometimes two. We'd throw them in a metal bucket, where they'd flop and snap a minute before going still. It unsettled me, the way their jaws moved as they died. As though they were carefully mouthing out a final message, a warning or prayer we lacked the ears to hear.

When the sun went down, we'd light a fire. As flames licked around the cast-iron pot, Ike would flick a little water in to see if it was hot enough—the droplets dancing across the metal like ball bearings, writhing and shrinking until they disappeared. We cooked the fish using nothing but a little salt, a little fat, and a few herbs from the greenhouse. When they were done, we'd chop the heads off—Ike buried them in his garden beds to fertilize the soil, the ground littered with skulls. He taught me to halve them and lift the bones away in a network of fine white pins. The fish could be delicious, though it always wanted lemon. The skin crisp, the flesh so soft it almost vanished on your tongue.

❧

My morning adventures got longer as I annexed more of the woods. I brought my cigarettes, but the thought of smoking one had started to seem unappetizing, my pouch of rolling shag nearly empty. Once, I crashed out of the brush and found myself at a bend in the river, maybe half a mile upstream from where Ike fished. The urge gripped me, raw and undeniable. I took my clothes off and crossed the bank quickly, hugging myself, still unable to feel I was truly alone. Twenty-four years old, and I'd never been fully naked in the sun.

I hadn't bathed since the motel. The river was colder than I'd expected, pinching at my calves as I waded in. Deeper, too.

After only a few paces, I was up to my shoulders in it. The dark, bracing currents stung my senses to life, gushing around me while I waved my limbs under the troubled surface, as if conducting an orchestra, grateful for the gift.

∽

Time passed that way awhile, with long, full days of work and walking, hours rolling by in the sweet, interminable way honey oozes from a spoon. So many little things, which now I barely remember: A lost family cemetery, all overgrown, with half-toppled, worn-away stones; a sudden clearing that brimmed with wildflowers; a huge wasp colony hanging from a branch in a paper lantern's shape. The way I'd catch Ike singing softly to himself now and then in what sounded like Spanish, or busted-up Italian, or even some invented language of his own, with notes he'd let trail off when he noticed me listening— leaving me to wonder where he'd learned the tune, what this private music was. He showed me how to load his processed fibers into the spinning machine, finished thread spooling out tight-wound and surprisingly strong while the great wheel turned. The stars at night were kingdoms of glittering buck-shot. I did think of home, of school, of the fact that I'd gone missing, of the people in my life and what my continued absence might mean to them—but those were thoughts I managed to bat away, like I batted away the mosquitoes that whined near my ear.

Through it all, Barry stayed loyal to his desk, ignoring us, his pencil scratching here and there as it flew across the page. We watched him closely, alert to the slightest shifts in his bearing or mood. His coiled presence haunted our days, this uneasiness in the air whenever we were near him—like waiting for a bomb to detonate, and it might be any second, though it could just as well be never.

And then something happened, a sign of things to come.

Ike and I were eating dinner by the fire when we heard him. A sudden scream, tearing the silence between us. Echoing across the meadow from the barn.

I stood up, but Ike lifted his hand to still me.

The scream again, a second time. It was Barry, clearly—a long, tormented howl. The clatter of metal, a tool hurled at the wall.

"See?" Ike said. "That's how it starts."

I looked over at the barn, candlelight shimmering in the windows.

"Should we do something?"

He shook his head.

"No," he said. "Just leave him."

So I sat back down, shaken. Ike watched my face with a knowing leer, a strange expression that was somehow both troubled and triumphant. The change he'd foretold was coming, and as ominous as that was, he was pleased to be proven right.

Ten

A sharp sound woke me, knuckles on glass.

It was morning, and I'd been asleep in the front seat of my car. I sat up. Ike was looking in through the window, his palm against the glass, his face tense with concern.

I'd gotten lazy about hiding the car in the woods, I guess. I'd just pulled off for the night on the side of their long dirt lane.

"Sorry," Ike said. He turned quickly, dropping out of sight.

I pushed the door open and rolled out, still half asleep. He started to walk his bike down the path, away from the direction of the house.

"Hey," I said.

We stared at each other.

"I saw the car," he stammered. "I was worried."

"I got tired last night," I said casually. "I pulled over and—yeah."

The question of my home—of where I went in the dark—had always been left unspoken between us. I'd never wanted to tell them the truth, which was that I could fit my whole life in a sedan. I preferred to let them imagine whatever they imagined.

"You slept here?"

I sensed him processing, trying to reconcile this information with what he already knew.

"Yeah."

That was when I noticed his bike's front basket was loaded

with wildflowers, long-stemmed plants with purple and orange blooms.

"What are *you* doing?" I said.

It was Ike's turn to look embarrassed. He shrugged.

"Flowers?"

He looked down at them, as if seeing them for the first time.

"I don't know," he said.

"You're—taking them somewhere," I offered.

The forest waited all around us, a cavernous stillness.

"I guess. Yeah."

"Can I come?"

This surprised him. He peered at me, flustered.

"Take me," I said. "I'll drive you."

I meant it. I really wanted to go.

He backed up against his bike and grabbed it, chewing his
lip. For a second I thought he might swing his leg over and race
off. But he didn't.

"All right," he said.

We left the bike on the side of the road, barely fifty feet
from the house. Then we were off. Ike carried the flowers on
his lap, their smell of dirt and honey sweetening the inside of
the car. He told me where to turn, and I pretended not to know,
and before long the water tower loomed up over the hills, just
as I knew it would.

❧

We cut across the graveyard into the wooded inlet where the
tower stood, baring its four-letter word to the sky.

"Look at this place," Ike said, carrying his flowers in both
fists. There was something reverent in his aspect as we stepped
into the clearing, the metal structure looming overhead. It unlocked some quality in him I never saw anywhere else, and I
wondered why.

I remembered what I liked about it, too: The tower was huge, the region's most visible symbol. And yet, standing beneath it, in the shadows, you felt like no one could ever find you. Fallen peels of blue paint lay broken in the grass, and tough weeds grew with abandon. I felt sure no one had been there since Ike and I had last left, the day my life changed.

"I love it," I told him, and that was true. I could still see where I'd pulled my car into the brush back then. A few branches snapped away, the vague outlines of tire treads in the soil.

"There's a thing I do sometimes," Ike said. "It helps me . . . I don't know. Think. Here, watch."

Something in his tone told me how serious it was, that it meant so much for him to show me this.

The flowers he'd tied on the chain-link fence—the ones I'd watched him tie before—had long since dried. He started to strip them away, throwing them into the forest. I joined in, using my nails to rip the dead stems away. The work of it left green stains on my hands.

Ike picked up a flower from his pile, one with purple bell-shaped blossoms.

"Like this," he said.

He showed me how he tied the stems on. He had long, intelligent hands—and in another life, he might have really used them. The bounce and wheel of a basketball, fingers pattering across the neck of a violin. This was what he had instead.

I picked flowers from his pile, and weaved them through the metal, our hands working together. I felt the meaning it had for him. We were paying tribute to someone, or something, I just wasn't sure what.

"Can I ask you?" I finally said. "What is it about this place?"

I glanced over at him, but he didn't look back.

"Did something happen here?"

Because it seemed obvious, suddenly, that something important had.

I'd asked as gently as I could—but even that had been too much, too fast. He finished the flower he was working on, and turned to me. Something in his eyes confirmed it—a bittersweet note of hurt, complicated by the first hints of a smile. There was real emotion there, painful and fond with memory.

"It's okay," I said. "Really. We don't have to talk about it."

His throat bobbed, and he nodded. He took me up on that.

We looped and tucked in silence, slowly filling in a wall of blooms. The tension drained away, until there was just the rhythm of it, this cool haiku-like calm. What was that feeling—there, receding only when I stopped to think about it? I was happy, I realized. For the first time in so long.

❧

I thought of something as we were walking back to the car, our fingertips stained, green under our nails.

"Hey," I said. "Let's get some food."

"Food?" Ike looked back at me, his eyes intense and curious.

My money had been sitting unused in the glove box. I led him down the street and across the intersection to the minimart. I'd forgotten how easily we could do that. A revelation, to remember food could just be had.

We went inside. Ike followed me solemnly, as if entering a temple. The older woman sat behind her counter, some news program on the TV glowing light back on her face. The sound was down, the beamed-in voices just a mumble. She peered at us over her glasses, with an expression like she was sniffing the air for a gas leak, before reluctantly returning her gaze back to the show. I don't think she remembered me, but the sight of us put her on guard. She didn't like our look.

I was too hungry to care. Ike followed me through the aisles as I took a sack of chips from the shelf, the package fat with air. A big bottle of Perrier. I plated up two cheese-smothered pizza slices, then we went to the register. She'd sold me a pouch of tobacco once, but I'd let my habit taper off—I didn't even feel the pull. There were better drugs than nicotine. I asked for ten bucks in gas at pump 2, and threw in a pack of Lemonheads on a whim. It had been so long since I'd tasted sugar.

∽

In the car, we divided up the spoils. Ike held his pizza by the bready edge and lowered it in from above. His technique needed work.

"Ahhm," he said, through his first mouthful. "Mmm. Wow."

"Like this," I said, showing him how to support the floppy part by putting a bend in the crust. I took a bite, my eyes closing helplessly at the taste.

"Oh," I said. The cheese was molten from hours under the heat lamp, but I tore another piece off anyway, singeing the roof of my mouth. I'd forgotten. My senses rang with it, overloaded by salt and fat.

"I can't believe," I said, "that I used to eat this all the time."

"All the *time*?" Ike said, chewing deliberately, unable to quite believe it.

I introduced him to seltzer—"It goes up your *nose*," he said, covering his face with the back of his hand, like he might sneeze—and then we ripped into the box of Lemonheads. His expression got comically serious, the sugar ball clacking against his teeth.

"I *love* this," he said, so earnest it hurt. His eyes went wide, the moment seared in. I could almost see his pupils shrink.

It felt so good to give that to him. It was only as we were driving home again that it occurred to me how cruel it might have been—to corrupt his palate like that, awakening his senses to what he hadn't known he'd wanted.

❧

We decided to check on Barry when we got back, and found him sleeping at his desk. His pencil—a piece of charcoal he cut to shape and whittled to a point with a knife—had fallen to the floor. His stained hands lay upturned on the table, as if he hoped they'd fill with something by the time he woke up.

Before I could do anything, Ike was nudging his shoulder. I didn't see the point in rousing him, but it was too late.

"Dad," he said, and Barry's eyes opened. He made a gruff sound, like a cough. Then Ike was offering to make him food, bring him water. He was asking him what he needed.

"Oh," Barry said, despair disfiguring his face as he sat up. "I'm lost, Ike. I hate to say it, but I've hit a snag. Ah, I don't know what to *do* anymore. Nothing I haven't tried already."

He turned to me, his chair scuffing loudly against the floor.

"I'm sorry, my sister," he said, grief choking out his voice. "I really thought—this last time, I thought—"

He hid his face in his hands and groaned.

"You should rest," Ike said.

"Rest," Barry said. "Yes, that's right."

He stood shakily.

"I'm just so tired," he said. "I have to clear my head."

As he limped to the door—a broken figure, shuffling slowly toward the light—I felt a rush of pity for him.

Ike followed out the door, and I did, too. I watched him try to help his father, but Barry shook him off.

"I'm all right," he said brusquely. "I just can't *think*, is all. I'm going to bed."

It was one in the afternoon.

We watched him lurch off toward the house.

"You see?" Ike said significantly. "It's happening."

"He seems so sad," I said.

"Another day or two like this," Ike said, "and we might really have a chance."

The screen door slammed.

"Oh," Ike said suddenly, tucking his hair behind his ear. He watched me, weighing what he'd say. "Don't do what you did last night."

I looked at him, confused.

"You can always stay here, if you want," he said, gesturing toward the barn. "Take the cot."

My ears burned.

"I—"

"Take the cot."

He'd seen through everything, my excuses about sleeping in the car. There was no point keeping up the lie. And when I thought about it, it did sound nice to have a bed—anything fully horizontal would be an upgrade.

"Barry won't mind?"

"No. I'll tell him."

He winced, putting his hands to his belly. I realized that he looked a little ill.

"I might go lie down, too," he said.

"Are you okay?"

"My stomach hurts," he said.

❧

I slept that night in the barn, done with the awkward ritual of excusing myself and slinking off into the darkness, collapsing the last boundaries between their lives and mine. Barry's cot was a fragile-feeling thing, with loud springs that echoed when I moved. The pillow smelled like dust, and was stuffed with chicken feathers—you could feel them inside, soft and bony, the quills sharp enough to poke through the fabric. There was just a single sheet to cover myself with, and it kicked up Barry's scent when I moved—a brief whiff of him, acrid with sweat. But it was good to lie out fully, my body finally stretched to its full length.

I wondered what it meant, as I fell asleep. We were supposed to be leaving, rescuing Barry from that place. I never thought I'd stay with them that long. And yet suddenly I'd moved indoors, more enmeshed with them than ever. Overhead, Barry's gliders swayed gently in the rafters. I watched them for a while, their white shapes muted by the darkness. Once, the sight had been so strange to me. But I got used to it quickly—we all did. Things feel new, unthinkable, and then they just become your life.

꙳

Barry's spirits sank in the days that followed, just as Ike said they would. He gave me reports, since Barry didn't leave the house.

"He won't get out of bed," he told me, as we sat by the fire. "He just lies there, groaning, until he falls asleep again."

"Is it time?" I asked him.

"Not yet," Ike said. "It's still going to get worse."

"How could it get worse?"

"You'll see," he said.

He insisted on it, the inevitability of this rock-bottom moment. Barry's will would briefly weaken—and with his stubbornness at its lowest ebb, we'd finally make our move.

Ike was almost ecstatic at the thought, convinced the two of us would do what he'd never managed alone: get Barry to abandon his crusade, if only for a little while. I'd try my best to help, of course. And yet I found myself wishing for the day never to come. It suited me, the life Ike wanted to leave. My long walks in the morning, time to do all the nothing I wanted. Fires at night. The river. Barry's beautiful gliders. Did I owe Ike that? To give up the peace I'd discovered so that he could save his life?

I consoled myself by admitting I couldn't stay there forever. Eventually, I'd have to go back. In a way, leaving Lack with Ike and Barry—as much as I couldn't imagine it—was probably my best bet, reluctant as I was. It was a lesson I'd learned in high school: parents can only be so furious with strangers around. If you're going to get in trouble, bring a friend home.

Besides, their presence would help make sense of everything. Without them, I was just a coward. A failure. But with them in tow, I'd be something else—an idealist, certainly. A Samaritan, maybe. Something almost like a hero.

～

When I opened my eyes in the morning, the first thing I saw was Barry's gliders overhead—bat-like and outstretched, an aching shape to their spans. It was early, dawn glowing in the windows. Through the closed horse doors I heard a sound in the distance: the faint, repeating whisk of Ike threshing flax through his hackle.

I got up, found my boots, and went outside, rolling the horse doors open. The sky was lovely, a dusky orange maturing into blue. Ike sat on a stump by the firepit, last night's firewood gone cold, and stopped his flax work when he saw me. When I waved, he waved back.

"Thank god you're up," he said. He set the hackle aside, the golden threads half pulled through its bed of nails. "It's time."

I knew what he meant: Barry had hit his low, the bottom we'd been talking about.

"You're sure," I said.

He nodded.

"He cried all night," Ike said.

"He's been doing that."

"He keeps asking for forgiveness."

This was something Ike had foretold, apparently a crucial tell.

"I say we go talk to him," he said.

I felt my chest tighten, thinking about it.

"You're ready?" Ike said.

I wasn't, but it wasn't about me.

"Are *you* ready?"

He looked down at his feet, the bristling fur of his moccasins.

"Yeah," he said, and got up.

We walked together toward the house, and I tried to memorize everything—the reedy stalks of grass spattered with tiny orange and purple flowers. That subtle smell of dew, cool and slick against my legs. The dark hunch of the house. A quickening brightness to the light. So maybe it all was ending, finally. So maybe this was it.

❧

I followed Ike through the crowded, chaotic rooms of their house to the staircase, which Barry had repurposed as a kind of filing cabinet, papers and notes tucked into the slats under the banister. I'd never been upstairs before, I hadn't had a reason to go. The old wood cracked and wheezed under our feet.

We entered Barry's room through a door in the cluttered hall. The first thing I felt was the overwhelming weight of the space—books, journals, paper, and newsprint, arranged in rising stacks around the bed, and on shelves over the mattress, almost in the manner of an altar. Years of his mental dreck. A single candle burned by the bed, and it struck me how easy it would be to tip it and burn the whole place down.

Barry lay in bed, orange light from the window bathing him in the sepia tones of an old photograph. His eyes were open, just barely, and his cheeks were wet from sweat or recent tears. He grunted, a scant sound of greeting, the only sign he knew that we'd come in.

I hated to see him like that, looking poisoned and drained. Ike sat on the bed.

"How do you feel?" he said.

Barry just lay there.

"Dad."

"Low," Barry said, his voice just a scrape. "I feel low."

Ike teased at the sheet with his fingers. He was working himself up, I could tell.

"Can I get you anything?" he said.

God, I thought. *Just go to it.*

"No," Barry said.

A long, empty pause.

"I had a thought," Ike said.

Barry lay there, still, his eyes open so barely he didn't need to blink.

"We should go somewhere," he said. "Get away for a while."

"Go somewhere," Barry murmured, his voice gruff and scornful. "There's nowhere to go."

"It'd be good for you."

Silence.

"Jane could take us," Ike offered. "She could drive." He turned to me. "Couldn't you?"

"Sure," I said.

Barry's expression didn't flutter.

"Drive," he said. "In a *car*? I'd rather die."

He said it sullenly, the sulky tone of a poor sport.

"But we could go anywhere," Ike said. "I was thinking—"

Barry's eyes opened a little, blue and symmetrical over his crooked nose. "I see what's happening," he said. "I see, now. You're giving up on me."

"No—" Ike stammered.

"You are!" Barry said, his expression wilting to a sorrowful wince. He started to sit up. "Both of you. You're giving up!"

Ike looked at me for help.

"Oh," Barry brayed miserably. "I've failed you, haven't I? I did. I did! It's over—"

"Dad," Ike said.

"A failure," Barry said. "All this time, and no closer than when we started. All this time!"

He turned weakly onto his side.

"My boy," he said. "I'm so sorry. I'm sorry I didn't come through."

"It's okay," Ike said.

"I know how much you wanted it," Barry said. "And I failed you. I *failed* you. I failed everyone."

His eyes flashed at me.

"You, too, my sister!" he said. "I hate for you to see me like this. Forgive me, I—"

His voice had reached such a high, plaintive pitch that I felt pinned, at the mercy of its force.

"Don't be sorry," Ike said. "Just come with us. A change, that's all. For a little while. Something new."

For a second Barry seemed to actually consider it. Then he shook his head.

"There's no point to it."

"Jane said she could take us to her house," Ike said. "Or, I was thinking—"

"You were thinking," Barry said.

"Maybe we could go to New York, to the city. We could even—"

"Oh, my boy," Barry said. "You don't want to see those monsters in New York. Those *terrible* people. You don't."

"But—"

"You don't want to go anywhere *near* them."

Ike turned to me again.

"Tell him," he said, desperation edging subtly into his voice. "Tell him how it could be."

I started to speak, but Barry cut me off.

"No," he said. "No. It's a ruse, Ike."

He lay on his back again, sitting slightly.

"The whole idea of it," he said. "A change of *scene*. My god."

He shook his head sadly.

"Don't be fooled," he said. "Don't think you can just *outrun* any of this."

He was content to leave it at that. A long pause followed, Ike fiddling thoughtfully with the sheet, before I realized I didn't know what Barry meant.

"Outrun what?" I asked softly.

He looked at me, a faraway note in his blue eyes.

"You couldn't know this," he said. "But we're doomed."

He lowered his voice, as if it were all too terrible for anyone to overhear.

"I've tried to explain to Ike," he said. "And I'll try to explain it to you. But I know—it doesn't sound real."

He sighed.

"All that decaying plant matter," he said. "Fossils, dino juice. It's built up over millions of years—a thick, murky layer of oil. And we burn it. Right? It powers everything, the furnaces of the world. The cars and planes, the power plants, the farms and factories, the whole damn city on a hill—all of it runs on *oil*. Liquid carbon. Fossil fuels."

He checked my eyes to make sure I was following.

"You know that," he said. "What you haven't thought of is the *cost*. Atmospheric gas is the cost of oil. We burn, and the resulting C-O-$_2$"—he spelled it out—"flies up into the atmosphere with the rest of it. That cloudy layer used to be our protector, shielding us from the fury of the sun. Now it's a bomb. Getting thicker and thicker each day we burn. Trapping the heat like a blanket. In other words, if we go on like this, we're going to *fry* ourselves."

"Right," I said. "Global warming." The term we used then.

Barry sat up.

"Yes," he said, suddenly interested. "*Yes*. You know this?"

I nodded.

"How?" he asked. "Who told you?"

I thought for a second. The question seemed mildly absurd.

"No specific who, really," I told him. "It's just something everyone knows."

"*Everyone* knows?" Barry said. "People talk about it?"

"Yes," I said.

His mood started to brighten, which surprised me.

"On the radio?" he said. "On the television? They talk about it?"

"Yes!" I said, happy to please him. "I mean, it's common knowledge. Something kids pretty much learn in school.

"Oh," said Barry, delighted. "Did you hear that, Ike? They teach the kids in school! And so—"

He turned back to me, his eyes all eager, waiting to hear more.

"—what are they doing?"

"Doing?" I said.

"Yes, right," he said impatiently. "What are they doing about it?"

"To stop it?"

"Yes," he said.

"Well," I said. "I'm not sure."

I thought for a second. It was still Bush II's first term, long before things ratcheted up, though even then people understood. Global warming, the greenhouse effect. We knew a new era was starting—and yet we spoke of it abstractly, as if it were on a separate plane, the fate of a different world somewhere else. Even *I* thought about it like that, to tell the truth. I couldn't come up with anything concrete anyone had done, besides talk about it. It almost wasn't the kind of thing you *could* do something about.

"So everyone knows," he said. "But nothing's changing."

"Pretty much."

His face darkened.

"Then it's worse than I thought," he said.

All three of us were still. Then Barry stood. So suddenly, I worried that he'd knock the candle over.

"Dad—" Ike said, standing, too.

"You go ahead," Barry said. "Really, I mean it. Go ahead. Enjoy the *scenery*."

He brushed past me, staggering through the papers on the floor like so many dead leaves. He turned around at the door.

"But tell them this," he said. "As it sounds like they haven't thought that far ahead. Tell them there's nowhere—*nowhere!*—for them to go."

He squared his jaw, his blue eyes flashing.

Then he was gone, the sound of his feet tramping unevenly down the stairs.

Ike sank down on the bed, the springs creaking, his hands in his lap. He blew the candle out, perfuming the room with smoke.

"I guess it didn't work," he said.

"I guess it didn't," I said, still a little stunned. Actually, as far as our plan was concerned, it had been disastrous.

"I'm sorry," I said.

I did feel sorry for him, a tragic angle in the way he hung his head.

"It's not your fault."

He seemed to be thinking about something.

"Next time?" he said, heartbreakingly polite. "Maybe don't ask him any questions. Questions get him . . . you know. All stirred up."

I hadn't thought of that.

"Okay," I said. "I really am sorry, Ike."

"It's okay," he said. "You couldn't know."

A pause.

"It might have happened anyway."

We waited in the silence for a minute, a spell in the room we weren't sure how to break.

"He's feeling better, at least," I offered, finally.

"Yeah," Ike said. "But for him, better's worse."

❧

I remember, afterward, really wanting to call someone. Too much in my head, too much for me to process on my own. For the first time, I regretted destroying my phone, that little portal to the other world.

I took a long walk in the woods that afternoon, alone. The deerflies picked up as I went, swooning clockwise around my head, and I swatted viciously at them. Something Barry had said stuck with me, this idea that there was nowhere to go. I wrestled with that notion as I walked, in no particular direction, and then I stumbled on a place I hadn't seen before.

At first I only noticed a collection of things, arranged with the unmistakable look of human art. Then I saw what I was seeing. Three figures sat in a circle, placed out in decaying chairs. Their bodies made from stones and sticks, crude faces painted on with red rock silt, almost too faded to make out. I didn't have to see their hair—made from combed flax threads and fixed with mud—to know the figures were Ike's. Something he'd made long ago and abandoned. Deprived of the family he wanted, so he'd imagined his own.

ELEVEN

I still remember pieces of the dream. The glow and the after-shame. We're at the Hearth at Pine Gables, in the dining room, and the whole place flickers with tea lights. Everyone's there. My mother looks beautiful in a black low-backed dress, her eyes glittering when she smiles. My dad's freshly shaven, his hair swept back with the comb-marks in. I'm pushing Ian over in his chair. A cake waits on the table with a single candle in it, a simple bobbing flame.

It's Ian's birthday, and we lift the cake toward him, singing and laughing and urging him on. Uneven light plays across his face—he knows just what to do. He shapes his lips into a beaten O and blows. The gust tickles my face, and the flame writhes and winks out.

We cheer. A string of smoke lifts from the burnt wick, signaling something. Ian's eyes shine, delighted, his face bent and dimpled by his smile. The thrill of it never gets old. A trick that borders on magic. The joy of it has no seam, is whole and door-less as an egg.

But something else is happening. Ian grips his armrests. For some reason, it's his hands I'm watching—his fingers as they clutch the black pleather that cushions the metal of his throne. His knuckles start to shake. Overhead, in big dark patches, the ceiling lights start going out.

I look up again, suddenly frightened. But Ian seems to be all right. He's still smiling, though there's something strange about his smile. Something so unlike him. What? Before I can say anything, my brother stands up from his chair.

~

I woke up to footsteps and the sound of tools. It was early in the morning, the sun barely a bright slit on the hill, but Barry had already come in. I sat up and felt bug bites on my arm. A mosquito had found me in the night. I vaguely remembered slapping something away from the bottom of a dream, fighting against wakefulness. A high whine near my ear, the brush of eyelash limbs.

"Don't mind me, my sister," Barry said. "Sleep."

But no one could sleep with him clomping around like that, and I felt self-conscious lying in his cot. I swallowed groggily and swung my feet to the floor.

"It's all right," I said, flustered, still trying to wake.

"In that case, come here," he said. "I want to show you something."

He had a series of plans spread out across the worktable. The headless figures all wore sets of wings, but the appendages got sleeker with each sketch.

"This was the problem Lilienthal was obsessed with when he died," Barry said. "Moving from a glider to a set of functional, flapping wings. People assume he died in the fixed glider. No! He crashed in his latest model, with movable pinions. Call it a failure—but somehow he got high enough to reach a killing height. So what was *that*?"

His glasses flashed at me, his language punctuated with their light.

"Another five years, and I believe he really would have done it. He was that much of a genius. It's taken me more than twenty, but here we are."

He explained that, for the human arm to truly mimic bird flight, the wing's inner ridge needed to be relatively stiff, moving out toward progressively thinner and more elastic ribs. When you watch birds fly, you can see that the widest portion of the wings, closest to the body, does very little work—while the farthest tip moves much more actively. Years ago, Barry said, he'd designed a system that could move a wing with that dynamic motion using just a single downstroke of the human arm. A more stubborn challenge was finding the right balance of graduated strength and flexibility along the surface of the wing.

"A lot of it has been trial and error," he said. "Trial and very *painful* error. But there's not another way."

He tapped the final drawing in the sequence.

"I have to thank you," he said, "for the conversation yesterday. Sometimes I let my feelings get the better of me. I really did want to give up. But to hear what you said. About the whole world just sitting there. Knowing, and *sitting* there! Too stupid or corrupt to care...."

He trailed off, letting it sink in.

"We have to try, don't we?" he said. "Come on. I'll show you how it starts."

❧

He had no plan, he conceded. But sometimes the only solution was just to try, he said—ideas came that way, too, through the doing. The first step was to take the damaged wings he'd fallen in, and strip them back down to the frame. Harvest all the parts, reusing what we could. We lowered them from their storage place near the ceiling, one wing still wounded from the smash-up.

We were disassembling when Ike appeared in the doorway

of the barn. I watched him take in the scene, Barry and me together.

"Oh," I said. "Hi, Ike."

"Morning," Barry grunted moodily.

Ike turned away, heading out into the meadow, and for a second I stood there, stranded.

"I'll be back," I said to Barry.

I was grateful that he said nothing as I left.

I caught up with Ike, who was headed in the direction of his woodpile.

"Hey," I said.

"Hey," he said.

"He was there when I woke up," I said.

"He shouldn't do that," Ike said. "He should let you sleep."

"He just came in," I said.

"What were you doing?"

"He wanted to break down the old wings," I said. "The broken ones, that's all."

"To build them back again," Ike said.

"I don't know," I said. "I don't think *he* knows."

Ike turned to me.

"Just don't get him started again," he said. "*Please.*"

"I won't," I said.

That reassured him, something shifting in his face.

"Hey," he said. "I was thinking."

He brushed his hair out of his eyes, then smiled so fully I saw his teeth, the wild, untended look of them.

"Let's go get more of those yellow candies," he said.

We'd torn through the Lemonheads already, the empty box burned up as fuel in one night's dinner fire.

I glanced back to the barn. I thought of Barry, the long day of toil ahead. I looked back at Ike, the pure anticipation in his eyes.

"Sure," I said. "Why not?"

❧

It was just a whim to let him drive. I'd seen how curious he was, the way he watched my hands on the steering wheel, his fascination with the on-and-off flick of the turn signal.

"Here," I said, when the Saab was in view. I held up the keys for him. "You do it."

"Really?" he said.

So we did. He learned to work the pedals slowly, a nauseating, stop-and-start saga. When he finally made his painful, halting way to the end of their lane, I turned the car around and made him do it all again. Two more trips, and he was good enough to coast out onto the road, which was always empty anyway. It was hilarious to watch him—his hands gripping the steering wheel with all their strength, his eyes wide with terror.

"It's okay," I said. "You can go faster."

He was barely pushing ten miles an hour.

The car lurched forward.

"Like *this*?" he said, his voice high and disbelieving.

"Even a little more," I said.

"But it's so *fast*," he said.

He wasn't wrong. Already we were racing far beyond bike speed, trees blurring on the roadsides into light. But he'd lose his fear in time, I knew. Practice would dull his senses, as mine had been dulled. We forget that terror, our grasp of fatal speed. People are wired like that: we get used to things. I knew Ike would, too, and he did.

❧

I think it was that day, though it could have been another day. We'd bought another pack of Lemonheads, to suck happily all the way home. Ike liked to eat them two at a time, one tucked into each cheek, so that he looked a little like a chipmunk. To even it out, he said.

I had the windows down, our hair blowing around. You could really feel the summer coming, a bottom-up warmth I associate with May.

"Hey," Ike said, a strange grin on his face.

"Hey, what?" I said.

"Go faster," he said.

I didn't do anything for a second. Just let the tone of his voice register, more challenge than command. Then I stomped the pedal down, the motor roaring. We felt the Saab pick up speed, the gathering rush of it. The car filled with wind, and Ike shouted joyfully against the sound.

We zoomed along the empty roads at a top clip, the engine straining. Speeding toward the final slope of a long, uneven hill, we briefly caught air. For a thrilling instant, all four tires left the road. We came down again with a muted *whump* and kept going.

I rolled to a stop. I looked at Ike and he looked at me, startled and openmouthed.

"You felt that?" I said.

"Yeah," he said.

I threw my head back, laughed. Then we pulled the car around and drove back up the hill. We did it again, and again, losing count before setting off for good under the trees. The buck of the engine. The thrust of gasoline as the distance peeled away. For a little while, these were the only miracles we needed.

❧

We slunk back in the afternoon, the sugar gone sour in our mouths. We were late preparing dinner, our stomachs dodgy and nothing made. The traps empty, our chores undone, we decided to kill a hen. It was something they avoided—the meat was rarely worth giving up a steady supply of eggs. We went ahead anyway. Ike chased the chickens around their yard for a minute before grabbing one, pinning its wings in a bear hug. We stuffed it into the slaughter cone, thanking the carcass while it drained. Then we took the body to the kitchen for plucking, an aggravating task that left my fingers sore. We were cooking the naked bird on Ike's spit when we heard a sound from the barn—the snore and wheeze of Barry's saw.

"So he's at it again," Ike said. "Building."

We went over to check on him. I could see right away that he was different. The lightning in his eyes again, blue and too big through his glasses.

"Where have you two been?" he rasped amiably. "There's been some progress—finally. It's been a day of breakthroughs! Come, look."

He showed us around the table, and explained a bunch of things I didn't understand.

"This is it," he said, a perceptible shiver in his voice. "This time, I can *feel* it. I feel it, I feel it."

Odd, the way he echoed himself, as if to burn off excess energy. I felt almost sorry for him. The grinding rise and fall of it, predictable as Ike said.

"Dad," Ike told him. "You should come eat."

To my surprise, he laid down his tools.

"Yes," he said. "We can talk about next steps."

❧

We ate. The meat was tough and smoky and unseasoned except for the salt we'd rubbed in. It could have been how hungry I was, but the taste sent me reeling, each bite exploding with flavor. I wiped dribbles of juice from my lips.

Barry set his plate on the ground, the fire's orange rush reflected in his lenses.

"Now," he said, his chin shining with grease. "We should talk about Friday."

I cocked my head at him, confused.

"The horse?" I said.

Barry wrinkled his nose crookedly, confused. Then he laughed.

"No," he said. "Not the horse. But the horse's *namesake*. Friday. Friday is what comes next. And it's been a long way to Friday—hasn't it—Ike?"

Ike said nothing, his silent self again. The timber flickered and spit.

"When we're finished," Barry said, "it'll mean the end of the world we've known. We can't even imagine, I don't think, what that will be like—though it's only days away. So it's important Jane understands the plan. Today, right now, before things get interesting."

He nodded to himself.

"We *crave* flight," he said. "You feel it, don't you? This hunger we've never had a way to feed. But soon—a matter of hours, now—we'll be able to *act* on the impulse. At that point, the whole emphasis will change. The flying man will not be bound by what he despises. The flying man will not permit an existence of apathy and abuse. We'll abandon that. We'll spread our *wings*, Jane. We'll feel the sun on our backs and go wherever we please. That way—and only that way—we can finally *start over*."

I'd hardened myself against Barry, reminding myself he couldn't be trusted. The high, fevered note in his voice I'd heard the day I first met him. He'd fallen just feet from where we sat, brutal proof of his madness. And yet I recognized it, what he was describing. It was something I wanted.

"It's the beginning of a beautiful long weekend, my sister," he said. "A global weekend, a weekend without end. *That's* what we'll do: grind the whole world to a halt, so something new can live."

He smiled dreamily.

"Friday," he said.

We'd move out across the countryside with the wings, he told us. We'd strike out north, toward Canada, stopping at all the little towns along the Black River, where the willows we needed grew abundantly, their canes teasing the surface of the water. Those towns were all forgotten places, he said, and that would help us. These hollowed-out spaces people had long ago stopped defending. There would be no resistance, no police, no rules or regulations to stop us. As we taught people how to build, freeing them one at a time with wings, the larger world would not take notice. Flight's revolutionary power would grow in the shadows, the way rot spreads through the weak parts of a tree.

The key was just to move fast enough. A seditious, north-ward charge. That way, by the time anyone noticed, it would already be too late. We'd cross the border then, soaring over Niagara Falls. The tourists gawking in their yellow slickers, snapping pictures through the spray. And then—like that—we'd be on the other side, the old rules falling uselessly away. Flight no longer something any one nation could govern.

Barry reasoned that if a thousand people, if five hundred people—maybe even just a hundred people—learned to build the wings, it would be good enough to set things into motion. Because no one can take away what can be easily built with basic tools. Knowledge can't be unlearned once it's known. Each successive person, changed by a new and animating cause—a rupture that turned student into teacher, servant into master, human into bird. What law could ban that trans-formation? What show of force could ever stomp it out?

We were trapped, he'd said, like microbes in a vat of cider. But the vat itself could burst.

❧

Barry spoke until he wore himself out. We sat there in the silence, so quiet you could hear the woosh and crackle of the fire feeding on the wood, a sound like an unending inward suck of breath. He finally stood.

"Good night," he said. "And get some rest, both of you. We have so much ahead."

With that, he picked his crutches up off the grass and limped toward the house.

"Wow," I said, when he was gone. I knew how crazy it was, everything he'd said. But it had been something to hear him. Painful and electric and forbidden, like sticking a fork into a socket.

"It's starting again," Ike said quietly.

"I can see that."

"He'll get worse. Just more and more of it. And then . . ."

He didn't need to finish. I understood, I'd seen it myself: Barry would build up a head of steam, and then go charging off a cliff.

Ike sighed.

"All that matters," he said, "is just to hold him back. As long as he doesn't *hurt* himself, that's all. Then it'll pass. It *will* pass, like it always does. And when it passes, we can try again."

It exhausted me, the thought of all that waiting.

Ike was staring at me very intently, then. I could see the fire reflected in his eyes, tiny twin flames burning at the bottom of his gaze.

"Don't let him fool you," he said.

"I won't," I said. I wouldn't. I understood.

I woke up suddenly, the sound of boots on the floor. When I opened my eyes, I saw a shadow in the doorway. The shadow headed for the worktable, and started futzing with some tools, a metallic clank and clatter. It was barely dawn.

"Barry," I groaned.

"Shh," he said. "My sister, sleep."

"What *time* is it?"

"*Our* time," he said. "It's our time."

I flopped over on my back. If he was going to keep barging in like that, I thought darkly, I'd be better off sleeping in my car. A loud scraping began, a sound I recognized—he was peeling the willow canes with a handsaw, stripping them to make them tapered and more limber. I lay there for a while, staring up toward the ceiling, winged shapes blocking a view of the rafters. Then I sat up.

The scraping stopped.

"Oh," Barry said. "You're up."

"It's pretty loud," I said.

"Hmm," he said, considering it. Then he shrugged and started in again. Shavings curled and fell.

"Now that you're awake," he said, "I wanted to ask you something."

He put the saw down.

"When they talk about it," he said. "The warming. Do they talk about refugees?"

I thought about it. I'd heard a lot about the planet, a lot about temperature. A lot about pollution. But I hadn't heard much about what would happen to *people*. No, I hadn't heard anything about refugees, and I told him so.

"So they're not making any preparations," he said. "None at all."

"I don't know," I said. "I don't think so."

"You'd know," he said. "*God.*" He spat the word out like a curse.

"Two degrees," he said. "Two degrees warmer—planetary average, which we haven't seen in a million years—and the entire *equator* gets unlivable. The earth's swollen belly. Where do you think all those people are going to go?"

He started scraping again, shaving away thin layers of wood in long, graceful motions as he talked.

"North," he said, "and south. They'll go where they have to, to survive. As I would. As you would. Anywhere but there— the hottest, most punishing part."

He looked over the top of his glasses at me.

"The question is whether they'll be let in," he said. "But not just them. All life, heading for the poles. The fish will go. Birds, insects. The *trees* will go. Did you know trees migrate? Slowly, but it's true. Everything will seek its place, the new place that's more like the old place, like the place that no longer exists. The question is only whether they'll move fast enough, or die first. And whether they'll be let in when they come."

He kept scraping.

"You'll see," he said. "Just watch, the Amazon will turn to desert before you're old. Just the natural order of things, a standard ecosystem for that climate. The forest will try to move, but that takes centuries. And now there's too much in the way."

He sucked loudly at his teeth, a that's-too-bad sound.

"North and south," he said. "Everything, in a race toward the poles. The last vestiges of the good old earth."

His tone had been almost jovial, but then it changed.

"Do you see what I'm saying?" he said. "People might be all right, if they're allowed to *go*. To flow, like rivers flow. To *migrate*. But, no. Power. It restricts everything, doesn't it? Borders—

they'll be the site of so much suffering. And death. Today's borders are tomorrow's prison walls. And the prison's much too hot, and there's nothing to drink."

It was horrifying to listen to him, unsettling and science-fictional. I didn't know if it was true, or just the kind of thing he said.

"Flight is the only antidote to all of that," he said. "A way we can move freely across a disaster-stricken earth. Become unbound from these failing human systems. You see that, don't you? So we *have* to try. We have to."

He slid his glasses back up the bridge of his nose and folded his arms.

"Come help me, my sister," he said.

He offered me a handsaw. I hesitated. I wasn't sure if I should take it—if it meant I was hurting him, if it meant I was betraying Ike. But Barry looked at me so insistently, and I sensed I had no choice. His will was a deep channel. It couldn't be stopped, only redirected, like water in a river.

I took the saw. It would be fine, I told myself. It was only morning. As long as we kept him off the ledge, he'd be all right.

⌇

Soon after, Ike came into the barn. He stopped when he saw me, a poorly disguised flinch. But, mercifully, he came and joined us at the table. He didn't look at me or speak. He simply pitched in as we joined the willow spars to the frame, drilling the holes and fitting the rods, the skeleton starting to take shape.

Ike worked with a methodical slowness that seemed outwardly like care, a measure-twice-cut-once intentionality in everything he did. But it was only subterfuge. I remembered his fingers in the dark, the whisk of his blade against the freshly sewn stitches. We both understood there was no point in taking Barry on directly. We could only work against him in the shadows, slowing his momentum, hoping the crash Ike warned about would come before he jumped.

I slowed my own work down a tick or two or more, easing into the subversive power of it. I know Ike noticed—in a silent way, we coordinated, a team of saboteurs. Barry only beamed, thrilled to see us all together, ostensibly bonded by his wish. I'd been so nervous for Ike to see me with him, but I started to relax. For a little while, I felt I'd won, delighted by the illusion that I could please them both.

～

We barely ate all day, besides the eggs Ike cooked and served us early, drinking cold water from the bucket to fill our stomachs. And as the sun started to fade, we were all exhausted and ready for a break. The underlying frame was nearly finished, including the delicate structure of hemp ropes Barry used to mimic the bend of actual birds' wings. While he gathered the cloth for sewing, Ike and I stepped outside to ready dinner. The sky was glorious, this aching mix of blue and orange, colors I somehow knew were inverses of each other, the sky a negative of itself.

"I'm sorry," I told Ike, as we walked down to the river to check the lines. "But he was there when I woke up! I couldn't just—"

He stopped me.

"I know," he said. I was grateful. I could see it was all right.

"What should we do?"

"Just slow him down," Ike said. "It's all we can do."

"But we can't slow him down forever."

"He needs us to help him—he can't get the wings on by himself," Ike said. "All we need to do is say no."

That was true. It was a final thing he needed from us, a trump card we could always play.

"Okay," I said, nodding. We would have to deny him—that was all we had. It was so hard saying no to Barry, but as long as there were two of us, I would do it.

&

That night at the fire, Barry almost seemed to crackle with energy. We were on the eve of our revolution, he kept saying. Friday. It had finally come. We'd bring the wings from town to town, a mutinous charge across the countryside, liberating all the sad country folk. Teaching them what we knew, the transformative knowledge of flight. Ike and I stayed mostly silent, letting Barry talk himself out. His energy was worrisome, culminating, an electric crescendo. All that emotion would need somewhere to go, and I braced myself for the confrontation I knew was going to come.

I listened to him, nodding politely now and then. Our dinner had been a meager thing that night, a soup of Ike's boiled greens, and my stomach was empty and resentful. Ike teased the flames with a stick, hunched and self-conscious. I think Barry sensed my doubt.

"Jane, my sister," he said, seizing on me. "I know—I *say* all this. But when I say the wings will *change* them, I really mean it. It's not *only* that they'll be able to fly, to escape, to move freely across the earth the way birds do. That's only one *part* of it. Try to understand—flight will truly *change* them. There'll be no going back to the old ways, not for any of us. And do you know how we *know* that? That no one would choose drudgery over flight, if given the chance?"

I had actually enjoyed being with Barry much of the day—learning to use my hands, the taut beauty of the wings themselves. But by that time of the night, he was almost beside himself, spilling over with missionary zeal. His language monotonous in its urgency, an exclamation point at the end of every sentence. I no longer knew what he was talking about.

"How?" I said, dutifully.

"Well, what do you know about deep homology?"

"Nothing," I said.

He took a deep suck of breath through his nose.

"My sister," he said, smiling kindly. As though he couldn't believe how lucky I was to be sitting there, about to hear the good news for the first time.

๛

Human beings—all of us, Barry said—are stuck in the wrong bodies. Thanks to biology, we're stranded on the ground. But we have this bone-deep need to pump our limbs, to displace air and rise. To propel through three dimensions using nothing but our own brute strength. To fly. Until we can, he said, we'll suffer, the anguish of a thing barred from expressing its true nature, the distress of stabled horses and shut-in dogs.

The impulse lies in a kind of genetic memory, imprinted at the level of our cells. No different from the way a newborn infant, still covered in birth fluid, knows how to crawl up its mother's chest to the breast. The way our twin lungs clutch for air without being told. Some things need no teaching, and this is like that. We're born seeking heat, hating cold, fearing pain—and thirsting, whether we know it or not, for flight.

Of course we do. Because, while people think of birds and humans as profoundly different creatures, we're really more like genetic first cousins, Barry said. Only five percent of the earth's species are vertebrates—and judged that way, the tortoise is not so different from the hare. We share eighty percent of our genetic material with birds.

Actually, we share a brain.

Humans didn't grow their enormous brains from scratch. Evolution keeps what it likes, building on successful adaptations, new structures on old foundations. Our brains evolved that way, like onions, piece by piece, successive layers added around an ancient core.

The brain's outer, and most recent, layer makes us uniquely human: it contains our language centers, our gift for meaning and math, symbolism and abstraction. The layer below that is the dog brain we inherited from early mammals—the part that craves constancy and rituals, that seeks patterns. And the layer below *that* is the primal node, just a lump at the tip of the spine, that we share with our even earlier ancestors, the reptiles and birds. That fleshy bulb is the seat of our emotions—where we nurse our deepest impulses and appetites. Desire. Fear. Hunger. Rage.

There, down in the bird brain, is where the urge to fly is rooted.

Viewed this way, the mind is like a set of Russian dolls, and the women stacked inside are the creatures we've been before. Each layer the mother of its shell. The innermost doll—the deep brain, the ancient brain—is where unspoken and profound aspects of us live. And that doll craves flight above all. To be human is to have a bird inside your head.

This is not a metaphor. It's biology. It's not even exceptional. There are other close similarities between our species. The more you look, the more you start to see that we and our winged cousins share uncanny genetic links.

Take speech and birdsong, for example. You might think they evolved independently, that birds learned speech-like behavior on their own. That they only by coincidence use their throats like we do, signaling their kind with pitch, inflection, and rhythm.

No.

Birds and humans share a common ancestor, a mother amniote a million years ago, who gave us both the language instinct—who gifted us both the same capacity for speech. The gift expresses differently in our very different bodies, but it comes from the same place. It's the same instinct, coming to life.

Evolutionary biologists call this "deep homology."

There are other examples—bats and birds, say. You might think each species evolved flight independently, through natural selection, in response to separate environmental factors. But that would only be half true. Bats and birds share a deep, cell-level flight *proclivity*, one forever rooted in their common genes.

We share it, too.

Somewhere in the dark recesses of our minds, in the most primordial place, the flying impulse lurks. There, with all the other invisible, irresistible messages—*breathe* and *eat this* and *kiss him* and *run*—a hushed voice whispers:

Spread your wings.

That whisper is forever in our ears, whether we listen or not. But once you hear it, you can never unhear it.

❧

I won't say all of that sank in, at least not right away. I mostly remember wanting to resist him, to prove to Ike—prove to myself—that I hadn't fallen back under Barry's spell. And though he wanted so badly to convince me, I could feel myself hardening against much of what he said. His language was intense and evocative but also unseemly somehow, cloaked in the language of science but clearly acutely personal, filled with so much emotion that you wanted to turn away. It didn't help that he spoke in a way that was quick, and darting, and bright—

somehow everywhere at once, and yet impossible to apprehend. The way a swung blade makes itself invisible, except for this blur of light.

It was Barry being Barry, wild and engaging and also not to be taken totally seriously. And yet, as the two of them walked back to the house for the night, and I went to my cot in the barn, I found his words echoing in my brain. Overhead, the gliders swayed from the rafters, their huge, serrated shapes animated by a barely perceptible breeze. Something about their scale, their height, the brazenness of their shapes spoke to me, then, and I felt my defenses crumble. I filled like a cup with longing. Was it possible, I wondered, that I'd always wanted what Barry wanted? That all my searching had forever been for this?

TWELVE

I woke up to the sound of rope sliding against wood. When my eyes adjusted to the candlelight I saw Barry moving by the worktable, attending to the wings. I watched him for a minute, then closed my eyes again. It was no good. He was making too much noise.

"Barry," I said.

He turned around.

"Morning," he said.

I tried to ignore the sound, muffled noises that came at odd intervals. Nothing you could get used to, but I tried. Then he started to use the sewing machine, filling the whole barn with its machine-gun tatter. I sat up and gave him a look.

"Sorry," he whispered, but he had no intention of stopping.

It must have been the middle of the night. I was so tired that I was almost able to drown out the sound, my mind half flooded with darkness. I drifted in and out of an uneasy sleep, the Singer's nattering monotone breaking in upon the quiet. Some time passed like that, I don't know how much. Then Barry started *talking* to me.

"Jane," he whispered.

I sat up.

"*What?*"

"If you're already awake," he said, "I could use your help."

I gave up. He wanted me to help him sew, so I took his place at the Singer.

"I couldn't sleep," he told me. "Not when we're so *close* like this. It's just *hours*, now—we're there, it's time—"

I was so tired that I wasn't thinking. I pedaled in a stupor, lulled by the rhythm of it, while he guided the wings in and out under the needle. I hung my head and barely watched, just focused on the motion of my feet. But after a while I started to come to my senses. Exhaustion had taken my brakes off. Barry had made so much progress in the night, while I was sleeping, and the new pair of wings was nearly finished. I started to feel painfully awake. Sitting there at the sewing machine, there was no easy way to change course—at least not without being more abrupt than I wanted to be. I was trapped.

In the candle's guttering light, I couldn't see exactly how much more needed to be done. I tried to think what to do, pedaling onward while Barry maneuvered the wings by their frame. Then he stood up, beaming.

"There," he said. "You can stop."

I let my feet slow.

"My sister," he said, "we're finished."

He didn't even pause to let the moment sink in. He lifted the frame and started to walk out with it toward the night.

"Barry," I said, but he didn't even answer.

I ran after him, following him around the side of the barn. He mounted the wings to the hook and started to hoist them, jerk by jerk, up to the platform. It was so dark. But he'd learned everything by memory, through years of repetition, and was literally able to perform the whole ritual with his eyes closed.

"You really want to do this?" I said. "Now?"

I looked back toward the house, a looming shape at the edge of the meadow. I wondered if Ike would hear me if I shouted for him. It was all happening so quickly.

The wings hovered above us in the air. Barry didn't answer me. He started limping over toward the ladder.

"Seriously," I said. "It's the middle of the night."

He paused, his hands on the rungs, and then turned to me.

"Jane," he said.

"It's dark," I said. "It's—"

"Listen," he said. "I know how you and Ike worry about me. It's very sweet. I am telling you—*there is nothing to be afraid of.* We'll fly tonight, right now, or I'll be absolutely goddamned. My sister, this is our moment—"

"I'd just feel better if we got Ike first," I said. "It's dark—"

"I know it's dark," he thundered. "Why in god's name does it matter?"

I fell silent, chastened.

"Look," he said. "I know. I *know* you're worried. But if you can trust anything in your life, trust this. The plans are good. We did our jobs. You'll see—"

"You can't do it without my help," I said.

I saw his teeth flash in the darkness.

"I don't need you at all," he said.

"But last time," I said, "I had to tie you in. I tied your hands and feet, your back—"

"Oh, you should absolutely do all that," he said. "But that's just for my safety. I can still fly without any of it, and I will. It'll just be that much more dangerous."

"But—"

"I'm going to do this now," he said. "You can come with me, and make sure I'm set up properly. Or else I'm going to rise a thousand feet above the earth with only my muscles to keep me from falling. It's your choice."

I looked back at the house.

"Go ahead," he said. "Go get him. But I'm going to do this now. And then you'll see how absurd you're being."

He seemed to think better of it, the words harsher than he wanted.

"I'm sorry, my sister—it's just, don't be afraid! You don't want to miss this moment, this gorgeous, history-making moment. But you can come with me or not."

"But—"

"I can't wait anymore," he said. "I've waited long enough."

With that, he started to climb the ladder.

I thought about screaming for Ike. But what could he do, even if he heard me? I wasn't sure how long I had—minutes, seconds.

Barry stood on the platform. He tied his ankles to the bottom of the hanging frame, and then, with his feet secured, he lifted the wings off the hook. He was going to go ahead with it, no matter what I did.

"Okay," I said. "Okay—stop."

Barry looked down at me.

"I'll do it," I said.

"Thank you," he said. "Thank you, Jane."

I climbed the ladder to the top. I helped him into the harness, cinched it up all along his back. I tied his wrists in, his ankles. And I stood back.

"Go ahead down," Barry said. "Be ready to watch, now. You won't want to forget this."

It was time. The stars were so unbelievably bright above us, like holes someone had poked out of the darkness with a needle, and on the other side was nothing but light. I looked up at the figure above me, Barry standing at the edge, his winged shape blotting out the cosmos. I wanted it, I realized, with a ferocity that startled me. Not just for Barry to be safe. But for Barry to be right. For us to be starting the first chapter in a new history, a better, freer era that would be born as I watched. I prayed for it, my whole body tingling toward the wish. I couldn't think what else to do.

He jumped. The wings beat once. A sound like the shake of

a great pillow. It was so dark, I couldn't tell what I was seeing, but his body seemed to actually rise. He pulled the wings back and clapped them a second time, and he rose higher, as if he were tugging himself skyward on a rope, like a piece of stagecraft. He flapped again, but by then the wind seemed to have caught him, and when he rose it was more like being blown, the way an umbrella is blown in a storm, carrying him higher. It all happened quickly, but by then it was clear something was wrong. My hand lifted to my mouth in horror—he was so high up. One of the wings wrenched out of shape, a shroud that wrapped him as he rose chaotically, and then he fell.

I caught only a glimpse of him as he plummeted downward, his legs swinging free, dangling helplessly. He hit the ground with a sickening crack.

Thirteen

Barry lay a good distance from the barn, our dinner fire still dying in the pit, a dim orange glow from its shuddering light. I ran to him. His breath had been knocked out—he was gasping for air, writhing inside the machine he'd made. I stood over him, calling to him, and he seemed to have no idea I was there. An awful sound escaped from his throat as he twisted in the grass, lost in a private universe of hurt.

Then I saw his leg.

It was bent at a wicked angle over the knee, a hinge no limb should have. Just one look and I thought I might vomit.

I shouted Ike's name, my voice ringing across the meadow with the full force of my lungs. But the house was a long way off, and I doubted he could hear. I looked down again. Barry's breath had calmed a little, and his eyes were open.

"Well," he croaked, as I stood over him. "That's that."

"We have to get you help," I said.

He didn't seem to hear.

"I managed to fall on my bad leg," he said. "That's good."

"We've got to get you to a hospital," I said.

"No!" Barry said, with surprising vigor, shaking his head. "No doctors, Jane. It isn't necessary."

"Please," I said. I kept my eyes averted from his leg. I couldn't handle seeing it again, smashed like a toothpick from the fall.

"Don't talk like that," he said, shaking his head.

"But your leg—"

"I'll be okay," Barry said. "It's not the first time I've broken a leg. Just listen to me. I need you to get me something. A candle. And the whiskey in my desk."

He told me where to find it. I went into the barn and grabbed the candle we'd left lit, and in his desk drawer I found a cloudy, unmarked bottle. I brought them back to him, lifted the whiskey to his lips. He slugged it down, a greed born of pain. When I pulled the bottle away, he seemed a little more lucid.

"Now," he said, "I'm going to need your help."

"I'm going to get Ike."

"Not yet. Do this for me first."

I did what he said, untying the ropes from his wrists. Barry was still lying on top of the wings, and his fingers dug into the cloth with how much it hurt.

"Now, my sister," he said, his breathing ragged. "If you could, please—take off my slipper."

I looked down at his moccasin, a tuft of fur at the end of the skewed, broken line of his leg. The horror of it welled up in me, and I froze.

"Jane," he said, clenching his teeth through the pain, pointing weakly to his foot. "The slipper."

I took his homemade shoe in my hands, soft with a long-dead rabbit's fur, and pulled it away as gently as I could. We both looked at his foot—busted and craggy-looking, the toenails odd and gloopy, as if they were made of poured glue.

"Please," he said. "Feel my toes."

I carefully put my palm on his big toe.

"No," he said. "Squeeze them."

I squeezed. He winced.

"Warm?"

"Yes," I said.

"Good," he said. "That's good. I can still feel them."

He grabbed the hem of his pant leg and started to tear. The fabric split, the sound of stitches coming apart. He tore until most of his leg was free, and then we saw the damage: his femur was clearly broken. Instead of a normal straight thigh, he had a crooked thing. Even in the darkness, I could see the skin was bluish and drowned-looking.

"God, Barry," I said tearfully.

"Stop," he said. "You think I haven't dealt with this before?" For the first time, his voice fluttered with the threat of tears.

He reached for the whiskey again and took another swig.

"Now," he said. "I'm going to need you to reset this."

"To do what?" I whispered. The nausea I felt just looking at it made me want to double over.

"We need to splint my leg," he said. "And first I'll need you to reset it."

"Reset it?"

"To correct the position," he said, shaking his head sadly, as if he knew it was too much to ask.

"I can't," I said.

"Of course you can," he said. "You will."

I looked down at his leg.

"I'll go get Ike," I said. "We'll find a hospital—"

"Jane," he said. "There isn't time for that."

⁓

Somehow, he talked me into it. He told me that a broken bone is like a puzzle piece, with two parts that want to fit back together. All I had to do was pull his leg out and align the pieces just right. But the pain seemed to be catching up with him. As he spoke, he sometimes had to pause and catch his breath, his eyes squeezed shut, waiting for the wave to pass.

I remember feeling like I might shatter with the stress of it.

My hands felt numb, just two latex gloves filled with ice water. Somehow, I did what I was told.

On the first try, he roared horribly, throwing back his head to let a guttural and wordless sound escape from him, a great discharging force. I had to stop.

"My sister," Barry gasped. "Please."

His voice was gentle then, almost serene.

"I'm going to scream—my body will make me. But that doesn't change what you have to do. It's the right thing to do. The only thing to do. So do it."

The second time, I pulled with all my trust, and I felt it— the give, like a loaded spring. He roared again, a glottal, tearing sound, but I suddenly sensed what to do. I pivoted his leg, with a noise like ice cubes cracking in warm water, and eased the bone into place.

Barry let his head loll back, gulping air through his nose.

"I'm sorry," I kept saying. "I'm sorry. I'm sorry."

"No," he said, when he could speak again. "It's better."

He showed me how to make a splint. We used two boards from the barn, and some torn cloth for fasteners, which we tied on either side of the break, enough to keep the rigid structure firm. By then my hands were shaking, a delayed reaction: my nerves had waited until the worst was over to fall apart.

Barry asked me to get his crutches from the barn, insisting that he wanted to go to the cot. I hated to move him, but I couldn't see just leaving him on the ground like that. So I helped him get up on the crutches, his breath heavy and ragged. The barn seemed so far away.

He lifted the wooden supports and brought them forward gingerly, a tentative first step.

"How does that feel?" I asked.

"Good," he said, after a pause. "The splint's holding."

We hobbled across the grass that way, passing in cautious

increments through the darkness. I steadied him with one hand, his shirt-back damp with sweat.

"Jane," Barry said. "You *saw* it, didn't you?"

"Careful," I said.

"But you did see," he said. "Didn't you?"

"See what?"

"That I *flew!*"

The word hung there between us. He took another step.

"I did!" he said. "A three-beat ascent. I got maybe forty feet in the air before I lost control. My sister—I *felt* it!"

"Barry," I said. To claim victory, after what had just happened, seemed absurd.

"Well, it's obviously not quite *there* yet," he said. "But the feeling—unmistakable!"

I wasn't sure what I'd seen. There had been a moment when it did seem like he was starting to rise. But that didn't mean anything. Did it? It could have just been the wind, lifting upward on the wings' twin parachute sails. What I remembered most was the way those first seconds morphed into something unpredictable and violent—how helpless he'd looked up there, snatched from the air and hurled toward the earth by invisible hands.

I helped him limp across the barn to the cot, where he collapsed in a wheezing of springs. He lay there panting, the mattress bobbing subtly against his weight.

The splint seemed to have helped him. But even with it on, I could see his leg had started to swell, like a second knee above his knee.

"I'm going to get Ike," I said.

"Oh, Ike," Barry groaned. "He'll be *heartbroken* by this."

"I know."

I couldn't quite believe it. Everything had gone exactly the way Ike had always warned me about, step by step. And it had finally happened on my watch. The thing he feared most, the danger to his father. I felt sick about it. The way I'd allowed Barry to risk his body, the way I'd betrayed Ike. Whatever had been beautiful about my time there, it was coming to an end.

I turned to go, the gravity of it all finally starting to hit.

"Wait," Barry said.

"I have to get him," I said. "I need his help. *You* need his help."

"Just wait a little while," Barry said. "Let him sleep. Let him find out in the morning. There's no point in waking him now."

"But—"

"I'll be all right," he said. "I just can't—I can't face him yet."

It was terrible to hear him say that. I understood, because it was the same for me.

~

Barry wanted the whiskey, so I brought it to him. He drank, the air potent with its astringent corn-sugar smell. He offered me the bottle, and I took it, the first sip like lightning and smoke. I felt it hurtling through my bloodstream, immediately intoxicating. It was a mistake to have any. I had to keep my head together, I reminded myself. I wouldn't drink any more.

The thought of Ike, still asleep in the house, totally unaware of everything that had happened, was miserable to both of us. Barry especially seemed haunted by it, bereft in a way I'd never seen before. The booze didn't help. He'd come undone. He was devastated by his failure, in unbearable pain, and somehow all of it was bound up in Ike.

"I'm a terrible father," he said. "I don't—there's no other way to say it. Tell me, Jane. What kind of dad am I?"

"I—"

"Don't answer that," he said. "Just *listen* to me. I want to tell you something."

It was almost dawn by then. You could feel a change in the

quality of the darkness, the world starting to come to life, frogs quibbling by the river in their electric tongue. I had a few candles going, and their light bobbed on the wall.

"It was a long time ago," he said. "Twenty years, more. I'd stopped building planes and I had the insight—that we might fly, that we could fly, that we *must*. The challenge terrified me. But there was no other choice. I was going to build a flying machine, or die trying to do it."

His breath was shallow, and I could tell it hurt him to talk.

"One day, I was driving back from somewhere. I still had a *car*, for goodness' sake. An old, worn-down Chevy truck, getting shakier all the time. Well, that afternoon as I passed the church, something caught my eye. This little bundle on the steps. And *that* seemed strange.

"I kept driving, but before I knew, I'd turned back around and had pulled into the parking lot. And there, on the stone staircase, was a child. Strapped to a car seat and wrapped in a crummy powder-blue blanket. He was all flushed with crying, tears still drying on his face. Just miserable. It was bright out, his eyes clenched tight against the sun. But when my shadow fell across his little body, I saw his face relax. And just like that, I had this feeling he was mine.

"Someone had left him there—to be taken, that was clear. I don't know. I never second-guessed it. I brought him home, and no one saw.

"I never knew much about kids. I was the youngest of three, always the baby myself. I guessed he was less than a year old, able to crawl a bit but still crying all night. I built him a crib and kept him in the room with me, laid him on a couple of folded sheets. After a few weeks, he started sleeping better.

"It was amazing, that will to survive. I fed him, and the rest he pretty much did himself."

He looked up at me, his eyes bright in the candlelight.

"So," he said. "That was Ike."

I stared at him, his bent nose casting a weird shadow across his face. Somehow I'd never imagined Ike coming to him that way, something between an adoption and abduction. I felt dizzy with the revelation of it.

"I named him," Barry said. "I did all the things that fathers do. For a while I was terrified that someone would show up and take him from me. But no one ever did."

He started to feel cold, so I got the blanket for him. A ratty grayish thing with patches of colored felt. I could see him shivering beneath it, the whiskey bottle held tight against his chest.

"At some point, the girl showed up," he said. "Charlotte."

He sat up a bit and swung the bottle upward, gulping the liquid down his throat.

"He'd started to walk, I remember that. He could amuse himself for hours in his crib, just playing with a piece of cloth. So I could finally work. By then I was working on a model of Lilienthal's glider, one of his early ones. I fell a few times. I broke my nose. All that."

He scratched his cheek.

"Well, one day this girl showed up. Out of the blue, like you.

"She was eighteen. A kid. In time, she told me that she'd won some kind of scholarship to college, paid in full and all. Except her father hadn't let her go. He wanted her to stay home and work the farm, a total dead-end life. I bet she did stay, in the end, and I bet the farm failed, too. But that was her little act of rebellion—coming to me.

"I was pretty well-known back then around here, for flying my Wright Brothers planes. I think it touched something in her. She wanted to fly so badly. Almost like I did. So I told her everything I'd learned—about the Wright Brothers, sure, but also about deep homology, and the craving, and how close they'd come to real human-powered flight during the age of steam. She'd help me build, or play on the floor with Ike and watch me, and all of it was useful. She slept out here in this very cot. But one day—it might have been after a couple of weeks—she wasn't there when I came out in the morning. She disappeared, and that was the end of it."

He managed a pained smile.

"I kept expecting you to leave us, too," he said.

He was quiet then, a silence long enough to drown in. It was strange, thinking of this long-ago girl who'd been so much like me. I felt kinship and revulsion—the resemblance was uncomfortably close.

"Mostly, I forgot about it," he said. "But not Ike. The thing was, he *remembered* her. Barely two years old—it was extraordinary. 'Who was she,' he'd ask, 'who I sat with, right there? Who was it I sat with, on the floor?' And of course there were mothers in all the books I read him. All the kids' books have mothers in them. You can't escape it. But a kid can only hear so long about mothers before he wants to know who was his.

"At first I told him the truth, actually. I didn't *know* who his mother was. He didn't believe me. He kept asking about his mother, asking about the woman on the floor. 'She had brown eyes,' he'd say. *Brown.* Like that proved something. So eventually this story kind of came together. Just a thing to tell him. There'd been a girl who fell from the water tower in town, a long time ago. A famous tragedy around here. That seemed like something to tell him. They started to get mixed up in my mind somehow. I'm not sure why. . . ."

"Does he know?" I said.

"Know what?"

"That you basically lied to him?"

It came out colder than I had meant, but it was the only way to say it.

"It's the funniest thing," Barry said, and his voice changed somehow, a softening tone of wonder in it. "He *knows* it isn't true. And yet he still kind of believes it."

He was starting to sound drunk again. He was still shivering. His eyes glowed in the dark like a cat's.

"I can't remember why I'm telling you all this," he said. "There was something . . ."

He went on awhile before I realized his story had no clear purpose. He was rambling, just saying whatever came into his head. His words started to slur, and I noticed he was sweating. I put my hand to his forehead, but quickly drew it away—his skin was fearfully hot.

Fever. He'd been so alert and talkative that I'd let myself believe he was basically all right. That our crude splint had somehow been enough. But this seemed to be a sign that things were serious, that he was getting worse. He shivered vigorously under the blanket. I filled his metal camping cup at the water pump and gave it to him.

"Here," I said. "Drink this."

His eyes were wide and haunted-looking, and he seemed not to know where he was. But he drank the whole cup greedily, water spilling from the corner of his mouth. I helped him lie down again. His eyes didn't close, and he seemed to notice the gliders swaying gently above him. His gaze locked in on them. His whole expression changed.

"Barry?" I said.

I can never forget the look I saw on his face as he lay there, slack-jawed and shivering in the bed.

A mixture of awe, and fear, and reverence, as if a portal had opened in the air above him and it was filled with light.

❧

By then I was really worried about him. I decided to go and get Ike—as much as I hated the idea, I didn't know what else to do.

Dawn had nearly arrived by then, the stars easing back into the pale glow of the sky. I went into the house and up the staircase. The old wood groaned against my feet.

I found his room at the end of a cluttered hallway. The walls and floors were bare, a stark contrast from the rest of the house. There was almost nothing inside except a mattress on the floor, with Ike lying on it, covered in a sheet of their wing fabric, the edges with the same ragged look as his clothes. He didn't even have a door. It was the one place in the house that was his, and he had nothing to fill it with—or maybe, I realized, he wanted to fill it with nothing but spareness.

I knelt down at his bedside. I almost wished he didn't look so peaceful.

"Ike," I said. I said it a few more times, until his eyes fluttered open. His face was totally still for a second, and then he smiled.

"Hi," he said.

"I'm sorry," I said. I felt like crying. "I'm so sorry, but—Barry. He's been hurt."

He sat up, still slow with sleep.

"What happened?"

"He *did* it again," I said. "I tried to stop him. But he wouldn't listen, he—"

"Is it bad?"

"It's bad."

Then we were running down the stairs, through all the rooms of his father's sketches, out into the grass.

Ike and I approached the cot. By then, Barry had fallen asleep. He snored lightly, a low dragging sound in his throat. His forehead studded with sweat, his cheeks slick and wet, his hair damp as if he'd just stepped out of a pool. I'd always known Barry to be in constant motion. It was unnerving to see him so utterly still.

Ike looked down to Barry's bare leg, where we'd ripped the fabric away, the tight clinch of the splint. He said nothing.

"His leg," I said. "He snapped it. When he fell. It just broke."

I hung my head, waiting for his anger. But it didn't come.

"Do you think he'll be all right?" Ike said.

"I don't know."

"Will his *leg* be all right?"

"I don't know. He says so. But it looked bad."

I couldn't believe how calm he was. But he hadn't seen what had actually happened, the violence of the fall. I didn't feel I could hide it from him. He needed to know the truth. So I tried to tell him what had happened, how his leg had looked when I first saw it. How he'd forced me to reset the break. I was shaking as I said it.

I'm so grateful for how he responded, even now.

"Listen," he said, when I stopped to take a breath. "It's not your fault."

"I tried to stop him. I really did."

"It's what was coming. It was always going to end like this."

❧

While Barry slept, we tried to figure out what to do. I wanted him to get his leg looked at—it didn't seem good to leave it like that, wrapped in a homemade splint. When he woke up, I thought, we could try to get him into my car. Take him to a hospital. But Ike wasn't sure.

"He won't go," he said.

"We'll make him go."

"He won't," he said. "I'm telling you, he won't."

"Then we can bring help here."

He looked at me.

"Who'd come *here*?"

I found the question heartbreaking, devastating in its earnestness. He simply couldn't imagine outsiders entering their kingdom against his father's will. I tried to explain to him that there were health care workers, people who were obligated by duty and law to help the sick and wounded, even those who refused help. This idea surprised and fascinated Ike. It was inconceivable to him that anyone could force Barry to submit. His world had been hermetically sealed. His father's authority had been that complete.

But neither one of us liked the idea of a bunch of strangers holding Barry down, forcing him into a stretcher. That didn't feel like the kind of help he needed. Maybe it was still possible he'd come willingly, I thought. I told Ike how filled with sorrow he'd been, how ashamed he was of what had happened. It was more than just the pain. Above all, he seemed to think he'd failed his son.

Ike seemed heartened by this.

"See—it's like I told you," he said, briefly excited—as awful as all of it was—that I'd seen things play out exactly as he'd described, with Barry's efforts becoming more and more frenzied and grandiose until they ultimately climaxed in failure, followed by bouts of doubt and torrents of self-loathing. Then Ike's expression changed, this look of guarded hope.

"He really said that? He was *sorry*?"

"Well," I said. "More or less." I wasn't sure Barry had apologized, technically. But clearly he knew Ike would be devastated. He sensed, in his own skewed way, that he'd let his son down again—though he'd construed it as a failure of the wings more than his failure as a man.

"Wow," Ike said.

He so badly wanted to believe it was a sign of something, the first stirrings of a long-sought change of heart.

We got hungry early, having eaten little the night before, and decided to make breakfast. I helped Ike gather some eggs from the hen coop, looking for the delicate ovals in the dirt, the pop of their speckled shells. We had the fire going and were getting ready to cook when we heard something from the barn, the sound of Barry's tools. We ran. Somehow, he'd gotten up again and was back at his worktable, where he'd started to take the willow canes out of the frame to file them down with some kind of chisel. Loose cloth spilled from the wings, limp as bed-sheets.

"What are you *doing*?" I said.

"I'm fixing them," Barry said, beaming. "Once and for all. Listen. While I was sleeping—I had a *vision*!"

I couldn't help it. I groaned.

"I saw the path forward," he said. "Everything laid out, as if on a piece of paper. The final alteration—it just came to me whole. And it's so *simple*. It's nothing. It's been in front of us the whole time!"

He said something about the proper convexity of the wing toward the outer tip, an adjustment of several fractions of an inch, and other things I didn't understand. Ike and I looked at each other.

"How's your *leg*?" I said.

"Oh, it hurts," Barry said. "Everything hurts! It's still ex-quisitely painful. But I'm able to work. That's the important thing, isn't it?"

I'd almost never seen him so animated. He had his leg propped up on a second chair under the table, where I couldn't get a good look at it. Other than that, he almost seemed normal—whatever normal meant for him.

"I'm even hungry, if you can believe it," he said. "You two should make breakfast. We're going to need our strength."

We walked out of the barn.

"I just don't understand it," Ike said. "How is he still *going* like this?"

"What should we do?" I said.

"He's going to get himself killed," Ike said.

We both knew it was possible. The manic energy was brimming in him still.

"Well, let's tell him," I said.

"Tell him what?" Ike said.

"That we're taking him to get help."

But when we looked in through the door again and saw how intently he was working—scraping away at the willow rods with his tools, thinning them out with fervor—we both started to feel he'd never give it up.

"He won't stop, will he?" I said.

Ike grimaced, all his sadness gathering in the crook of his mouth.

"Should we go get help?" I said. "It's time, isn't it?"

Ike looked through the door at Barry, looked at me. It was what he wanted, even if he couldn't bring himself to say it.

❧

We decided we couldn't leave Barry alone, not in that state. So Ike stayed behind to watch him while I drove out to the gas station, where I thought I'd seen a pay phone. I only had the vaguest outline of a plan. I'd call 911, those three forbidden digits somehow a relief. Then I'd explain our compounding emergencies: a man was injured, he was having some kind of prolonged episode, he wanted to jump from the roof. I imagined a composed voice on the other end of the line—a voice that knew what the options were in a situation like ours, a voice with the power to intervene. A dog lay tied to the stoop of a blighted house as I raced by, the roadsides thick with stemmy plants. Before long, the water tower loomed up in the distance, the swimming-pool-blue that tried and failed to match the color of the sky.

I pulled into the parking lot, relieved to see the pay phone I'd remembered, nestled into its oblong metal housing. When I picked up the receiver, I heard nothing, but I put a quarter in anyway—still nothing. The coin clanked back down the chute. It was broken, or had been decommissioned. It was dead.

I walked over to the mart, but the door was locked. I realized it was likely still very early in the morning. Most of the outside world wasn't awake yet—being up since before dawn had warped my sense of time. A sign on the inside of the door posted the hours. The place didn't open until nine-thirty, ten on weekends. I had no idea how long that would be to wait.

The analogue clock inside my car dash had long been broken. The hands stopped moving every time I turned the engine off, and their angle bore no relation to reality. I switched the radio on and waited for a human voice, hoping I could catch someone announcing the top of the hour. But I only found ads and bad music swimming in the static. I got out and paced around the parking lot, hoping anyone might come, feeling foolish and helpless and sick.

I started to regret leaving Ike alone so long with Barry. I knew exactly how things would play out: his father would finish his latest pointless adjustments, and then he'd try to climb the ladder again. Ike could physically stop him, but I wasn't sure he would.

How long did we have? With no way to know what was happening at the barn, it was hard to decide if I should rush back or keep searching for help. I consulted the crumbling asphalt, the phone poles that stretched out into the distance like crucifixes on the road to Rome, the empty shrill of insects in the brush. But nothing was revealed.

Somehow, I remembered the motel where I'd stayed once, in the beginning. It was five miles past the turnoff in the other direction, but someone would surely be there, and it would have a phone.

I wasn't sure if there was time. With Barry in that state, every minute mattered. As I pulled out of the lot, I decided I'd stop by the house first, just quickly, in case things had escalated. Ike might need my help, and it was sort of on the way.

⌇

I banged through the screen door and walked into the meadow. The sun was still coming up—a lemon wedge at the edge of the sky. As if overnight, the dandelions had started bursting open into seed heads, so many ghostly halos ready to be blown. I saw Ike first. He stood in the middle of the field and waved, pointing. He shouted something that sounded like "gold and light."

Then I saw Barry. He was standing on the roof of the barn, the wings stretched outward in a huge span of white cloth that trembled in the breeze. He was kind of balancing on one foot—even from a distance, I could see they'd tied something fat and cushioning around his broken leg. He shuffled toward the ledge. Before I could shout, he bent his one good knee and leapt.

Wind thumped in the cloth. The wooden frame creaked and held.

And he flew.

Each wingbeat threw him higher in the air. I watched as he became a kite—and I couldn't unclench my fists, as if I held the string that moored him to the earth.

I rubbed my eyes and scanned the air for tricks. Maybe he was held aloft by tiny wires like a pageant angel.

It was no dream. There was only Barry, the wings, and the wide blue sky.

Ike stood planted in the middle of the meadow, staring, his hands bunched and raised like a boxer's. When I looked up again, I saw Barry swooping in a downward arc, and realized he was falling, quickly losing height. I cried out. He came down with the smooth glide of a parachute—and right before he hit the ground his legs somehow swung free. He bounced on one foot before turning a high somersault and landing on his back in the grass.

Ike ran. The pale bottoms of his feet blinked in rhythm, and I ran, too.

Barry lay sprawled out in the clover. The wings weighed down his arms, and he was helpless as a capsized insect. But I saw his rib cage heaving. He'd survived.

He raised his good leg in a victory salute and tore the air with an ecstatic shriek. Ike and I fell down beside him. He was crying, he was laughing, he was calling our names. I couldn't help it—I kissed his forehead like he was my child. When I looked up at Ike, there was the strangest expression on his face—he looked ashamed or triumphant, depending on the angle of his head.

"It's just how I thought it would be," Barry said, gushing. "The *feeling*—! My god, it's finally Friday—it's Friday—"

We lifted him by the armpits, careful not to bounce his broken limb. They'd swaddled it up nicely, a splint of pillows and willow cane that ran from his thigh to his ankle.

"How did this happen?" I said. "I don't understand—"

"I told you!" Barry roared. "It just *came* to me, finally—I just saw how it needed to be—"

The seconds all tumbled together, a joyful delirium.

"Is your *leg* all right?" I said.

"It hurts like hell!" Barry said. "But nothing could blunt the thrill of this. Jane! Grab the champagne—we'll celebrate, the three of us. And Ike—help me out of these wings—our beautiful, beautiful wings—"

I helped Ike lay Barry down in the grass, then ran back to the house, down into the dug-out basement, where a single champagne bottle sat with the cider jugs on an old wire rack. While Ike undressed his father, I pulled the cork and tumbled fizzling gold into each cup. Then we hoisted him up, balancing him on a crutch, so that we could loosen the corset-like harness.

"To flight," Barry said, raising his mug. "*True* flight. And to Friday."

We clunked our cups and drank deep. The first sip prickled to life in my mouth, a taste like oats and apples.

"Still delicious after all these years," Barry said, resting on one crutch. "And it's just as sweet and fresh as . . ."

He trailed off, staring at me funny.

"Jane," he said. "*You* should fly."

"Me?"

"Yes, of course! Don't wait even another second!"

"What about you?" I said, to Ike.

Ike's eyes went wide. Wordlessly, he shook his head, pure refusal on his face. I sensed he hadn't fully reckoned yet with how much had just changed—he was still conditioned by the past, by all those years of saying no.

I drained my glass.

Rung by rung, I scaled the thin silver ladder bolted to the side of the barn. The roof was steeply sloped, and I had a terrible feeling I'd catch a toe on one of the shingles and fall to my death. My vision swooned. I'd never been great with heights.

Ike pulled himself onto the roof and handed me the harness.

"Step into this," he said.

I held the harness up and gawked at it.

"Hey," Ike said. "You're shaking."

I guess I was. A chilling wind blew, and the hairs on my arms became tiny erect bristles, and my legs felt like they'd turned to columns of Vaseline.

"Here," Ike said. He held my waist steady, as if we were about to dance.

I lifted my foot—the world reeled for a second—and piloted it through one of the leg holes. Then I did it again. I pulled the harness up until it was snug, and I stuck my arms through the arm-slots. Like putting on a one-piece bathing suit.

"Now go stand at the edge," Ike said.

I shuffled over to the ledge, my sneakers scraping over the shingle grains. My kneecaps wouldn't stop twitching. Far below, Barry cheered and waved, hoisting a crutch in the air.

"I'm going to vomit," I said.

"No," he roared back, "you look great!"

"Okay," Ike said, behind me. I felt him pull the harness, a corset's slow tightening as the fabric hugged my chest, my ribs. A strap tightened around my waist. Then Ike took the wings off the pulley and set them behind me.

"Lift your arm," he said, so I did. He fit my hand into a sleeve-opening in the cloth, and slid the wing down along my arm, all the way to my shoulder.

"Now spread your fingers," Ike said, so I did—and he slid a glove onto my hand, wooden rings at each knuckle. He knotted loops of string around each ring. I was tied in, and suddenly the wind began to clutch at me—I feared I'd be blown into the air.

"Jane," Ike said. "It's going to be all right."

He had me lift my other arm, and he slid the wing down—like pulling on a sleeve. Again, he tied my hand. And I felt the power tremble in my arms, as if coursing through my wrists out the tips of my fingers.

Breeze pooled in my sails. I waited to be bowled over. And yet, strangely, my arms felt stronger than they ever had. If a sudden gale blew, I sensed that I could stand my ground against it.

"Pull your hand toward your chest," Ike said.

"Which one?"

"It doesn't matter."

The wing beside me shifted with sudden, terrifying strength.

"Try the other one," Ike said, and I pulled that one, too.

"That's all it is," Ike said.

Down below, Barry used the flat of his hand like a visor against the sun. Ike knelt and tied my ankles with rope to the frame.

"When you're going to land, pull this cord," he said, gesturing to a rope that dangled above me. "It'll let your feet hang down for landing."

"How do I land?"

"The best way you can," he said. "Ready?"

I looked down.

"I can't," I said.

"You don't have to," Ike said, his voice low near my ear.

But I was already wearing so much rigging. The ground was so far away.

"What do I *do*?" I called down to Barry. I started shivering so hard I could barely grip the knobby wooden handles he'd instructed me to hold.

"Do?" Barry called back. "That's the beauty. You already know!"

I looked down at their crop of little sheds, the chicken coop, the billowing trees, the river seething beyond them in its channel.

"I can't," I said, frozen.

"Jane!" Barry roared. "Just do it."

So I stepped to the edge of the world, and jumped.

At first, I fell.

But then I managed to bring my arms together, and something burst behind me in a great rush of air—like a parachute opening—and suddenly I was flying.

❧

The wind snatched my voice out of my throat. My eyes dripped with tears from the speed. I forgot who I was. There was just the blurring ground, the ocean sky, the sun—nearer, warmer—and the lulling rhythm of the wings.

Air rushed in torrents and beat in brisk waves. Somewhere, someone was screaming. Somewhere, someone was laughing.

I looked down, giddy with height: the trees a mash of green, the roads long scars, and Barry's compound just a few scraps of shingle tumbled across the round green world.

Then a thought jolted me—I could fly off on the wings and make them mine.

I never had to go back. I never had to come down.

But I didn't abandon them.

I flew until my arms strained and burned, my lungs raw as a sprinter's. Until every muscle nursed an urgent, mutinous ache and I thought my armpits would tear. Then I couldn't stand it anymore. Somehow—there wasn't time to think too hard about it—I knew to lift the wings into an erect posture, thrusting me into a dive. I started to fall. Faster, until the meadow spiraled toward me with nauseating speed. I held my arms out in a way I guessed would slow me, and my speed tapered in the seconds before I crashed.

The impact knocked the wind from my chest, the whole world turned a somersault, and I was flat out on my stomach, wheezing and laughing and drained. Blood thudded in my cheeks, my chest, my limbs.

"... great up there, god, Jane ..."

They pulled me to my feet, but my legs had turned to dough. I stumbled forward, almost fell. Ike held me up, and his and Barry's fingers played at the harness clasps.

"Did you *feel* it?" Barry asked, his blue eyes flashing at me. I knew exactly what he meant.

When they pulled the wings away, I felt small and fragile—a crab or snail all naked without its shell. But they held me steady, and the three of us embraced. I really needed them to help me stand. We held each other, swaying, in the pollen-sweet air.

"Now me," Ike whispered. "Now me."

PART
TWO

So may it be; let us hope that the advent
of a successful flying machine, now only
dimly foreseen and nevertheless thought
to be possible, will bring nothing but
good into the world; that it shall abridge
distance, make all parts of the globe
accessible, bring men into closer relation
with one another, advance civilization,
and hasten the promised era in which
there shall be nothing but peace and
good-will among all men.

—OCTAVE CHANUTE,
PROGRESS IN FLYING MACHINES, 1894

I prayed for wonders instead of happiness,
Lord, and you delivered.

—ABRAHAM JOSHUA HESCHEL

FOURTEEN

We took turns flying. One by one, until our muscles gave out and we'd fall back toward the meadow to collapse in the grass—spent as lovers, clammy with sweat. I'd rush toward the arched white bat-shape as Ike or Barry came in for a landing, giddy with knowing I was next. Everything surged toward the moment when they'd tie me in again, my limbs bound by ropes to the frame, the wings' uncanny strength suddenly my own. You rose, utterly alone, the only thing of your kind in the sky, and flew until you couldn't anymore.

I didn't want to stop. But it wore me out, all that strange motion. Somewhere between a breaststroke and a crawl. The pain was almost pleasant at first, new muscles aching as they started to wake up. Then slow fire gathered in your armpits, radiating out toward your elbows and down through the bones of your hands. The heat ate along the wicks of your nerves until it became too hot, too bright, and you were inevitably forced to swoon back toward the world again, down and down, where it was always someone else's turn.

Was it everything I'd hoped for? It was more. Like stepping into my body for the first time. No, like stepping out of my body altogether. There was nothing but the rush of wind in my ears and a sense of life-giving speed. The air was different up there, clean and cool as satin, and when I closed my eyes to blot out the world below, time itself seemed to have no beginning and no end.

Finally, I had everything I wanted. I was happy. I was whole.

The sun dropped down, heavy and orange, and as night fell we finally rested. We were exhausted, too afraid to keep going, not yet ready for the spooky, dislocating thrill of flying through the darkness. It was only once we put the wings away, stashed carefully in a corner of the barn, that we realized how hungry we were. A rabbit had wandered into one of the traps, huddling behind the wire walls of its cage. We killed it, and while I built the fire, Ike stripped the skin, prepped the carcass, and stuck it on the spit. I'd never been so eager for a meal. We watched with almost frantic anticipation as the raw flesh cooked, the small, headless body weeping lines of grease as it turned over the flame. When it was time, we ate like beasts. The night filled with the sound of our teeth tearing meat, and then it was quiet. I licked my fingers in the dark.

Later, I fell asleep in a dip in the meadow, too tired even to crawl back to the barn. Too tired to worry about the others, or wonder where they were. I felt the earth's coolness through the matted-down grass, could smell the moist soil's loamy perfume. *The world can be restored*, I thought. *The sky is ours.*

Bright wings beat under my eyelids all night long.

～

When I woke up, everything hurt.

I squinted up at the light, too bruised and wrung-out to move. A bug clicked near my ear. Then I remembered: the sky overhead was a towering blue vapor, transformed forever by our bodies, and I was in love with the way the air held me, with how obvious it became that I belonged.

Words kept chattering in my mind: *We flew, we flew.* That was the truth, no less electrifying after a night's sleep.

When I started to get up, my muscles screamed with the

effort. I could barely pull my fists away from my chest—my limbs stiff and achy, like the day after a workout you've put off for too long. Somehow I managed an awkward sit-up, and after a few tries staggered to my feet without using my arms. I was sorer than I could ever remember feeling, sore in tendons I didn't know I'd had. And yet, as I stood, I felt taller somehow, my posture corrected. My spine as straight and limber as a dangling string.

I crossed the meadow and nudged open the barn's sliding doors. No one was there, but the wings still leaned huge and imposing against the far wall—the cloth stained with our falls, hashed with grass-colored skids. I lingered in the doorway and let myself remember. God, how it *felt*. Height, speed, light, combining in a wordless blur. Desire gathered in my temples, a cherry-sized knot of want.

I felt this urge to touch them then. To feel the cloth's rough weave under my palms again, my fingers tracing down the willow's knuckled canes. To lift them, to feel that weight that was barely weight at all. But I collected myself. I summoned my will and turned back toward the house.

❦

I found Ike and Barry in the kitchen, the cast-iron pot filled with scrambled eggs. They cheered as I came in.

"My sister!" Barry roared, beaming. He lurched forward on his crutches, his eyes their gas-fire blue, and touched his forehead to my shoulder. I think he wanted to hug me, but couldn't quite figure out how without letting his crutches go. Ike stood at the sink behind him, smiling as he polished a plate.

"Thank you," Barry said, when our eyes met, though he couldn't have been thanking me specifically—he was paying tribute to the gratitude we all felt, a deep-down gladness that suffused everything, the bones in my shoulder and the silver cups on the shelves, the tree rings in the table, the ancient windows paned with runny glass, and beyond them the summer air alive with birdsong.

We clattered about the room, clumsy with joy, making as much noise as possible as we plated the food. The wattage just thrummed in our veins.

"Careful," I said, when Barry thumped against the table. "Barry, your leg!"

He moved so quickly, as if he'd forgotten he was hurt. Our rigged-up splint still guarded the healing bone, but I didn't want him knocking into things. I asked him how he was feeling, the first night behind him after the break.

"Well, I'm a little banged up," he said. "But, really—I've rarely felt better!"

There was nothing but earnestness in his face. It was true: the harrowing bit of wilderness first aid he'd coached me through seemed to have had near-miraculous results. The day before, when we were flying, my lungs would catch each time he floated down toward the earth again. But he always managed: his legs would swing free and he'd land expertly on the good one, graceful as a stork, before crumpling safely to the earth. Ike and I, on the other hand, smashed down too hard and fast, skidding chaotically through the grass. Barry looked well, he had years of practice with his gliders, he knew just what to do. Maybe it was reckless to let him fly with his leg like that, but it seemed his mastery was total. We could all feel his complete control.

We sat down to eat, incoherent and giddy, the conversation heartfelt and animated and yet we barely knew what we said— like the moment a drug kicks in, the rush of each instant washing away forever the memory of five seconds before. Barry was explaining how it all would be, how that very morning we'd strike out into the countryside and do the thing we'd promised to do for so long. At one point, he got so worked up that he pushed his chair back and stood, careening into a fully blown speech.

"Rousseau put it best!" he thundered, leaning on a crutch. "Man is born free—but everywhere he is in chains!"

He nodded in agreement with himself.

"Today that changes. Today we start the long process of unshackling. Today is *Friday*."

I heard an ecstatic note in his voice, like he'd taken too much speed. His teeth were practically chattering. But we all felt the radical force of it, how the wings would split the old world open like a fruit.

His hair almost glimmered as he moved, the color of a penny turning in the light.

"Now is when we start to *change* things," he said. "Finally! We'll spread the way rot spreads in a sick old tree—growing in the weakest places, flowering in the seams. All the left-behind people in the left-behind places. They're *waiting* for us. Even if they don't know it yet."

He looked at Ike, at me. I felt lost in the disorienting brilliance of his eyes.

"Are you ready to teach them?"

I was. The readiness throbbed in my heart. I pushed my chair back forcefully and stood, Ike following suit in a scrape of wood.

For a second the three of us looked at each other. Then, unexpectedly, Barry fell quiet. He shot a baleful glance at the half-eaten eggs on his plate.

"Dad," Ike said, concern prompting him to speak. Something was troubling him.

"Ike, my son," Barry said, his voice lowered, a confiding growl. "My sister, Jane. We're *soldiers* now. You know that, don't you? No matter what happens, we've got to see this through. Promise me you'll see this through."

His hands were shaking. From the expectant way he looked at us, I could tell he really needed our assurance.

"I promise," I said.

"I promise," Ike said.

Barry was quiet for a moment. Then looked up at us again, and it was the most wonderful thing: he smiled.

"Let's go save the world," he said.

❧

That was how it started.

We found Friday the horse munching grass near the edge of the woods and hitched her to their old Amish wagon. She patiently took the bit between her teeth, the saddle on her back, as if she understood it was finally her time to be of service. Then we set off down the road. I took Ike's bike, and Ike rode Friday, who pulled the wagon cart behind her on strands of rope, and Barry sat up in the wagon's wooden seat, his hair wild and his glasses flashing, a triumphant grin on his face. Behind him the wings lay stretched across the mouth of the buggy, giving the whole thing the look of a bird-like boat.

I pedaled along beside them, Friday's hooves clopping briskly against the asphalt. By then it was starting to feel like summer, the air so thick with buttery light you could almost scoop it with your hands. Barry sat up in his perch, nodding approvingly at the trees as we passed. From time to time our eyes would meet, and he'd grin down at me. Ike kept glancing back, too, as if to make sure we were all still there. We seemed to need to reassure each other, to confirm it was really happening, to persuade ourselves that this was finally real. But the intoxicating truth was that we were ready, that the world was unprepared for us and we could do with it what we wanted.

We rode fast enough to outrun the deerflies, and the wind smelled clean and pure.

"Someone's coming," Ike said.

He was right: a car was zooming toward us in the distance, twin headlights bright against the day.

"Flag them down!" Barry shouted. Ike drew Friday to a stop. So it was finally happening. I straddled the bike in the middle of the road, waving my hands.

"Hey," I shouted.

The car didn't slow, only honked out a warning. As the headlights drew closer, I realized it wasn't going to stop. I lost my nerve and pedaled off onto the shoulder. Ike followed suit, trotting Friday into the grass, Barry and the wings rolling along behind.

"Hey!" Barry roared. "Slow down!"

But the car just whisked past, blaring speed-warped notes from its horn.

"Where do you think they're going, in such a hurry?" Ike said.

"They only drive like that because they can," Barry said. "Cars—what an absolute *menace*."

❧

We tried the first few houses, a sequence that started a mile or so down the road—squat, forlorn-looking hovels clapped together with shabby white siding, their windows dirty and nobody home. Driveways were empty, tire ruts worn in the too-tall grass. A dog howled madly behind a door.

Ike didn't hesitate as he rushed up to their stoops, while Barry looked on proudly from the wagon. I sensed Ike had always wanted an excuse to do something like that, close the distance between himself and the world beyond his father. But I felt less sure myself. It was one thing to talk about outsiders in the aggregate—the *people*, we'd always called them—but trespassing onto their lawns like that left me breathless, unnerved by the specificity of their lives.

It was slow going, and though we tried to seem cheerful, it started to become clear how vast our challenge really was. I didn't know then that Bell Valley is the least populous county in New York State, just four people per square mile, not a single traffic light in any of its three hundred thousand acres. You could feel the isolation. Each house sat in its own kingdom of thirsty grass, sited to avoid all contact, as if there could be no worse fate than the sight of other dwellings out your window. That old American taste for self-reliance, the freedom to suffer on one's own. A woman told us through the window that she didn't open the door for strangers, and it didn't matter if we knew she needed what we had.

Eventually someone in one of the houses came out.

A middle-aged man, wearing flannel pajama bottoms and a stained white T-shirt. He was holding a cup of coffee. It was still early in the morning, I realized, startled that I'd lost all sense of time.

Ike and I were on the stoop, close enough to smell his acrid breath. I watched him take us in—Ike in his ragged clothes, broken-legged Barry, the actual horse on his lawn.

"What the . . ." he said, stepping back in alarm. His eyes darted from my face to Ike's, as if he expected us to attack him, or burst into song.

"Tell him!" Barry roared, from the cart.

"Look," Ike said, smiling. He pointed back to the wagon, where the wings stretched out on either side, giving the whole thing a bat-like appearance. Friday swung her head impatiently, jingling her reins.

"They're wings. We built them. We *flew*."

A woman came up behind him, silently peering over his shoulder. Her lips a grim line, her gaze fixed and unfriendly.

"I know it sounds crazy," I started to say. "It *is* crazy. But what he's saying is true. We can *fly*, and what we want to do now is—well, to teach people. How to fly and how to build them—"

"Are you with the people across the street?" the man demanded suddenly. I looked back: a little ways down, a dilapidated house sat back in a junk-strewn patch of earth.

"No, we don't know them," I said. "We're from a few miles down the road—"

But their expressions only hardened.

"Come and see," I said. "Just let us show you."

"They're for you!" Barry roared from the wagon. He was standing by them, waving one of his crutches, his improvised splint in full view. "It's all for you!"

"Sorry," the man said. "We can't help you." They both looked at us sadly—convinced of the con, hurt that we'd try. He shut the door, and it was quiet.

"But we're the ones helping *them*," Ike said.

Barry brushed it off. Though it stung, I could tell.

"It's all right, it's all right," he said gamely. "They'll see, in time. Let's try the other house."

We pulled up, and Ike and I walked through the yard, which was covered with mechanical debris. A rotted-out child's play set, the carcass of a car up on bricks. The man who answered was stringy and muscular, his teeth stained with tar. He regarded us first with bewilderment, unable to hide his surprise that anyone had come to the door.

When I pointed to the wings, a flicker of interest flashed across his eyes. Something about the shape of them registered with him, the born curiosity of a tinkerer. That gave me courage, but when I tried to coax him down the steps he seemed to collect himself. He sniffed the air, a suspicious glint in his eyes.

"I want you off my property," he said.

"But—"

"I don't know what your game is," he said, "but I ain't playing."

He looked this way and that, as if he expected someone to jump out and brain him with a wrench. Then he shut the door, and we were alone again.

Barry stood in the wagon, watching.

"He won't come?" he shouted.

"No," I said, though it was obvious.

"Then we keep going!" Barry shouted. "We'll find someone else! Someone who hasn't been seduced into utter helplessness, someone who isn't—"

Behind us, the door opened again.

"I swear to god," the stranger said. "I'll call the damn police."

❧

We finally found her in a house much like the others, a squat ranch set back in the grass. A few rosebushes suffered out front. Pale, sickly blooms dangled from the thorns.

By then the mood was grim between us. The joyous rush of the first few hours had dwindled into something hard, stubborn, and silent. Ike hopped down from the horse, and as I got off the bike to join him, Barry stopped us.

"We can't go crowding up to people's doors like a bunch of home invaders," he said. "We're *scaring* them."

He took off his glasses to polish the lenses on his shirt, looking down at us from the wagon.

"You do it, Jane," he said. "Alone. We'll wait here."

I glanced at Ike, who shrugged back with forced nonchalance.

"We'll wait here," Barry said.

It was true our approach hadn't worked, and Ike's appearance could be striking—his unmannered energy, the homemade clothes that made him look like a marooned sailor and also vaguely religious, some kind of hard-pressed Hare Krishna. I'd caught him staring unhelpfully into other people's houses as we made our pitch, and while I knew it was just innocent curiosity, his hunger to understand what other lives were like, he appeared to be casing the joint.

Or maybe it was about something else altogether—the squeamishness Barry sensed in me, a tendency to flinch I had to overcome. I'd never handled rejection well, and already I felt deflated and ready to quit. But I did what I was told. I walked up to the door alone.

I knocked, and the sound set a dog off. Explosive yapping, scrabbling of claws. Then the door opened, and a woman peered out, pale as a pressed flower. A tight, silver-blond braid fell down her shoulder to her waist, her jeans thin in the knees.

Quickly she took in the scene: two men, me, a horse and buggy with a huge kite spread across.

"What is it?" she said, startled, her eyes meek and wide.

The dog was a noisy little thing, a spluttering frenzy of fur. She held it back with her foot.

I swallowed.

"We're going around to all the houses," I said. "We built something. A pair of wings you can *fly* in. Look."

It sounded ludicrous, even to me.

Her eyes flicked to the wings' flat white shape.

"Fly?" She said, squinting, the word weird in her mouth. From where she stood, they could have been a collapsed tent, some kind of double sail. Ike was fussing with the ropes that held them down, while Barry watched us silently from his perch.

"We want to show people," I said. "Because—well, it's amazing. Honestly. It's so unbelievably good we *have* to share it."

I hated the hesitant note in my voice, clear as the chime of a bell. But I drew myself up.

"Come and see," I begged her softly. "Please. The only way to understand is to just come see."

I had this sudden urge to touch her, to lead her by the wrist down the porch steps.

"I'm sorry," the woman said, and she really did sound sorry—sorry that basic good sense forced her to reject us. She moved to shut the door. But just then, Ike lifted the wings away from the wagon, and the wind blew them wide for us to see: the broad serrated frame, the cloth stained with use. I loved the way the white cloth caught the light, half memories of what flight felt like swooning back.

The woman's eyes quivered in her skull. She saw that they were truly wings—how strange that was, somehow familiar and yet totally unexpected. The audacity of a shape like that, too intricate to be a ruse. Her mouth hung open in this funny, awestruck way, a trained soprano before she starts to sing.

"Come and look," I said. "Come on. I'll show you."

To my amazement, she actually did it. She followed me down the steps.

We crossed the lawn together. It felt strangely wedding-like—our slow procession, Ike's expectant face, Barry smiling proudly on his crutches. The slow dawning sense that nothing would ever be the same. You could almost hear music.

"My sister," Barry said, so warmly that for a second I almost wondered if they knew each other.

"What *is* it?" she asked. Ike held the wings before us, a thing of tension and complexity, the cloth trembling in the wind. She wanted to reach out and touch it, I could tell by the expression on her face.

"What we're going to show you is the end result of thousands of years of trial and error," Barry said. "It's what I've worked on all my life, like so many before me. And it's for you. It's all for you."

The woman pressed one hand against her neck, where the skin had flushed to a cooked-looking pink.

"Me?" she said, suddenly confused.

"It's for everyone," I clarified. I was used to Barry's elevated language, but I saw the way it spooked her. "He only means we want to share it. That's why we're going around—"

But she was still staring upward, toward where Barry stood on his crutches in the wagon. Something had changed in her face, this look of recognition setting in.

"You're him," she said. "Aren't you? The man who builds those antique planes—the man down the way!"

Barry smiled, blushing. She turned to me.

"I used to see him fly," she said. "I was younger then, like you. You'd see him cross the sky, until you couldn't hear the motor anymore, and then the plane was gone—"

She stopped, suddenly embarrassed. But I saw it was meaningful to her, the memory of Barry coasting freely through the clouds. One of those images the mind collects to return to, vibrant and yet poorly understood.

"My sister," Barry said again. "This here, what we've done—it's so much more than any plane."

Her dog was yapping behind us, a ruckus muted by the door.

"I should go," she said. "I—my husband isn't home."

Except she didn't go. She lingered, her eyes pale and curious, her face somber with interest, almost daring us to make her want to stay.

We had her, I realized.

From there, it was easy.

Her name was Diane. I helped her into the wings while Ike set up a ladder she'd left resting against the side of the house. She stepped into the harness, pulled it up against her hips, and slipped her hands around the wooden grips. I tied her wrists, and then we held the ladder steady. She tottered to the top, step by step, swaying like a person on a tightrope, each tremble of her arms magnified by the sheer size of the wings.

Once she stood on the last high stair, Ike and I tied her ankles to the frame, the sailor's knot Barry had taught, which was tight but could pull free. We explained how she could yank the rope to let her legs swing down again, so she could land on her feet. She nodded thoughtfully, her cheeks all flushed, and I could feel her trying and failing to memorize all the instructions she'd been given.

We looked up at her, marveling at what we'd done. She'd been transformed. The wings' arched shape made her huge, their wooden bones registering even the smallest movements of her hands.

"What do I do?" she called down, this spooked look in her eyes.

"Just jump!" Barry shouted. "You'll know."

This look of concern was frozen on her face, as if she had started to suspect that maybe she was dreaming, but couldn't say for sure.

"I can't," she said.

"My sister," Barry said. "Look up."

Diane looked up at the sky above us, still and blue as a pane of painted glass. The light, as it beat against her face, gave her skin the ashy translucence of parchment. She almost seemed to glow.

"Don't think," Barry said. "Jump!"

I'd felt the same fear. The terror of leaving what you knew behind, the old, familiar physics obsolete. But I'd trusted Barry, and I'd jumped, and I was better for it. As I watched Diane wrestle with herself, wincing doubtfully at the sky, I felt impatience ripping in my chest. I looked over at Ike, who was gazing up at her and murmuring words of encouragement:

"You'll be all right," he kept saying, an improvised mantra. "You'll be all right."

I placed my hand under one of the ladder's metal steps. Slowly I lifted upward, just barely tilting the angle of the top platform where she stood. It was enough. Diane stumbled forward with a cry, and I let go, shocked and immediately regretful as a child who's pushed a glass off a table, not believing it can actually break.

It happened quickly. Diane tumble-jumped off the ladder. The wings beat once, a blast of air that rushed across my face and bent the grass. She rose upward in a bobbing motion, as if yanked up by a rope, the bounding ascent of a butterfly.

Then she was flying.

Barry, Ike, and I looked at each other, and then up again at her. Neither of them seemed to have noticed what I'd done, the audacity of it still pounding in my chest. Barry roared words of encouragement. We cheered, a loose chorus of shouts.

Overhead, Diane's form beat in the air, throbbing in rhythm like a vein. Something burst from her lungs—not quite a laugh, not quite a sob—and the sound fell down around us, eerie and far away.

"Would you look at her!" Barry shouted, his voice hoarse with emotion, a tenderness that bordered on grief. "It just came so *naturally*, didn't it? Just like we knew it would!"

Ike watched, too, his face raised toward the light, his eyes trembling and wet. Barry grabbed his shoulder and shook it vigorously.

"My son!" He said. Ike turned to him and grabbed him in a crushing hug. They swayed together in the grass.

By then I think all three of us were crying. You could feel how good it was, the door we'd opened into a new world, its potential barely glimpsed.

We watched her fly awhile, looping this way and that overhead. It was impossible to mistake her for a bird. The way the wings lit up like panes of frosted glass when they hit the light, the pair of human legs aloft behind her.

We did it, I thought.

There was no going back.

FIFTEEN

I still remember those first minutes the way I wanted them to be: the three of us on the ground, the woman in the sky, everything arranged as if in a diorama, all of it perfectly foretold. Light played against the leaves, crooked tree limbs tunneled through the air, and beyond it all she flew under clouds of godlike size, their white heights so soaked with sun my eyes started to ache. But every time we thought she was coming back for a landing, she'd pass overhead and continue on— higher, farther, soaring out of the frame. We staggered around backward with chins lifted, trying to keep her in our sights, as if directed by her through an awkwardly blocked-out dance. After completing a last, widening circle, she finally sailed off in a straight line over the treetops, like a rock whirled in a sling and thrown.

She'll loop back, I told myself, but she didn't. My palms broke out in a sweat. By then the wings were so high and far away they'd shrunk to the size of a dime.

We'd all assumed she'd float back down to us, loyal as a trained bird. But the truth was bigger, and more unruly: Diane could go anywhere she wanted.

"Barry," I said, my voice brittle with concern.

From his perch in the wagon, Barry glared up silently at the sky. Whole seconds passed.

"Let's go," he roared, finally, "or—damn it, we'll lose her!"

We left too fast to put her ladder away. I looked back and

saw it unattended in the driveway, an abandoned staircase to the sky.

The pursuit took us down a random series of country lanes, a wooded maze that mapped poorly to the path of her flight. The wagon rolled down the road and I pedaled beside it, flushed and winded, straining to keep up. The pursuing deerflies found me if I slowed down, and once after waving them off I looked up again and couldn't see Diane. For a wild few seconds, I scanned all that emptiness, afraid we'd finally lost her.

"Where'd she go?" I called out, a choke in my throat.

Barry peered down at me from his perch, and then pointed.

"There!" he said, directing me back toward the figure in a corner of the sky.

When the road insisted on angling in the wrong direction, we'd race at double speed toward the next turn. Friday nearing an all-out gallop, Ike's hair blowing back as he hugged her neck. It was dizzying, scary, a joy that bordered terror. The day was hot, and the pace was brutal, and at times I wanted to burst, inexplicably, into tears. But when we drew close enough to slow down, the wings plainly in view—god, the audacity of it!—I'd be filled with an unfamiliar happiness, as if I were finally bearing witness to the events of my own life.

We passed a house. An older woman stood out by her garden, patiently misting her flowers with a hose.

"Look!" Barry roared, lurching upright in the cart. He pointed to the sky. I pointed, too, as I whizzed by. The woman lifted her chin, squinting against the light.

"She's flying!" we called out. "*Flying!*"

It took a second, but we saw that she understood. You could tell by the way her body changed, her head cocking in fascination. She stopped watering and cradled the sprayer to her chest, the way you'd hold a wounded bird.

She knows, I thought. *She knows. She knows.*

Barry whooped. I looked up again and tried to see Diane the way the gardener must have: an elaborate kite moving through the sky, its wood-and-cloth wings two sunlit panes, with a human form just barely visible between them. And then we were past her. There wasn't time to stop. There was just the chase, the rushing fervor of it, because we could imagine nothing else except to follow her, to give over to an instinct we didn't fully understand.

Ike shouted something, gesturing upward with his hand. In the distance, Diane was losing height. The wings started to falter, each flap weaker—I recognized the way her muscles had burned past exhaustion into numbness. My arms still ached with the same strain.

Diane dropped lower and recovered, lower and recovered, as if passing out and waking in midair. She fell slowly and then quickly, and then she was plunging past the tree line with a sound of tearing branches, where she vanished from our sight.

We pulled off the road and stopped. It was suddenly quiet, no sound but Barry's breath wheezing through his nose, the sighing of the horse. Sweat wept from my forehead. Ike looked flushed and sticky.

"Well?" Barry said. "Go get her! I'll wait here." He paused. "It's just, my leg."

Ike and I glanced at each other, and I thought I caught a glint of worry in his eyes. It was easy to forget Barry's leg, splinted with the break still new. He seemed all right, but of course it was best for him to stay back. We ran into the woods.

The forest was huge and ancient and smelled like moss and rust. The quiet pines all draped with icicles of light. At first it seemed crazy to think that we could ever find her, but then we heard something. A low, throaty groan from somewhere in the trees.

We found her tangled in a grove of saplings, young trees bent under her weight. They were limber enough to hold her, and she hung suspended a few feet above the ground. Sun poured in where she'd punched through the canopy, lighting up the cloth. Her eyes were closed, and she was smiling, sweat beaded over her lip. As she breathed, she bounced subtly, like a moth strung in a web.

"You're all right," Ike kept saying, as we pushed through the brush and tried to lift her down. And she really did seem to be, if a bit raw with branch scratches. She looked half asleep, in the palm of some good dream, and as I remembered how it had felt for me—a trance-like place beyond exhaustion, all emptied out from the rush of it—I felt a jolt of want.

We managed to pull Diane free and laid her on the forest floor, her body something you could pour. Her braid had loosened, half undone. When we tried to hold her upright, she slumped against Ike's chest and tumbled onto the ground. She lay there on her side like a slain deer.

"It's like she's still asleep," Ike whispered, waving the bugs away.

"You remember," I whispered back. "Don't you?"

Ike had come down that way, too—I'd seen him in the same stumbling, dream-like state.

He paused, his gaze hardening as he thought back, and nodded.

"Come on," he said. "Let's lift her."

As we bent to pick her up again, I noticed a mosquito had touched down on her cheek, its little tube engaged. Sunlight passed through its belly, a pulsing, blood-filled jewel. I tried to brush it away and crushed its body without meaning to, leaving a small red smear by her eye, my fingers stained.

"You had a mosquito," I said, unsure if she could hear me.

"Mm," Diane said, as I wiped the blood away.

Her face had changed, I realized. The worry furrows on her brow had smoothed, and she somehow looked much younger. I caught a glimpse of the person she'd been, of the girl's face that was still there under her face.

We lifted her by the armpits and threw her arms over our shoulders, carrying her like army medics out of the woods. Her body surprised me with its weight. The way this tiny person took both of us to move, all our combined strength. *We're such large animals*, I remember thinking. We see people as essence and spirit, the body incidental. We forget how much of us there is, the sum of our bones and muscle and blood.

❧

It was brighter out by the time we pulled Diane from the woods, heat shimmering up from the asphalt. Barry had gotten down from the wagon somehow and was standing on his crutches by the forest's edge, peering uncertainly into the darkness between the trees.

"*There* you are," he said, hobbling toward us. I heard relief in his voice. "Good—you have her."

As we started to help Diane across the road, her head still slumped against my shoulder, we heard the rush of an oncoming vehicle. A pickup truck swung around the corner, blurred with speed. I held Diane tighter. Barry lifted a crutch and waved it wildly, hollering something against the roar. But the pickup barreled indifferently onward, and then we were alone again. I tasted dust, the air sparkling with kicked-up grit.

"If you want proof of how *broken* things are," Barry raged, "look no further. We're carrying an unconscious woman out of the forest, for goodness' sake. Wouldn't any decent person stop, slow down, ask some questions, try to help?"

We maneuvered Diane's body into the back of the wagon. She showed no sign of waking, only lay collapsed in a heap. Ike smoothed her out, gently arranging her limbs until she was flat on her back like a doll. All three of us stared down at her. The top buttons of her shirt undone, her silver-blond braid coming loose, stray tendrils of hair matted to her cheeks.

"Look at her," Barry said into the quiet. "She looks so *happy*. Doesn't she?"

It was true. The tension had seeped out of her, this contented smile on her face. Her prone, spooky beauty filled me with a longing that bordered on jealousy—because I knew what it was to be wrung out like that, to feel nothing and everything at once, the wordless joy plants must feel as they ache toward the sun. Flight restored you to something pure and fully sated, a kind of infancy. And we could give people that, a way to feel those things again. I wanted it for her. I wanted it for me.

"What do we do now?" I finally said. I turned to Barry, ready for his orders. Instead, he flinched. Quickly, but I saw it. For a split second, the confidence fell away. A swallow in his throat. And then it passed.

"We take her home," he said softly. "Come on, now."

"Home?" I said. I felt a pang of disappointment, I wasn't sure why. It felt too small somehow, a simple out and back, when I craved something much more radical, a culminating march into the new.

But Barry had become himself again, the old knowingness renewed. He grinned at me slyly.

"Not *her* home," he said. "*Our* home. We'll take her back with us. We'll teach her how to build."

That stopped me for a second. It caught me by surprise, the idea that we'd bring her with us, lifting her wholesale from her life and placing her down again like a chess piece. So why did I feel we had permission? Like we already knew what she wanted? Where did it come from, the knowledge that she'd only tell us yes?

"Listen," Ike said. "She's saying something."

He was right: Diane was murmuring softly, her mouth struggling to shape the words.

"Thank you," she was saying, quiet as a prayer. "Thank you. *Thank* you."

Back into the meadow. The wagon bounced over the uneven earth as we rode on with a joyful, almost delirious feeling—things were under way, we'd brought a stranger home. Diane and I stood in the back of the wagon, poking out between the edge of the wings and the lip of the wagon, hidden from the waist down by the frame. I found myself thrilling at the wild scale of the place, the details new again: a crook of land rushing out past the wooden storage hovels and the barn, the tall, tufted grass bursting with dandelion heads and sprays of rust-colored flowers. Hens waddling, circled by wire. The forest's nearness, and its smell. It was a universe, our universe, and its population was growing.

Barry wanted to show Diane the remains of his old plane. So we followed him around the side of the barn, Diane glancing at my face for cues. The old ruin sat half consumed by the forest, a barely recognizable wreck.

"There she is," Barry said, leaning against his crutches, still catching his breath. We all fell silent looking at it, a low breeze in the leaves. Saplings shot up through gaping holes in the fabric, the lower carriage bushy with ivy.

"I guess it's fallen apart," Diane said softly. She sounded almost hurt. I felt her weigh the decaying hull against the soaring thing in her memory.

"It doesn't matter, my sister," Barry said. "We let it go! I love to watch it rot. Come on. Let's show you what you're really here to see."

We took her into the barn. Barry's gliders dangled from the rafters and Diane walked cautiously beneath them, her braid still loosened by the wind, jolted into reverence by their other-worldly shapes. I still remembered my own first day, how it felt to have Barry's work thrust upon me. Like walking into a cathedral for the first time, your senses assaulted by the mad, dizzying scale of it. Light filtered through the stained-glass windows, throwing vivid smudges on the floor, and as dust danced up toward the high painted ceilings you were reminded of something: the capaciousness of the soul. Maybe there was a door in you that could open. Maybe the godlike force had been there all along, waiting for you to say yes.

∽

We taught her how to make the wings, a pair she could take with her. By then Ike and I knew how to cobble the basic frame together, so we started there. As we worked, Barry drew. He slumped against the table, half supported by his stool, sketching in real time as we went along. The wings on paper engrossed him at least as much as the real ones we were building, this air of quiet intensity about him as he penciled in the lines. He must have noticed me watching.

"Like a manual," he said. "Step by step by step. Will make it easier to show others—something to just lay it all out."

A blueprint started to emerge across his stack of loose pages, and he pivoted between drawing and building, pausing to direct our work or take up a tool. There was something intoxicating about his energy, his ability to keep track of both things at once, like watching someone compose a symphony at the same time they were building a boat.

The old wings leaned against the outside wall of the barn, stationed there like a sentry, a bit scuffed up from Diane's landing but otherwise fine. I found excuses to go outside and look them over from time to time, reminding myself what we'd suddenly made possible. We crafted the new frame from pine, peeling the willow struts and drilling their holes. I watched Ike with fascination, a new side of him unleashed. I'd always known him to be surly at the table, working at a pace just shy of outright rebellion. But that had changed, the old stubbornness drained away. His movements were lively, his fingers skillful with all he'd reluctantly learned. He seemed to love going back to Barry for approval, asking him to check his work.

"Dad," he'd say, "how's this?"

"Dad," he'd say, "does that look right?"

And Barry would lean forward to look with barely disguised pleasure, a new kinship between them.

Diane, it turned out, was also good with tools—her hands moved with practiced grace. She must have noticed the way I watched her work, envious of the ease she showed in bending the wood to her will. Her father had been handy, she volunteered. All her childhood she helped him out with projects around the house—making shelves, hanging cabinets, laying deck. She seemed to relish the memory, even if—or because—that part of her felt banished to a long-gone past. These days, if something needed fixing, her husband did it.

"Your husband," Barry said, suddenly interested. "Where *is* he? My sister, he should join us!"

I'd forgotten that she'd mentioned him during our encounter on her steps, her feeble excuse for why she couldn't come outside.

"He's a long-haul trucker," she said. "I'd imagine he's crossing Iowa by now."

"Tell him to come home," Barry said. "Can you reach him? For god's sake, he doesn't need to do that anymore."

"But he can't just come home," Diane said, a smile faltering on her face.

"Of course he can!" Barry said. "Really, what's stopping him?"

"Well, I mean . . ." Diane said softly, shamed by the obviousness of it. They needed the money, of course. They relied on that job, so the work—though it took them away from each other, though it frittered their days into long, empty hours—was justified. Anything could be justified that allowed for survival. But I saw her flinch anyway, newly unsure of herself. With Barry's eyes on you, all that disorienting blue, it was hard to remember what anything else was for.

In the awkward silence that followed, we heard a scraping sound. Everyone went still. There it was again: the low, repeated scrape of metal against wood. Something raking the barn's far wall.

Ike and I ran outside, racing around the corner of the building. In the rush of things, we'd forgotten to unhitch Friday—horse and wagon were still tethered together. She stood there, pushing insistently against the bit with her floppy pink tongue, trying to force the metal from her mouth. The barn bore scars where she'd scraped the bit against it, streaks in the paint. We were not that unalike, I thought, as Ike whispered to her, fiddling with the clasp. We only wanted to be free from the things that contained us.

～

We worked until the light shifted, shadows growing on the floor. The barn's stale air cooled as night fell. Barry had grown distracted by then, retiring to absorb himself in sketches. He lay propped up on a pillow on the cot, with a flat circular mirror Ike had dredged up across his lap as a makeshift desk. At times he seemed totally engrossed, drawing each step from memory, annotating details in his careful script. The blackened wad of putty he used as an eraser sat there on the glass, unused. From time to time, when we asked for help, he got up slowly and reluctantly, hobbling toward the table to tell us what to do.

Night started to flood in. We lit a couple candles, ready to make a push for it, rushing toward completion. No one wanted to be the first to say that we should stop. Then Diane lay down her drill. She stood up stiffly.

"Oh," she said, startled. "My gosh."

She needed to go home right away. She'd forgotten to feed her dog, the little defensive one we'd seen yapping by the door.

"He likes his dinner punctual," she said, a hint of apology in her voice. "I can't just let him wait."

I almost had to laugh. Hours earlier, she'd traced a radical path through the air. Tasted heaven, the sky no longer forbidden to us. And still she was worried about kibble, windows darkening on an empty bowl. Miracles happen in the world, empires rise and crumble, but nothing will keep a dog from getting hungry.

We left the frame half finished on the table, and I drove her home—passing in silence the occasional houses, strangers sheltered behind doors. I wanted to reach through the walls and grab them. To tell each one what was coming, except I didn't quite know. Only that my heart hurt with impatience and desire. Whatever came next, it would be better than what we had: weedy plots connected to fueling stations by ancient asphalt, no one else in sight.

We pulled up to her place, the ranch with the eaten-up rose-bushes.

"I'll see you tomorrow," she said, her voice somber and truthful. A promise. I met the force in her powder-blue eyes.

"Tomorrow," I said. It happened fast. Connective tissue could form from nothing, the first stirring of a bond. We owed each other something already.

The barn was quiet by the time I got back, darkness gathering in the rafters. A few candles guttered on the sills. Ike was gone. The half-made wings sprawled unattended on the table, and Barry had fallen asleep. He lay on the cot with his sketches spread out around him, a pencil loose in his hand.

"Here," I whispered. I neatened his pages into a stack, setting them on the floor. I took the pencil, too.

"Barry," I said, and he seemed to know I was there. He grunted softly, a throat-clearing sound, and without opening his eyes let me maneuver him onto his back. His battered face blessed with a childlike calm. The day had asked so much of us. His body needed time to heal.

I lingered there a little while. The thin gray blanket rose and fell in rhythm with his breath. Once I was sure he wouldn't need me anymore, I got up and went outside.

I found Ike in the garden, pulling summer squash in the twilight. The vines burst with green pendulous fruits that hung by the dozens under wide-brimmed leaves. We took as many as we could carry, chopped them, and cooked them over the fire until the pale coins went soft and translucent. The result was delicious but made almost of nothing. I got hungrier with every bite I ate.

Ike insisted on bringing a bowl to Barry.

"He barely touched his breakfast," he said. "We have to remind him—or he'll just go around not eating."

So we approached the cot. Ike carried the food and I brought a candle to see by. Barry snored softly, breath dragging against the back of his throat.

"Dad," Ike said. Then, more forcefully: "*Dad*."

Barry's eyes cracked open. He swallowed.

"What?" he said. He turned his head toward us, his eyes struggling to focus.

"We made dinner," Ike said. "You should have some."

He held the bowl out toward him.

Barry made a face, repulsed.

"No," he said. "Put it on the floor."

"But—"

"It's not important."

"Dad—"

"I'm asleep," he mumbled, which wasn't true, and then it was.

Ike and I looked at each other. He put the bowl down on the floor, defeated, an offering to go neglected through the night. In the candlelight, I saw a stray page I hadn't noticed, down by Barry's knees, and picked it up. It was a section from his blueprint, the wings still early-stage. As always, his work was ornate and almost eerily lifelike—precise as architectural renderings, evocative as portraits. What surprised me was how much prose there was, directives written out in Barry's script.

The ribs and stiffenings of the wings should be fitted near the leading edge, he'd written. And elsewhere: *The broader wing portions near the body should be moved as little as possible and act chiefly as supporting surfaces.* And also: *The wing must show a curvature on the underside, a camber about 1/12 the width of the wing.*

"Ike," I whispered. "Look."

He came closer and peered at the page.

He didn't see anything unusual. He'd grown up surrounded by Barry's sketches, and was numbed to the sight of them. Even I wasn't exactly sure what I wanted to show him as we huddled there in the darkness. It was something about seeing Barry's plans so polished, so close to final form. The way those words were written for an *audience*. He'd distilled his vision into its essence, and soon anyone would be able to hold the wings' secrets in their hands.

"Do you see it?" I asked. "Do you know how beautiful this is?"

He shrugged. I felt electrically awake. We couldn't keep building without waking up Barry, and it was too late to go knocking on doors. But I couldn't imagine quitting for the day, not yet. By then I was almost bursting with restless energy, my nerves charged with a power-line hum. I still had so much more to give.

"What now?" I asked Ike desperately. "What should we do?" He thought for a second.

"We could go sit by the fire," he said.

There was a time when I would have enjoyed that, to sit and watch the fire burn with Ike. But not then. The idea felt comically meager, insufficient for the moment we were in.

"No," I said. "That's not enough."

I put the page down with the others on the floor. Out of order, to sequence later. Then I stood and faced Ike in the wobbling light. "Come on," I said. I blew the candle out and pulled him by the sleeve to the door.

Outside, the night was dark and cool and filled with sounds of life. The stars were out, so much silvery dust. And the original pair of wings still leaned against the barn, right where we'd left them.

I just beheld them for a second. Their radical, intricate shape evoked so much, desire deepened by the memory of desire. I went over and put my hands on the frame. I loved their responsiveness, the way they twitched like something living as the wind bucked gently in their sails.

"Feel it," I told Ike, and he held on, too.

For a minute, the two of us just stood there and held on. Always that sensation, like a too-stiff breeze might suddenly lift us. Friday stood sleeping in the yard nearby, nickering through some horse dream.

"Ike," I said. "Let's fly a little."

He swallowed.

"Let's do it," I said. "You can go first."

"But it's dark," he said.

"It's all right," I said. "There's plenty of moonlight."

It was true: you could see fairly well. The night held a radiant half-moon, and soft, glittering light fell down from it like rain.

"What about him?" Ike said, gesturing through the wall toward Barry. "We can't just *leave* him."

"We won't leave him," I said. "One of us will be right here the whole time."

Ike chewed the inside of his cheek, thinking.

"Please," I said. "I'll do it, then. Please just let me do it."

So we agreed. I climbed the silver ladder to the roof, and Ike came up behind me. We hoisted the wings up on Barry's hook and pulley and padded across the shingles to the wooden platform Barry had made. I slid the harness up around my hips, and Ike tied my wrists. When he knelt to tie my feet to the frame, his hands brushing my ankles, it felt like a benediction.

You knew when you were ready from the way the wind pooled in the cloth. You could feel its power swelling in you, the strength of ten men in my arms. I edged my toes over the lip of the plank, and the night bugs clicked and sang.

❧

I flew as high as I could, higher, swirling and spinning, gulping dark air. I could shut my eyes or open them, it hardly mattered— it was all the same sea of shadow and starlight. I closed my eyes to feel it fully. The way my whole self swooned into each dive.

I let the rush of it unmake me, dissolve me. I emptied out, becoming nothing but wind.

Time passed.

I forgot myself completely until my arms started to give out. The ache was low at first, a molten, intensifying heat that stretched from my armpits toward my elbows. I couldn't ignore it forever. Slowly, the pain made me myself again.

When I opened my eyes, I had no idea where I was.

The feeling must be common among the drowned. To become lost in the sea's rhythm, oblivious that you've stroked too far from shore. This was like that. I looked down into blackness and felt the swimmer's terror.

The trees below, all flecked with silver from the moon, pulsed like anemones on the ocean's floor. Otherwise, the ground was a blankness, laced with dark canals of unlit roads. Wind tore at my clothes with cold hands. My elbows hurt, my armpits screamed, as I scanned the night for signs of home.

I almost closed my eyes again, let myself drift down toward wherever the earth would greet me.

But then I saw it, far away: something bright and twisting, a little ring of fire. A knot of flame that chased itself, tracing phantom letters that glowed and disappeared. I fell closer until I finally saw the sloped, familiar jut of the barn. A lonely tree circled by meadow. I didn't have the strength to think. I just aimed my body at the flame, dancing and bright. I let it call me downward.

I crashed to the ground with a bone-jouncing shudder and slid through the grass to a halt. Hands felt at my shoulders, my neck, my back.

"Jane!" Ike's voice.

I moaned. It was all I could manage.

"I thought you were lost," he whispered. His lips near my ear. "I couldn't see you anymore—"

There was something in his voice—an exasperation rising out of jealousy or fear—but I was too tired to tease it out. I was limp, utterly wrung out. Sweat poured from my hair. My tongue seemed to fill my mouth, and I couldn't speak. What remained was the feeling of it, better than I'd remembered it to be. I would not forget again. A promise had been made. My vows renewed. I knew I would do anything for this.

Sixteen

I woke up sideways on the ground, my cheek pressed to the dirt. It was morning and my whole body ached, a full-body throb. My first thought was that I'd been punched in the face. I checked my nose for blood, but my fingers came away clean.

I lifted my head, squinting against the sun. Ike lay a few feet away on his back, his fists balled like a baby's. Dead leaves clung to his hair. We were in a forest clearing—a place I knew, not far from the house. One of Ike's woodpiles sat stacked at the edge. The wings lay nearby, too. Cloth billowed subtly in the wind.

I couldn't remember how we got there. My memory, cut like a strip of film. I lay still until the night started to flood back in little snapshots, single frames I could pit against the gap of time. A rush of air. The smell of smoke. A shadow plummeting toward me through the darkness, quickly growing in size. Exhaustion, and relief.

A story started to come together. Ike had flown after me. Then me again. Then him, then me, on and on like that until we lost track. I'd waited for him, a burning torch in my hand. A beacon lifted to the night and waved at the stars. It was something we'd improvised to guide each other. You stared up at the darkness, and waved your torch, and hoped the other person would come back.

I tried to stand. The flight muscles across the top half of my body—my arms, armpits, and chest—threatened to tear when

I moved, heavy with lactic acid. My arms too sore to straighten. I rocked myself onto my knees and then stood, one leg at a time.

"Ike," I said, walking unsteadily toward him. His hair spilled out around him, littered with dead leaf fragments I wanted to pull away. I nudged him with my toe.

"Hey."

He groaned and shifted. I nudged him again, and his eyes cracked open slightly. His face twisted into an affronted grimace, as if the sun had no business being that bright.

"Hey," I said again.

"Aghh," he sighed, starting to wake up.

"Hey."

I couldn't reach for him, my elbows all rusted shut at the joints.

"My arms," I said. "I can barely *move* them."

It was the same for Ike. He finally tried to stand, but was stuck like a beetle on his back. Our eyes met, and it dawned on us. A slow, giddy realization: we were powerless to help each other.

"Um," Ike said.

He tried getting to his feet. Playing up the awkwardness of it, failing to launch himself with his elbows. He rolled onto his side and groaned in mock-agony. I started to laugh, drunk with how new it was, our bodies rearranged. Ike flopped around clownishly on the ground, then started to push himself across the clearing on his back, pedaling with his feet. I could barely breathe, it was so funny. He slithered backward up a tree trunk and leaned there, panting and flushed. My belly hurt with laughing.

We left the clearing with our arms folded helplessly, the wings still lying in the dirt. We'd have to go back for them. They'd carried us all night, but we were too sore to return the favor.

Diane had come back, just as she'd promised. She sat with Barry at the worktable, wearing the same clothes she'd had on the day before, her silver-blond braid still loosened from flight. They turned to us as we came in. Diane smiled at me proudly. Barry felt around for his glasses, hanging from their lanyard on his chest.

"*There* you two are!" he said. "I was wondering when you'd show up. Come—look how much we've done already!"

He peered at us.

"Why are you *standing* like that?"

Ike and I traded glances. Our arms folded up against our chests, forming collars made of knuckles. I saw no reason to hide it. As we explained how we'd flown through the night, Barry's eyes brightened, their blue intensity magnified by his glasses.

"It must have been *wonderful*," he said. The thought of it softened him, briefly, something childlike in his manner. "Was it?"

"Yes."

"I'd like to try that. To fly in all that darkness, with the stars out. Maybe tonight. But here, come help us. We're nearly through with the frame."

"We can barely move," Ike groaned.

Barry smiled.

"It's good pain. The tissue tears and grows back stronger. You're building muscle where you'll need it. Oh!"

He turned to Diane.

"Tell them what you told me before," he said.

"Which thing I told you?"

"You know!" he said. "About the *call*."

She put her hands in her lap, a sly smile spreading across her face.

"Well," she said, "last night, I spoke to my husband. He calls every night when he's on the road. I just couldn't *wait* to tell him. Before he could even say anything, I was talking. I told him about flying. About the *wings*. About you all. Everything in one big rush. And when I got finished, there was just *silence* on the line. And then he said, 'Di, have you lost your god-damned *mind*?'"

She wreathed her fingers, laughing silently, her pale eyes dancing.

"I couldn't get him to believe me! He thinks I've gone *crazy*!"

Barry shook his head.

"People can't fathom it," he said. "They really can't. But we'll show him. Soon, we'll show everybody."

∽

What would it be like to get a call like that, I wondered, out of the blue? To hear someone you love tell you in a steady voice that the impossible was happening?

I hated that Diane's husband had brushed her off like that. I nursed an exasperated, bee-stung feeling while we worked, my thwarted instinct to defend her. I imagined him in carica-ture, too confident in his own confidence, too ignorant of his own ignorance. Clinging to his sense of the way things are, while the ground shifted under him.

But I wasn't sure I'd fare any better, if I was honest. I imag-ined calling my parents. I tried to think through a faltering script, searching for words to make the miracle real. But I could only hear my voice going high and thin as I told them about flying, about wings, my throat catching at each fanciful detail, my case absurd and badly made. They wouldn't believe me. Their minds weren't prepared for it, and nothing could change that. Nothing except the sight of someone flying, the wings an ornate kite, rising on their own strength over the hill.

The most visceral thing, that's what was needed. The wordless, transformative, lived experience of watching us actually *do* it.

I burned to show people. Until they saw, we couldn't inhabit the same universe: you knew it was possible, or you didn't, and the gulf between those two worlds was wide. An entire day had passed already, and we'd converted one person, which was good. But the wider revolution, the thing we'd promised ourselves, hadn't really started yet. I found myself chafing against the minutes as they passed. As if the four of us toiling in the barn—the same way we always did—were anywhere near enough.

The barn started to get hot, filled with its pencil-shaving smell, and when I started to taste too much sawdust I stalked out into the meadow for some air. The sky overhead, blue and alluring, an endless satin sheet. Then Barry was beside me on his crutches in the grass.

"What's wrong?" he said.

Without my realizing it, he'd pushed away from the table and hobbled out. Our eyes met for a second, but I flinched and looked away.

"It's nothing," I said.

"Jane."

I felt him next to me. Leaning on his supports like that, he was almost my same height.

"Tell me what you're thinking about."

I took a deep breath, starting to speak before I knew what to say.

"It's just—" I said.

"Yes?"

"—do you think we're moving *fast* enough?"

He was quiet for a moment. The wind swelled, bending the grass stalks, stirring in his beard. He nodded.

"I know," he said, softly. "I feel it, too."

"You do?" I said. A relief, to hear it from him. "I was thinking—"

"Don't think," he said abruptly. "You're right. We're in this now. We have to work quickly. I—" Here his voice became hoarse, subtly frayed at the edges. "I got—well, distracted. Just a little. This is all so *wonderful*, isn't it? But we've lost focus. Thank you for keeping us on course."

I was somewhat taken aback by this—his intensity, the surprising display of emotion. The sudden urgency after all those torpid hours of work. The suggestion we'd done something wrong without knowing. Was it going to be that easy to make mistakes?

"Quickly, Jane," he said. "Don't forget it. Don't let *me* forget it. The point now is to touch as many people as we can. No matter what happens. Whatever it takes."

He lifted a crutch, shaking it for emphasis.

"It may not seem like it yet, but we're at *war*. A war on the way things are. We could still lose at any second. And we can't win soon enough."

He looked straight into me with his intoxicating gas-blue eyes.

"So what will you do, my sister?" He said. "What will you do to help us win?"

⁓

I wasn't sure how to answer him. The question felt rhetorical, but also genuine—though maybe he was testing me somehow, or simply trying to goad me into action. Before I could say more, Barry turned and went back into the barn, his crutches thudding against the wood. Suddenly I didn't want to be alone. Without even really thinking, I followed him inside.

"Jane's going out," Barry announced, nodding at the others.

"We still need to alert as many people as we can—that part really can't stop, even though we also need to build. She's going to find people, bring them back here."

This wasn't something I'd volunteered to do.

"I am?" I said.

"Yes," Barry thundered. "Aren't you? So, go. It'll be a help to all of us."

Ike and Diane looked at me from the worktable. I shrugged at Ike, made a face that let him know this wasn't my idea. That these were Barry's stage directions.

"What do you think?" I asked him.

"I mean . . ." Ike said.

"What, Ike?" Barry said.

"Well . . ."

"*What*, Ike?"

He swallowed.

"I just thought we were going to stay together."

For whatever reason, I'd thought so, too. I'd always imagined the three of us working like a unit, a special task force deployed to the hills.

"Stay together," Barry said dryly. "And what purpose would *that* serve?"

Ike glanced at me.

"What purpose would it serve for him to stay?" I said. I didn't say it belligerently, but there was the hint of a challenge in my voice. He'd asked me to be strategic, after all. At that moment, wasn't the most important thing to be out there recruiting others to the cause?

"Well," Barry said. "I'd just wanted to finish my sketches, is all. I'll be slowed up with Ike away. But, sure. Go, the two of you. It will all take longer, but Diane and I can finish here."

Ike stood. So we'd do this together.

"Are you going to take the wings with you?" Diane said. "Like when you came to me?"

"Yes," I said, realizing that we would. It pleased me, the thought of being close to them again. A satisfying click, the turn of a key in a lock.

"Could I see them one more time?" Diane asked, folding her hands over her chest. "Just once, before you go?"

❧

The three of us entered the clearing, where the wings had blown up against Ike's woodpile, the cloth grass-stained and powdered with dirt. We'd left them on the ground, and it was eerie to find them transplanted, as if by their own volition. I made a mental note: If we left the wings out in the open, they could move. There was always a chance the wind could steal them from us, carrying them toward the heavens like a runaway balloon.

"There," Diane said. "God. *Look* at them."

I knew what she meant. The shorthand your brain developed was never quite enough: in person, the wings were always more than what they were in your memory.

She wanted to touch them. We let her run her hands across the frame, her fingers sliding against the wood. As she felt at the cloth, the ribs, I thought of statues in the shrines of old Europe, their feet worn away by pilgrim kisses, the stone carved smooth with wishes.

Diane looked back over her shoulder. Her hair was such a lovely silver color. I hoped mine turned that way when I grew old.

"I forgot what it was like to *see* them," she said, her eyes sparkling. "I guess the ones we're building are just the same, but—"

She turned to us.

"I want to fly again," she declared suddenly, like it was a conclusion she'd reached after a long period of thought. She looked back and forth between us, nodding steadily, as if to say, *I do, I do.*

I glanced at Ike, not sure how to respond. We let the question hang a beat too long.

"Please," she said, her voice rising with need. "There's time, isn't there? We could be quick about it."

Ike shrugged, ready to let her. I tried to read the resistance that I felt, decouple it from the unseemliness of asking, from the soreness that still ached dully in my arms. Of course, it wouldn't hurt. Wasn't that the whole point, anyway: to give folks flight, and let them revel in the gift? And who were we to refuse her, anyway? I wanted her to want it. I wanted it, too, the day's first pangs like icicles hardening behind your eyes.

But I also felt this need to move, to strike quickly the way Barry had said. We couldn't lavish all our time on just one person. And once we put her in the wings, part of the day would inevitably be swallowed—I already saw how unpredictable it was. Flight was a door you opened, though you never knew what would come out.

Diane sensed me hesitate, and that seemed to sap her will.

"I'm sorry," she said. "It can wait. Of course it can."

"Are you sure?" I said.

"Of *course*," she said. "It's fine, it's fine."

She helped Ike and me carry the wings out of the woods, a breeze lifting subtly in the cloth.

❦

Ike and I trailed along the meadow's edge, looking for Friday. Ike called to her, a clicking sound made out of one side of his mouth, percussive and startlingly loud. The forest responded with cavernous silence. The horse was nowhere to be seen.

"What do you do when this happens?" I asked him.

"There's nothing you *can* do," he said. "Just wait for her to come back."

"We can't do *that*," I said. "Waiting around for a horse to show up—can you imagine?"

The idea struck me as absurd.

"Yeah," Ike said. He clicked his tongue and teeth as we walked onward, the noise echoing in a woodpecker's staccato. He was pondering something—I could tell by the contemplative way he tucked his hair behind his ear.

"What if we took the car?" he said suddenly.

For some reason, this hadn't occurred to me. I glanced toward the barn's open door, knowing Barry would hate the idea. His wings, carried by the car. Symbol of all we wanted to overthrow.

But Barry had also tasked me with reaching as many people as possible, and quickly. Driving would help with that. *We're at war*, he'd said. *Whatever it takes.*

What was I going to do to help us win?

I'd burned so much gas in my life. A little more wouldn't hurt, even if flight was supposed to end all that.

Ike and I carried the wings out of the clearing and through the meadow, tall plants swiping against our legs. I thought I'd worked through most of my muscle soreness, but as I lifted I felt the ache again, burning in my armpits and shoulders. Pain I wore like a backpack.

The Saab sat waiting for us where it always did, at the end of the dirt road. As it turned out, the original owner's neglected kayak rack made for a perfect way to secure the wings. We tied them down and stood back to admire our work: The wings lay evenly across the roof, the jutting metal bars no longer a pointless adornment. They transformed the car into something potent and unrecognizable, a vision of a flying machine ready to be steered through the air.

I thought back to the man I'd met, a lifetime ago. Near a bridge somewhere in Jersey. He'd been so animated, so earnest, as he'd tried to convince me to buy his car and its bulky metal fixture, as though a kayak rack were something he absolutely knew I needed. It had seemed so silly at the time. How wonderful, that he'd turned out to be right.

～

The homes looked empty. Shades drawn in the windows, cars gone from the drives. We piloted the Saab slowly along the forested streets, watching for signs of people. When Ike got out and knocked on doors, nobody came.

The houses passed in sluggish tempo, spaced a half mile apart from each other. With the wings tied to the roof, I was afraid to go any faster. At thirty-five miles an hour, I could feel the frame drag in the wind, a new stubbornness in the gas pedal. I worried the Saab's relentless, inhuman speed might tear the cloth, or bend the willow canes past the breaking point.

"Look," Ike said.

Someone was sitting on a porch. So still, I hadn't seen. I pulled over, nosing into the shoulder. Before the car had even stopped, Ike was out the door.

I got out and followed him across the road. It was an elderly woman, her hair a white shell, frowning at us against the light. Ike addressed her, pointing back toward the car. She was sitting in a wheelchair, I realized. An electric one with a little joystick jutting from the armrest. Claw-like hands lay weakly in her lap. I wondered if flying might be out of the question for her, just physically. But Ike had already launched into the pitch.

". . . it's easy," he was saying. "You'll just know how, you'll see. . . ."

She squinted at me.

"Wings?" she said, as if the word were new and unfamiliar in her mouth.

"Yes," Ike said, nodding.

"And you're coming to *me* with them?"

"We're going to everybody," Ike said.

She peered across the road. We were quiet for a second, letting her take it in. The wings looked huge and imposing on top of the car, something from another world.

"You just, what," she said. "You *built* this?"

"Yes," Ike said.

She stared at the wings warily, her chin high and quavering, as if to appraise their worth. And then, something wonderful: Her face softened, the expression shifting to one of sly delight. She smiled, gums exposed where the teeth were missing. She was with us. She believed.

"You kids," she said, her voice hoarse with wonder. "You're something."

I blushed, pleased by her earnestness, by how easily we'd reached her.

"Come with us," Ike said. "Come see."

"My dear," she said. "I can't."

"You can't?"

"Parkinson's," she said sadly. "I've slowed to a crawl."

Of course it was that, I realized. Her uncanny stillness, her trembling chin. Ike looked at me for help. There were so many things he'd never been told about.

"My grandmother had it, too," I told her. "I know."

"But you could help me," she said. "You could go and get my book. It's dropped where I can't reach it."

I pointed to the door.

"Inside?" I said.

"Yes," she said. "Right there in the kitchen."

"I'll get it," I told Ike.

I was happy to help her, and curious, too—it's always interesting to see what a stranger's reading.

Stepping into her kitchen was like getting slapped in the face. The counters were cluttered with food garbage, open tin cans and take-out containers, crinkled-up plastic bags. A kitten on the windowsill over the sink stood and mewled at me, its tail in the air, and hopped to the floor with a thump. Dried cat-food pellets lay tumbled about everywhere. A musty sour-milk smell.

I saw the book lying on the linoleum, a thin one with blue binding. I picked it up, and a pen fell out. *100 Intermediate Word Searches*. On page after page, she'd pulled clue words from a chaos of random letters, claiming them in spidery circles of ink. The cat swerved once against my bare legs, its fur rough and silty with dander. I quickly backed away.

Outside, a crow had alighted down in the yard, and the two of them were watching it, Ike sitting on the porch railing. The bird had found a piece of wire somewhere and was toying with it, flinging it up in the air with its beak, as if that might somehow turn it magically into a worm.

"Here you go," I said, offering her the book, the pen hooked neatly onto the outside cover.

"Thank you," she said, and her arms lifted in shivering slow motion to take it.

"Are you going to be all right?" I said, sounding more concerned than I meant to. "Can we do anything else to help?"

"No, no," she said. "My son is coming. Later this morning. He comes every day. Sometimes *twice* a day, if he can."

I was relieved to hear she had someone, even someone who would let her live like that.

It was time to go. I looked back at the wings, how the radical fact of them made the Saab otherworldly, an alien craft. I swelled with longing then—the sudden desire to let her see how flying worked. We could at least do that.

"We could fly for her," I said to Ike. "Just for a minute, just to show her."

I watched Ike do a rapid calculation. The porch was deep, its overhang blotting out the sky, with piles of detritus at either end—rusted-out lawn chairs and other junk that would be hard and unpleasant to move.

"If we could help her down the stairs . . ." Ike said, wincing.

"Miss," I said. "If you come out into the yard, we could show you. A demonstration, so you can see for yourself. We'd just need to get you down the stairs. . . ."

She smiled sadly.

"It's best I don't," she said.

A car whisked past, a roar that grew and peaked in a blur and was gone. I could see that she was right. The chair looked too heavy to lift. There wasn't a ramp.

"But I can imagine it," she said brightly. "*Flying.* A great white kite."

I brimmed with a feeling I didn't fully understand, something about the way she said it. Barry had triumphed too late in her life.

"We'll come back and see you," I said. Suddenly it seemed important to promise that. "We pass through this way sometimes. We'll come again."

I meant it, in the moment. It wouldn't have been hard. But

so much was changing, and so quickly, and before long I forgot what I'd told her. The truth is that we never did.

✌︎

It was Ike's idea to go back to the house—to the woman we'd seen watering her garden during Diane's long flight the day before. I'd forgotten this until he said it, but remembered with a jolt he was right. Hadn't she looked up when we called to her, standing there as spray misted from her hose? Hadn't she seen Diane high overhead, a winged form we chased across the sky? Unlike everyone else, she wouldn't need to be convinced. She already knew what we knew.

Slowly, we found our way back. The house was like so many of the others: a one-story ranch clad in dull white aluminum siding, its windows flanked with dusty shutters. But she'd made a lovely garden. Rows of bushy green plants burst with delicate flowers, their bright cups brimming with bees. I marveled at a plant that hoisted huge thickly veined leaves on reddish green stalks.

"Look at those *leaves*," I said to Ike. "Big as couch cushions if you flattened them out."

"Rhubarb," Ike said.

Her doormat was a faded scrap of brush, the words YOU ARE WELCOME HERE still faintly visible. I hoped it would be true. But I felt nervous as we waited. I couldn't help it: to cross someone's lawn uninvited still felt illicit to me, no matter how important it was. Ike, though, seemed to be enjoying himself. He knocked a second time, without hesitation, like we were simply calling on a friend. Had it been a lifelong fantasy of his, to knock at a stranger's door and be let in?

There was a clatter by the window. Behind the glass, a hand parted the blind slats. Someone's eyes appeared in the slit.

"She's *here*," Ike said, beaming.

The blinds went smooth again, a beat of quiet. Then the dead bolt slid back and the door opened. A woman stood there, the one we'd passed the day before, a smallish person with a nimbus of gray hair. I could tell by her face she'd seen the wings through the window. They were still strapped to the Saab's roof, plainly visible behind us.

"*You* again," she said, peering at us with a haunted expression. "You passed through here, yesterday. . . ."

Her voice wavered, as if she couldn't be sure anymore how long ago it was.

"Yes," I answered. "It was yesterday, and you were outside watering your flowers. They're beautiful, by the way."

"What are you doing here now?"

"We're going to everyone," Ike said.

"I'd started to think I'd dreamed it up," she said. Her voice broke subtly, catching with real emotion. "It just didn't—I couldn't—"

She shook her hair, the springy gray sphere. The sight had left her shaken, I realized. Of course it had. Nothing could prepare you for it: the way the known world tore open suddenly before you, upending all you took for granted. She stood on her tiptoes to see more clearly, looking past us toward the car.

"So what *is* it?" she said.

"It's what you think," I said. "They're wings. To fly with, just like you saw."

"But it's not possible," she said softly, as if to be sure no one would hear. "You can't just . . ."

She trailed off, in conflict with herself, witness to what she knew couldn't be true.

I smiled at her, having felt it, too: the fear and wonder made you like a child again, no longer sure what could be.

"Come on," I said. "Come with us. We'll show you."

Ike followed me back down the steps.

"Keep going," I muttered to him. "Let's just give her a minute."

We started untying the ropes while the woman lingered in the doorway, watching. Slowly, curiosity got the better of her. By the time the wings were free, she'd crossed the grass. We held them up for her to touch. Standing in their shadow, she ran her hands along the frames.

"How did you *do* this?" she said.

"We built them," Ike said, grinning, like that explained everything.

"*Why?*"

The word burst out, exasperated, a capsule for her disbelief. It stopped me. Why *had* we done it? For no reason, for every reason. To save ourselves. To change everything, because everything so badly needed changing.

"My sister," I said, surprised to hear myself slip into Barry's cadence. But we *would* be like sisters, once she knew. "The only way is just to do it. Here. Put them on, we'll help you. And then you'll understand."

I wanted it for her. To have what we had: This glorious loophole, a way to slip outside yourself and all that had shaped you. To be freer, wilder, than anyone had ever let you be.

"Me?" she said. "You want *me* to do it?"

"Yes," I said. "Yes, yes, yes."

She lifted her eyes, took in the wings' full span. We had her, I thought, but then she stepped back.

"No," she said, grimacing. She laughed ruefully, just a puff of breath through her nose. "I couldn't. Really, I . . . shouldn't."

She turned and started back toward the house. But her movements held the slightest hesitation, as if she expected me to call after her. As if she were bracing for the command that would override her will, freeing her to take what she wanted.

"Wait," I said.

She stopped. By then she'd reached her stairs, one hand on the railing. She didn't turn around, not right away. She only stood there, her back to us, letting the moment pull loose like a bow. Nothing to break the silence except the hum of bees.

～

She needed something to jump from. Ike suggested we use the Saab. I helped her balance as she stepped from the bumper to the hood, from the hood to the roof. The huge bat shape loomed over me, briefly dimming the sun.

We tied her ankles to the frame. Her sneakers scuffed and dirty, shedding crumbs of garden grit. My fingers brushed the skin above the low-cut socks she wore, the flossy hair on her legs. For most of my life, I couldn't have imagined touching a stranger like that. But flight collapsed the distance between us. You learned to do things you never thought you'd do.

I stood back.

"You're ready," I said.

The woman paused, a nervous swallow in her throat.

"I can't believe this," she said. "I feel like I'm dreaming."

She shuffled forward, the roof's white metal dimpling gently under her feet, and balanced at the edge, knees bent. Time stretched like dough, the seconds pulling thin. I was about to cheer her on when she jumped.

The wings clapped with a gust of warm wind, and then she was flying. She rose and circled the house twice in a slow, dizzy loop. Then, a scream. The noise reached us as an echo of itself, a sound made tinny by the height. But we heard what it was: a long, full scream from a purging part of the throat.

Ike and I looked at each other. His eyes were wide.

"Wow," I said.

She wheeled around for a third time, screaming again, and again, her voice shifting and softening each time it reached us, until it was no longer a scream at all: she was crying out with pleasure, with gratitude, a sound so pure it was almost erotic, so unguarded it shamed me to overhear. I'd done that, too, I realized in a snap of recognition—I flooded with a sense-memory of rushing through the air, half-sung words escaping from my mouth. My eyes prickled with tears. Nothing like this had existed in the world before, not even close. I stood in the grass with Ike and let her sound float down around us, the call of some new and undiscovered bird.

SEVENTEEN

She flew in a listless way, tossing like a boat lost in a tide. Ike and I kept up easily on foot, trailing along below as she pitched about. She'd float off in one direction and then seem to think better of it, doubling back—it was nothing like what Diane had done, the frantic chase that followed. For the first time, I could really just watch the wings transform a stranger: her enjoyment obvious even at a distance, her aimless swimmer's pleasure, something waking up in her.

Ike and I walked down the middle of the road, weaving back and forth over the faded yellow line, drunk on the lawlessness of it. Every now and then our eyes would meet and we'd grin at each other in silence. I felt intensely bonded to him then, grateful to share in the moment, a witnessing too vast for just one person. I loved the faint, exuberant note of apology in his eyes, his mild embarrassment at the way words failed him. But I had no language for it, either, and we walked on in silence as the woman crisscrossed the sky above us, as if taking a switchback pass up an invisible mountain.

Then she started to lose height.

"She's coming down," Ike said, and it was true—she'd swooned into a last, low dive. We sprinted under her shadow, trying to keep up. For an eerie half second her body was almost close enough to jump and touch, and then she overtook us. She hadn't pulled the cord, the one that would let her legs swing free for landing. I realized that in the rush of getting her into the wings, we'd forgotten to show her how, so she didn't even know she could. I winced, too late. She was going to belly-flop full-tilt into the earth.

"Hey," I shouted. I didn't even know her name. I tried to yell out some last-second instructions, but she was falling too fast.

"She'll crash!" Ike called out, panicked.

My hands flew up instinctively to block my face, as if I expected an explosion when she landed, a piercing rain of light. I looked again in time to see her skid to a stop on the asphalt. We ran, no sound except the patter of our feet on the road and the rushing of our breath.

The fall had winded her, and she writhed there gasping in the street. The wings shuffled about awkwardly, on top of her. Ike fell to his knees, his hand on her back, murmuring to console her with words I couldn't quite hear. When she'd recovered, we tried to help her stand, hoisting her up by the armpits.

"We're going to lift you," Ike said.

"Yes, yes," she said, nodding, almost impatient with fatigue.

She'd regained her senses quickly—she wasn't so woozy and drained as Diane had been, probably thanks to the relative shortness of her flight and the violence of the fall. It was only then we saw how much skin she'd scraped away. On her shins, on the underside of both arms, long friction burns oozed painful whey.

Ike looked sick.

"You're hurt," he said, distraught. "She's hurt."

But the woman didn't seem to mind, or feel any pain at all. She offered us a dazed smile, blinking away tears.

"I didn't . . ." she managed, before her throat creaked shut. "I never thought . . ."

She shook her tears away and tried again.

"That was *wonderful*," she said, her voice weak, her cheeks pink with the effort. Ike and I traded glances. She didn't notice the damage to her body until we started to untie her, the skin minced raw, specks of grit stuck in the blood.

"Oh, that's a shame," she said absently, peering down at herself. "See what I've done. . . ."

Then she laughed, the sound eerie and soft.

"What should we do?" Ike whispered.

"I don't know," I whispered back. And I didn't.

We decided to bring her back to her house and clean her up. We couldn't just leave her like that, dumping her back on the porch all mussed and bloody. So we left the wings by the roadside and helped her limp slowly down the street, her limbs ginger and unsure. A sequence of half embraces, clutching at each other for support. It was almost comical how the gliding form above us had been reduced to this: three people, joined awkwardly at the hip, hobbling down the shoulder in the heat.

∽

The woman still wasn't quite herself, even by the time we reached her house. She seemed mild and drained, her head lolling sleepily, like she might wilt the second we stepped away.

"We could take her inside," Ike offered.

I looked up at the front door. Three concrete steps rose from the walkway where we held her steady, our arms all wreathed together.

"I think we have to," I said. We were so close I could smell her soap, a dignified mineral scent.

"We're going to take you in," I told her. Declaring it felt better, something closer to consent.

"Yes," she mumbled. "Do that." But she seemed to hardly know what she was saying, and I felt she would have agreed to almost anything.

We helped her up the steps and went in through the unlocked door. Then we were in the hallway, a jumble of shoes by the door. Big ones, small ones, the bright sneakers kids wear. It suddenly occurred to me that someone might be home.

"Hello?" I called out. No one answered. The place was empty.

We steered her down the hallway, through a kitchen, onto a couch in the den. She dropped backward into the cushions, landing with a huff. Her scrapes looked terrible, livid spills of open skin. Her eyes stayed closed, even though she wasn't really asleep. She was resting, and that took all her strength.

We stood back and regarded her.

"All she had to do was pull the rope," Ike whispered to me sorrowfully. "How? How could we forget to tell her?"

It had been careless. I felt chastened and sorry.

"I know," I conceded. "But, here—let's get her cleaned up."

Ike went back for the wings while I raided the medicine cabinet in the bathroom off the den. I hadn't set foot in a normal American household in months, and was amazed at the scope of their stash: dozens of over-the-counter bottles filled with potions, creams, and pills for every ailment. I found some bandages and disinfectant and returned to the couch. She sprawled back with her eyes closed and her palms cradled upward, as if she'd fallen out of a tree.

I knelt on the shaggy rug and uncapped some rubbing alcohol, wincing at its chemical stink. I stuck a cotton ball into the opening and inverted the bottle, the little cloud slicked with germ-killer.

"This'll hurt," I said, softly.

But I couldn't make myself touch her. I'd never cleaned another person's wound before. I was only playing at what I'd seen others do—my mother, the school nurse—rehearsing their methods in a poor performance of care. I wasn't actually ready to sweep the cotton wad along her exposed tissue, to wake her with the sudden sting. So I put the bottle and cotton aside. I sat on the carpet again, my hands cupped uselessly in my lap, and waited for Ike to come back.

❧

"I've never felt anything *like* it," the woman said.

We'd nearly finished bandaging her up—or Ike had, anyway. Given his history with Barry, he knew exactly what to do, while I just knelt beside him trying to be useful. She'd become herself again. Talkative, with dancing points of light in her eyes.

"It was . . . wow. I mean, I can't describe it. I just remember thinking, *There's nothing like this. There is nothing like this.*"

She wrinkled her gray eyebrows thoughtfully.

"Was I . . ." A delicate pause. "Making *noises*?"

I shrugged, giving her room to deny it.

"I mean," I said. Her look of mock horror made me smile.

"Argh." An embarrassed groan, throaty and deep. "I knew it. But I—it just felt so *good*."

"There you go," Ike said brightly. He'd finished wrapping the bandage around her arm, a cotton pad with first-aid tape. I hated that we'd let her get scraped up like that, but she seemed to take it in stride, as if it were the least noteworthy part of what had happened.

"Wait'll I tell my husband about this," she said. "I did tell him about the other day, you know. That I thought I saw someone flying, but I wasn't sure. And he said that was impossible—which, right, I know. So I thought there had to be some other explanation. . . ."

She trailed off.

"Who *are* you? How did you *do* this? I mean, my husband's a contractor. And he could *never*—I mean, never—make something like this."

"A man made them," I said. "His name is Barry Haliban."

"That's my dad," Ike said.

"He spent years designing them. And they're going to change the world."

She studied us.

"Yeah," she said finally. "You might be right about that."

〜

Her name was Grace. I remember how fluidly her responsive face shifted from surprise or concern to knowingness and laughter, and how her bristling halo of gray hair shook with emphasis as she spoke, and how she held worlds of feeling in her slate-blue eyes. We told her all about the wings, and Barry, how he and Ike had worked for years until he finally had a breakthrough, this fever-driven vision I had witnessed but still barely understood. Then I noticed she was looking at me funny.

"What?" I said.

She leaned closer to me, staring intensely, her irises flat as paint.

"*What?*"

"I've *seen* you somewhere before," she said.

"Me?" I said.

"Yes," she said. "Turn your head like that again."

I just did it, made obedient by surprise.

"Like this?"

"Yes," she said, nodding eagerly. "Yes."

I held my chin in the direction she wanted, glancing at her sideways. It was hard not to laugh. Ike sat beside her on the couch, bewildered, looking like he didn't get the joke.

"Jane," she said. "That's your name, you said. Right?"

"Yes," I said, relaxing out of the pose.

She didn't seem to blink, her eyes all wide with revelation.

"So it *is* you," she said softly. "You're the missing girl, aren't you?"

❧

"I'm not missing," I said.

"Honey," she said. "It's you. You're *her.*"

I tried to stammer out some words in my defense, but Grace seemed to see right through me.

"I can't believe it," she said. "I can't *count* how many times I've seen your picture on TV. A student gone, no explanation. Never showed up for her exam. Her kitchen burned. I saw an interview with your *parents*, those poor people—"

She stopped.

"Oh," she said. "I'm sorry. I'm upsetting you."

She and Ike faced me from the couch.

"No," I said. "It's just . . ."

It had all happened so quickly: The revelation of who I really was, the invocation of my parents, a sudden torrent of pent-up guilt. What had they said about me? And my *parents* had done an interview? I tried to imagine the camera crew crowding into their living room, my father's wrinkled shirt. My mother crying, his arm wrapped stiffly around her. I wasn't ready to face them yet, face anyone. How many strangers knew my name?

"Listen," she said. "If I know one thing, it's this: when people run away like that, there's usually a reason."

She nodded, wanting to comfort me.

"I foster kids," she said. "You'd be surprised how many of them have done it. Sometimes that can seem like the best option left. To run."

"You foster kids?" I said, glad to put the focus back on her. The cavalcade of shoes we'd seen suddenly made sense. She had to be prepared for any feet that might come through the

door. Or maybe growing kids who lived with her left them behind, shedding sneakers like old skin.

"Yeah," she said. She pointed through a glass-paneled door
to a side office, where a desk and file cabinet were visible next
to a bulky gray photocopier. "I have all their folders in there.
Their histories. You'd be surprised, how many runaways. One
in ten, something like that. And you know what? When you
find out what they're running *from*? I totally get it."

She was trying to make me feel better, and I loved her for it.
But it wasn't the same as what I'd done. The kids she dealt with
surely came from the worst situations, homes of violence,
squalor, and despair. What was my excuse? There hadn't been
anything like that. Just this sense of the world ending, of my
light dimming, of the walls closing in. Just wanting—
needing—something to change.

"Do you have one with you now?" I said. "A kid, I mean?"

"Yes," she said. "Two. From two different families. One's
been with us six months. The other, just five weeks. You
wouldn't *believe* what she's been through. . . ."

Emotion welled in her briefly, this mix of anger and pity.
But she tamped it down, collecting herself, knowing the story
wasn't hers to share. It struck me as incredibly noble, to open
up one's life like that. To risk all kinds of heartbreak and trouble. In a way, it reminded me of what we were doing as we
knocked on the doors of strangers' houses—to enter the mess
of other people's lives, for no reason except you knew you had
to. You had to, or nothing would ever get any better.

"Your parents," Grace said. "Are they decent people?"

"Yes," I said, without hesitation. They weren't perfect, they
were as flawed and lost as any of us. But I knew that they were
decent, whatever she meant by that.

"That's good," she said. "You should call them. Why not let
them hear your voice?"

It was still a question I felt unprepared to answer.

Grace touched my arm.

"I know," she said. "Scary. But they care about you, right? They just want to know you're safe. I think they'll understand."

Once, I would have burned to hear this. That I could take what I needed without guilt, a freedom that was free of consequences. That my parents would forgive me: my unreasonable actions dissolved by their illogical love. She was trying to absolve me, I saw that.

But I also knew I wasn't ready yet. How could I explain so soon, in the first hours of something that radical and new? It would be worse than pointless, after all my absence, to call out of the blue—talking about flying, about wings. What would that do except worry them? How could they possibly understand? No, the best thing would be to wait. Because our progress would be bolder with every day that passed, and before long we'd accomplish something unmistakable—enough to justify the pain I'd caused them, if anything could.

"I will," I said. "I can't—not yet. But soon. I promise, I will."

She nodded with a wistful smile, one that made pleasant creases in the corners of her eyes.

"All right, honey," she said, nodding. "Just be sure you do."

⟡

She had to kick us out. She wanted to change her clothes—pants and long sleeves would hide her bandages, the signs of damage from her fall. Her kids would be home soon, she said. It was a long ride on a short bus chartered especially for them, a high school sophomore and a five-year-old, ferried back and forth to their distant schools for continuity's sake. There was such a shortage of credentialed foster parents that the state housed kids where they could and figured out the transit.

But before we left, Grace insisted on feeding us. We looked

hungry, she said, and she was right. She had a pie in the fridge wrapped in tinfoil, a strawberry-rhubarb she'd charmed out of her garden, the crust thick and flaky with Crisco.

"Will there be enough left?" Ike asked, as she sawed our pieces out. "For the kids?"

She smiled. "I can always make another."

I closed my eyes and let the flavor soar through me. Ike looked down, crestfallen, at the last crumbs on his plate, the end of his life's first slice.

Then we were outside. The Saab was in the driveway, the wings lay flat across the roof. It was a sight to stop traffic, but if anyone had passed they'd just breezed on. You could sense the day starting to end, the blue sky tinted with gold.

"We still have a few hours of light left," I said, as we drove off. "Let's make the most of it."

"Make the most of it how?"

"There are others, just like her," I said. "We have to find them. It's up to us."

"I was thinking we could go back," Ike said.

"Already?"

"I wonder how my dad's doing," he said. "And Diane. And the wings they're making for her."

I hadn't really thought of the new wings as hers, but of course they would be.

"It's only been a few hours," I said.

"A lot goes on in a few hours."

I sensed time slipping away from us, a window closing as the world tilted toward night. If we went back, the day would be over, those hours lost to us forever. But I saw how much Ike wanted to return, how tethered he was to Barry. So I relented.

We drove. I started thinking of my own parents, the forlorn image of them sitting on their sunken couch, surrounded by cameras.

Almost as if he could read my mind, Ike said: "You never told me you ran away."

It wasn't an accusation. He was just telling the truth.

"Where did you think I came from?"

"Everybody comes from somewhere," he said. "Running away means how you go."

It was hard to argue with that.

"I don't feel like a runaway," I said. "I feel like I'm where I should be."

He was quiet for a second, warm wind from the open windows fluttering his clothes.

"I'm glad you did it," he said.

For some reason, this made my throat tighten. Just the humble goodness of him, the unguarded way he spoke. But there was more, I realized. He was saying something that wasn't about me.

"I thought about it, too," he said. "For years, I wanted to. Winter after winter, I thought about just getting out. Leaving him."

He fell silent, chewing pensively on his lip.

"But I never could. I just knew that even if I left, he'd still be with me all the time. He'd be everywhere."

❧

Barry and Diane were still at work, the new wings nearly complete. Diane was stationed at the sewing machine as Barry helped guide the fabric under the juddering needle, stitching the outside seams.

"Tell me all of it!" Barry said. I was disappointed with our progress, just one person after all those hours. But Barry's eyes lit up greedily at the news. Each successive flight was a new miracle to him, as much cause for wonder as the first. He listened with great enthusiasm, roaring out praise and encouragement as we explained how Grace had flown. The story seemed to set him off in a different direction, and he tottered back to the cot to work on his sketches.

"You can see her through," he told us, nodding at Diane. "It's just the stitching now. The hard parts are behind her."

So we did, sewing while Barry drew. In time, we carried the finished wings outside. Daylight was fading, the sky the color of ash. Ike and Diane climbed the ladder while I fit the wings onto the pulley hook and hoisted them up. As I crawled up to the roof to join them, the whole thing had the familiar shape of ritual—like monks that wake each day with chanting, like mixing a relied-upon drink.

Barry stood below, watching eagerly on his crutches, his hair distressed with wind.

"It's been so long now," Diane said. She was shaky, expectant little jitters in her limbs. "I've almost forgotten what it feels like."

Ike cinched up the harness along her back while I tied her wrists and ankles, the tender, joining places we used to strap ourselves in. When she was ready, we went down to watch with Barry. Poised at the ledge, she looked huge, her body centered darkly in the giant frame. The lines connected to her hands thrummed with power, all her timidness gone. She'd been transformed. It was unthinkable, it really was, the way we let ourselves stay so small for so long.

～

We watched her a little while, and then Barry said:

"Come! I want to show you what I've been working on."

He started swinging on his crutches toward the barn, his gait a broken gallop.

"Wait," Ike said.

Barry turned back, his eyes twin disks of blue impatience.

"What about her?" Ike said.

Diane was by then high above us, the wings a twisting shape, two oak leaves lost in the wind. She was getting farther out over the trees.

"What *about* her?" Barry said.

"We'll lose her if we go inside."

"What did you think we'd do?"

"We went after her before!"

Barry cocked his head.

"Well, we had to, didn't we?" he said. "Those were *our* wings. Not ours, exactly—but our first, the demonstration pair. Our calling card. These ones are *hers*."

"But where will she go?"

"Wherever she wants to!" Barry said, cheerfully exasperated, as if trying to share good news with someone in a language they didn't speak. "That's the whole point. It's up to her now. She's complete."

"I just thought . . ." Ike looked at me, trying to tap me in.

Complete, I thought. It was an interesting word, and one I wasn't sure I'd heard him use before. It was true that we had nothing left to offer her, her training finished. But I sensed that he meant something else, as though the wings had completed her in some larger, more existential sense. Instinctively, I got that. I almost felt jealous of Diane: left alone with wings of her own, and all the sky she could drink.

"It's all right, Ike," I told him. "We can let her go now."

In a way, we already had. As we talked, she'd soared so far out that I wasn't sure we could catch her anymore even if we wanted to.

"The point isn't to get people to hang around with *us* forever," Barry said. "It's to set them *free*."

We watched her go, a shrinking dark speck distantly above us.

"It was nice having her here," Ike said.

"And she'll come back, if she wants to," Barry said. "But there's going to be others, Ike. More than you can count. Now I want to show you something."

He turned to me.

"Shall we?"

⁓

We followed him back into the barn, where sketches lay all over the cot. Barry carefully lowered himself onto it, the springs creaking under his weight, and started to gather the pages. Ike knelt and helped him collect them into a stack.

"Look," he said. "I'm nearly finished. Just one more page to finish in the morning—it's almost done already. And then we'll have it: our first blueprint."

He grinned.

"Everything we know, distilled into sixteen pages. Look!"

He held the drawings out to me and Ike, and I leafed through. They were just as extraordinary as they'd seemed to me before, like a child's flip book that brings a dancing man to life in a breeze of pages, except what emerged here was intricate and radically original, a miracle that came to life in sequence. By the end, the full wings were ready to embrace you—the half-finished drawing surrounded by white space, already stunning in outline.

"I'm going to let that one sit without commentary," Barry said. "No instructions there—they're not *needed* there. Just a last, detailed rendering of the whole thing, to consult and ponder, surrounded by silence."

"It's perfect," I said. Truly, I felt honored to hold it in my hands.

"If anything should happen to the three of us, this is what's left," Barry said. "Besides the wings themselves, this is everything. The seed of it. We should guard it with our lives."

The words hit strangely, spooky in their implication. What did Barry think might happen? But he was right. We'd entered a great new unknown—we couldn't know what tomorrow or the next day would bring. In a war on the way of things, nothing was certain.

I handed the pages back to him, the light sheets heavy with value. *I'll protect them*, I promised silently. Conviction aligned in me like stars. I would do whatever it took.

⁓

We made another meal. The squash again, this time with dandelion greens. The dandelions were no longer the mild, tender plants I'd first eaten; they'd grown, their leaves ridged and spiky as nettles. We cooked them in rabbit fat with the squash, until they softened into dank, dark twists that stubbornly held their bitterness. It was fuel my stomach would tear through, enough to quell the hunger that was always at the edges, if not for very long.

Barry was too excited to eat. We sat at his bedside, the cot covered in the day's new sketches, his bowl cooling in Ike's lap. He made us recount the day to him again—how we'd gone to see Grace, and how she'd flown. I noticed that we both left out how brutally she'd fallen—how, in the rush of everything, we'd forgotten to give her full instructions. But it didn't seem worth distressing him with that news. We were ashamed already, and it was a mistake we wouldn't make again. Besides, a detail like that threatened to overwhelm the fuller picture, detracting from the bigger, truer story of her progress through the air.

We talked until late, with Ike occasionally reminding Barry to eat, holding out forkfuls of food in his direction. Eventually Barry's features sagged and he started to fall asleep.

"Barry," I said. I didn't feel ready to face the night without him. Not with so much unresolved, and so much still before us.

His eyes opened.

"Hmm?"

"Tomorrow," I said. "What should we do?"

"Do?" He sat up slightly.

"For next steps," I said. "For the cause."

He relaxed back into the mattress, a shiver of springs.

"We'll figure tomorrow out tomorrow," he said. "It's been a *marvelous* day, my sister. Unprecedented in every way. I need to rest."

He closed his eyes, considering the conversation finished.

Ike and I sat in the silence awhile, hugging our knees, listening to him breathe. I wanted to appreciate it, this quiet moment to ponder and venerate, to literally sit at the feet of a master. But I was too filled with kinetic voltage, this desire to go and do what needed to be done. When I couldn't take it anymore, I stood. Ike looked up at me.

"I'm going," I whispered. "Are you coming?"

I didn't know where I was going, just that I was.

"What if he needs us?" Ike whispered back.

"He's asleep."

"He might need us."

"So you're going to stay here?"

"Yes."

"All right," I said.

I walked out into the night air alone. Overhead, a gibbous moon swelled toward the blackness, a portal rolling open. The meadow's tiny citizens whirred and creaked in a symphony of life. It felt good to be outside. And though it was too dark to do anything but sleep, I wasn't ready for the day to end. I had to find some way to let myself down, to burn off all that energy like fuel.

I looked up at the stars. The sky felt different, closer and more intimate, a border I had crossed. I wondered if Diane was still up there somewhere, winging darkly over the earth, indulging in the reverie we'd promised. Or if she'd returned home already, and was talking with flushed cheeks to her disbelieving husband on the phone. I imagined her in bed, propped up on a pillow, a finger twisted in the spiral cord. And his silence on the other end, as she tried to match what could only be felt with the words to make it real.

How were we going to shake the world into wakefulness?

It struck me that I no longer had anywhere to sleep, even if I'd wanted to. Barry had taken over the cot. So I decided to walk out to the car, still the one place in the world that was only mine. Maybe I'd even think of something useful, a late-hour adventure for the cause. If not, it was simply where I'd spend the night. I could roll down the dirt road to where the first wisps of a radio station started to come in, lull myself off on oblivious music.

I walked around the side of the house, the shrouded path our feet had beaten through the plants. Then I saw something I hadn't expected. The wings were still tied to the top of the car, the wind in their cloth a barely perceptible flutter. We hadn't taken them down when we got back, and they'd waited there, patient and perfect, a pair of pale hands bleached white by the moon.

∽

I was able to tie my ankles in. I pinned the wings against a tree with my back and reached down in a toe-touch, looping ropes around the jutting bones. There was no way to put the harness on—the strings needed to be pulled through and knotted on the other side—and I could only tie one of my wrists. But I wasn't sure it mattered. I was unwilling to let anything stop me from communing with the night awhile, to burn off the restlessness running through me. I craved the feeling that came after, how you felt clean and emptied out, like a dishrag wrung of all its dirty water.

I thought I'd use the car as my jumping platform, the way Grace had done. Trussed and hobbled, I made my way in a series of shuffling hops to the Saab. I'd pulled myself up onto the hood when I heard something nearby. I looked: Ike had emerged from the darkness, and was standing there in the road. I saw him mostly in silhouette, the outline of his hair.

"What are you *doing*?" he said.

"I'm just . . ." I said, kneeling exposed on the metal, my free hand slapped against the windshield's sticky glass. It was obvious what I was doing. "What, did you come out here to check on me?"

I felt bruised, exasperated. Accusing him of something helped to stem my thwarted rage.

"I just decided to come with you, is all," he said. "I could hear you."

"You heard me?"

"You were being sort of loud," he said.

It wasn't like I'd tried to hide what I was doing. It was more like I'd forgotten about Ike and Barry completely. The rest of the world dropped away, leaving just me and the urge to sate my private want. I hated to think what he'd overheard, my gasps of exertion, the first hollow booms of my knees on the metal. But I didn't stay shamed for long.

"Ike," I said. "Here—help me. Help me get up onto the roof."

He picked up the discarded harness, looked at it as if for the first time, and then looked back at me.

"Just give me a push," I said.

"Jane," he said.

I stopped.

"What?"

"It's dark."

"So?" I knew it was dark.

"Last night," he said. "I couldn't see you! I didn't know where you were."

"I followed the fire," I said. "I came back."

"It scared me."

"I didn't get lost," I said. "I was fine. We both were."

"Don't," he said. "Don't do it. Not right now."

He was serious, and it sobered me. I remembered how I'd felt during his turns, looking up into the night sky with no idea where he was. Only trusting that he'd see the torch as I waved it back and forth through the night—that it would guide him, that he'd still want to be guided. I'd been anxious, too.

"Wait until tomorrow," he said. "Please."

Something shifted, the urgency flooding out of me.

"Okay," I said. "Sure—no, you're right."

❧

Ike knelt to untie my feet, and then I was free. As we secured the wings to the roof again, I noticed how vigorously he knotted the rope. When we were through, I opened the driver's-side door and looked at him across the hood.

"What are you going to do?" he said.

"I don't know," I said. "Try to sleep."

"You're not going anywhere?" Ike said.

"No," I said. "It's too late to do anything."

"You shouldn't sleep out here."

"Well, Barry's in the barn."

"So stay with me," Ike said.

This surprised me.

"You don't have to be so alone," he said.

I gawked at him. *So alone*: as if "alone" were a way you be-haved, and not a thing you just were. But before I could say anything, he came around to my side of the car and linked his arm in mine, the insides of our elbows touching, our shoulders both sore the same way. He was leading me toward the porch, away from the solitary night, and whatever that meant, I was grateful for it.

I don't think I'd ever been inside the house so late. Silvery light floated in through the windows, barely enough to see by, and in the darkness the place felt more claustrophobic than ever. Paper brushed my legs as I followed Ike through stacks of pages and folders of notes, the too-full archive of Barry's mind. We reached the staircase that Barry had repurposed as a make-shift bookshelf and filing cabinet, just a narrow trail upward through space Ike had cleared in the middle of each step.

The second floor was lofted over the tree line, high enough to let some moonlight in. We passed down the chaotic hallway and into Ike's room at the end.

We lay down in his bed. The mattress was a slab of some thin, hard material, covered in rough cloth. He handed me a pillow, a sewn-together sack of feathers, to lay my head on, and we pulled the covers over. He'd made the sheets himself, I real-ized—I recognized the wings' same fabric, knew by heart the rough boat-sail quality of it. At first this made me terribly sad for Ike: He'd never been free from Barry, even in sleep. His fa-ther's craft came first, and he eked out bare necessities with whatever was left over. But the cloth also reminded me viscer-ally of flying. It was such a stirring, tactile reminder that—if Ike hadn't been there—I would have been driven back out into the night, to where the wings lay waiting.

I was glad he had brought me with him, even if there wasn't really room for both of us. The mattress wasn't standard-issue size. It smelled like an antique, and seemed to be something between a twin and full, its dimensions punishing and Victo-rian. We shifted around politely, trying not to jostle each other, trying not to touch. Eventually I gave in to comfort and convenience. I pulled Ike close to me and held him from behind, my fist in the hollow of his chest. He was right, I had been too alone.

The closeness of our bodies released a pleasant flood of brain chemicals, and I felt my spine unclench. It had been so long since I'd held someone. Ike put his hand on mine, his palm over my fist over his heart, as if to be sure I couldn't leave him. We stayed that way awhile, no sound but our breathing and the rustle of leaves near the open window. Then it blessed me, the mind's slow unwinding. Consciousness coming undone. A memory I couldn't place. The long cast of a fishing line over an endless lake, arching out across the water until I fell asleep.

Eighteen

I had an idea in the night. It came to me suddenly: I opened my eyes to the darkness, and there it was, fully formed, as if my brain had been working out the problem while I slept.

I'd rolled away from Ike at some point and lay facing the wall. He'd sprawled out on his back, taking up most of the bed, more selfish in sleep than in life. I almost didn't care. I fingered a fold of the bedsheet by my ear, let my skin remember the wings' lovely surface, all loaded with tensile strength.

This is it, I thought. Finally, I could see a way forward.

~

By the time I woke in the morning, Ike was gone. Or maybe it wasn't morning at all. Light streamed boldly through the windows, a mature quality to the sun, the day in full swing. It had been so long since I'd slept like that, and I felt restored, an inch taller, like after a river swim. I got up—my arms were better, the soreness gone—and made my way through the page-strewn hall to the stairs.

"Jane!" Barry roared, when I found him in the barn. He was lying in the cot, still drawing on his mirror. "Look what we've done!"

I was as glad to see him as he was to see me.

He gestured me over to the cot, and brandished his sketches for me to see. They'd been stitched together like a book.

"I finished them this morning and had Ike sew a binding on," he said. "It's *wonderful*, isn't it?"

I skipped to the last page, where the final image waited, finally complete: the wings in miniature, as they were in life, real enough to fly off the page. I felt even more convinced, then, of what I'd realized in the night: the plans would be key to everything.

"Let's bring them with us," I told him. I felt a strange, kinetic buzz, as if a church organ were playing nearby. "To show people, when we go out to recruit. Don't you think it would help? To show them it's not just something to fly with. It's something to *build*."

"Yes," Barry said. "Yes! Take it with you. It underscores the larger point, doesn't it? That this is only the beginning. . . ."

I started to say something and stopped, catching the hint in his pronouns.

"So you aren't coming?" I asked him.

"Me? No," he said. "You and Ike go ahead."

So he really did expect us to carry on without him, at least for now. This wasn't something I'd considered fully. Barry bristled with authority, odd as he was; his forceful, compelling manner made it hard to just dismiss him. It also helped that he was older, this winning mix of harmlessness and gravitas. I'd always imagined him right there with us in the trenches—our avatar, our asset.

Disappointment must have flicked across my face.

"It's my leg, Jane," Barry said confidingly. "I can't be charging around all over in this condition. I'm healing still. I need to rest, I can feel it."

I glanced down at his leg, which was still clapped together in the increasingly dirty and tattered-looking splint. He was right, of course. He was just so vigorous that it was easy to forget how badly he'd been injured, how much he needed rest. In a way, it was the most important task of all: giving Barry everything he needed to recover.

"How do you feel?" I asked, scanning his face. He did look thinner, maybe a little pale, though it was hard to tell with his beard. His eyes burned bright as ever. But we'd asked so much of him.

"I'm more tired than usual," he said. "A bit sapped. But I'm healing, that's what matters. I can tell you that."

"Does it hurt?"

"Sure it does. Less each day, though. I'll be fine. But listen, you don't need me as much as you think you do. And I promise, I'll be useful. I can stay here and keep drawing, which is about all I feel up to at the moment."

That, I didn't understand.

"What's left to draw?"

Barry laughed.

"You really think it's a good idea," he said, smiling wickedly, "to start this revolution with just a single copy of our plans?"

"Right," I said, with a little shiver of recognition. It was almost spooky, because I'd been thinking the same thing. It was like he'd sensed the idea I'd had in the night, but hadn't quite seen yet what was possible—for once, I was two steps ahead of him. So, while I'd planned to tell him right away, I decided to wait. It would be better as a surprise.

"I have a good feeling about today," I told him, beaming. "I'm ready to get going. Where's Ike?"

"Oh, he wandered off somewhere," Barry said. "See if you can find him. It's *hell* keeping that boy on task."

❧

I found Ike in the river, fishing, knee-deep in the water. He waved when he saw me coming, and I waved back. Did it change anything that I'd fallen asleep with him, his skinny frame wrapped in my arms? No, there was only what had always been: something delicate and good that resisted explanation. It was Ike, and I was simply glad to see him.

"Look in the bucket," he said, smiling.

A large fish of some kind flopped around inside, its scales shining and prismatic as if they'd been brushed with oil.

"A big fat one," he said. "Breakfast."

"Ike," I said. "I figured it out."

He looked at me sideways.

"I know what we're supposed to do."

I sat down on the rock next to him, and explained. It all came down to the photocopier we'd seen at Grace's. If we made copies of Barry's plans, we wouldn't need to convince people right there on the spot. We could leave something with them, a reminder to contemplate. And when the time came—when they finally looked up to see a real human body winging through the sky—they would understand what they were seeing. Even better: they'd have a full set of detailed instructions.

Instead of being excited, Ike just looked confused. I almost laughed: he had no idea what a photocopier was. It sounded almost mystical, the way I explained how a gray box with a glass top could scan pages and reproduce them a hundred times, a thousand times. It was magic to him, but I took it for granted. That was our issue, too. Flight seemed like sorcery at first. We had to make it concrete and explicable, familiar as a habit.

The way things were going, it would take weeks to reach everyone in Lack, a single town in the middle of nowhere. But distributing Barry's plans en masse—at sixteen pages, the most radical text I knew—would supercharge our efforts. It was the missing middle step, a way to change people's awareness before we even met them, and to leave an impression long after we left. I was so busy saying all this that at first I didn't notice what was happening in the river.

"What *is* that?" I said.

Thick clumps of whitish foam were drifting past us, towed quickly by the water.

Ike shrugged.

"It happens sometimes," he said.

They almost looked like whitecaps. But the uneven, sudsy globs were something much more unnatural: wads of froth, the kind stirred up in a bubble bath, that rode the water instead of cresting with it.

"It's polluted," I said, feeling sick with the realization. This was the water we bathed in, that we ate from; the river, nearly sacred to us, had been desecrated.

"Is there a factory or something upstream?" I said. "Do you know? What's near here that could do this?"

Ike shrugged uneasily, suddenly aware of how serious I was. He had no idea. In other words, it could have been anything.

It shocked me to see the dark hand of industry even there, in a spell of river miles from anywhere. Part of me had really come to believe that Barry's homestead was an oasis, pure and self-contained. I was startled, even horrified, to realize it was not the paradise it seemed—that nowhere is, or can be very long, if we go on like this.

I told Ike not to eat the fish. When he cooked it anyway, I said I would abstain. But then its body was on a plate, filleted in two with one half handed to me. The flesh delicate and pink, the skin a brittle, richly colored crisp. I was so hungry. *This is what we're trying to kill*, I thought, as I raised a morsel to my mouth: *the system that spreads poison everywhere, then forces us to consume it.*

❧

But first we had to do something about Ike's clothes. His strange homemade garb wasn't helping our case. In my suitcase I had a shirt I loved, a vintage black Pixies tee I'd found in a thrift store back in New York. It had always been a little too big for me, so I mostly wore it to bed, but I thought it would fit Ike. I got it from the trunk and gave it to him.

"So we look more like one of them," I told him. "I hope it fits."

Ike wasn't offended—he seemed downright pleased, and I couldn't believe I hadn't thought of it before. He stripped his muslin tunic off and slid into my shirt, then turned to me for a look. It was only concert merch, swag from a band whose music he'd never heard and couldn't imagine, but it transformed him. I caught a glimpse of the kid he might have been without Barry, the stung loner with headphones on. I filled with yearning for a past that didn't exist: a past where we'd met earlier, two freaks trapped in a high school somewhere. We could have saved each other.

❧

When we pulled up in front of Grace's house, she was outside watering her garden. Mist blew in a wet puff from the hose. She turned and saw us coming: my Saab with the wings attached, crawling along at half speed.

She dropped the hose and ran over, lowering her head into Ike's open window.

"*There* you are," she said. "I was hoping you'd come back."

Her voice went soft, conspiratorial.

"I told my husband everything," she said. "He's not sure what to think, but he knows *something* is happening. He said to call him if you all came back. He wants to see them, too."

She was wearing jeans and a long-sleeved shirt, her outfit too warm for the weather. To cover her scrapes, I supposed.

"Show her," I told Ike. He had Barry's pages in his lap, and he lifted it to her. Grace took them and straightened. For a minute we watched her flip through them, her head out of the frame, just a view of the pages turning one at a time. Then she bent down again.

"I'll be damned," she said. "A set of *instructions*."

She shook her hair.

"Gene's going to love this," she said. "Do you have time to hang here? I want to call him."

"Sure," I said. "Actually, we have a favor to ask."

◈

She took us in through her garage. They had a workshop in there: planks up on sawhorses, tools hung on pegboard, a scorched smell like gasoline. It was nothing like Barry's workspace, but instead was all machines and clean lines, an orange extension cord snaking around on the floor.

We walked into the living room, past the couch where we'd tended to her scrapes.

"It's in there," she said, pointing to the side office. "But you knew that already."

She opened the door, and I saw what we'd come for: the photocopier.

"There's some extra paper next to the desk," she said. Packages of unopened stock sat in a cardboard box, stacked like bricks of gold. Tantalizing, all those untouched white sheets.

"How many reams can we use?" I said.

"How many?" she said. "Oh gosh. I don't know. Three? Definitely leave a few. You wouldn't believe how much paperwork we do for the state. I'm going to call Gene."

She shut the door behind us, and Ike and I were left alone with the xerox machine. Ike held Barry's sketches in his hands, approaching cautiously as if the machine might wake up and snap at him. I lifted the lid. Our faces peered back at us from the dark photo chamber, reflected darkly in the glass.

"I've never seen anything like it," Ike said, his voice hushed and reverent.

The first thing to do was take out the stitches he'd made, so we could feed the pages individually through the chute. I felt a little bad destroying the binding, tearing the thread apart with a letter opener on Grace's desk. But Barry knew better than anyone: you break what exists to make room for the new.

I punched in an order for several hundred copies, each button-push sounding a little electric chirp. Our pages slithered through the slit and landed on the tray. Then fresh copies started spitting out as the scrolling bar of jewel-green light passed and went dark, passed and went dark.

The copies turned out beautifully—the lines lighter and slightly thinner somehow, but otherwise the same. We marveled at the growing stack of blueprints, an immaculate conception, the beginning of something to last a thousand years.

"Barry's going to love this," I said.

"Feel it," Ike said, lifting a fresh page to his cheek. "They come out *warm*."

⁓

Copies spat out in a smooth, brisk cadence, fresh sheets steadily filling the tray. The photocopier seemed to exude something unmistakable: this aura of profound contentment. Maybe it was strange to detect emotion in a mass-produced machine. But isn't that a version of what happiness is, a thing excelling at what it was built to do?

We'd made maybe forty reproductions of Barry's book, Ike and I stapling each one three times along the edge, when Grace came back into the office.

"So, he's on a job about an hour away," she said. "And he can leave in about forty-five minutes. That would put us about two-thirty this afternoon, which isn't long before the kids get home. But it doesn't have to take long. He just needs to *see* those wings of yours. If there's time for him to try them, all the better."

Her dark, expressive eyes implored us.

"Can you stay that long?"

There was no reason not to, except the hugeness of what lay ahead. But while I had this feeling we couldn't delay, no one was actually waiting for us. We needed Grace and her dependable photocopier. Also, I wanted to please her. I wanted her husband to know she was telling the truth.

"We can stay," I said.

"Good," she said. "He says don't go anywhere."

She looked at the uneven stack of copies that was growing on her desk, the pages slanting down toward the unstapled side.

"What are you going to do with all those?"

"We're going to give them away," I said.

It sounded so small when I said it. But there was magic in those pages, I could tell. I tried to explain to her how I thought we could distribute the plans quickly, before hitting the houses: how they'd give the more competent people what they needed to build, while priming others to be ready for us. She listened carefully.

"Why *do* all that?" she finally said. "I mean, you're famous! Everyone knows you disappeared, at least around here. You could have a camera crew here in an hour. This could be international news by tomorrow morning."

This was something we'd discussed with Barry, again and again.

"We don't want that kind of attention until we're ready," I said. "So many things could stop us. The police, the government. Is flying *legal*? Well, who knows? Do you want to wait around and find out?"

Ike kept working while we talked. He'd learned to staple the pages as fast as they came out, his hands doubled up and thrusting, the impact registering each time in his hair. The air smelled like toner, a scent almost like sunlight.

"No," I said. "What we want is to spread this far and wide in all the places where no one's paying attention, where people have been forgotten, where flight is needed the most. And by the time it's clear what's happening, it will be too late for anyone to stop us. Cat's out of the bag."

Grace picked up one of the pamphlets and started leafing through it. There was something almost tender about the way she turned the pages.

"You're approaching it like a war or something," she said softly.

"That's exactly right," I said.

"But what are you at war with?"

"Everything," I said. "Well, not everything. But—you've done it. You know what flight *feels* like. We're at war with everything that isn't that. Everything that's old, and constraining, and filled with despair. We want to replace all that—we *can* replace it—with what's new, and joyful, and free."

She put the pamphlet down, laying it gently on the stack and patting it once with her fingers to make it stay. Her hands betrayed her age, speckled and heavy with rings. Her fingers returned to the page again, caressing the lines, as if trying to erase Barry's markings with her thumb.

"You know," she said, "we don't have to just *wait* in here. The three of us crowded in my office. Maybe . . ."

She trailed off.

"Maybe what?" Ike said, looking up, flushed from stapling.

"Well . . ." she said. "No, it's nothing."

"What were you going to say?" I asked her, though I could already feel a script unfolding in my mind, and then we became the actors in it.

"It's just, while you were talking," she said, "I started to think how much I'd like to *fly* again. If it's all right. Maybe we could . . . you know. Fit it in."

I recognized the depth of need I heard, barely hidden in her voice.

"Just a fast one," she said, her voice rising with the intonation of a question.

I glanced at Ike. He shrugged, as if to say it wasn't his decision. Because who were we to tell her no?

"Just a fast one," I said. "Let's do this."

❧

You started to forget what it felt like, and then there was this hunger to remember. It took almost no time to get her into the wings, though I could tell by the way she moved that the scrapes under her clothes still pained her. We helped her up onto the roof of the car, and Ike tied her ankles in. That time, I explained how to pull the rope that loosed the knotted bow that let your legs hang free, and I made her repeat it back to me so I was sure she understood.

She needed no encouragement, she knew just what to do. As I was walking backward from the car, she jumped and flapped and flew. She screamed again as she rose, a long, delighted peal that broke three times for breath. Her voice echoed strangely across the height.

"There she goes again," Ike said, smiling.

We watched her for a minute, satisfied. A shifting, bird-like glyph making for a corner of the sky. If you listened closely, you could hear her muted yelps of pleasure and effort break against the silence, noises that reminded me of the defiant cries tennis players make in a stadium's quiet—the same unguardedness, the same tension and release. It was a transformation I never tired of watching. Who could explain the way a human being lifted? How could anything stay the same, after this?

~

That time, she didn't merely circle over the house. She was a bullet, and we had to chase her in the car. We followed her way out, deep into farm country. Sheep roamed the hills behind electric fences. Ike gave directions while I steered. Occasionally, unable to help myself, I'd take my eyes off the road to seek a glimpse of her in the sky. I nearly crashed into a tree at one point, its girth enough to end us.

"Just watch the road," Ike said, shaken. "I'll watch her."

"I know, I know," I said, but it was so hard not to look, so hard to accept his eyes as mine.

Grace's body failed before her will did. We saw the telltale motions, by then familiar: her arms pumping as best they could with their strength gone, a stepwise descent toward the ground. I pulled over to the side of the road and we got out. There were a few red barns in the distance, and everywhere the air had a sweet, fetid smell. We hopped a fence and then were running down a gently sloping hill, grass flicking at our ankles. By then she was only sixty feet above the ground and dropping quickly. I saw from a distance as she came in with great speed, bounced once, and was still.

We ran to where she lay, wings crumpled against the earth. She'd fallen on her stomach, her entire body covered by the frame except the very top of her head. Ike and I got her to her feet. The flight had exhausted her completely. Sweat poured from her forehead, her damp gray curls flattened to half their usual mass. With her eyes closed like that, she looked pale and feverish, the face of someone dreaming about a fire.

We untied her, misjudging how ready she was to stand on her own, and she toppled forward. Ike reached for her, but it was too late and she dropped like a sackful of stuffing into the grass.

"Here, let's help her up," Ike said.

We were trying to lift her when we heard something, the sound of a motor. A man was riding some kind of vehicle toward us across the field—a strange-looking thing, like a lawn mower or Zamboni, but fitted with a number of ribbed suction tubes.

He was a stocky guy with close-cropped hair, wearing work boots and coveralls, a few stray pieces of hay still stuck to his clothes. He got down from the cart looking awestruck, his mouth open, alarm snapping in his eyes. His wonder made him like a dancer, circling us with slow, purposeful movements, as if the scene had been pre-choreographed and his feet knew every step by heart. The seconds oozed by as he looked back and forth between the wings, and us, and Grace wheezing facedown in the grass.

The man started to speak in Spanish. I didn't understand him, but I recognized the emotion that reduced his voice to a whisper, this mix of fear and reverence.

To my absolute astonishment, Ike spoke back to him in Spanish—his words fluid, his accent convincing. Ike lifted the wings, encouraging the man to touch them in words I didn't know. He came forward cautiously. But when he was close enough to touch, he ran his fingers down the frame.

"He saw her," Ike said. "He saw her fly down from the sky."

"Ike," I said, still flabbergasted. "How . . ."

"How, what?"

I couldn't imagine how a second language had found him. He'd never used basic office equipment before that morning, yet there he was conversing nimbly in Spanish. It was its own small miracle, one I wanted him to explain. I thought suddenly of the songs I'd heard him singing now and then, under his breath, with words I hadn't understood—I had so many questions. But I decided clarity could wait.

"What's he saying? Does he want to try them?"

"I'll ask him," Ike said, and he did.

The man wiped his forehead and looked back anxiously toward the barns. He said something I didn't understand, and then a wide grin spread across his face.

"He does," Ike said, delighted. "He wants to try. But he only has a few minutes."

∿

While Ike and the man carried the wings toward the car, I stayed back with Grace. She was still exhausted, just completely physically spent. I knew the feeling, like trying to pry yourself out of a deep, delicious sleep. I knelt and put my hand on her back, the outlines of her shoulder blades pressing through her shirt like shrunken wings, but she didn't respond. I rolled her over, trying to be gentle. Her eyes opened slightly, squinting against the sky.

"How are you feeling?" I asked her.

"Hmm," she said, a drowsy smile on her face.

I started to rub her shoulder, a form of touch I imagined would feel comforting as it lulled her her back to life.

"Come on, Grace," I said. "Wake up."

She lifted her arm and put her hand on mine. Maybe it was her way of letting me know she could hear me, a gesture of reassurance. Or maybe she just wanted me to stop rubbing her shoulder, it was impossible to tell. I sat with her another minute, her hand warm on my hand, waiting to see what would happen.

"Thirsty," she said finally. I hadn't noticed the dried spittle in the corners of her mouth, like two dabs of Elmer's glue. I wished I had something to give her. I was trying to get her to sit up when I heard something in the distance, a faraway shout. I looked and saw the man was flying. His body rose, the sky a sea, the clouds a peaceful archipelago. For a second I forgot everything—there was only the play of light and shadow, the sense of weight falling away. It didn't matter how many times I'd seen it before: it felt miraculous when gravity proved to be so fragile.

The man soared over our heads, out deeper over the field. Ike came running after him down the slope, a frantic figure who grew in size as he drew closer. The scene played out in a pleasing, painterly way: the sun in the grass as Ike raced closer, the man sailing off overhead, all the primal urgency of motion. Ike reached us, and dropped to his knees.

"There," he said, panting. "We did it."

We followed the man with our eyes a little longer, the wordless exhilaration of watching someone fly, the body reduced to a couple pen strokes in the blue. But we both seemed to realize at the same time that we'd miscalculated. The man was moving quickly, at a right angle to the road. I felt myself compute how long it would take to get back to the car, factoring that against the man's speed and the fact that there was no easy way to chase him—not without driving the car through the fence and down the hill.

"Ike," I said. "We should follow him."

Ike chewed his lip. He saw it, too.

"What about her?"

I shook Grace's shoulder, more roughly than I had before.

"Grace," I said. "Grace, please."

She moaned.

"So *thirsty*," she said.

"What should we do?" Ike said, nerves pushing his voice into a stranger, higher register.

It would set us back a whole day to lose the wings—our only pair, our first. I felt the afternoon slipping through our fingers.

"We have to go," I said. I looked down at Grace. "We can come back for her."

But I turned against the idea before I'd even finished saying it.

"We can't just leave her," Ike said, saying out loud what I'd already decided.

"Then you stay," I said. "I'll go get the car and follow him, and we'll meet back here."

"No," Ike said, with a force that surprised me. "We have to stay together."

Alarm flashed in his eyes, little sparks of light. Was there a reason we shouldn't split up, some rationale I'd forgotten? I didn't think so, but there wasn't time to argue.

"Okay . . ." I said, thinking. The man was getting smaller, a silhouette that drew tighter as it sailed toward the horizon, his edges smoothing out. He'd be fine—better than fine, he was lucky.

To lose the wings right then, just as we were starting to gain some traction, would be a setback. But we owed Grace something, too. I looked down at her prone, sapped form, weighing her comfort against the greater cause.

My brain raced helplessly. "Let's carry her," I said.

Ike nodded. We lifted her to her feet and slung her arms over our shoulders, then started up the hill. It was slow going, her feet dragging senselessly, the upslope working against us.

"Stop," she groaned finally. "Stop."

We looked at her.

"I'll walk," she murmured, but when we stepped away, she

tumbled to her knees. I didn't dare to look out into the distance, afraid to see how far away the man had flown.

"Here," I said, offering Grace my hands.

"It's too late," Ike said, looking back over his shoulder. "He's gone."

⁓

We drove around for a while, searching. Ike leaned forward in his seat, peering up through the windshield; Grace was slumped against the cushions in the back, trying to rest. Without the wings tied to the roof rack, I could speed down the country lanes, and for a little while I thought we might actually close the gap between us and the flying man. But the sky was too huge, and the man was just a speck in the middle of it somewhere, getting more distant with time. He'd be almost impossible to spot.

"We *have* to find him," Ike kept saying.

"We can build the wings again," I finally said. "It'll just take time."

"He said he only had a few minutes," Ike said. "He has to go back to work."

In their short walk up the hill, Ike had learned that the place was a dairy, with hundreds of cows inside the complex of barns. The man had a job there, a shift to finish out.

"Wherever he is," I said, "I really don't think he cares about that now."

"He just kept saying he needed to get back."

"But that's the whole point," I said. "Isn't it? Does he really need to spend his life milking cows all day?"

I let the question hang there between us.

"We just gave him something so much better," I said.

"Yeah," Ike said. "I guess we did."

By the time we found our way back to her house, Grace had become herself again, sitting anxiously at the edge of her seat, her hands on the backs of our headrests. A truck was in her driveway, one that hadn't been there before.

"It's Gene," she said. "He's home!"

She was embarrassed that we'd lost the wings, that she'd made him come all the way back and would have nothing to show him. But at least Ike and I were there, witnesses to make the whole thing seem more real. We walked in through the open garage and found Gene in the living room, a freshly printed stack of Barry's plans laid out on the coffee table. He stood to greet us—a man of Grace's age, still wearing his work belt, hammer and tape measure and other items hanging off the side. His face looked much older than his dark, straight hair implied.

"Grace," he said, his voice strained with emotion. There was so much packed into that single syllable: confusion, longing, apology, wonder.

"You're the ones she told me about," he said to us.

"Yes," Grace said. "It's Jane and Ike."

"But you're just kids! How did you *do* this? I'm looking through, and I understand it completely. I can see how it all comes together. It's . . . genius. It's—"

He broke off.

"The wings," he said. "Show them to me."

"Oh, honey," Grace said. "A man wanted to try them. I wanted you to see them, but he flew off. . . ."

"A man," he said.

"It was our fault," I said. "Mine and Ike's. We let him fly too far ahead, and we couldn't catch him."

Gene's eyes bulged, the expression a frog makes in your fist. It was all so much to take in.

"Someone could make a million bucks selling these," he said, "if they work the way you say."

"Yes," I started to say. "But they're not for sale, they're free—"

"The children," Grace broke in, suddenly very serious. "Do we tell them about all this? Do we tell them, Gene?"

The conversation had quickly become heated, disjointed, the feel of a stone running away from you down a hill. We were following three different threads at once, overwhelmed by the sheer number of things we needed to talk about.

"The children?" Gene said. "Well, I don't see why not."

"But," Grace said, "I don't know—are they ready for it? For something so . . . *big*?"

She turned to me.

"Would they even be able to do it?" she said. "Their arms are so much smaller than ours. I don't think they could reach, it wouldn't work."

This wasn't something I'd considered, how a child's proportions might warrant a new design altogether. She was probably right. But that was different from what she'd first asked, which is how a young mind might react to the revelation of the wings. That was something I'd given zero thought to, and wasn't prepared to answer. I stuck with her more literal question.

"They'd probably need something specific made for them," I said. "I'm not sure—we could ask Barry."

"I'm wondering if they need to know yet, then," she said. "Why tell them, if it's just another thing they can't have? Let's not, Gene. They've missed out on so much already."

NINETEEN

We couldn't wait. We stapled together all the blueprints we'd printed, then went out to paper the countryside. I drove and Ike hopped out at every opportunity, rushing back and forth across people's lawns with Barry's blueprints in his hand. He stuffed copies into mailboxes and slipped them under doors. He tucked them through fence links and left them pinned by welcome mats. I loved navigating that way: no route in mind, just going wherever people might be, waiting for the thick roadside foliage to part and give way to a dwelling. Places to survive in, clawed out of the woods. I tried to imagine the faces of the people inside, and I couldn't.

We must have hit a hundred houses. Forlorn hovels in various phases of decay. A car carcass jacked up on bricks in the yard. Cheap swimming pools choked with dead leaves. It didn't matter that we didn't find anyone at home, everyone was too busy with the chore of making a living. The plans—when the people found them, whatever they made of them—were the first step in a larger unwinding. They signaled that something bigger existed. They stood at odds with everything the postal truck brought, the bills and junk mail that could find you even at the ends of the earth, that wanted your money and already knew your name. They came from a place beyond all that, telegrams from a better world.

Ike leapt onto porches, sprinted across rows of old flag-stones. We even hit the old motel I'd stayed in that one night, dropping copies at the door to each room. Day was ending, the blue sky tinted with gold. Deerflies seemed to find us whenever I slowed down to let Ike out—they circled the car as if it were meat, hurling their little bodies at the glass, until he trotted back, waving them away, and we blew off in a burst of speed.

∽

We needed gas on the way back, the Saab's fuel needle sagging low into the red, so we stopped at the little mart near the water tower. The lights were on, fluorescent overheads with a harsh, sickly glow.

"Someone's *here*," Ike said, grinning.

By then we were really ready to see someone. We'd driven for hours around a mostly empty landscape, no sign of a human being anywhere: just the crows that pecked roadkill on the roadside, people's captive cats eyeing us from the windows of their homes. But it was to be expected. The only place you could count on to be open, for miles around, was the store that sold sugar and fossil fuels. "Let's do this," I said.

I felt my heart start to beat louder, the rhythmic thud of feet on a staircase.

We took a copy of the plans and went in, the door sounding its dull electronic chime. I knew the woman behind the register: she was the younger of the two I remembered, the one with the disappointed face. She sat there ruminating, staring at the payment counter as though there was a stain on the wood that particularly troubled her. Our entrance, apparently, wasn't a good enough reason to look up.

"Pizza," Ike groaned, longing in his voice. Two last slices wheeled slowly on their tray behind the glass, pepperoni curling upward in the heat.

"God, yes," I said. I slipped them both onto a paper plate and left the carousel empty.

"Hey," I said, approaching. "These slices, and I need twenty-five in gas."

Back then, that could fill your tank, almost. She handed me my change and announced the total, somehow managing to sound sarcastic, as if she'd actually given me much less.

"We have something for you," I said then. No one else was there, but it came out quietly, confidentially, words for her alone.

The woman looked up, her eyes flat and unsurprised. She waited without anticipation, expecting nothing more than the latest insufferably stupid thing.

There was no way to be subtle, no preamble that could naturally pave the way.

"Ike," I said. "Show her."

Ike offered her the plans.

"Go ahead," I said. "Look."

She took the pamphlet almost without thinking, and placed it in a cranny beside the register. People had given her stuff before, clearly. Probably missionary tracts and handmade ads for services.

"No," I said, "please—really look at it."

She sighed and picked it up again, lifting the first page back. Then she turned another page, which I took as a first flicker of interest.

"I know how it sounds," I said. "But we've done something incredible."

I tried telling her about the wings, about the cause, about the power of what she held in her hands. But her face only got stonier the longer I talked.

"Well," she said finally, "you know what my dad always said."

"No," I said. Of course I didn't.

"If it sounds too good to be true, it probably is."

She gestured toward the door, making clear that was the end of it. So we shuffled out, Ike and I, though we left the plans with her. It was all we could do without the wings on hand. We could only plant a seed.

I couldn't help glancing back through the window as we walked out to the car, the pizza plate warm in my hand. To my delight, she was still looking at the drawings. An intense look on her face, as if she were conjuring a hidden picture from a book of Magic Eyes. Like the page might shift if she loosened her gaze just right, and a scene would be revealed: a boat, or bird, or lofty fortress in the clouds.

⏤⏤

By the time we got home, we only had a few dozen copies left. Just enough for a private cache, held in reserve for safekeeping. It was almost dark by then. We walked in elated silence through the meadow, a pleasing lushness to everything, thrilled with all we'd done. Progress, the rush of it unmistakable. You could really feel the circle widening, our influence starting to grow.

As we headed for the barn, I took a tentative inventory, like a child counting on her fingers. There had been the three of us, and then Diane, and then Grace, and then the man at the dairy, and then Gene, who hadn't flown but clearly wanted to. And then all those plans passed out, surely more than a hundred of them. It was nowhere near enough, but the paradigm was shifting. Barry would be pleased. I couldn't wait to tell him.

But Barry was asleep, we discovered. We found him lying in the cot, a candle carelessly left burning on the floor, his torso covered in new sketches. I was glad that I could free him from that, the need to shackle himself to his notebook all day. There was another, better, faster way, and it would give Barry back to us.

"Should we wake him up?" I whispered.

"No," Ike whispered back. "Let's let him sleep."

He was right, of course. My excitement had warped my intentions, making things seem urgent that could wait until morning. We left the remaining copies near the bed, an offering and tribute, the first thing he'd see when the sun opened his eyes. Then we ventured out into the meadow again. In the distance, under the sound of tree frogs, you could hear the river rushing, a subtle and powerful hush. I felt a throb of sadness when I remembered the soapy foam blobs floating past, the water desecrated. The great wheel mindlessly turned. We couldn't move fast enough.

❧

It was too dark to do anything useful. We gave up on the day. I slept again in Ike's room, the top floor of the house musty with stifling heat. We left his little window open, letting in a torrent of night sounds but only the weakest breeze. I tried to sleep, but I was uncomfortable and much too warm, and my thoughts raced as if with fever. I kept returning to everything that had happened that day, and I found myself wondering about the man we'd seen by the barns. How simple it had been with him: he'd seen Grace flying and immediately understood, he'd needed no convincing. If only every time could be like that, I thought, and then I remembered something.

"Ike," I said.

"Hmm?" he said. He'd been half asleep, having run himself out in a hundred short sprints back and forth from the car.

"That man today," I said. "The way you spoke to him. How did you do that?"

"Who?"

"The man from the barns," I said. "You spoke to him in Spanish—how?"

He was quiet for a second.

"Someone taught me," he said.

"Barry?"

"No," he said. "Someone else."

It took a few more questions to draw it out of him, though once he started talking he didn't want to stop.

He had met someone, a few years back. Sometimes, when he'd bike out to the water tower, he would pass a boy about his age walking in the other direction. Sometimes the boy would be with an older woman who shared his features, but he also would come alone. Once, their eyes met as Ike whisked past, connecting with an intensity that surprised him. The boy called something after him, a word he couldn't quite hear. Ike rode on anyway, his heart pounding in his ears. Then Ike found himself biking out around the same time each afternoon.

It didn't take long for them to find each other again. When Ike saw the boy coming in the distance, he slowed, light-headed with knowing his life was about to change. They stopped in the middle of the road, and by the familiar glimmer in the boy's eyes, Ike could tell that he'd been waiting, too. His straight black hair was parted on one side, a line neat and pale as a scar, and his teeth were brilliant and white. He carried water in a plastic thermos.

They started talking. A faltering conversation that Ike experienced as awkward, in part because he found the boy a little hard to understand. At first, the words came out twisted and much too fast, the syllables piling up unrecognizably. This wasn't something Barry had prepared him for. He'd always assumed that words flowed between everyone easily, as naturally as we share breath.

Then, somehow—it happened fast—the boy had asked him for a ride. This unsettled Ike at first, and then it overjoyed him: Ike would have taken him anywhere, he realized.

The boy showed him how two people could ride a bike at

once, with Ike standing while he pedaled to free up the seat for a passenger. They rode away like that, and as they did he'd occasionally put his hands on Ike's hips to steady himself, or reshift the balance of his weight. It was brief, pragmatic contact, but it made Ike's head buzz.

The boy's name was Jaime. He lived in a small two-bedroom rental near town with his mother and his uncle's family. During the day, he worked with his mother in the same motel I'd stayed in, cleaning rooms. They were in the business of invisibility: erasing all the human signs that people left, remaking things until it seemed no one had ever been there. In the late afternoon, he'd walk home. On days his mother got a ride to a second job she worked, restocking shelves at a grocery store forty miles away, he'd walk alone.

The house was too cramped for them to spend any time there, but they had the whole forest to be in. I listened, fascinated, as Ike explained how they'd walk around for hours, exploring, talking, laying down to rest in a glade. At first, conversation was difficult: they had very different families, and very different dreams, and Ike's Barry-inflected English was so unlike the language Jaime had learned from working and TV. But they started to teach each other, new words in English and in Spanish, trying to bridge the gulf. There was something Edenic about it, the way they wandered through the woods, naming the world for each other—soil, water, tree, clouds, sun, sky. So many different ways to describe the way light could look. Everything made new again, like they were the first two people. Eventually the verbs started to come, deeper nuances of grammar. I sensed without Ike saying it directly that they'd been lovers, too—that physical intimacy had been another language for him to learn, one with similar risks and rewards. There was the same fear of doing or saying anything wrong, of accidentally heightening one's aloneness while attempting to connect. But desire tended to outweigh fear, the way a touch could kiss the skin and open like a word in the mind.

Jaime hid all this from his family. They knew about Ike, had seen the boys riding around together. But Ike sensed how furtive the whole thing was—he hadn't told his father, either. It was moving to hear him tell this story, because his reasoning was so pure; his secrecy had no hint of shame. He hid it for the same reason he kept his seedlings in the greenhouse until they were strong enough to be replanted outside, for the same reason you'd shield anything newborn and delicate from the wind and the rain and the light.

As the day ended, they'd make sure to be close enough to the house that they could hear Jaime's aunt calling to him through the woods.

"Hiiiii-may," she'd call. "Hiiiii-may." And then, "Hi-*may*!"

Jaime would cradle Ike's head like a bowl, draw him close, and kiss him one last, long time.

"Tomorrow," he'd say. He'd taught Ike the Spanish version of the word, but the greater concept—that they could count on each other to be there, sure as sunrise—they'd learned from each other.

"What happened to him?" I whispered.

"I don't know," Ike said.

"You don't know?"

"No," Ike said.

"One day, I didn't see him on the road. I biked back and forth, looking all over. He wasn't anywhere. When I went to the house, it was empty."

"You never found him?"

"No."

"You never saw him again?"

"Never."

A severing, inscrutable and final. The word held so much hurt.

⌇

Our conversation slowed and petered out, but neither of us could sleep. Eventually I surrendered to comfort and asked for what I needed. I turned over and held him, my fist again in the hollow of his chest. He put his hand on my arm. I felt the slow seep of something chemical, my brain starting to relax.

It wasn't really sexual, holding Ike like that. I won't say there was no charge to it, but there was also something else. Something that wanted nothing, except to be allowed to be what it was. A togetherness that asked for nothing back. I lay there and basked in the slow, recovering feeling.

I was almost asleep when I realized what it reminded me of, lying there with Ike. I was nine or ten years old when my brother Ian had his first seizure. A violent, consuming thing to witness—an exorcism or electrocution. It happened early in the morning, everyone asleep. I woke up to my father shouting. The sudden lurch of something wrong.

In the weeks that followed, I started sleeping with Ian in his bed. Not every night, just sometimes. I didn't tell my parents, though they found out quickly—I'd forget to get up, and in the morning they'd find me there asleep with my brother. They disapproved at first, then decided it was harmless. To me, it was more. I thought I could protect him. I convinced myself my presence did something to ward off the seizures, as if they were evil spirits I alone could dispel. I'd put my hand on his chest and feel his breath rise and fall. Sometimes he put his hand over mine, his fingers often pressed into strange and evocative shapes, like I might make to cast shadow puppets on a wall. I imagined some power in me, conveyed to him through the skin.

Of course, I couldn't cure Ian. He would go on to have a second seizure, and another after that, and he still sometimes has them now. And while I believe I was a comfort to him, it strikes me I was also there to work through my own fear. Being close to Ian helped disarm my terror of uncertainty, of the pinch in my father's voice as he shouted, of sudden terror in the night. So maybe it was Ian healing me.

I pulled Ike closer, my fist against his chest, my face against his neck. I held him like he was my brother.

❧

I woke up late again, a morning that left port without me. Ike was already in the barn when I came in, stationed with Barry at the worktable. The first thing I noticed was the new frame that had started taking shape across the wood. To see them building again was a sudden, delirious jolt.

"Jane!" Barry roared, nearly knocking over his stool as he launched onto his crutches and came at me, swinging wildly across the room. "Ike told me everything! It's wonderful—it's—"

He was talking about the stack of photocopied plans, I realized, which were by then sitting in disarray on the floor by his cot, as if he'd scattered them in a mad search for something. Ike seemed to see them with fresh eyes, and ran over to neaten the stack.

"It would have taken me *months* to draw that many," he said. "And Ike says you've already passed out hundreds of them?"

He knew already, but wanted to be told again. It didn't matter that he'd inflated the number, the moment too radiant to quibble with details.

"Yes," I said. I couldn't keep my mouth from curving with pleasure, a smile I tried to rub from my face with my hand.

"It's brilliant," Barry said. "It's *won*derful. All those copies, every one of them the same."

The approval that beamed from Barry's face was the only reward I needed. But I was relieved, too. I'd half expected him to give me a lecture on the importance of abstaining from electrical tools, or even on the evils of photocopiers in particular. But he seemed to understand this was a needed compromise, and that scaling our ability to reach others—more people faster—outweighed his standard concerns.

"I think this marks a turning point for us," he said. "*Hundreds* of people now understand what's at stake here. They may not even believe what they're seeing, yet. But it doesn't matter—they have the *means*. And that's what matters. Now we only have to show them it's real. Show them how *easy* it is."

His face was close to mine.

"How many more do you think we can make?" he said. "The woman Ike mentioned. What can you talk her into?"

"I . . ." I said. I wasn't sure, but I was ready to try anything.

"As many as she'll let you," Barry said, answering his own question. "Go and make her see she has to let us do this. And then—then, when the new wings are built—we can really start. Friday! We're going on a journey. We'll leave as soon as this is done."

"Leave?" I said. Ike and I glanced at each other.

"Yes!" Barry cried. "You didn't think we'd just stay here forever, did you? Isn't there a whole world out there, just waiting for us?"

❧

When I pulled up to Grace's house, the garage door was open, and someone was moving around inside. I'd brought Barry's original blueprint along, and I took it with me as I got out, announcing myself with a knock on the side of the house. Grace and Gene looked up from the worktable. They both seemed exasperated, flushed and shiny with sweat. It was sweltering in there, the air so thick with sawdust that I thought I might sneeze.

"It's *you*," Gene said.

It was clear what they were doing. There, on the table, was the beginning of a frame, that unmistakable initial shape like a guillotine minus the blade.

"We're *building*," Grace said giddily, mopping sweat from her face with a cloth. "We thought, let's try it—why not? It's been a bit . . . well, complicated, but—"

"It's not complicated," Gene growled. "It's just *hot*."

A fan rattled uselessly in the entryway, its blades a blur.

"Look," Gene said to me. His cheek was smudged with some kind of ash. "Does this seem right to you? Are we getting there?"

I joined them at the table and looked down. I wasn't the best judge, but the frame basically looked like what I knew.

"I think you're good," I said.

Gene nodded, satisfied. He rubbed his chin, and a dark smear came away on his skin. He must have had something on his hands.

"Then, for the wings, it says we need to use *willow*. A particular species, *Salix luna*. I have no idea what that is or where to find it. Do you?"

"It grows by the river," I said. "And we have plenty back at the house."

"The house," he said, squinting at me.

I explained we had a workshop of our own, outside of town.

"Does it matter, anyway?" he said. "Can't I just use something else?"

"I'm not sure," I said. "Barry says it has to be willow."

"Barry?"

"Yeah, he—" I stopped short, trying to think how to describe him. "He's the inventor."

"Well, can I come get some when we're ready? We'll need it soon. . . ."

"Sure," I said. "But I have a favor to ask."

I held up the blueprint.

"I was wondering if I could make a few more copies."

Gene cocked his head at me, and then he sighed.

"Are you sure you want to do that?"

"Of course I'm sure," I said.

"It's just—really? You're really just going to go around giving them away for free?"

"We really are," I said.

"You don't worry that devalues it?"

I laughed.

"No," I said. "That literally *is* the value."

"What can people even do with those instructions, anyway?" he said. "I mean, I make things for a living. I've got all the tools. And this is tough, even for me. So what are most folks going to do? They can't even hang a picture."

"That's why we're going to teach them," I said. I knew he had a point, but I wasn't going to think too hard about it, because thinking might keep me from acting, and above all we needed to act. Besides, Barry had a plan and had surely thought of this. All I needed to do was ask him.

Gene wiped his cheek thoughtfully. Every time he touched his face, he made it dirtier.

"This isn't, like, a kids' craft project. This is challenging stuff."

"Hon," Grace said. "I think she just wants to use the copier."

"Fine, fine," Gene said. "Do whatever you want."

I had the copier running, the green light sweeping back and forth, when Grace came in and shut the door behind her. Her face glittered with sweat, her crow's-feet tiny diamond seams.

"I just wanted to say," she said softly, "I hope Gene didn't offend you."

"No, no," I said, "of course not." I was self-conscious about how much paper I was using, but she didn't seem to mind.

"It's just," she said, "he really does think it's foolish to give all these plans away. He thinks there's money to be made. Now, I know. I *know*. But listen."

"I'm listening," I said pleasantly, though I didn't like where she was going.

"Gene's a good man," she said. "I know it sounds selfish, when he talks like that. But it's not just about him, not just about us. You have to understand. The kind of people we deal with, the parents of our kids, they get thrown in jail because they can't pay a forty-dollar parking ticket. Or for stealing school supplies from a Walmart. These kids, they come to us hungry most of the time.

"All I'm saying is, a little money can do some good in this world," she said. "We can only spend so much on ourselves. If this is a chance to generate *real wealth*—I mean, we're good people. We give back. If this all works the way Gene thinks it can, we *will* give back."

I realized, by the tone in her voice, that she wasn't just explaining. She was asking permission.

"I won't let him do anything unless you say so," she said. "But he wants to send in a patent application. If *you're* not going to, I mean . . ."

She trailed off.

"I won't let him do anything until you say so," she said again.

I smiled at her sadly. Barry was right: The world had its way of imposing limits, of nailing things down, of walling off everything that came for free. Humans took things and exploited them to the edge of ruination, it was what they did best. We would need to move quickly, if we were going to outrace the forces of domination and inertia and simple dumb greed. Grace didn't realize it, but she was issuing a kind of challenge.

"I'll think about it," I said.

"Yes," she said. "That's all we ask, that you think about it. Here, I'll leave you in peace."

She opened the door and stepped through it, before turning back one more time.

"He's a good man," she reminded me, one last time. "If you understood him like I do, you'd know he really is."

❧

It took three trips to carry all the copies to the car. Each load high and heavy, the top tucked under my chin. As I came in and out the front door, the sounds of power tools kept exploding from the garage. Grace and Gene didn't seem to notice that I was heading out, and I didn't say goodbye.

The copies sat in five tall stacks across the backseat. I sped away with the window up so the papers wouldn't be disturbed, the trapped sun baking me pleasantly with heat. I decided to hit up a few houses on the way back, and got so lost in the rhythm of it—drive, idle, rush out to leave a blueprint on a stoop, drive off again—that I surprised myself with the familiar sight of big red barns emerging down the hill. The dairy! I was suddenly excited. Here was a target unlike the others: a place where people were likely to be, and where we still had unfinished business.

I parked and crossed the road with a few copies in my hands. The air smelled loamy and fertile, the mind-penetrating scent of dung. One of the barn doors was wide open. The idea of going inside scared and delighted me, another threshold to cross.

I'd never been inside a space like that before, an alien mix of biology and industry. Two rows of raised pens ran the whole length of the building, a kind of subdivided platform with a cow in every stall. The animals were parked with their noses to the wall, so that their udders hung near eye-level as you passed through—swollen pink sacs that bulged with veins, bigger than I ever imagined. Each cow was hooked to a sucking machine that clung like an octopus to her teats, pulling milk into pipes under the floor.

I stared in disbelief, taken aback by the science-fictional underpinnings of plain old everyday milk. I walked through slowly, fascinated, horrified, and humbled by the scale of it.

"Hello," I called out.

There was no response except the sound of shuffling hooves and the gentle crush and mash of their chewing. Tails swished everywhere, flicking flies from their mud-spattered legs. Then I realized two men were lingering by the stall, huddled together and looking at me. I waved. I was grateful to have Barry's sketches with me. They could do the talking.

"I was here yesterday," I said. "I wanted to bring you something. Look."

"Come," one of them finally said, beckoning. The other nodded, as if agreeing for me. They pointed out the back door of the barn.

"Come where?" I said, following as they started to head out.

"Yes, yes," they said. They seemed excited—there was something they genuinely wanted to show me, something I needed to know.

We walked past a dull pool of mud or liquid dung, where the smell intensified and the air turned poison, attacking the eyes. I coughed, resisting the urge to lift the neck of my T-shirt and breathe through it like a gas mask. Next to the path, a large mound rose from the earth—a huge white tarp weighed down by dozens of car tires. Loose grain spilled from the sides. Up ahead, a woman walked stiffly toward some rows of small huts, buckets hanging from each hand. One of the men shouted something, and she turned to look. She set her load down and ran to join us.

The huts, it turned out, housed calves—spotted cowlets, thin and leggy as Dalmatians. They lay there in the dust, chained by their necks. As we passed, a calf bounded out of its hut with a rattle of metal, then ran back in and was still. I hadn't known that cows could jump like that, or that dairy calves were kept in doghouses. I hadn't suspected anything like it could exist on planet earth.

The grass thinned into mud and gravel, and then I saw where we were going. Down the path, a few trailers sat behind a chain-link fence. A scuffed metal sign hung up with zip ties said NO UNAUTHORIZED VISITORS. We walked through a hole between fence posts where a gate would normally be. Some men were sitting on the steps drinking coffee, getting ready to start work. They looked at me and fell silent.

Someone from our group spoke. A volley, back and forth. One of the men brandished the plans I'd given them. The men put their coffee cups down and started to bang on the door and some windows, and other people started to come out. It surprised me, how many people lived there.

Then I saw him, rushing with the others down the plywood stairs: the man from the day before, who'd flown after Grace had. When he saw me his eyes lit up with pleasure and surprise. He started shouting to the others. An image of him flying off flashed into my brain, still and bright as a Polaroid, the memory a vicarious thrill.

There were maybe twenty of us then, my guides and a larger group of them facing us down. They started to walk between the trailers toward the back of the fenced-in area, and it was clear I was to follow. A few lawn chairs sat by an ash-caked charcoal grill, the hulking structures blocking out the light. There was a garden, too: lush rows of peppers and beans and corn, and other crops I didn't recognize, all of it green and swelling toward harvest. Then I saw what we'd come for. I recognized their color before I saw their shape, an alluring whiteness that shone up from the shadows.

I was so glad to see the wings again. It didn't matter how far I'd strayed from what I knew. Wherever they were, I was home.

We arranged ourselves in a circle around them. Someone pointed, said something. One side had been shattered, the willow splintered and torn. The man must have fallen. He tried to tell me, in a faltering mix of languages, how he'd smashed off-kilter into the ground, and at great speed. He made a nose-diving motion with his hand. I saw quickly he'd already become famous among them, the way they went silent as he spoke, though he must have told the story many times already.

I knelt down to look more closely, fingering the splintered ends.

"Can you fix it?" someone said.

I looked up. I couldn't meet everyone's gaze at once, so many different stories in their eyes: excitement, desire, amusement, caution, alarm. A lurching heave of emotion caught me off guard.

"Yes," I said, and I meant it. Finally, a promise I had no doubt I could keep.

Twenty

When I got home, I took a two-foot heap of photocopies from the backseat and carried them out toward the barn. I should have left them in the car—I'd just have to bring them back again—but I wanted to show off. To let Barry marvel at the bulk of it, his vision multiplied beyond all imagining. Abundance conveys permanence, and in the riffled white column of pages I hoped to prove that Barry's dream could never die.

Ike and Barry were at the table, working on the newest set of wings. Ike was still wearing my Pixies shirt, and I found myself briefly startled to see him look so disarmingly normal. I walked toward them, the papery load straining my hands.

"You did it, didn't you?" Barry said eagerly. "You were gone so long!"

I thumped the pages down on the table.

"There's ten times this amount in the backseat of my car," I said, beaming. "More than enough for everyone in Lack."

"Would you *look* at them!" Barry crowed. "Look at them, Ike!"

He grew quiet for a second.

"Jane," he said. "You don't know what a *comfort* it is to me. To have these."

"But that's not all," I said.

I told them how I'd started to distribute copies, dozens of them, and ended up back at the dairy where Ike and I had been the day before. I explained how I'd gone inside to hand out the plans.

"And?" Barry said. His eyes seemed to grow brighter and brighter as I spoke, as if my words nourished their light.

"There was a surprise," I said. "Come on, and I'll show you."

Too giddy to wait any more, I grabbed Ike's hand and pulled him out into the sunshine, racing toward the road. Barry swung after us on his crutches, shouting for us to wait up. We could see the Saab parked there as we ran around the side of the house, shadowed by the toothed, unmistakable shape of a wing.

Ike slowed to a trot and stopped, a dazed smile on his face. I could see his mind fitting the pieces together, his recognition that the broken wings were ours.

"So," he said, delighted, "he came *back*."

❧

Fixing the wings turned out to be easy. The frame itself was intact, unharmed; we only needed to tear the torn, fluttering cloth away from the broken wing and replace the willow canes along that side. Barry directed us, occasionally making a correction or adjustment. But mostly we worked in a frenzy of silent coordination, the way ants work, as if our thoughts beamed around the room in little bolts, messages sent and caught by antennae.

I couldn't wait to get back to the dairy. I was still raw from the encounter, my thoughts returning again and again to the scene by the trailers. So many people crammed together in a few rusted-out double-wides, two hundred feet from the stink of the barns. Life separated from work by only the flimsiest barrier. And though they weren't captives, not exactly, it was not an existence you would choose unless your options were so limited. Circumstances drove you there, a destination reached through a sequence of small rational decisions, of cascading least-bad-things, each one eroding slightly one's power to reject what one would otherwise refuse.

I hated it, the idea of anyone being that vulnerable. But flight was the great dissent. When the wings clapped, a thundering *no*, the forces that bound us finally fell away. Flight was the only thing strong enough to keep humanity from going where it was headed—to a fate shared more and more with the poor cows I'd seen in the barn, hooked up to the machines that ceaselessly ruled them, their bodies reduced to mere fuel.

It was glorious to repair everything so quickly. The cloth was discolored where it was old, and bright where it was new, the look of a patched garment. And then we were finished, and Ike and I were carrying the wings out to the Saab again, and it was only late afternoon.

❦

We brought the wings back to the dairy. I'd already described the inside of the place to him, but I could tell the sight stunned him anyway—the number of animals, their smell, the sheer volume of machinery, the long rows of muck-clotted hooves.

"There," I said, pointing. Thirty feet down the corridor, someone knelt in galoshes on the raised platform, decoupling a cow's udder from the sucking hoses. The man looked our way, and his eyes went wide with recognition. His boots slapped against the floor, and then he was reeling down the stairs.

He skidded to a stop before us, close enough to touch, and lifted a finger to his lips to insist on silence. Then he said something in hushed Spanish, and Ike spoke back in a whisper—his cadence more halting than I'd remembered, but enough for an understanding to pass between them.

"He says the *owner* is here," Ike whispered. "He says to

leave right now, and only come back when the truck out front drives away."

So then we were running, out into the sunlight and across the road. I hadn't noticed the red Ford pickup stationed there in the dirt, hulking and washed to a shine, mud flaps dangling over its tires. We drove down the road and pulled the car under some trees.

"Wow," Ike said, still short of breath from running. "He really wanted us out!"

"We're not supposed to be there," I said.

We were quiet a little while, waiting.

"What do you think would happen," Ike said, "if the owner saw us, whoever he is?"

"He'd probably make us leave," I said.

"But we could show him the wings," Ike said. "Maybe he'd—"

"No, Ike," I said, shaking my head.

His innocence pained me.

"Why not?"

As I grasped for an answer, I saw he had a point. Maybe we did have a responsibility to the owner, too. And maybe the wings would bring out the best in him, as they did in us. But I doubted it. The strangers we'd encountered had already been so resistant, so defensive, even when they had nothing to lose and everything to gain by talking to us. I couldn't imagine the man who owned the dairy would want us approaching his workers—the people who ran his operation for him, who financed his expensive truck—with the promise of something new.

"Some people don't *want* anything to change, Ike," I said. "Why would they? Why would this guy, when his staff does all the work, while he collects the checks?"

"The . . . checks?" Ike said, confused.

"The money," I said. "He keeps all the *money*. He *likes* the way things are."

Ike shifted in his seat, thinking it over.

"But maybe," he said, "if we just *talked* to him. Do you think? If we just talked to him, do you think he'd understand?"

❧

It wasn't long before the truck pulled away. It veered way out over the dotted yellow line before correcting back into the proper lane, racing off in the other direction. We waited a few minutes to be sure.

"Let's go," I said.

By then, word had clearly spread. A small group met us near the door, led by the man we'd seen. I saw a few others running toward us through the barn. We led them across the road, where the wings waited for us on the Saab's roof, their striking outline filled with sun. No one said anything, the scene as silent as a photo on a postcard—the sky a lucid blue, the clouds pulled wool.

People gathered around the car, touching the wings, examining their craft, murmuring to each other. Ike was talking with them, and the fact that I couldn't understand added to the dream-like feel. A few last stragglers rushed across the road to join us. I gathered that the man who'd flown already was volunteering to demonstrate. The others seemed cautious, electrified, still unsure what they were about to see.

As I helped Ike dress the man, I noticed his skin had puckered into little goose bumps. He trembled, all his systems firing, almost feverish with expectation. He shook like he was cold.

We helped him onto the roof of the car. When he jumped, the wings beat once, a ripple like thunder, and he was rising. This collective suck of breath, an accordion wheeze. Then came a spectacular chaos: voices ringing out, some shouting, some pointing at what we all saw, or crying out as if to beg everyone to look harder, someone groaning as if sick, someone's sharp, alarmed staccato, someone laughing, someone praying, a mindblowing explosion of sound.

A man had fallen to his knees, his eyes upturned to watch the shrinking dark form that played against the blue, almost far away enough by then to be mistaken for a bird. He saw me notice him and smiled back tearfully.

"Un milagro," he said, nodding. For me, the word registered strangely, a mix of *mill* and *crow*, and yet I somehow grasped the implication: a miracle, a marvel. Someone was running down the road, shouting. I heard Ike's voice in the mix, trying to explain. I could hardly think from the rush of it. *This is real*, I reminded myself. *This is real.*

∿

Their faces run together now. I didn't know most of their names. What I remember most are their arms: arms that were smooth or ruddy, arms that burst with coarse hair, arms adorned with faded tattoos, arms that had wrinkled subtly with age, like the skin that forms on the cooling surface of a bisque. Flight belonged to them; we let them have it. Ten flights, fifteen, more. And when they flew too far, we chased them down in the car—the backseat crammed and the passenger doors open, folks riding along on the outside of the car, hanging on to the roof rack. It was reckless, giddy stuff, no one wanting to miss a single second, our lives changing with every passing breath.

I'd been demoted to chauffeur and getaway driver. It was Ike who spoke to them, who marshaled them, who translated and filled me in. It was wonderful to see him so at ease, smiling and laughing and whooping with everyone, a role he'd rehearsed for all his life. We stopped only when night fell, and though some of them begged Ike to keep going, he wouldn't relent.

"Mañana," he kept promising them, his cheeks flushed from laughing.

We dropped everyone off at the entrance to the dairy, and watched them go, hurrying down the hill in a group. Their voices rang out over the asphalt, a buoyant mix that faded slowly as the distance grew. We waited for a minute, sorry to see it end, the planet's very turning finally able to dissuade us.

Ike and I drove home in silence. Talking seemed beside the point, an insult to the stunned, exhilarated quiet. The wings were tied to the roof overhead. I felt their presence in the bones of my foot, a stubbornness in the gas pedal, their telltale drag. I went slower, I always did, because I didn't want to hurt them. Our pace had a gentle meandering rhythm, and I let my thoughts wander. Circling like a bug sucked in water toward a drain. Just a stirring first, the tug of undertow. But it grew stronger, your whole being caught up in the pull. I finally turned onto the shoulder and slowed the Saab to a stop.

"What?" Ike said.

"Please," I said. "I know it's late. But—"

"Jane," he said softly, getting ready to deny me. I felt my pulse start to race, my coursing and indignant blood.

"We'll be all right," I said.

He bit his lip, shaking his head.

"We were fine before. We flew all night, remember? Remember how we flew all night and woke up safe? How good it was? How *sore* we were," I said, smiling, shifting my tone midstream, ready to cajole him or berate him or say anything as long as it worked. "I just want to feel it again, that's all. We can light a little fire—just like we did before, we can follow the light."

Ike was quiet for a second.

"We have to go back tomorrow," he said. "Everyone'll be waiting."

"And we will go back," I said.

"Jane."

"There's enough time for everything," I said. "There's time, Ike."

"You keep saying there *isn't* enough time."

"It's getting late," I said. "There's nothing else to do."

"If we get out of this car," he said, "we don't *know* what'll happen next."

"Of course we do," I said.

"We *don't*," he said. "I can't follow you in the dark."

"But I'll come back," I promised. "I swear I will."

"You promise?" He hesitated.

"Yes," I said. "Yes."

Except he knew I didn't mean it. I couldn't mean it. We both knew things shifted when you were up there, how easily you lost your way, because nothing mattered more than your body moving through miles of empty space, the rush of it addicting and radically new. It *was* possible I could forget about Ike. About Barry. Even about the cause, our North Star, and the grand, rickety plan we were building to promote it.

"Don't," Ike finally said.

He'd refused me before. But I could see something else was happening, something more sober and permanent. Self-sacrifice would be needed, if we were really going to do this. It was a new part of the challenge we'd been tasked with: to give away what we most wanted, and lavish on others what we denied ourselves, until the thing was finished.

TWENTY-ONE

Barry was lying in bed when we came in, candles set out recklessly on the cot, pooled wax ready to tip. He was drawing. For the first time, I saw there was no practical purpose to it anymore: we already had all the plans we needed. He kept at it because that was what Barry did—he drew, to be Barry was to draw. It was a compulsion for him, a way to scratch some inner itch, and nothing we'd ever accomplish could change that.

"Barry," I said, and it broke the spell. He looked up and watched us approach.

"We met people, Dad," Ike said, unable to hold it in any longer. "They flew, so many of them. . . ."

"How many people?" Barry said. He took the news voraciously, wanting to know everything. He wasn't spending enough time outside, I thought—even in the dim light he looked pale and drawn.

"A dozen?" I said, guessing. "Maybe more. Flight after flight after flight. Barry, I—it was *incredible*. You should have seen them."

"It's *glorious*," Barry said. "Today, fifteen—tomorrow it's *fifty*. Soon it will be fifteen hundred! But Jane," he said, his voice sliding into lower register. "What will you do next?"

He grinned at me slyly, testing me. I knew the answer should be obvious, something right there in front of me, but I felt disoriented by his intensity and couldn't think what to say.

"I don't know," I said finally. "What do *you* think we should do?"

"The only thing we *can* do," Barry said. "Don't cater to them. The goal isn't to *amuse* them. Bring them back here. We have to train them, teach them. That's the only way to really *change* them."

He cleared his throat loudly and shifted, the cot springs screeching under his weight. I turned to Ike.

"Do you think they'll come?"

"Sure," he said. He looked excited, his eyes glinting back candlelight. "Sure they'll come."

"So do it," Barry said. "It's as simple as that."

♈

Barry wanted to keep drawing for a while. We decided it was better not to leave him. He insisted on keeping all the candles lit, and Ike was afraid he'd fall asleep and set the cot on fire. So we sat nearby on the floor, ready to be of service if he needed anything.

I wrapped my arms around my knees and huddled at the foot of the bed. Something about curling up like that made it easier to ignore how hungry I was. I still had so many questions, but Barry made it clear he wasn't interested: he was completely absorbed by his sketches, working at them with a quality of concentration so pure, so complete, that I felt it would be profane to interrupt.

I hunched there, listening to the insistent scratch of Barry's pencil, until he took pity on us.

"I'm going to keep at it a while longer," he said. "Why don't you finish up?"

He gestured to the new set of wings, which lay mostly assembled across the worktable.

"Let me know if you get stuck," he said. "But I'll bet you can do it."

Ike and I wandered over to the table, both of us glad for the change. I saw that all but a few of the struts had been fitted. We set to work preparing the last pieces of willow, a copy of Barry's plans laid out on the table as our guide. With the hardest stuff done already, we made satisfying progress. It surprised me, how much I enjoyed being given a simple, straightforward task. The cause felt huge and open-ended, almost debilitating in its scope. But I could follow directions. I could take things step by step.

"Look," Ike said.

Barry had fallen asleep, just like we'd feared. His head slumped forward on his chest, his glasses balanced at the end of his nose.

"Shh," Ike said, stalking quietly to the cot. One by one, he lifted the candles and blew them out.

～

"Wake up," Ike said.

I opened my eyes. It was morning, a bird's two-note song lifting in through the window. I could smell the meadow, that scent of dirt and honey.

"Here," he said. "I made you breakfast."

I sat up. Ike handed me a plate with some eggs on it. He'd made them scrambled with zucchini and dandelion leaves, which had dyed them green, like something out of Dr. Seuss.

"Eat," he said. He didn't have to tell me twice. I attacked them, though the eggs were pungent with plant flavors and—like everything Ike cooked—needed salt.

Ike sat down on the bed.

"It's early," he said. "But I think we should go as soon as possible, don't you?"

He seemed excited, this joyful energy bounding through him. He just wanted to see people, I realized, the anticipation simple and sweet. I shoveled down a few last forkfuls of breakfast.

"Let's go," I said.

We walked out to the car, where the newly fixed wings were still hitched to the roof rack, the two-tone cloth joined by a jagged seam. I started to take them down, untying the knotted rope.

"Wait," Ike said. "What are you doing?"

"We don't need them," I said.

"We don't?"

"It'll just be a distraction, having the wings around," I said. "We don't have to let them fly around all afternoon. They need to learn to build."

"But don't you think they'll *want* to?"

This stopped me.

"Well, of course they'll want to," I said. "But . . ."

I couldn't untangle my thoughts fast enough. It was true, he'd caught me: I was trying to shuffle people around the board like chess pieces, without thinking enough about what we might owe them in return. But we couldn't think too much about that, or the whole thing would slow unbearably, the ground turning to mud under our feet. That was what it meant to have a mission: it was a plan you trusted enough to implement, so that you didn't *have* to think when thinking got too hard. I told Ike that. I made him help me hide the wings in the woods.

❧

I try to imagine how we seemed to them, the group we spoke to in the barn. Two skinny kids, just shy of starving, in stained, sweated-through clothes. The boy in animal-fur slippers, whose shorts looked like they were torn from a bedsheet, grasping for sense in secondhand Spanish, pushing his black hair away each time it fell over his dark, keenly shining eyes. The girl standing there in idiot silence, a missionary's suspect smile frozen on her face. We wanted them to trust us so badly.

"They don't want to come back with us," Ike told me finally, in the same low tone.

"They don't?"

"They want us to bring the wings *here*."

"But we don't have them here."

"Well, they want us to go get them," Ike said.

"Did you tell them we can teach them?" I said. "If they'd just come with us, they could build their *own* wings. Then it wouldn't matter if we brought them or not."

"I told them," Ike said. "They don't care about that."

Another tense, hushed exchange followed, incomprehensible to me. Ike seemed to make no progress. Eventually we turned away. We left the barn in defeat, walking back up the hill toward the Saab.

"I didn't think it would be that hard," I said. "Not after yesterday—"

"Look," Ike said.

Someone was running up the hill after us, waving for us to stop.

~

Four of them came with us, in the end, squeezed into the back without seat belts on. I stole glances at them in the rearview mirror. One was older, his hair shot through with gray. Two of them were obviously brothers: they shared the same aquiline nose, the same bemused grin, and both looked younger even than me. The fourth, who seemed to be between the others in age, was the quietest, with an expression like he was forever weighing two difficult choices. It was unclear if their decision to come with us reflected some change of heart within the group, or if they were outliers, or if they'd simply decided—at the last moment, one by one—that they couldn't pass up the chance. Ike spoke back and forth with them, but didn't seem to feel the need to fill me in.

We pulled up to Barry's, and Ike and I got out. But the four of them stayed in the car, peering up in horror and fascination at the old farmhouse, dark and haunted-looking even in broad daylight. I heard a shift in the timbre of their voices: *Maybe this isn't such a good idea.*

"Come on," I told them. "It's okay."

Ike and I traded looks. It was clear they were hesitating. Then Ike was running off into the woods.

"Ike," I shouted after him. "What—"

As I listened to him crash through the branches, I realized what was happening. A huge white shape floated up between the trees.

"Ike," I said, but by then it was too late. He came out of the forest, the wings retrieved from their hiding place and hoisted over his head, this goofy grin on his face. The men saw him through the windshield, and then they came spilling out the doors. A chorus of shouts, eager and joyful. They were already arguing about who was going to go first.

"What are you *doing*, Ike?" I muttered.

"They're saying they want to do it now," he shouted to me. "They don't want to wait."

They had him surrounded.

"Can't we at least bring them to the barn first?" I said. But it sounded hollow, even to me. The men had already started to fit one of the brothers in the wings. They didn't need our help, or our permission. It was a lost cause.

"I just wanted to show them," Ike said apologetically. "I wanted them to feel at home."

"I know," I said.

"I just thought—"

"Don't worry about it," I said.

৵

I walked back through the meadow, their shouts fading behind me in the trees. In the barn, Barry still lay in his cot, surrounded by sketches, the thin blanket covered in paper. He looked up as I came in, his eyes bright half circles over the rim of his glasses.

"Jane," he said. "What's wrong?"

He must have seen it in my face.

"Where's Ike?"

"We were *this* close," I said, holding my fingers out a pinch apart, "to getting somewhere." I told him how we'd brought back a whole carload of people, but that Ike had derailed everything by getting them all riled up with the wings. He watched me, his eyes burning merrily, an amused look on his face.

"It's not funny," I said, offended.

"No," he said, though he clearly thought it was. "No, my sister. It isn't funny. But listen. You're taking it too hard. So they want to play a little. Let them. Everyone's going to have their process."

"But—" I began.

"It doesn't matter," he said. "There must be a hundred other people in the surrounding five square miles. So find some of them, and bring them back here."

"I just *did* bring people back here." I groaned. "That's what I thought I was doing."

"Then bring more," he said.

I tried to tell him that I didn't know where to start. That people at the dairy had actually flown, and even *they* were reluctant to get into the car and come with us. So much still lay ahead, the scale of it overwhelming, an entire world out there for us to change.

"Sometimes I don't know what to do," I said, starting to feel shaken.

"Jane," Barry said, "you're doing *beautifully*."

"Am I?" I said. "How do we know we're going about this right?"

"You don't need me to tell you," he said, smiling.

"What if I do?"

"My sister," he said, "you're selling yourself short."

❧

By the time I walked back to the Saab again, Ike and the others were nowhere in sight. I thought I heard voices somewhere far away, but it was hard to tell. I scanned the sky and saw nothing—just the clouds, all heavy with sunlight, almost too brilliant to look at.

I did the only thing I knew how to do: I went out driving, hitting up houses with copies of the plans, which were by then tumbling around in the trunk. It felt like scanty progress, but I hoped by going through the motions I would settle on something bigger and bolder, the kind of effort Barry seemed to think I was capable of. At least that time I saw a few people, spoke to them directly about what I was giving them, knowing how absurd it sounded. One lady held her copy dangling between her thumb and forefinger, as if it were soaked in pee. An older guy kept winking at me, grinning crookedly, as if we were merely conspirators in some ludicrous joke. I offered to take them with me and teach them how to fly, of course I did, though I knew before speaking what the answer would be. As I made my pitch, I found myself hoping that Ike or one of his friends would interrupt me, screaming above me across the sky. They never did.

I tried to drive out farther than I ever had before, to find houses and people we hadn't yet encountered. But I got turned around somehow, and found myself heading back toward Barry's on roads I knew. I was close enough to Grace's that I decided to stop. It would be good to see a familiar face.

Gene was in his workshop, stooped over his table, the garage door open to let in cooler air. I knocked on the side of the wall and went in.

"Hey," he said.

Right away I noticed his face—a nasty bruise all along one side, a contusion the gray color of liver. Burst blood vessels branched out below the skin, and his eye on that side was all red, like the eye of a cyborg.

"What happened?" I said.

"It's better than it looks," he said.

"But—"

"I fell, okay?" he said. "I jumped off the car, like Grace said I should. And I fell right on my damn face."

He put his drill down.

"Listen," he said. "I was hoping you'd come back."

He gestured down at the wings he'd made. They were finished, but they looked off somehow, like a child's model of the real thing.

"I think it's the spines," he said. "The pieces that give the wings their shape. I didn't use the willow like the instructions said. I didn't have any. I lathed the wood down, thin as I could, but I think it's just too heavy. I can't get them any thinner, but it's still too much weight."

The swollen eye made his gaze look weird, off-kilter.

"The willow," he said. "The *Salix luna*. You said you had more of it?"

～

That was how I ended up taking him back to Barry's. Grace had gone out somewhere, so he came alone, trailing me down the country lanes in his truck. He pulled up behind me at the end of the dirt road, his enormous vehicle kicking up dust and exhaust, then killed the engine. I stood in the tall plants by the front porch, waiting for him.

"*This* is the place?" Gene said, looking queasily at the house.

"That's right," I said.

"Looks abandoned," he said. "Is it safe? Do we know it's structurally sound?"

"Of course," I said. "Barry would know if it wasn't."

"Listen," Gene said. "There's no judgment here. I just want to make sure you kids are safe."

He looked at me over the top of his glasses. It was sobering, how much the house seemed to unnerve him. But his concern was also comical, since he was the one with the busted face.

"You can come stay with us anytime, if you need to," he said. "That goes for Ike, too. You understand? *Any*time. We have room—we can be ready at a moment's notice."

"Thanks," I said. "We're all right."

I decided it was better not to take him through the house. We walked around the side, out toward the meadow and the barn.

Ike and the others weren't back yet, but Barry sat up from the cot as we came in.

"And who is *this*?" he asked me hoarsely, delighted to see I'd brought him someone new.

"Barry's the one who created all this," I told Gene.

"Welcome, friend," Barry said. I felt newly sensitized to Barry's appearance—his dirty, wrinkled clothes, his pallor, the way he was lying in the cot in the middle of the afternoon. At least his splinted leg was under the blanket. The two men eyed each other—one disheveled and feral, the other clean and prim—then seemed to recognize each other by some unspoken craftspersons' code. Then Gene noticed the gliders on the ceiling.

"My god," he said, thunderstruck, as he gaped up at them. "It's incredible. . . ."

He walked slowly across the floor, glancing back and forth between the evocative winged shapes overhead and the equipment we had strewn around the barn—the loom, the Singer, the handsaws on the table. He stopped by the worktable and stared for a while at the wings that were coming into being, a hard, intentional gaze, as if he'd be grilled on his impressions later. From the cot, Barry watched him greedily. I could tell Gene was awed by the workmanship, and I swelled a little, validated in ways I didn't know I needed.

"You did all this here?" he said finally. "With just these tools?"

"Yes, of course," Barry said. The question almost seemed to bore him.

❧

Night came, and Barry and I were alone again. I'd helped Gene carry some armfuls of willow to his truck, loading up the bed with long, tapering spines; when we were done he set off absently, without really saying goodbye, his mind already elsewhere. There was still no trace of Ike or the others. I'd stayed alert for any sign of their return, but I heard no voices warbling distantly in the forest, saw no passing shadows in the sky— they were gone. It was just me and Barry, Barry and me, as darkness fell like a cloth over the world.

Barry wanted to work on the wings again, getting up from the cot with great effort to join me at the table. We had all the soft parts left to make, the ancillary rigging that added tensile strength, the harness and the long bit of rope that tied it in. I sat at the sewing machine and pedaled while Barry measured and cut strips of fabric, guiding the pieces under the needle when he was ready, his movements silent and masterful. I kept expecting to hear Ike at the door—the swish of his moccasins, the thump of his companions' boots—but no one came.

"Where do you think they went?" I said finally.

"Who?" Barry said, lost in the rhythm of our work. He leaned against a high stool for support, his crutches resting against the table's edge.

"Ike," I said. "And the others."

He shrugged.

"There's no telling," he said.

"But it's dark," I said. "They've been gone so long."

"Hmm," Barry said. We were sewing the final covering by then, the wings' white expanse slowly coming into shape. I pedaled on, my hands rising and falling as they rested on my knees.

"Only another hour and we'll be finished," Barry said.

I could feel him wanting me to nod in assent, to show some ardor for this latest milestone. But I couldn't do it. In the darkness, with everyone missing and so much unsettled, I simply couldn't do it.

"*Less* than an hour," Barry said. It was his way: always pushing, trying to outdo himself, swelling with promises and pronouncements. I felt the words coming up like vomit, rushing out before I knew what they'd be.

"And then what?" I said.

I saw him flinch, surprised.

"I mean it," I said. I stopped pedaling, and the needle's antic rhythm went slow and then still. "We'll finish building these, and then what? What will we do then?"

"Well . . ." he said, and he paused a bit too long.

"Barry," I said. I felt my voice start to break. "What should we be *doing*?"

He cocked his head at me, as if I had suddenly and unexpectedly become an object of intense interest, a butterfly alighting on the windowsill.

"Are we doing this right? Are we moving *fast* enough?"

"You're doing wonderfully, my sister," Barry said. But it sounded glib to me.

"Am I?" I said. "You can say that, but I don't know. There's so much I feel like I don't understand, Barry—"

"What don't you understand?"

"Well," I said. "How we're going to *do* this, to start with. How we're going to touch the lives of thousands—or really millions—of people. How we're going to get enough momentum going to actually change anything."

"You can see it, can't you?" Barry said. "Can't you already see it starting to happen?"

"I guess a little bit," I said. "In this one tiny corner of the world. But what about everywhere else?"

"We go there," Barry said. "We go and we bring flight *to* them. Like we've always said we would."

"But when?" I said. "When do we start?"

"We've started already," Barry said. "We bring them copies of the plans. When people are ready to fly, we let them fly. They'll seek it out, Jane. Once they understand, they will. And we'll just widen the radius, every day, and our influence will grow . . ."

"But Barry," I said, "should it really be this hard?"

"Hard?" he said. "Who ever said it would be easy?"

"We can't build pairs of wings for thousands of people," I

said. "They have to learn to do it themselves. But, look at Gene today. He has the skills, the tools. And even *he's* struggling. He didn't know where to find willow, this basic part of the design—he didn't even know what it was. What do we *do* with that? Is it really enough just leaving plans on people's doorsteps? Don't we owe them something more than that?"

Barry opened his mouth, and I waited for him to speak. Instead his face changed slowly, so gradually I didn't at first realize what was happening. His eyes squeezed shut, his face hardening into a pained grimace. He fell backward against the table, clutching at his leg.

"Barry," I said.

I lurched over to him, holding him steady so he wouldn't fall.

"What's happening?"

He rocked back and forth slowly, his face frozen in a silent scream. And then, gradually, it passed.

"I'm all right," Barry said hoarsely, trying to catch his breath.

"You don't *seem* all right," I said. "What just happened?"

"I have these bouts of pain," he said. "Now and again. It's nothing to worry about."

"Your leg?"

"Yes," he said. "The pain just . . . flares up. But, well—it's over now." He was still breathing hard.

"That looked terrible," I said. He sighed heavily through his nose, brushing his hair back with his hand.

"Please," he said. "Listen, will you? It's fine."

"So it's happened before?"

"Less and less now," he said. "Look. I'm resting. I'm recuperating. I'm doing what I'm supposed to be doing."

There was no convincing him otherwise. And in a little while, after he'd had time to collect himself, he really did seem to be his normal self again. He felt good, he said. So good that he wanted to keep working.

"We're so close," he said, his eyes bright in the candlelight.

"That scared me," I said softly.

"I'm *fine*," he said. "Come on, let's just finish up here. Before it gets any later."

I looked at him skeptically.

"I have a plan," he said. "We'll talk it all through, everything. But we can't do much without a finished pair of wings, can we? So first things first. Then we can iron out next steps in the morning. Ike will be back, I hope."

"You think he will?"

"I hope so."

"But what if he isn't?"

"Well," Barry said, "let's just wait and see."

Until then, I hadn't let myself entertain the possibility that Ike might not come back. But Barry was right: we really couldn't know what would happen, a thought that banished all hope of sleep.

I figured I might as well help him, rather than lie awake with all my questions, wondering. So I went back to my station at the sewing machine, and Barry and I started fixing up the cloth together. I watched him carefully, looking for any sign of injury or distress. But aside from the awkwardness of his splinted leg, and the way he leaned heavily against the table for support, you would never have known there had been anything wrong. Whatever had afflicted him had passed. He was a master, his whole being channeled into his craft, and it was a joy to watch him.

"There," Barry said, after some time had passed. I let the needle slow and stop. We were finished.

"Let's go outside and test them," Barry said, his voice an eager whisper.

Of course I wanted to. But something held me back.

"It's dangerous at night," I said. "What if—"

"We'll be fine," Barry said.

Ike was still out there somewhere. I couldn't stand the thought of losing Barry, too, even for a little while. The thought of staying down on the ground while he flew, just praying for him to come back, made me start to feel insane.

"Barry, please," I said.

"Oh all right," he said, grinning roguishly. "I'm tired, anyway."

Then he stopped—he must have seen something in my face.

"My sister," he said, "it's going to be all right."

"I know," I said.

"You're exhausted," he said. "I am, too."

"It's true."

"Look," he said, his voice suddenly gentle, confidential. "I know you're worried. Don't be. You want direction, fine. I'll give you all the direction you can handle. In the morning, okay? We'll map out the plan."

I felt myself flood with relief.

"Okay," I said, smiling. To know we were doing the right things—it was all I wanted.

"Tomorrow, then," Barry said. "Let's get some sleep—we're going to need it."

TWENTY-TWO

"Wake up," a voice kept saying.

I opened my eyes into the darkness. I couldn't see much, just the outline of his hair.

"Ike," I said. For a weird, unmoored moment, I thought I might be dreaming. But no—I was lying in Ike's bed, grateful to discover that he was really there. He crouched on his hands and knees, looming over me.

"We lost him," Ike said. "He didn't come down again, and we lost him."

"Lost?" I said. "Who?"

"Chava," he said. "We flew too late, I should have stopped them. It was so hard to see. . . ."

I propped myself up on an elbow.

"Where are the others?"

"They wanted to walk home. What should we do?"

"What can we do?"

Ike sat back on his heels.

"Gabi—his brother—thinks he'll come back tomorrow."

I was still half blasted with sleep, and I struggled to absorb the news.

"I'm sorry," Ike said. "I shouldn't have gone off with them like that. I just—"

"It's okay," I said. "I know why you did it."

"I let the fire out," he said.

"The fire?"

"The fire-coal. I left it too long and now it's out."

"We have my lighter."

"I know," he said. "But I'd kept that one going for so long—"

"So start again tomorrow."

With that, Ike seemed to realize how tired he was. He flopped down in stages—hip, shoulder, head—the way an old dog lies down. I lay down again, too. It was quiet for a minute, nothing but the night bugs blaring.

"We flew," Ike said, his voice an adoring whisper. "All of us. Me. One by one by one. We ran so far, chasing each other . . ."

He rolled over on his side to face me.

"Tomorrow, when Chava comes back," Ike said, "we'll try again. We'll really teach them, this time. I told them all about my dad. They *want* to build—they're ready."

He lay down again, pulling the sheet up to his chin.

"They get it now—they really do. They see how it can be."

∽

Ike fell asleep almost immediately, worn out from miles of running and countless flights. But I found I couldn't sleep— as if he'd sucked up all the melatonin in the room, leaving none for me. Something gnawed at me, low and wordless as a headache. Part of it was jealousy: that Ike, the scold, who'd held me back so many nights, who'd insisted that we all needed to stay together, had abandoned himself to flight with his friends. A reverie so long and lasting that only night could stop them. I didn't blame him for doing it. I hated that I'd been left out.

But there was something else. I lay there, trying to understand the nagging feeling, until I realized what my brain wanted to tell me. I got up, as quietly as I could, and left the room. I felt my way through the hall—a slow, blinded fumble— Barry's papers brushing at my shins.

I burst out into the meadow. The stars wheeling and vast overhead, their light as hard and tight as diamonds. Absurd how they came out every night in all that glory, while everyone slept through it. I would have watched them for a while, if I didn't have something else to do.

In the barn, Barry lay asleep in the cot, snoring unevenly. Our finished wings still right there on the table. I lifted them as quietly as I could, though it didn't really matter if I woke him. I knew without asking that Barry would approve.

I took the wings outside, their white cloth canopy blocking my view of the stars, and carried them across the meadow to the woods. The reality was that I no longer trusted Ike, at least in one small way. He'd shown me he couldn't say no—to the others, at least, though he could to me. But if he couldn't be strong, I'd be strong for him.

I walked into the woods, the dead leaf litter soft and damp on the naked soles of my feet. Low-hanging branches scraped at the wings, scratching and snapping off as I passed. I'd have to take them way out to really hide them, since Ike knew the woods so well. I stumbled on for a long time, with no clear idea of where I was headed, wondering how much deeper I should go.

❧

For once, I woke up before Ike did. I lay there and watched him breathe a little while, glad to have him back. His eyes closed, his eyelashes long and still. His mouth finally relaxed in sleep, something I rarely saw in life, thanks to his thoughtful scowl, his chewing at his lip. He was pretty scuffed up, I realized. His arms and neck scored everywhere with thin scabbed-over scratches. All that hard flying and running through the thicket. I felt a jealous throb for the escapade he'd had, while I toiled in the barn.

"Hey," I said. I put my hand on his bony chest. His eyes cracked open subtly, a glimmer in the slits.

"Hey," I said again. "Let's get going. Let's go to the gas station and buy a huge, disgusting breakfast."

I woke up craving something carb-heavy and sweet, the opposite of Ike's meager, earthy meals. But I also wanted to make a gesture, to show him we were okay. That I forgave him, even if I couldn't fully trust him.

I shook him gently with my hand until he sat up. His arms tucked feebly against his chest, his frame all twisted and sore.

"Aghh," he said.

"Come on," I said. "Work through it."

He groaned again, rubbing life into his biceps.

"I mean it," I said. "Let's go. Let's *eat*."

He smiled.

"Mmm," he said, blissing out to some junk food vision.

I helped him up. We were standing on the mattress when he stopped.

"Do you think we need to tell my dad?"

"Tell him what?"

"That I came back."

He let his palm slide slowly down his face.

"Ugh, I can't face him yet," he said. "I'm . . . embarrassed."

"Don't be," I said. "It's all right. Besides, he knew you'd come back."

"He said that?"

"Well, no," I said. "But I could tell. He knew you wouldn't really leave us."

"I wouldn't," he said, his face slack and earnest. "We got carried away, was all. But I always meant to bring everyone back."

He stood straighter then, startled by a thought.

"Chava," he said.

We hit up the gas station first. The car had turned out to be crucial to our efforts, but I was forced to admit that my stash of cash was dwindling—I could probably only afford a few more tanks of gas. What would happen when we ran out of money? I could no longer imagine a wagon-powered revolution, the cause pulled onward by a wayward horse. We had so much distance to cover.

It was another thing I'd have to ask Barry about, I thought. But I was too hungry to conserve the cash I had left—one meal wouldn't make much of a difference anyway, and I'd already promised Ike. We spent with abandon. My hands shook with anticipation, drunk on the promise of easy calories. We bought pre-made breakfast burritos, the kind you could microwave at the store yourself. Two big bags of chips, large and puffy as pillows. I wanted some chocolate Little Debbie cakes, and Ike got a cherry hand pie and a box of Lemonheads. To top it off, we poured ourselves two suicide-style fountain drinks, different-colored syrups bubbling in our cups.

The older woman was behind the register again, watching her muted TV. I decided not to tell her about flying. Ike and I had never splurged like that before, and it wasn't a good look for the cause.

The whole thing cost less than twenty-five bucks, cheaper to fill ourselves than feed the car. We sat in our seats and feasted, progressing from savory to sweet—first the thick, steaming burrito. The chips shattered between our teeth, loud in our skulls, until my senses rang with salt. Then dessert. I unwrapped a pack of Swiss Rolls, marveling at their delicate intricacy: two sleeping-bag curls of cream and cake, coated in a tender chocolate shell, all wrapped in a square of cellophane. A minor miracle of science and industry, small enough to hold in your palm. The chocolate broke gently in my mouth, the frosting a slick fluff on my tongue. It was gone in two seconds. The soda was its own tantalizing finish, almost a form of torture: there was so much of it to drink, but each swallow only made you thirstier.

By then the car was strewn with shiny plastic trash. Ike took a loud suck on his straw, swallowed, and sighed.

"I feel *sick*," he said, laughing. This was only half a lament: it delighted him, too, that we could do this to ourselves.

Ike. I wanted to tell him that I was angry, but also that I understood. That I forgave him, but he had to be more careful now. And that I needed him, that I couldn't do any of this without him, that he'd scared me more than I was ready to admit. But I didn't have the words for that, not then. So I spoke in the language of our shared deprivation, the grinding hunger of our days. It was how I showed what I wanted to tell him: one day, when all of this was done with, we would not always be wanting.

&

From there, we drove out to the dairy. I could tell Ike wanted a do-over, a chance to absolve his guilt at bungling things the day before. We agreed we'd bring folks home with us again— but this time, rather than let them fly right away, we'd teach them how to build. I didn't have a better idea, anyway. And, really, we owed them that. We'd come to them, we'd given them a taste of flight, and now we had to see it through. I also knew Ike wanted to check for Chava, to see if he'd come back yet.

I still wasn't sure what we were doing, how we would take our efforts beyond an initial handful of people. But I did believe in that, in flight's radical, world-altering potential. I believed in the feeling I'd had when those four men had crammed into my car, ready for the drive to Barry's—like a dam had burst, newness and potential flowing irreversibly through the break. And I believed in Barry. I believed in the problem-solving capacity of his astonishing mind, in his ability to find the best way forward.

~

As soon as we stepped inside the barn, I could tell something had changed. Someone saw us and word started to spread, their voices bouncing off the concrete floor, all magnified by wet, cave-like echoes. This time, when people approached, I saw need in their eyes. It was like their memories of flying had only grown stronger and more urgent with time, the way some memories do. A new energy had started to kick in. They no longer wanted to refuse us.

There were maybe ten of them, mostly men. Someone was running down the wide corridor in silhouette, sunlight slick on the floor. Cows shuffled and groaned. Everyone seemed to know that Ike was the person to talk to, and they were all talking at once. I felt thirsty and foggy-headed, my sugar rush crashing, watching helplessly as Ike fielded their questions and demands. A dazed smile on his face. One hand raised weakly in the air, a gesture like a conductor's trying to quiet an orchestra. When he glanced sideways at me, I could only look back and shrug.

Someone tugged at my sleeve.

"Please," a man said. His eyes burrowed imploringly into mine. "Take me."

"We want to take you," I told him, smiling in a way I hoped was kind. "We want everyone to come. . . ."

I felt overwhelmed, as if my very self might blow away like dust, pulverized by their collective need. I snuck a look at Ike, who was talking heatedly with Gabi, Chava's brother. The young man's eyes were wide, distressed, almost unblinking, and he emphasized certain words with his hands.

"He wants us to take the car and look for Chava," Ike told me quietly. "He wants to go find him."

"And the others?"

"They want to fly again."

"They'll come back to the house?"

"Whatever it takes."

I didn't know how to weigh these competing needs—what Gabi wanted, what everyone else wanted. I sensed our loyalty was to the crowd, to do the most good for the greatest number, in service of the larger cause.

෨

We brought as many of them as we could, seven of us in the car. Four men in back, including two from the day before—the older gentleman, and the man with the thoughtful light in his eyes—and a woman, squeezed up front between me and Ike. She sat on the center console, hunched over to keep her head from hitting the ceiling, gripping the headrests for support. Her sneaker rested against my leg, the sole treads shedding dried mud on the edge of the seat. No one spoke, silence that stemmed from a shared recognition: we all knew what was about to happen. Warm air roared in through the open windows. At first I fretted vaguely about getting pulled over, we were so blatantly over capacity. But I'd never seen a cop anywhere near Lack, and I sensed it wouldn't happen. There was no one to tell us no. I decided to stop worrying, thrilled to feel the car so filled with life.

When we pulled up, the house again seemed to spook people. Its dark shape, looming and shabby. Its many shades of disrepair, of brokenness left too long. An uneasy murmur spread among the group, but Ike and the two returning men seemed to talk them through it. We walked into the tall plants around the side of the house. In the distance, we could see the barn, a painterly red splotch set back in the green.

Barry sat up in the cot as we came in, his glasses glinting in the darkness. He set his drawings aside. He scanned us, quickly reading the scene, then started to clamber out of the cot, sweeping his crutches up with one arm.

"My friends," he said hoarsely, hobbling toward us in a thud and swish of crutches. "Welcome—welcome!"

∽

A change came over them. Something about the gliders overhead—their vivid shapes hanging out of reach, the scale and hush of the barn. They fell silent as they started to look around the room, reverent and a little daunted, whispering to each other like guests on the exhibition floor of a museum. Barry's mastery was obvious. They finally saw how serious it was.

While they were distracted, Ike asked me where the wings were, the ones we'd been working on.

"They were almost ready when I left," he said.

"Yes," Barry said. "They're finished now, more glorious than the first. As of last night!"

"I thought we agreed," I reminded them. I didn't want to say too much in front of everyone. But Ike didn't catch the hint, and I had to spell it out.

"We said we'd teach them how to build before anything else. Remember? So it wouldn't be like last time."

"I know," Ike said. "But they're *here* now."

Our guests noticed the shift in the way we were talking, and their attention swiveled away from Barry's gliders back to us. Suddenly, there was so much tension in the room—I could hear every creak of the floorboards.

"That's not what they came for," Ike said.

In my rush to convert everyone, I'd been unclear about our intentions. I could see that. They'd come expecting to fly right away, a repeat of the earlier free-for-all. Because Ike hadn't done anything to tell them otherwise, and I hadn't thought of it, they were unprepared for the long day of building I'd planned.

It hadn't been malicious, but we'd brought people back under false pretenses. Everyone's eyes were on us, then.

"Just tell them," Barry said. "Make them see they're here to *learn*."

"But the wings," Ike said. "Where are they?"

"They're gone," I said.

"Why?"

"They're just gone, is all," I said. "For now."

Ike stared back at me, a little hurt, still not ready to believe I'd deal with him so sternly.

"So there's nothing we can do?"

I shook my head. I hated to be so firm with him, but I wasn't willing to abandon everything we'd discussed. We'd already delayed the larger mission for too long.

Ike's face fell. He knew when he'd been beaten.

"But what am I going to say?"

❧

Reactions to the news varied. I saw disappointment, confusion, even anger in their expressions as Ike tried to explain. There were some negotiations, things that went over my head. Some pointing to the gliders—I think they didn't understand, at first, why they were different. In the end, he found a way to smooth things over. Our guests weren't happy about it, but all of them stayed.

We showed them how to build. I gave them each a copy of

the plans and they started on five different pairs at once, each of them with their own. Barry, Ike, and I floated between them, helping out, showing by example. Our guests were good with tools. In a few hours their basic frames were made and we were drilling holes for the struts. We showed them how to prepare the willow, bending the canes first to make them limber, while Barry roared encouragement. His voice warm and vigorous, filling the room to the rafters. Some of them had a little English, but it almost didn't matter whether they could understand him.

Time passed, the sun rising higher, and soon the barn was warm with feverish heat—but we kept going, hungry for progress. We drilled the frames one at a time, our bodies spattering the table with sweat. On a trip back from the water pump, the woman found some feathers a crow had dropped in the meadow—big glossy black quills—and lay them out on the windowsill, emblems worth displaying. It surprised me later when I noticed someone had sewn them into the fabric so they dangled from the edges of the wings. This was an adornment I never would have thought of, but I loved that subtle alteration, which I saw as testament to the creative, anticipatory buzz I think we all felt in the air—and Ike was in the center of it, conversing and decoding, giving instructions, laughing at jokes I couldn't catch but that made me smile anyway.

Barry kept trying to catch my eye, and when I looked at him he'd nod significantly, as if an understanding had passed between us. At first I just thought he was expressing his approval, his enthusiasm for what was happening. I was excited, too: the barn was by then a bustling hub, the frenetic atmosphere of a factory. I only wished there were more of us, that Barry and Ike and I could multiply ourselves, or find others like us, just as dedicated to the cause. I still didn't see how we were ever going to scale our efforts up, when what was needed was so far beyond what three people could do. But I tried to take heart in what was happening, the sudden formation of our little task force, our eight minds and sixteen hands.

Once, as we passed each other, Barry pulled me aside.

"Look at them!" he said, a low growl, for my ears only. "This is *exactly right*. And only possible because we did it, because we hid the wings like that. . . ."

It seemed so long ago that I'd carried the finished wings into the moonlit forest, a memory from a parallel life. Mostly I'd been hiding them from Ike, with his instinct to please the crowd. But Barry was right. When flight was off the table, delaying the immediate payoff, we all worked so much harder. Maybe it had been manipulative to hide them from everyone, but I was coming to peace with that. Sometimes people need to be manipulated, I thought, if only for our own good.

❧

We wouldn't finish building before the sun went down, that much was clear. By the time the light started fading, the four frames still lay out half made, still hours away from final form. We were hot, our clothes soaked through, the barn musty with a mild human stink. Most of all, we were hungry. All through the day, no one had consumed anything except the endless buckets of well water that Ike and I hauled in from the pump, placed on the floor to scoop out with camping cups. We were close enough to hear each other's stomachs guttering, a famished irritation gathering behind our eyes.

There were limits to what we could do in a day. We all had other needs the wings couldn't fulfill, no matter how much we wanted that to be the only thing.

Ike tried to get them to stay. I watched him negotiate, making earnest promises of dinner. But I think everyone sensed we couldn't really feed them. We couldn't offer much beyond a plate of wild, half-foraged scraps, barely enough for half our number, and a hard barn floor to sleep on. Whatever waited for them at the dairy would be better, surely, and not just that: for a little while longer, still, it was home.

"They want to go back," Ike told me finally, as if even he saw the logic in it.

So we loaded everyone into the car again. It would have made more sense for Ike to stay behind, freeing up a seat. But everyone seemed to assume that he'd come with us, as I did. The men crammed into the back, the woman climbing to her perch on the console, and no one seemed to question it. We no longer expected comfort.

∽

We pulled over in front of the dairy, and everyone burst out the doors, running out into the night. Some muffled talk of tomorrow—tomorrow, tomorrow. Their shoes echoing on the road. New bonds formed quickly, like they had with Diane. We hadn't known each other a few days before, confined to parallel lives. Now, suddenly, we depended on each other, promising to be there when the sun came up.

Ike and I drove home, pleased with the day's work, drained and satisfied and sore. He wanted to revisit all the little details, things I can't even remember now. I was listening—I was happy, too—but before long I found myself wandering into the woods again in my mind. I could almost feel the branches scratching at my arms, superimposed on the dark state route, the bright blur of its double line. To step into the clearing and see the wings, two great cloth pockets filling with moonlight, dark in the bones. I would reach out and touch them.

"I wanted to ask you," Ike said.

"Ask me what?" I said.

"That pair of wings we'd almost finished," he said. "Why they weren't in the barn."

It was if he'd read my mind, as if some subtle shift in mood had revealed the cast of my thought. I hesitated, I couldn't help it.

"Yeah," I said. "They weren't."

"So where are they?" he said. "They were almost done...."

I felt my pulse kick up a notch, a sudden lurch in tempo. What was I so afraid to tell him?

"I hid them," I said. "So nobody would know."

He was quiet for a second.

"Yeah," he said.

"All of it," I said. "Everything we did today. You know it would have been different, if I hadn't done that."

Ike sat up straighter. At first I thought he was shifting in his seat in anger, his affronted reaction to what I'd done. But then he leaned forward slightly, to better peer through the windshield.

"Look," he said, and at the very same time, I saw it.

There was something in the road. My headlights hit a mound where there should have been asphalt and yellow lines.

"What is it?" I said.

I slowed. At first I thought it was just trash—some garbage blown into the street. An abandoned tent or tarp. But as we got closer, the broad, serrated shape was unmistakable.

A pair of wings lay spread out across the road.

❧

"Stop," Ike said, and I hit the brakes. The tires rolled a few more times and were still. By then we were just feet away. The Saab's headlamps turned the cloth an obliterated white.

We stepped out of the car, the engine still on.

"Hello," I said.

Exhaust rose all around us in chilly columns of smoke. A warning bell chimed somewhere—I hadn't shut the door.

Someone was in the wings, I realized. The frame rose and fell subtly in the rhythm of a person's breath. Someone was in there, lying underneath.

"Hello," I said.

"Chava?" Ike said.

A low, muffled moan sounded from beneath the wings. I thought I would be sick.

"Chava," Ike said. He turned to me. "It must be him."

The wings shone wet with light. We were almost close enough to touch them.

"Hey," I said, but the flier didn't move.

"Should we lift him?"

Ike nodded. He grabbed one side of the frame, and I grabbed the other, and we heaved. We pulled the wings upright, revealing the body attached to them.

Two things happened almost at once. I saw the leg first, bright under the headlights. The femur had broken like a toothpick above the knee. It stuck out at a stomach-churning angle, bent the way no limb should be. The sneaker on the end aimed cruelly outward.

Then I saw his face, or what should have been his face. The man's forehead had been cut somewhere, and blood, fresh and still shining, blacked out his features. In the darkness, he looked like he'd been smeared with motor oil.

Ike shouted, terrified. A pair of eyes opened, bright ovals that shone out from the dark smudge of his face. He started to fight our grip, the wings slashing wildly. All three of us fell backward, staggering a few paces until we fell against the hood of the car, the metal still warm from the engine. For a second the man lay on top of us, pinning us. The wings' cloth pressed close to my face, the suffocating smell of grass.

"Stop," Ike shouted, too close to my ear. With a cry of pain or anger, the man pushed off the front bumper with his good leg. I reached for him and fell sideways into the road, landing hard on my side. It happened fast, a disorienting rush of movement: the wings snapped once, a single thunderclap, and he was lifted.

It had all taken only a few seconds. In a few more, we could no longer see him. I heard a faint creaking of wood, but that was all—a sound like coming down a staircase in an old house—but even that grew fainter, fainter. Then there was nothing overhead except darkness and a frozen spray of stars. It was almost as if he'd never been there at all.

Twenty-Three

I sat up on the pavement.

"His leg . . ." Ike said. "His face . . ."

He was still pressed against the hood of the car, sprawled out on his back. He leaned forward and offered me a hand, both of us still shaking. We ran into the road and shouted at the darkness, pleading with the night.

Come back, come back.

Our voices rang strangely against the asphalt, wobbling echoes that carried around the hills. I blasted the car horn a few times, hoping that might jar the man from his trance and bring him down. None of it did any good. We were alone.

I fell into a crouch, winded, our hearts knocking against our ribs.

"I think I'm going to throw up," I said, my tongue thick and languid in my mouth. But the throwing-up feeling just stayed there, trapped in me, a nauseating clench. I could feel the world rushing out around us in every direction, bigger than it had any right to be. It sickened me to think about: a broken body dangling under the stars, lost in all that ink.

"What should we do?" Ike kept saying, his face slack with worry. "What should we *do*?"

~

We raced down the dark roads, the car in its little half bubble of headlamp light, the whole world blacked out past ten feet.

All I could think of was to go back to the barn, confront Barry with what we'd seen. He would know what to do—he'd have to.

"Do you think it was Chava?" Ike was saying, as I bent over the wheel, trying to see through the glare.

I didn't want to think so, though it was hard to know. I tried to remember what he'd looked like, days before, when I'd first driven the four of them in my car.

"But it had to be," Ike said. "It couldn't be anyone else!"

I took a quick inventory of everyone it could have been. Diane. Grace or Gene, maybe. Chava. The person we'd just seen didn't look like any of them. His body had been different, somehow larger and more muscular. His face unfamiliar, even through the mask of blood. I wish I'd had more time to see what he'd been wearing. Had there been anyone else, someone I was forgetting? Time seemed to swim. I no longer knew.

"But it *wasn't* him," I said.

"It had to be," Ike said, his voice an anguished moan. "Who else is there?"

❧

We parked in front of Barry's and rushed back across the meadow to the barn. Candles flicked on the floor near the cot, and in their light we saw he had been sleeping. He looked pale, his face in contrast with the darkness, his forehead smeared with damp tangles of sweat-darkened hair. His hand lay on his chest, rising and falling with his lungs, and in the rhythm of his breath I heard a subtle creaking of the cot's springs.

Ike gently rocked his shoulder, massaging the bone with his thumb.

"Dad," he said. "You have to wake up."

Barry stirred, and his eyes fluttered open. His gaze wandered at first, slowly sliding into focus. With great effort, he sat up.

"What is it?" he said, looking back and forth between us. "What's wrong?"

We told him about the man, the awful angle of his leg. The way he'd pushed us off when we'd tried to help, escaping to the sky.

"Ah," Barry said, wincing. He closed his eyes, breathing deeply through his nose, and finally opened them again.

"A shame," he said. "I wish you could have helped him."

He looked up at me, his blue eyes deadened by the darkness.

"Do we know who it was?"

"Ike thinks it might have been Chava," I said, "but—"

"Chava?"

Barry had never met him, I realized. The name meant nothing to him, so I explained.

"But I don't know, Ike," I said. "It didn't look like him. He was . . . different."

"I didn't get a good look," Ike admitted. "But who else could it *be*?"

"Not what's-his-name," Barry said. "The man who came here the other day."

"Gene," I said, trying to think what he looked like. I couldn't map his badly remembered features against the suffering face we'd seen.

"No," I said, "I don't think so."

"Hmm," Barry said, his eyes narrowing thoughtfully.

"What should we do?"

He stopped, the question catching him off guard.

"Do?" he said.

"We have to do something!"

"But, my sister," he said, "what *can* we do?"

"It's just . . ." I turned to Ike, whose eyes reflected back my own alarm. Still, I knew what Barry meant. We could search all night until the sun came up and still find nothing. The man, whoever he was, had moved beyond our reach.

And yet I couldn't imagine just doing nothing. Not with the way his eyes had opened in that bloodied mask. Not with the jutting bone of his leg, its soul-jarring angle. It threatened to ruin everything, to know the sky held suffering like that.

Barry studied our faces.

"I know what's happening," he said, the triumphant note barely hidden in his voice. "You feel . . . guilty! Don't you? Is that what it's about?"

I glanced at Ike, who looked back wretchedly at me.

"Yeah," I said softly, hanging my head. "I guess I do. . . ."

I did feel guilty, and the admission ripped at me, a sensation like grass being torn from the earth. But my answer also fell flat somehow, the dissatisfying ring of something not quite true. Mostly there was the anguish of it, the pure emergency of the body. It almost didn't matter who had brought him to that brink.

"I just want to fix it," I said. Ike stood next to me wordless and sorrowful, his eyes just quivering jelly.

Barry groaned, a gentle, scolding sound.

"Ike," he said. "Jane. *Please*."

With great effort, he pushed himself up until he was sitting fully.

"Everything in this world can hurt us," he said. "Were we ever trying to change that, the fact of our soft bodies?"

He let the question hang unanswered.

"No," he said finally. "We *can't* change that. But—listen to me, now. Our enemy isn't pain. It isn't death, even. We're fighting what is worse than death, which is the degradation of *life*."

He shifted toward us in a wild echo of cot springs.

"You see that, don't you? These people have a chance to *live* now. Free, the way we're meant to be. Untethered from the forces that numb us to what we love above all—the feeling of being an animal, alive and unconstrained, on a green planet. *That* is what we have to give. And it's worth any price."

"You should have *seen* him," Ike said, his voice a trembling mess.

Barry closed his eyes, as if to summon patience. Candlelight wavered on his face. His eyes opened again, his gaze fiercely bright.

"This is a revolution, Ike," he said. "Not a *picnic*."

"But—"

"Don't," he said roughly. "Don't do this. Not when, at this very second, cars are smashing into bodies all across the world. Ruining them. Maiming them. Killing them. *Children*. But not just people. The roads are an endless cemetery, murdering everything they touch. You've seen them, Ike. The bodies of deer, burst like they've been dropped from a thousand feet. What kind of culture would *accept* that? As the cost of doing business? Well, hold that up against this person's broken leg. It's *nothing* in comparison. We're pure and blameless as a baby."

He looked back and forth between us.

"We can stop it," he said, his voice straining with urgency. "That's the goal, to free ourselves from this rotten way of life."

He leaned back against the wall. The tirade left him spent. He was quiet for a minute, then turned to us and smiled.

"You saw how *joyfully* they worked today," he said. "All day. All *invigorated*. It's beautiful, isn't it? To want something so much?"

I could feel myself pulling away from him. I'd heard him say those things so many times before, and they didn't have the effect he wanted. *He didn't see it*, I told myself. *He doesn't know what it was like.*

"My sister," Barry said, as if he'd heard me. "Ike—my son!

Don't let *pain* turn you back. Pain isn't the right metric for measuring goodness against badness. What matters is life, only life, life in harmony with itself. What matters is ending the way things are now, these systems that threaten *all* life. You see that, don't you? How we won't stop? Will not, will not, though every passing day the world gets hotter? Setting the planet on fire, the whole earth choked with ash? We're killing ourselves, and not even that slowly. We don't know how to stop."

His fever was coming back, I realized. Sweat had started to glisten on his forehead, catching the candlelight like tiny webs of stars.

"We have nothing to lose," Barry said. "Not when so much has been lost already! But we have a world to gain. *That's* what matters. In the wings—in flight—we have a world to gain."

He lay down again, his voice lowering to the gruffest part of his register.

"Please," he said. "Bring me some water, will you? I just— I'm terribly thirsty. This headache. My mouth is filled with paste."

❧

Barry's cup lay on the floor, sideways and empty. When Ike took it outside to fill at the pump, I followed him, almost without thinking—my thoughts still reeling, just wanting to be led. We propped Barry up, and he downed the water in greedy swallows. He wiped his lips, eyeing us intently.

"I know who he was," he said. "Your mystery man."

He handed me the cup again, and I took it. It seemed impossible that he could know, and I had no idea what he would say.

"Listen," he said, his voice low and confiding. "It's—well, it's *wonderful*, really. It means we're doing even better than we knew."

"Better?"

"Dad," Ike said, his voice chiding and exhausted. He looked so tired, his eyes all squinty with unhappiness.

"It was no one we recognized, right?" Barry said. "Well, of course we didn't. Because it wasn't anyone we know."

"But—"

"The plans," Barry said, wagging his head sagely. "The ones you've been handing out all over. Well, they finally did some good! Someone, we don't know who . . . just followed our instructions. Without us even knowing. Don't you see? It worked!"

I couldn't believe I hadn't thought of this before. Though I could hardly admit it to myself, I'd started to write off the photocopies—doubting how useful they could be for people who lacked the tools, and the supplies, and the skill, and who still didn't understand that flight was real, here, now, and not a dream. But Barry had to be right. Even disfigured by darkness and blood, that much was clear: the face we'd seen had been a stranger's face. So someone had figured it out on their own. They'd followed Barry's instructions, and why not? That's what instructions were for.

I felt this sudden need to know who it had been. Which tenant of which overgrown house, on which god-forgotten lane? When they came home and found the strange drawings tucked under their welcome mat, or sandwiched between the screen door and the jamb, had they started building right away? Or had the plans slowly gnawed at them, sitting out on the kitchen counter, a curiosity that the mind couldn't quite parse and so returned to?

"Jane, my sister," Barry said. "Don't look so distraught. You see what this means, don't you? It worked! All that outreach, it worked exactly as we hoped it would!"

It did seem almost miraculous, viewed in a certain way.

That a stapled stack of pages could inspire someone to change their life that profoundly, empower them to build something so radical with whatever poor tools they had. But it was more than that, which was what Barry was saying: It meant we had a playbook. Because if it had happened once, it could happen again. People just aren't that unique, I thought.

The implications were huge, actually: It meant we could paper a neighborhood and know that a certain number of people would take the directions and successfully *use* them. For a fraction of the time and energy it took when we went door-to-door. It reduced the whole thing to a numbers game. The only question was how quickly we could move.

Barry seemed to sense what I was thinking, that my realization paralleled his.

"See?" he said proudly. "It's what I told you. You don't need my help, either one of you. You're doing this exactly right."

I wanted to believe what he was saying. That it wasn't our fault the man had gotten hurt so badly. That it wasn't our job to protect everyone from danger—and that, on the balance, the misery we'd prevent, and the joy we'd create, would far outweigh any suffering we'd cause. Maybe I did believe that, even. And still I sensed the end of something. That sense of shining purity I'd had was gone, replaced with something aching and delicate. The trade-offs were more complicated than Ike or I had realized. It would all be so much harder than we thought.

∽

Later, Ike and I left the barn and wandered slowly back toward the house. He was very quiet. We were still shaken, the memory of what we'd seen pulling at us both with tidal force.

"We could go back out," Ike said weakly. "We could try to find him."

But I think he saw the absurdity of that, even as he said it. We stood there for a minute in silence, looking up at the night.

"Who do you think it *was*?" he said.

I couldn't answer. There was no way to know.

Overhead, the constellations glowed at full wattage, the glittering astrological outlines of heroes and demigods. If you stared long enough, other, fainter stars started to peep out of the murk, a tapestry made from incandescent dust. There were even stars between those lesser stars, only visible if you kept still, until what at first looked like darkness revealed itself to be a thing of crystalline light, of infinite depth. The darkness really wasn't darkness after all. I tried to take heart in that.

⁓

I woke up alone, sunlight warming Ike's room. The window was open and a fly had gotten in, an insistent buzz of wings. I watched it bump stubbornly against the ceiling and tried to decide how to feel. The memory came back readily, almost cinematic in its force: how the eyes in the blood-smeared face had opened. But the terror of the night before had curdled, and what remained was grief. Ike and I had fallen asleep on opposite sides of the bed, not speaking or touching the way we often did, a new sorrow between us.

I heard a shuffle in the hallway, and suddenly Ike was there. A mound of scrambled eggs on a plate, cooked quickly and without adornment, with two forks for us. He sat next to me on the bed.

"Eat," he said. "Then we'll go."

"Go where?"

"I could hardly sleep all night," he said. "Just *worrying*. But it's still early. Maybe we can find him."

"Ike—"

"And Chava. We still don't know if he's all right."

I took a bite of eggs, gamy lumps that badly wanted salt. Their egg flavor uncomfortably strong, a repugnant whiff of the hen coop. For once, I had no interest in food, hunger rendered pointless by the clench in my gut.

"I don't know," I said. "Do you really think—"

"I don't think anything," Ike said, setting the plate down on the bed. "I just keep remembering that man. How his leg . . ."

Stress choked out his voice.

"Me, too."

I put my fork down, too, a tiny metallic clank.

"But," I said softly, "he could be anywhere by now."

"I know," Ike said. "That's what's so horrible about it."

"Do you really think we'd ever find him?"

Ike looked right at me, his eyes bleary and sorrowful.

"We have to try," he said. "Don't we? Have to try?"

❧

So we drove out. The awful thing was, it was a glorious day. The clouds hung in thick lacerated sheets, like tattered treasure maps, brilliant blue poking through the holes. The sky felt huge and generous, the trees prayerfully lifting their leaves to its light. But we saw no sign of anyone, not even after miles and miles of looking, and that made the beauty somber, a facade we couldn't trust.

"Ike . . ." I'd say from time to time. Trying to be gentle, giving him an out.

"Not yet," he'd say. "We can't give up just yet."

I wasn't sure when it would end, or how he'd know we'd finally done enough. But I drove on dutifully, scanning the sky until my eyes ached from the sun. Eventually we ran low on gas. We'd gone far enough to reach a different gas station, one I hadn't known about, where a gallon of standard fuel came eighteen cents cheaper. At first this made me wistful, knowing how much further our money could have gone. But then it occurred to me: while the gas cost less, the longer drive would have meant wasting more gas. I weighed the factors for a minute, straining toward a calculation. I didn't get anywhere. It was pointless to wonder, I decided, the kind of thing you never figured out.

~

We drove for hours, our only plan to watch the sky and cover ground. I felt tiny in comparison, dwarfed by all that blue, the earth's entire surface no match for so much three-dimensional depth. And though I truly wanted to find the broken stranger, it also scared me to think what might happen if we did. I dreaded the sight of his smashed limb, snapped like a wooden puppet's leg. We would have to help him, we'd find a way. But, confronted by the sight of all that damage, I feared I'd have no idea what to do.

The car tore through its fuel, the red needle steadily dropping. Now and then, I'd ask Ike if it made sense to keep going. He always insisted that we should. But I noticed something new in his voice each time, a slow hollowing out, as the minutes chipped away our hope.

It was afternoon by the time we got back home, haggard and empty-handed, a golden tinge to the clouds that promised dusk. We both were heavy with the failure of it, a feeling in my stomach like poured lead. Still, the time hadn't exactly been wasted. I felt a little better knowing that we'd tried, that at least we'd done everything we could.

We walked through the meadow. The tufted grass stretching upward in weedy stalks, the wildflowers busy with bees. The sight of all that—the good old earth, persisting as it should—cheered me a little. That brimming-over beauty, what justified all of it. Then Ike stopped short.

"What—" he whispered.

It took me a second to see what he saw. There, on the roof of the barn: a white winged shape punched out of the forest, backdropped by dark pines. Ike dipped his head and kicked into a run, and then I was running, too.

There were people in the yard. Maybe a dozen of them, with Barry in the middle, the eye of the storm. He was shouting something, one of his crutches hoisted in the air. On the roof, someone edged to the lip of the raised plank, the wind thumping and cracking in the cloth. I recognized faces from the dairy—the people who had come with us before, but also many others. Barry saw us coming, but our arrival barely registered: everyone was focused on the winged figure overhead, who I realized was the older man from Ike's original group. A few feathers hung from the lower tips of the wings he wore, and the dark, knife-like ornaments he'd added somehow channeled the skyward wish.

"There you are!" Barry said. "Where've you *been*?"

The older man—they called him Tato—was caught up in some kind of back-and-forth with the others on the ground, calling down from his perch on the plank. Shouting, as if something still needed to be negotiated. Then Ike joined the fray, his voice raised with the others'.

"What's happening?" I asked Barry, still out of breath. "How—"

"We've been building all morning!" Barry crowed. "Where were *you*?"

"But how did everyone get here?"

"They just *came*," he said. "I don't know *how* they came. But all day people have been showing up. We've finished so much work. Look!"

He pointed upward. Overhead, someone was flying already, a shadow opening and closing like a pair of hands. After all those hours of scanning the clouds, the sky ruthless and empty, the sight struck me with almost physical force. This knotted jolt of feeling, too tangled to sort out. My nerves worn down to the nub. The sudden urge to weep.

"But Jane," Barry said. "Where *were* you?"

"We were trying to find him," I said, and cleared my throat.

"What?" Barry said. "Find who?"

"The man," I said dismally. "From last night. The man who got hurt."

Barry's face fell.

"Oh, my sister," he said. He shuffled toward me, stopping a few paces short. "Let him go."

Their voices seemed to tilt toward a crescendo. Ike was really shouting, I realized. Then Tato jumped off the roof. The wings snapped, beating as he rose. How quickly gravity lost its hold, the body unbound from the forces that ruled us.

"Jane," Barry said, his voice raw with feeling. "Look!"

My eyes strained against the height. With an electrical surge, I realized what he meant: For the first time, two people were flying overhead, drifting together in a newly crowded sky. Two winged bodies, locked in choreography. This delicate, evolving dance, this fresh interplay of scale and distance, so different from the isolated figures we'd grown used to. Barry grimaced at me meaningfully. We were entering a new phase of our history, he seemed to say, something starting right that second.

Tato was disappearing, his form shrinking slowly. Some of our crowd drifted back toward the barn, ready to keep working, but a smaller group crossed the meadow toward the house, and beyond it the dirt road, looking up and pointing. They were following him, I realized. I couldn't tell if they were chaperoning him, or if they simply wanted to be there when he came down, so they could be the next to go. Or maybe some more basic attraction pulled them after him—maybe their eyes, like mine, were simply greedy for the sight.

By then Ike had come back to us. "I tried to tell them," he said, crestfallen. A few stragglers were taking their last looks, then heading back inside. "They wouldn't listen."

He chewed his lip, his scowl thoughtful.

"They said they *know* it's dangerous," he said, wincing. "We all do, I guess. But they're not worried. They just think—"

I could feel him appealing to me, as if I had some power he lacked.

"They didn't *see* him, Jane. They didn't see what we saw. If they'd seen it—"

"Ike," Barry said, and I sensed him summoning some oratory, one of his speeches coming on.

"Try to tell them," he said to me, his eyes bright and urgent. "Try to make them understand why all of this is worth it."

But Ike was too focused on the group of people trailing Tato's path through the air, the way they'd crossed the meadow already and had almost reached the house in their pursuit. He left us without another word, a brisk walk that broke into a run. Barry sighed, annoyed, as we watched Ike join the others. I could see him talking to them, his words too far away to hear, and then they stepped behind the house and were gone.

～

I spent the rest of the afternoon with Ike's appeal needling at me, stuck like a fishbone in my throat. But I didn't know what I could tell the people at the compound that he hadn't said already, and no one seemed to want to talk. Everyone was working, their smudged copies laid out beside them, frames taking shape on the table and on the floor. I tried to think what the previous night's incident changed, really. The more I thought about it, the less I was sure. So I let Barry do the talking, lurching between the groups of them to give pointers and make corrections. He seemed so moved by the sudden flood of people. Sometimes our eyes would meet, and his gaze was fierce with emotion, this note of something I didn't understand.

Another person flew, and another. They worked more quickly than we ever had, all those pairs of hands. Each time, I felt something slipping away—my chance to come through for Ike somehow, though I'd promised him nothing. But I didn't see what choice I had. The thing we'd built was bigger than any of us, vibrant with a momentum of its own.

Once, I decided to follow one of them. His name was Alfred. It wasn't something I knew I'd do before I did it. We were watching him, the temporary way we always did, our eyes drawn to the carefree loops and turns he made as his body got smaller, slowly absorbed into the blue. But when everyone else lost interest, filing back into the barn again, I felt this impulse to go with him. Maybe I felt responsible for him, the way Ike seemed to. The specter of injury, the nightmarish angle of a stranger's leg. But that instinct was hard to untangle from something else—this intense curiosity to know what happened each time someone finally let go. Given all that time and space, what did a person do?

I made it out to the Saab without losing track of him, somehow, and shot off down the road in a cloud of dust. I trailed him intensely, my whole being trained on his body, until my eyes ached from the strain. Sometimes I almost forgot I was trailing a flying human being in my car. It could feel more like being towed, a distant speck pulling me onward through all that ocean-blue. This made for a dangerous kind of driving. Sometimes I'd veer into the opposite lane without knowing it, looking down again in time to course-correct. A truck blew past, the warning whine of its horn.

He came down on a loping country road, the shoulders

bedded with goldenrod and Queen Anne's lace. I pulled over and got out, listening. We'd passed a few houses along the way, but no one seemed to be around.

Tiny clustered flowers perfumed the air, their smell like honey and rust. I plunged in to find him. Plants whisked at my hips, painting my jeans with pollen. As I came closer, I could hear his breath, harsh against the nattering of bugs. Grasshoppers and crickets flung themselves out of my path as I passed.

Alfred. He'd fallen on his back somehow, and lay there, slack and flat, his T-shirt so soaked through with sweat I could see his skin on the other side, the fabric sticking to his chest. He still had his baseball cap on, the fit so neat it had stayed on through all those revolutions in the air. His head crowned with flowers, gold dust in his beard. With his eyes squeezed shut like that, his breath coming in hoarse drags, you would almost think that he was sleeping. Lost in the drama of some dream.

So this is what it is, I thought. The state Ike had always been there to hold me back from. I didn't have to linger long to know he'd eventually come to his senses, rested, and fly another time. Living from one ecstatic rush to the next. The only question was how one would sustain oneself—but the earth was rich, still. And the more of us there were, the more bountiful it would be, as we abandoned the poisonous logic of commerce to rise instead like birds, to sleep like babies in the grass. This was the deeper transformation Barry had promised, the mass-scale backing away that everything depended on. It looked the way Alfred did in that moment, finally content, drunk on sky and earth.

Desire knifed through me again, fiercer than I remembered. A jolt of hunger, startling as a bee sting, gilt-edged with anger. *How dare you make me feel so much*. God, how I wanted it.

I left him there, satisfied by what I'd seen, and went back home to help. Intellectually, I didn't want to rest until I'd seen all of them through, and I hurled myself for hours at the task of building. But at a certain point, I was too hungry to keep at it. All other needs eventually fell away, subservient to the stomach.

I wandered out to the garden plot where Ike's squash grew in whirls of heart-shaped leaves. The vines were bursting, orange blossoms that dangled like wilted starfish. Zucchini, so shiny, a green that was almost black. I knelt in the dirt and ate. The raw fruit had a grassy taste, its skin squeaking against my teeth, the flesh spongy and brittle. But it was something. All I wanted was to fill myself like a bowl—everything else could wait.

I broke another squash off the vine, able to think more clearly with each bite. I should cook something for the others, I realized. They'd spent all day in the barn's stifling heat, and surely Barry hadn't given it a thought. I didn't know how to wrangle up a meal for the eight, nine, ten people who remained, the way Ike could always seem to wrest dinner from the earth. But something was better than nothing. There had been times I would have given anything for a small, hot morsel roasted over a fire.

I finished the squash and chucked its tough butt-end into the leaves. Then I heard someone coming. I froze, ashamed to be caught eating by myself. There it was: a swish of feet in the grass. I looked up, and Barry was there, pausing on his crutches at the end of the row. He looked down at me and said nothing. But before he took off toward the woods, he gave me a long, significant glance that made it clear I was to follow.

I stood and went after him, just in time to see him swing in his hobbled way toward the trees. He didn't need to look back to know I was there. Then I was at his elbow, walking beside him through the woods. He was looking for something, I could see that. It was so quiet that I could hear the breath wheeze in his nose.

I saw it, then: a splash of white through the trees. This snap of recognition. I'd almost forgotten how I'd left a pair of wings in the woods—what was it?—days before, the ones Barry and I had finished together. My heart started to race. Up ahead, sunlight gathered in the space where the trees thinned. It was shameful, almost, how paltry my hiding place had been.

The wings lay right where I'd left them: they leaned up against the edge of the clearing, their white shape bright and perfect. My mouth actually started to water. One of Ike's woodpiles sat nearby, the logs neatly arranged. In the darkness the other night, I hadn't even noticed the woodpile was there.

Barry turned around to face me, and finally spoke.

"Here we are," he said, all out of breath.

He was smiling, but he looked terrible, his appearance more alarming in full sun. Even through his beard, his cheeks were hollow pockets, sucking in against the bones of his face. His skin looked like it had been powdered with talc.

"How did you know these were here?" I said softly. I hadn't really meant to whisper.

"Ike told me," Barry said. I was reminded of the way information flowed effortlessly between them, though they barely seemed to speak. So Ike had found them easily, I realized, embarrassed by my own scheme's crudeness.

Barry paused, still winded, trying to collect his breath.

"Jane," he said finally. "My shoe's too tight. Help me with it, would you?"

I hesitated, surprised. He'd never asked for this before.

"Go ahead," he said.

With great difficulty, I helped him lean against a tree. Then I knelt and took off his moccasin. What I saw underneath was horrifying. His foot had blackened from the toes halfway down to his ankle, as if it had been dipped in ink. The rest was puffy and irritated, with scaly greenish splotches that marred the swollen flesh. The smell was foul.

"Barry—" I said.

"Shh," he said. "Now—my splint. Take it off."

"But—"

"Jane, my sister," he said. "The splint."

Tears wet my eyes, a sting like cutting onions. I thought back to the night he'd fallen, how I'd gritted my teeth and set the bone. He told me that I'd saved him.

I loosened the knots that tied the splint to his leg, and pulled it away. His thigh was horribly swollen at the break, the thick, dark clot wider than his knee. Heat radiated from him. He was sweltering with fever.

"Oh my god," I kept saying. "Oh my god—Barry."

"Listen," he said. "It's going to be all right."

"You're not even close to all right!"

"Well, *I'm* not all right," he said, grinning weakly. "But that hardly matters anymore. Here, help me."

He set off with great care, his naked leg hanging, swinging on his crutches in the direction of the wings. I watched him go, stunned.

"What are you doing?"

He reached the wings, and turned back to me.

"Come on," he said. "Help me into these."

"But—why?"

"Why else? To fly!"

"Barry," I said. "I don't understand."

"There's nothing to understand."

"I can't do that," I said.

"Of course you can!"

"Look at your leg," I said. "You need *help*. How can you talk about flying, with your leg like that?"

"Because it's what I want," he said. "I want it very much."

"Why didn't you *tell* us?" I said. I felt sick with pity and horror.

He smiled sadly.

"My sister," he said. "I hate to say this. I hate it, because you tried so hard. But, Jane. It's over for me." He drew a finger gently across his neck. "I'm all toxic with infection now, I can feel it. My kidneys ache. It could be compartment syndrome. I don't know. Gangrene, definitely. But it doesn't matter. I just—it hurts so much. There's no saving me. I know that."

"Don't *say* that," I said. I stood up, starting to panic. All around, the air felt thinner. "We can get you to a doctor right now. My car is right outside the house—"

"Jane," he said. "Enough."

"I'm going to find Ike," I said.

"No—!" he said. "Don't do that."

"Barry—"

"Don't let him see me like this," he said. "It won't do any good."

"He would never let you do this to yourself."

"He won't be thinking clearly."

"We're getting you to a hospital," I said. "And that's it."

"It won't make any difference," he said sharply. "Do you hear what I'm saying? I'm through! It's too late. All we can do now—"

He hung his head, and I heard a strange, muffled noise. He was crying, I realized, though I couldn't see his face. He wiped his eyes with the heel of his hand. It was so quiet—every movement of his body, each rustle of his clothes, registered above the faint, slithering hush of the woods.

He dropped his glasses onto his chest and looked up at me, his cheeks wet, his eyes shrunken from crying. Grief had distorted his features so much that I briefly hoped it might all be a horrible dream, my mind glitching as it tried to summon Barry's face. But no, it was actually happening—reality was sliding off the table, toward darkness, everything in free fall.

"I just want you to help me," Barry pleaded. "Help me end it on my terms, that's all. The way you would for anyone else."

"But—"

"Jane," he said. "You're the only one who will do this for me."

"I won't abandon you like this," I said.

"There's no one else I can ask."

"I can't."

"It's too late," he said. "I'm done, Jane. Don't haul me into a hospital! I don't want to die in a windowless room somewhere—a cot behind a curtain. I want to be out *here*. Up there. Knowing that we did it. I just want to fly a little longer, while I still can."

"I can't."

"Sister," he said. "You'll be amazed what you can do."

He cleared his throat.

"You'll help me," he said. "Won't you?"

I could already feel the ground shifting subtly, the world-warping might of his gaze. I looked away.

"Please?"

The plaintive note in his voice forced me to turn back to him. His body was ruined, his face twisted with pain. But his eyes were bright as ever.

"I am only asking you to give me what I want," he said.

The wind picked up, a stirring in the leaves. The sense of a parachute opening.

"I'm begging you," he said. "It hurts so much."

I bit my lip so hard it hurt.

"All right," I said. "I'll do it."

❧

He balanced on his crutches while I helped him into the harness. His bad leg was terrible to look at, like something unburied from a swamp, and I had to turn my head while he slotted his feet one at a time into the holes. I pulled the harness up against his hips. His leg hurt too much without the splint, so he had me tie it onto him again, a process that left him agonized and gasping. Somehow, we got through it.

He gripped the hand supports while I fastened his wrists. The last step was to tie his feet to the frame so that they wouldn't hang free during flight, using the special knot he could pull from above to loosen. Everything in me rebelled against the idea of tying his distended, blackened ankle to the wood, securing it with rope. But I pushed down the pity that was swelling in me, and I did it.

I stood, and we were face-to-face.

"Here we are, Jane," he said.

I couldn't help it. I was crying openly by then.

"It's going to be all right, my sister," he said. "We're just people. That's all."

It started to dawn on me how final this was, that we were really saying goodbye. I started to feel cold, an electric tingle in my arms.

"What are we going to *do*?"

"Do?"

"What do we do next? Where do we go from here? How will we know . . ."

My voice trailed off.

"That," Barry said, "is what you'll have to figure out."

"But—"

"I trust you," Barry said. "Look what you've done already! It's *wonderful*. You'll manage beautifully."

"It's fifteen people," I said. "Maybe twenty. Twenty people in one tiny remote county. We have so much more to do."

"That's true," he said.

"But don't we need a *plan*? Don't you have one? You were going to tell us. . . ."

"Everything I know," he said, "I've shared with you already."

The admission crushed me. Laid me flat. There was no playbook. It was really only up to us.

"Tell me," I said. I wanted to grab him by the shoulders, shake some kind of wisdom from him. "Just tell me what to do."

His eyes flashed, two indignant jewels.

"I gave my life to this, damn it," he said. "What am I supposed to do? Everything?"

It hurt so much to hear him say that. I couldn't believe his vision could be so vast, but his imagination—when it came down to it—could be so narrow. I'd always believed that Barry would lead us into the remade world we wanted. I couldn't find the way there on my own.

"I'm sorry," he said, and his face softened. "The pain gets bad. All I mean is, it's your turn now. Not mine. How could I tell you how to be? It's your time."

"We can't do this without you."

"Jane," Barry said. "Look at all those people in the barn. *You* did that. Not me. You'll figure it out. You're very good at that."

He smiled.

"Besides," he said, a hint of wry pleasure in his voice, "the wings have a momentum of their own. Now, listen—we don't have much time."

He straightened, the wings snapping to attention behind him, the giant frame all alert to his movements.

"There is one last thing," he said, emotion ripping into his voice. "Tell Ike. Tell Ike I love him, that I've always loved him. My boy. He has to know that, or . . . well."

He started to recover, but I was losing it.

"I know you can make him see that."

"I'll go get him," I pleaded. "You can tell him yourself right now."

"No," Barry said, and I sensed that it was final. "Don't do that. He'll never let me go."

He looked up at the sky once, then back at me.

"You'll have to throw me," he said. "I'm going to lean into you, and when I do, grab me by the armpits and toss me as high as you can."

He'd need to launch himself upward—already there was something I'd forgotten.

"I can't," I said. I couldn't believe how much was happening, and how fast.

"Jane," he said.

"But I'm not strong enough. I'll hurt you."

"You can do it," he said. "You will, because you have to."

He shifted onto a squat pile of logs, balancing on one foot. I knelt down halfway, ready to throw him upward with my hands. His arms spread wide. I sensed his muscles tensing for the jump.

"Wait," I said.

He looked down at me. His eyes twinkled, cut from summer blue.

"Don't you want your glasses?"

"I don't need them," he said. "Not anymore."

So I lifted them from him, and laid them down in the pine needles.

"Are you ready?"

"I think so."

It happened faster than I expected. He fell toward me, the wings' huge bulk shifting with him. I pushed up against his chest and lifted with all my strength, shouting as I thrust upward from my legs. A cry of joy and pain burst from his mouth, and with a rush of air, he was rising.

Up, up, he went, looping in concentric circles, the floating path of a leaf as it spirals down from a tree, but the opposite way. I felt my brain go funny—as though the top of the world were the bottom of it, and rather than flying he was sinking deeper and deeper. I watched him go as if from a great height.

How quickly the distance erased his identifying details— the copper glint of his hair, the scar hidden in his beard, the brokenness of his nose and teeth, the splint on his ravaged leg, all the specific damage of his body. He rose, and soon I could no longer tell he was the man who'd changed my life. For a brief moment, he could have been anyone. Then he was gone.

TWENTY-FOUR

When I looked down again, the forest was empty, hushed, and still. The woodpile sat there mutely, the naked cords dirty and dead. There was an odd calm, like the first second of boiling water on your hand—the cold before the scald. I lingered there for a minute, my eyes raw with crying. I'd slipped into a numb reverie by then, a moment's shell-shocked peace.

I didn't move until eventually I heard something. I held my breath and listened. There: a cracked twig, the slash of a branch, the rhythmic sweep of feet in the woods.

Ike burst into the clearing. Immediately, I was glad to see him. My friend, my companion. Out of habit, I flooded with relief. We'd consoled each other for so long.

"Ike," I said gratefully, and I started to walk toward him.

"He's gone," Ike said, and the illusion fell away. The whole sequence had the logic of a dream, the way a scene can lurch on a dime from fantasy into nightmare. I wasn't ready to tell Ike anything. How had I thought—how had I ever, ever thought—I could face him?

"He's . . . gone?" I said. The cold fact of it an icy fist in my gut. He didn't seem angry, the way I'd feared. Just resigned, more tired than I'd ever seen him, his cheeks flushed from running. How could he know already?

"Tato," Ike said. "We lost him."

So then I understood. Of course, of course. We hadn't gotten to the worst part yet.

"They saw you two go back here," he said. "Where's my dad?"

"Ike," I said, and no other words would come.

"Where's my dad?" he said, his voice tensing with the first hint of alarm. "Where are the wings?"

"I'm sorry," I said, starting to panic. "He talked me into it. I don't know how—I—"

"Jane—"

I staggered forward tearfully, grabbing at him in an awkward, desperate hug, but he fended me off.

"Where's my dad?"

I couldn't force myself to say it. Slowly, I lifted my hand and pointed up.

Ike's face went blank with shock.

"How long ago?"

A basic, concrete question, and it stunned me into sense.

"I—I don't know," I said. "I guess it's only been a few minutes."

"A few *minutes*?"

He lifted his gaze toward the tree-lined circle of sky overhead, a pane of pure, unbroken blue. For a half second, all was quiet. Then he turned and ran, without waiting for me, looking up frantically through the gaps in the trees.

I rushed after him, sprinting toward the meadow to get a clearer view. Ike's presence had knocked me back on track, righting what had gone badly askew. We wouldn't let Barry fly off without us, we just wouldn't. We'd bring him down again, and when we did, we'd find some way to get him care—and then he'd get better and be our leader as before, our guide and beacon as we unmade the world.

I started to feel relieved. Nothing had happened we couldn't undo. It was like Barry always said: you always had more power than you thought.

We ran out into the grass and scanned the sky. I didn't see

anything at first, just clouds sliding over a vast sheet of blue. I was frantic for a glimpse of him, staring upward, refusing to believe he really could be gone.

"There," Ike said, pointing, as if to grant my wish.

He was right: in the distance, way out over the dirt road, wings beat darkly against the air. I didn't see how he could have flown so far already, but the shape was unmistakable.

We raced toward the house, rushing past it toward the old dirt lane. Ike outpaced me, and by the time I reached the road he had already hopped on his bike and was pedaling madly down the lane, his ragged clothes fluttering with speed.

～

I'd never catch him running on foot, so I took the car. That would give us a better shot anyway, I figured, the Saab faster and more ruthless in its motion. Ike was still biking full-tilt down the road by the time I reached him, his chin tilted upward, his hair blown back.

"Get in," I shouted through the open window, my voice blown to bits in the wind.

He looked over at me, saw the car rolling next to him, and kept pedaling as the realization sunk in: he had no choice. We slowed and threw his bike in the back, driving off with the trunk still open, the bike's back half resting on the stacks of plans we had in the back. So it would ruin some of them. Xeroxes we could replace. Barry, we couldn't.

Ike collapsed into the passenger seat, so shiny with sweat he looked like he was melting. He took a minute to collect himself, then sat forward to look up through the windshield, his palms leaving wet prints on the dash.

"There," he said. "A little closer, and we'll be right under him."

I held steady on the gas, looking up when I could for a glimpse of Barry's shadow in the sky. The shame of what I'd done still felt raw, but I channeled it into driving, speed burning away the guilt like fuel. The chase was all that mattered, the only way to take back what had happened in the woods, the dire mistake I'd made, the anguish in Ike's face.

As we got closer, it started to seem less and less like Barry could escape us. The path of his flight became haphazard, contradictory, drunken: he'd struggle higher, higher, as if to taste the sky, then fall in a long, swooning dive toward the earth while his straining muscles rested. Each time, he pulled out of the drop at the last second, until he finally didn't.

"He's down," Ike said.

We pulled onto the shoulder, along the edge of an old cornfield. It was summer, everything lush and green, but the stalks were beige and dead. Someone had let them grow in a bygone year, then decided for some reason that the crop was not worth harvesting. Barry had gone down somewhere in that sea of spear-length stalks, each one taller than us both, and we were going to find him.

The corn was dry, and it made a terrible clatter as we pushed through it. The leaves were brittle and sharp, scoring our arms with scratches. Insects buzzed and trilled. It was hard to know where you were going—we could only run madly, blindly, a strategy based on hope and sweat more than any kind of sense.

"There," Ike shouted finally.

He pointed—a splash of white, shining through the forest of spears.

We came to where the wings lay suspended on an angle, lifted by dense, dead rods of corn.

"Dad," Ike said, the threat of a sob in his voice.

The wings didn't move, and neither did the body inside. We felt along the outer ridge of the frame, pushing the stalks away, trying to reach him. Then we saw something so strange that my eyes rejected it at first. Where Barry's head should have been, there was instead a mass of dark hair.

Ike and I lifted the wings, pushing at the shoulders. It took a second to sink in: The man in the wings, he wasn't Barry. We'd followed someone else. I recognized him, someone from our group. He must have flown earlier that day. His face hung off his skull like a mask—his cheeks slack with exhaustion, his jaw hanging open, every muscle spent and sliding toward the earth. Breath scraped back and forth through his lungs in a loud, unguarded way.

I turned to Ike, feeling sick.

"But . . ." he said.

He shook his head, as if to ward it all away.

"No," he said. "No, no, no."

I watched him scan the sky again, but it was empty. When he looked down at me again, his eyes were wide with panic.

"What are we going to *do*?"

His voice plaintive and musical, the last syllable rising to a howl.

"We can go back," I stammered, trying to sound stronger than I felt. "It's not too late. We can still find him."

But the words rang hollow, even to me. We both knew the sky could resist all our searching, a merciless expanse just made for getting lost in.

"Why did you let him *do* that?" His voice pitiful, lacerating. "*Why?* Why did you let him go?"

He was begging me, as if the answer actually mattered. Like I could still say something to make it better, as if he still had faith in that.

〜

By that point, we needed every second. If we were going to have the faintest prayer of finding Barry, we had to go back right then. But there was also the man we found, and Ike refused to leave him. We spent many long minutes lugging him through the corn, hope slipping away with the time as it passed.

Eventually we reached the car. The man had started to stir. He groaned, though I couldn't catch the words, which might not have been words at all. Ike said something to him in Spanish, his voice low and reassuring. I opened the door and we managed to lift him in, dumping him onto the backseat. Ike ran around the other side and started to drag him by the shoulders, his body limp as a sack of laundry.

Without fully realizing what I was doing, I ran back into the corn. We had to bring them back, too, I thought. The wings too precious to leave behind. I figured I had maybe sixty seconds. If I could get back fast enough, the extra time would still be justified. I ran as hard as I could, pushing my body to its limits, fighting desperately through the corn. It was the urgency the moment demanded, even if we were already too late.

〜

We made it all the way home without any sign of Barry. Our one brief flutter of hope—*There, there*, Ike shouted—had turned out to be nothing, the specter of a passing plane. Then came the moment I'd been dreading: when we reached the end of the dirt lane, nowhere left to search, and I was forced to shut the engine off.

Ike burst out of the car, glad to be free again, and ran for a few paces, looking up. He still couldn't tear himself away, animated by the last dregs of hope. But the sky was an empty blue channel, placid between two rows of silent trees. I went after him, with the man we'd found still lying half-conscious in the backseat, our car doors both left open.

Ike stood motionless in the road. Still as a picture, with his back to me. Light and darkness, a study in contrast—the back of the black Pixies shirt, with its list of cities and dates, the off-white rags of his shorts. His rabbit slippers, the worn gray fur crosshatched with white. His hair a rich and tangled blackness. His skin the color of spun flax.

"Ike," I said. "I'm sorry."

The words felt puny, just painfully small, a handful of pebbles tossed down a gorge.

"He was sick," I said. "His leg almost decaying already. Had you seen it? I hadn't until today, it was horrible. . . ."

I just wanted him to turn around, so I could tell him face-to-face.

"He was *dying*, Ike. He wanted to leave on his own terms. But he loved you so much, he wanted me to let you know that. He made me promise to tell you how much he loved you."

Nothing.

"Still, I don't know why I listened to him, I—"

Something in me collapsed, this rush of shame and horror that threatened to suck out all my breath.

"I'm so sorry."

For an awful, drawn-out moment, Ike didn't speak. Then he turned to face me. There was a blank look in his face, the slackness of uncomprehending grief.

"It's over," he said, his voice raw with disbelief. "All of it, finally. It really is, now. It's *over*."

"Nothing's over," I said pathetically. "It's not, Ike."

I wasn't disputing what he was saying, really, as much as the tone in his voice: the hollowed-out sound of it, all emptied of hope. I knew as well as he did that something had ended.

"No," he said. "No—it's over."

Confusion startled his face, a new sorrow hitting.

"How will I ever find them?"

"I—"

A bird twittered across the lane, splashing him quickly with its shadow. You could hear birdcalls echoing everywhere, all spooky and disembodied.

"I'm nothing to them without him," he bleated. "Nothing, nothing."

I had no idea who he meant by *them*, I realized. I'd assumed he meant Barry and the others who had flown off on our watch, Chava, and Tato, and Diane, and all the others who'd left us. But it was clear he was talking about something else.

"I don't understand," I said, as gently as I could. Sorrow had reduced him to some basic, combustible state, and I sensed that all my words were flammable, dangerous as lit matches.

"I was going to make him take me to New York," he said. "One of these days. To see the family. To *meet* everyone."

I'd forgotten about the plan he'd had. New York, the relatives he pined for there: all that had slipped away with our first flights, no room for anything in my mind except the cause.

"If—he'd been so close to giving up. He *would've*, if all this hadn't happened. He would've. We could've left this place."

He hugged himself, suddenly cold.

"I'll never find them," he said. "They don't—"

Our eyes met, a pleading darkness in his gaze.

"I don't know who they are!"

I wanted to run. I wanted to die. What I'd done was unforgivable, a betrayal that left him orphaned twice.

We stared at each other, frozen. Then he stumbled forward and grabbed me, so suddenly I gasped. His arms crushed my ribs with alarming pressure. For a second I thought he was really trying to hurt me, and I would have let him. I would have let him do anything. But then I heard him crying softly, near my jaw. His fists bunched in my shirt.

"I don't have anywhere to go," he was saying, a strain in his voice like he was lifting something heavy. "I don't have—"

He held me tighter.

"—anything."

I held him back. I felt his tears spill warm against my neck. When we finally looked at each other, he seemed so different—the face I loved all hard and rearranged. His pupils seemed to have swallowed the rest of his eyes. Two black pools, reflecting back some interior darkness so dense that no light could escape.

"I want to fly again," he said.

It was the last thing I expected him to say.

"Right now?" I said, my voice the meekest thing.

He nodded, his dark eyes glassy with want.

"But—"

I still felt the lure of the moment, the urgency of Barry having gone missing, the call of everything we'd left undone. But desire was its own current, too, the pull of blackish water.

"Please," Ike said. "Please, it's the only thing I want."

I'd hung from the cliff face of self-control for so long already. I could feel my fingers slipping.

"Please," he said again.

What would I become without Ike to hold me back?

I was shaking as we walked back to the car, the wings bouncing subtly in the roof rack, registering every tiny shift and gust of breeze. We started to untie them. By then the man in the back was starting to revive. He'd gotten his door open somehow, so he could sprawl more comfortably across the seats, his chin in the air, his face upside down. Too tired to talk, he grinned at me. A blood-drunk, satiated smile.

We pulled the man out, laying him on the ground as gently

as we could. I hated to abandon him like that. But as I turned back toward the car, this rushing sensation swept away the shame I felt, the little twist of guilt. So much was happening so fast. Our hands, untying the wings from the roof. Ike pulling the harness up around his hips, his motions all jerky, made awkward by desire. I knew we should delay, that I should force us to wait, find some way to hunker down and let the storm of our emotions pass. But he needed it so badly, his grief as deep as thirst. He wanted to be free from everything awhile, that was all. At the very least, I told myself, I owed him that.

TWENTY-FIVE

Something happened while you were up there. Like sliding through the ocean—eyes closed, lungs clenched, beating blindly against the surf. Then bursting up again to gasp for breath at a weird angle to the shore, with no idea where you'd left your towel.

This was like that. You might close your eyes a minute, surrender to the wind, and then look down to see you'd flown farther than you knew. Nothing below but a strange clutch of houses and the snake of an unknown road. Sometimes I forgot about Ike entirely, trusting he would always find me. Or maybe I lost the part of me that needed to be found. Whatever it was, I abandoned myself to the rush of it. The air slithered around me like cool sheets.

I want to write exactly what it felt like. But the truth is, I don't remember. Certain details come to mind: how I blinked away the tears as they leaked down my face, or how my features sometimes hardened as I fell, an openmouthed rictus of awe. My breath seemed like one long unending inhale, a way to suck at the whole sky with my lungs. The experience can't be paraphrased. It's the kind of memory that only comes back by doing, so you live it again and again and again.

That's what we did.

❧

That first time, I drove off with Ike's bike still in the back, its handlebars lolling out of the open trunk like the antlers of a wounded thing. Then I chased him to the ends of the earth.

I drove beneath him, hardly daring to blink, because if I did I might lose him, and I couldn't bear the idea of losing him, not with Barry gone.

He came down again, far away from anywhere we knew. Sweat poured down my face—I'd had to leave the car and hop a fence to keep up, running below on foot. I found him crying softly in the clover. I lay with him awhile, his tears mixing with my sweat mixing with his sweat, then started to unbind him from the wings. When he could finally sit, he seemed a little better.

I wanted to be better, too.

Then my arms were sliding against the cloth again, as Ike tied my wrists, tied the lace down against the notches of my spine. I loved the way the wings enlarged me, became me, as the smallest movement of my hands quivered in the wing-bones, a spider sending tingles down the plucked lines of its web.

A tree had crashed over at the edge of the woods, lying there craggy and dead. Ike took me by the ribs and lifted me onto it. Wings outstretched, I walked toward the thickest part, where the trunk had broken away in a wild nest of exposed roots. Little green chutes sprouted where the trunk had been. He knelt and knotted up my ankles.

I looked up, the sky patient and enveloping. It had been so long. For a second I wasn't sure I'd remember how to do it. It still seemed crazy that I could jump and be lifted, that flight was inside me and my body just knew.

I jumped anyway.

When I leapt from the tree trunk, my limbs didn't fail me, and the wings held strong. The infinite air took care of all the rest.

Yes, I felt a little guilty as the world swirled below. The trees like rows of broccoli, Ike a dwindling speck. People needed us. There was something about a cause. But it could wait a little longer. *There's time for that,* I thought.

I lifted my eyes to the sky, and as my head filled with sunlight and forgetfulness, it felt like we had all the time in the world.

Things went on that way.

Him, then me, then him, then me.

No thinking, only motion.

The day finally ended, the air a summer dark. Our day might have ended, too. You came crashing down again, the earth a hard reminder, and for a little while you were satisfied. You started to remember the things you needed to do, pieces of the larger plan. But then it was the other person's turn, and the sight of them flying woke up the want in you. Every time, like that. It felt dangerous to fly at night. But Ike and I whetted each other's appetites, and we had no simple way to stop.

We pulled a couple tree limbs from the woods and set them ablaze for torches. I still had a lighter in my pocket. That felt lucky, as if I'd smoked for years just to have a ghostly white Bic on hand when I needed it.

"Don't lose me," Ike murmured, his lips brushing my ear, as if he were trying to speak directly into my brain. I took off from the gentle slope of a hill. "Keep your eyes open," he said. "Keep looking down."

It was so hard to remember. I had to pry my eyes open in the air, an act of will that took everything I had, like bench-pressing weights with your mind. But I would do it, briefly. I'd see the flaming tree limbs wheeling slowly down below, two chasing circles of flame, before surrendering again to the night.

Sometimes I think that's all we can be to each other, really: a bit of offered light to follow through the darkness.

~

I woke up with no idea where I was.

Lying on wild ground, thick with scratchy plants. Ike lay next to me, sleeping, his hair half covering his face. His pupils flicked behind his eyelids, in the middle of some dream. Or maybe his mind was only blank, like mine had been, blackness brushed with the occasional glitter of wings.

I sat up, rubbing the old ache away from my arms and shoulders. Pain at the pivot points like the tearing loose of stitches. Our charred tree limbs scattered nearby, next to the wings. We'd come down near some power lines, huge metal towers draped with wires. I thought I remembered running through the darkness, plants whipping at my legs, as the girded structures loomed up suddenly against the moon. I called out, afraid Ike would get tangled in them on his way down. Then a warning chuff, a stir in the thicket. Elegant, departing shapes that bounded away from my voice. I'd spooked a herd of deer. I hadn't seen them, but they'd listened to me coming. Frozen and unsure what to do, until they heard me scream, and then they ran.

The power lines filled the air with sound, a taut, insistent hum. Each metal structure tall and latticed like an Eiffel Tower, a sequence that stretched to the horizon, thrumming with strength. Who had agreed to their audacious march across the landscape? Nobody had. But that was what the wings were for: to break apart old systems, the kind set in motion by no one living and yet that forced each new generation to consent.

"Ike," I said. I touched his shoulder.

He drew air in loudly through his nose. His eyelids fluttered and settled again.

I shook him gently.

"Hey," I said. "We should get going."

He lifted his head, squinting against the light, his eyes rheumy and shot. This disappointed expression on his face, as if he hated to wake and find the world still existed.

⌒

I tried to get us back on track, I really did. We carried the wings on our shoulders, lumbering in the heat toward the Saab. The asphalt had been newly poured, tiny diamonds shimmering in the tar. It amazed me. The houses were falling apart, the people sick and despairing, but that section of the road was new.

"There," Ike said, once we were driving. He tried to point, lifting his arm in a way that made him look maimed. We were both so sore. Up the hill, there was a house. So we stopped.

I walked up to the porch while Ike untied the wings and pulled them down. I already felt better. It had been so hard alone. I thrilled with knowing that together we could do it, the old sense returning. We still couldn't be stopped.

Ike leaned the wings against the car and joined me on the stoop. But no one answered. There was no car in the driveway, I realized. Almost without thinking, I tried the door. It was unlocked, so I pushed it open.

"Hello?" I called inside. "Hello?"

I looked back at Ike. Our eyes met. We were so hungry, so parched. My mouth was a pocket made of paste.

So we went in. It was an ordinary American house, on the shabby side. But the kitchen had a stocked pantry, the shelves lined with goods. My eyes nearly bugged out of my skull. While I drank at the kitchen faucet, Ike pulled the tab on a can of pork and beans. We took turns slurping it cold, like a Coke, not even bothering to find a spoon. I beat back the guilt I felt. This was food they wouldn't miss, I told myself, and it was a feast to us.

We ate an entire cylinder of Ritz crackers, gulping directly at a jug of milk to wash down the grit. In the refrigerator, we found a half-eaten sheet cake in a white box, some occasion's inscription carved out and unreadable. I pulled a knife from the drawer and cut us both a long, cool slab. It had been sitting there awhile, too much of it to finish: the cake had hardened at the edges, the frosting starting to sour. We ate it anyway, the sugar too precious to resist.

We walked out onto the porch again, stunned and heavy with food. A strange feeling warped the air, this mix of triumph and shame. The wings leaned there against the car. If we hadn't untied them, it might have been different. But now we would have to touch them, bind them to the car, deny ourselves first before we could move on. And that, I knew, was going to be too much.

It was almost like they were waiting for us.

I looked at Ike, recognized the wanting in his eyes. It was amazing what the sight woke up in us. A slant of wood and cloth against a car, and all your neurons fire. Strange how desire works. A simple thing like that, and you're lost.

∽

I'd told myself that I wanted to save the world, to tear like fire across the map and let new life grow from the scar. But maybe that wasn't true at all. Maybe all I really wanted was to be inside the flying machine, to feel my arms turn into wings again and glide awhile through the sky. I loved each part of it: the gathering corset-tightness as Ike laced up my back, the way my limbs took on new length, new strength. I loved the way wind lashed the cloth, the coiled strength of the willow. The way my gut dropped with each leap. I loved how the blood shuddered in my veins once I was flying, thick and intoxicating as wine. Speed-muffled shouts flew unbidden from my throat, discharging dead sorrows through a buzzing door in my skull.

But we always came down again. Hunger brought us down, exhaustion brought us down. I found myself wishing I could change my body, the endless way that it wants. If only I could teach myself not to need food, not to need sleep, I thought—then I could finally give myself over. I wondered if it was possible, that kind of living: to need only what the wings needed from us.

～

Days passed, nights. We learned to hide ourselves in the woods, staggering sleep-heavy through the darkness, so that no one would discover us in the daylight and interrupt our rhythm—the flow of him and me, then him, then me. We woke up in the strangest places. I remember an old abandoned house, three walls fully cobwebbed in ivy. An algae-scummed bog. We stumbled onto some old railroad tracks out in the woods, barely visible in the dirt, like proof of a forgotten civilization—a thing that would have seemed impossible if it weren't real.

Our plan, if we got separated, was to meet back wherever we'd left the car, my keys left atop one of the tires. Or, if that didn't work, back at the barn. Once, only one time, we saw another flier. A single soul in its own kingdom of sky. It wasn't a bird. You could tell in the moment the light hit the wings just right: the starfish outline of a human body dark against the cloth.

I stood there marveling at the beauty, reveling in the surprise. But when I glanced over at Ike, he looked stricken, clearly grieving, beating back the hope that it might be Barry. And maybe it was. The afternoon took on a different pallor then, a cloud sliding over the sun: the notion that the dark winging shape might be our father, our brother, our leader, forever lost to us, and we would never know.

Flight had delivered us from ourselves, from the old narratives of our lives. But that didn't mean Ike had forgiven me—I could tell he hadn't. When I heard him crying in the night, he cried alone. He didn't care if I heard him or slept through it, because he wasn't crying for me. So, while I knew that part of him still hurt—wounded, gaping, sore—it was something he no longer let me access.

Mostly, though, he was quiet. His moments of acute suffering got rarer, leaving just the dull, pained glint in his eyes. That expression was always there, as it was when we stood on the hillside and watched the distant flier soar way beyond our reach. A look about him that suggested nothing mattered. Nothing mattered anymore, since nothing could be done about it.

☙

We were by a roadside somewhere, not even trying to hide. No one around to interrupt, and the few cars that passed swished by quickly—the sight of the wings strange but not arresting, never enough to slow the wild momentum of their lives.

I pulled the frame away and Ike lay there, still groggy, crashed out in the grass, a bruise blooming on his cheek. I said his name, rubbed his shoulder, tried to be patient, because I knew how it felt to come down again all numb and dreamy, too wrung out and sore to move. The world like an alarm clock's blare, when all you wanted was sleep.

I told myself to breathe. I ignored the way my hands trembled, swallowing the impulse to shake him roughly into action.

It was important to be gentle, even though every moment felt intolerable and much too long, as if I were trying to wake him underwater, holding my breath beneath the waves.

Eventually I had him sitting up again on the ground. His eyes squinted against the light.

"I'm *thirsty*," he croaked.

I was, too. I dimly remembered stealing water from the side of someone's house, drinking greedily at the garden spigot.

"Come on," I said, trying not to sound frantic. "Let's go, Ike—please."

I'd stepped into the harness already, my bare arms ready for the wings.

But he lay back down again with a groan.

"Oh, no no," I said. "Don't do *that*."

I knelt next to him.

"Please," I said, the words tumbling out faster than I meant them to. "I've waited, I—"

His eyes didn't open.

"I *can't*," he mumbled.

"You what? Of course you can!"

His eyes opened a crack, two bleary slits, the light still too much for him. He muttered something, a word like "emerald." His eyes closed again.

I sat down on his chest.

"Look at me," I said. I knew how hard it was, what we asked of each other. The long, unbroken bouts of flying and following. It took all of you, and nothing less.

I patted his cheek, hard enough to sting the skin. His eyes opened again.

"Ike—it's my turn."

"I can't do this anymore," he moaned.

"Please," I said, not meaning to sound so desperate. "Just one more time, for me."

Sometimes, when we got so exhausted that we lost track of whose turn it was, when nothing mattered except rest and sleep, some kind of end to all that motion, we'd collapse together and wake up later, huddled in the darkness on the ground. We woke up in all kinds of permutations: Ike on his back, still all tied up in the wings, me sleeping on his chest. Both of us free, each person lying on a wing. The wings on top of us like a tent, our arms laced together through the frame. Maybe we slept that way for comfort, the reassuring closeness of our bodies. Or maybe our trust had already corroded. Maybe pinning the wings down physically was the only way to know for sure we wouldn't wake alone.

My sleep was mostly dark and dreamless. But now and then a noise would pull me back toward the world, the muffled sound of Ike crying. Sometimes I'd leave him alone, or reach for him if he was near, or try to talk him through it. I was glad it mostly happened in the dark. That way, I didn't have to see him—his mouth open in a frozen wail, his crooked teeth visible to the canines, his eyes shut so tight it was like he was trying to squeeze tears out with the tension in his face.

"Ike," I said, once, crawling toward him in the dark across the surface of the wings.

"I'll never find them," he kept saying, one of his usual refrains. It could be hard to know if he meant the family he imagined in New York, or Barry and the other fliers we'd left behind—or who'd left us, I wasn't sure anymore. Or maybe he meant all those things at once. I'd started to think they were all connected for him, different parts of the same unbearable whole.

I moved closer to him and he moved away. I moved closer and he moved away, jerking his shoulder roughly to turn his face from me. He had always tolerated my nearness before.

"What is it?" I said. "What are you doing?"

"Don't follow me anymore," he said.

"What?"

"In the morning," he said. "When it's my turn again, don't come after me."

"Ike," I said.

"Don't," he said. "Don't, don't. Let me go. I want to be alone with this."

What I'd done to him was unforgivable, so maybe it was that. But I had felt the same thing, too. This desire to lift away. Sharing the wings was so much work, all the running, the chasing, the waiting. The waving of torches in the dark. So he wanted to be alone with them, that above all else, and I had felt it, too. To hurl ourselves toward the last horizon, freed from our last commitment, no longer pinned down by the only thing that held us back. Alone with the sky and free to drink, drink, drink.

He'd apologize later, in the morning. He'd say he didn't mean it. But we were pulling away from each other, I sensed that. It was only a matter of who would do it first.

❧

It finally happened at night, when I was flying. The world below nearly as dark as the sky I was in, nearly as dark as all the outer space above it. Only the tug of gravity, always in the same direction, could tell you which was which. I looked for the usual sign, when my body failed—a spinning torch to guide me home. But the light was out. I looked again, newly alert, trying to pull a self together from the shards of me. No, I was alone. The land below empty and dark, he was gone. What I didn't know—what I still don't—was if I'd abandoned him, or if he'd finally escaped.

Twenty-Six

Wind. The smell of honeysuckle. Manure, hay. Wet night grass. A moon like a nail clipping. The joined rhythms of heart and breath. Daybreak. Cowbells, a distant chorus. Clouds bright enough to blind.

I let the wings take me. I don't know how many days. Flying until small fires spread along my arms, a slow detonation. Eventually I'd have no choice except to plunge down again and rest wherever I fell. Crashing full-tilt into the earth, because there was no one to tie me back in if I let my legs swing free. Falling hard into the grass and rough brush. The pastures and cornfields. There was so much open space out there, endless earth and endless sky, and I was always alone in it.

Except once, or only one time I remember. I lay there on my chest near the top of a small hill, my mind waking up again. Then I sensed something, the chill of human presence. I lifted my head, my chin in the dirt. Down the slope, a house sat surrounded by sickly grass—a single prefab unit, set up on concrete blocks. The windows had a dull, plastic look. Then I saw the kids. Three of them, in various sizes, army-crawling toward me on their elbows. They stopped when they saw me looking, frozen in the grass and gawking back. They had no idea what to do next.

It took all my strength to get up without help. With your ankles tied to the frame, your wrists strapped in, you had barely any range of motion. The only way to stand was a tricky kind of push-up, lifting with your elbows first and then forcing the wings themselves to lift you, the willow rods straining at an awkward angle to the ground, until you feared the whole thing might tear apart. But it was possible. And I did it. I was standing, near the top of the hill.

The oldest boy stood, too.

He shouted something: "Identify yourself!"

A dumb line, cribbed from some war film, but said with feeling, more plea than command.

As I spread my wings, he aimed something at me—a play rifle, small in his hands. A BB gun, maybe. But nothing would stop me. I bent my knees and jumped, the thrust so delicious my eyes rolled back, and then I was passing over them, over their house, beyond all of it, leaving them forever with the problem of explaining what they'd seen.

I flew. An endless map, green and supple with hills, scarred by houses and highways. Nights swallowed the days and were banished by light. There had been something I'd wanted to re-member. A prickle at the base of my skull. A fleeting itch that came and was gone.

❧

I was lying on my chest somewhere, grass brushing my cheek. I couldn't open my eyes at first, the lids stitched shut. Every-thing was darkness.

My arms thumped with blood and everything hurt in a wrung-out way, a rag twisted and emptied. My kidneys ached, my ribs all bruised with falls. A rotten taste filmed my tongue.

I was so thirsty.

When I finally did open my eyes, the sky felt harsh, too filled with light. I looked down along one of my arms, my wings. My bones bulged under the skin, a skeleton revealed. I caught a whiff of something, the acrid musk I'd known to clear a subway car. It was my smell, I realized. I'd soiled myself, and flown that way for days in the sun.

Ike was gone, and I couldn't remember how I'd lost him.

Water. I was so dehydrated that my veins had started to shrivel, my mouth a sticky pit. I feared the sides of my throat would cling and flatten, choking out my breath. I couldn't go on like that. My body wouldn't let me ignore it anymore, no matter what I wanted.

I lay there, stuck, too weak to stand. Little sparks flew in my vision when I moved my head. My brain no longer seemed to control my limbs. With terrible effort, I induced a twitch in my shoes. The wings' scant weight had become too much. I was pinned like a moth to a board.

I tried to stand. Again, again. When I called for help, the sound of my own voice scared me, my shouting winnowed to a barely audible rasp.

To sleep, that would have been the easiest thing. To bow my head and sink under again.

But I sensed that, if I did, it would be the end of me. I didn't want it to be the end. Not then. A comfort, to know that still was true.

I felt blindly for the cord that would free my ankles, found it, and pulled. Then, shaking with effort, I managed to push myself to my knees. From there, I stood, the wings still balanced on my back, my arms tied in.

I was in a seedy backyard behind a little house. A round swimming pool sat there, swamped in last year's leaves, the water clogged and dead. A tree flowered overhead, the air sickly with honey. When I looked up at the sky, the urge gripped me again—to leave all that, to jump another time, to lose myself forever in the cathedral of the air.

I might have done it, too, if I hadn't seen the water spigot. Ike and I had learned to look for them at the base of houses: knuckled metal handles, so often painted fire-engine red.

I shuffled across the grass, the little gusts of wind that gathered in the wings almost enough to bowl me over. Finally, I collapsed against the side of the house. I tried to lower my mouth to the pipe, sticking my neck out, shaking with exertion, ready to nudge the handle with my chin. But it was no use. The wings were too big, blocking me from kneeling the way I wanted to. No matter how I moved, I couldn't reach it. I couldn't wear the wings and also drink.

I kept on that way for a few minutes, pushing myself downward, the willow canes straining as they bent against the ground. It was hopeless. I slumped against the wall, defeated. A piece of vinyl siding edged into my forehead, my face a mask of want. It was over. I'd been beaten.

I knew what I had to do. It was that or death.

I stepped backward, turned sideways, and pressed the tip of one wing into the house. Then I started to push. The thin struts, light as bird bones, started to bend. I pushed harder, the willow curving at a merciless angle, until something snapped. I did that again and again, each time a wallop I felt through my whole body. The wing lost its shape, became nothing but a frayed rag tied to some broken spears. I stepped on the dangling cloth and tore it, and then my arm was free.

When I'd broken myself out, I rushed to the spigot. I fell to my knees and drank deeply. The water had a copper taste, but it was beautifully, numbingly cold. I splashed my face and drank some more. I'd been spared. I was saved.

When I finally turned around, I saw what I'd made of the wings. A busted mess, the ruined tangle of what had been. Regret kicked in right away—I had nothing without them. I'd exiled myself, banned myself from the garden. But I tried to greet that feeling, sit with it, welcome it into me as the beginning of something. It meant I'd survived, that I was coming back to life.

⁓

After the thirst came the hunger. I was frantic with it, need pushing me toward recklessness. I knocked on the back door. When no one answered, I found it was unlocked. On the kitchen counter, a few clementines sat in a bowl. One of them had started to go bad, unnoticed, the rind powdered with whitish green mold. I ate the others, devouring them right there on the linoleum, juice running down my wrists. They were sickly things, the segments pale and tough, as if they'd somehow fruited in winter. But to my starving body they made an ample feast.

I left through the front door, defiant. Food is yours once you swallow it; no one can take it from you. The orange smell lingered on my skin.

I walked along a lonely, overgrown road, some ancient phone poles draping a black cord through the maples. With a little food in my belly, I could finally think, and because I could think, I started to worry. It had been a close call. I'd let myself get so weak I could barely stand, overpowered by the wings' scant weight, my body's systems shutting down. It registered at first as a horrible failing, the kind of self-loathing that comes parceled with strong hangovers. But with a sickening rush, I realized I might not be alone. All that flying weakened you—any of the others could have wasted away, too. It would be so easy for them to get stuck, the way I almost had, trapped by the thing that freed them.

What had happened to everyone else?

It was a scary realization, a jolting lurch of worry. I started walking faster, thinking myself in circles, asking myself if what I feared was possible, if it could really be. Without each other, the wings became too much. You needed someone at every step: to tie you in, to lift you up, to hold you back, to let you out again. I'd let myself believe other people would always be on hand ready to help, unable to fully imagine what would happen once they were gone.

I'd watched Barry do that, too, totally unaware of how dependent he was on Ike, oblivious to the way his grand, thundering vision became possible only thanks to a million unacknowledged forms of support. I'd resented that in him, but I'd gone and done a different version of the same thing—and this time it had almost cost my life.

Barry. I remembered what I'd helped him do with a sense of gathering horror, worse the more I thought about it, a darkness so potentially consuming I had to bat it from my mind to starve its power. And Ike. How had I allowed us to get separated? To not know where he was, or if he was okay—it all pulled at me, a miserable tide.

A two-lane state route, the distant hills sloping and shaggy with trees. I headed north, slinking behind the guardrails. Eventually I found a sign that measured the distance to three places, including mine: Lack, still twenty-one miles off, and nothing to do but hack away at the distance one step at a time.

I was so hungry. When I saw a cluster of bright red specks by the roadside—wild strawberries, in little clumps of vine-like leaves—I fell to my knees and ate. They had the taste and texture of Styrofoam, like movie set fakes, and only the slightest whiff of strawberry flavor. But what I needed most was to fill my stomach, pleasure an extravagant afterthought. Ike had taught me to eat the pungent carrots at the root of Queen Anne's lace, which you could tell apart from poison hemlock by their hairy stems and the tiny dark flower in the center. I pulled them up, my hands tugging at their stalks like rope, and ate the fibrous roots, always dirtier than I could clean off with my shirt. Sediment crackled in my teeth. But it was something, the meager meal I foraged, and I hoped it served as proof: that the others had been able to fight their hunger, too, that there was still enough left on earth for us.

A few miles in, something had been killed on the road. A crow flapped away as I came closer, the stench of rot still lingering. There was nothing left but a flattened blast of blood and fur. The destruction total, its very being vaporized. It was impossible to tell what kind of animal the animal had been.

∽

It took the better part of a day to get anywhere I recognized. I wandered around looking for the Saab, trying to remember where Ike and I had left it, the recollection partial, and painful as squinting at the sun. I finally saw it in the distance, parked crookedly on the side of a random road, and started hobbling faster, my legs wobbly and too sore to run. The doors were locked, but I found my keys were sitting on a back tire, just as we'd always planned. This leftover sign of Ike cheered me up a little. Our contract honored. Like it could still be possible, everything we'd promised each other.

∽

I drove back toward Lack, my eyes scanning the roadsides, the sky, unable to stop hoping I might see one of them. I checked Ike's water tower first, parking near the old graveyard. He wasn't there. As I peered up one more time at the flaking fake-blue basin, I had the urge to scale the ladder—maybe I could spot him from up high. But I didn't indulge myself, the act as pointless as a wish.

From there, I went to check their house. Ike would have gone back there. If not him, surely somebody would be around. So I found myself driving down the hidden dirt road again, the ruined house throwing heaps of shadow across the end of the lane.

I checked inside the house first, shouting Ike's name. The place was empty. But people had been there. Some of Barry's papers had been pushed carelessly to the floor, tracked over with dirty boots. There was a new element to the usual chaos, an unsettled look to everything, as though it all had been rummaged through by a dozen ferreting hands.

As I made my way out to the barn, I kept seeing feathers on the ground, silver tufts and little clouds of fluff trembling in the grass. As I got closer, I realized that the gate to the hen yard had been left open. Something had gotten in there—a fox or coyote, a cluster killer. Ike had always warned me it could happen, how some predators go wild with bloodlust, murdering more than they could eat. The birds were dead: I could see their torn forms strewn darkly across the dirt. I closed the gate, though there was no longer any point, and felt sickened by the senseless waste of life.

The barn, too, was empty, and in total disarray. Barry's gliders pulled down and scattered everywhere, trampled scraps of fabric lying about in twists, everything broken and looted-looking. People had fouled the place, the thing people do best. I wished I could have seen it one last time the way I remembered it: a temple to an idea, quiet as held breath, winged shapes hanging solemnly in the gloom. But the loom had been shattered, the Singer pushed on its side. The destruction had been willful, a form of sabotage, a decision to lay waste. Somehow—and I couldn't know why—the communal scene

I'd abandoned had shifted, morphing into one of resentment, defection, rage.

❧

I drove around until dark, seeing no fliers in the sky, no sign of anyone. Eventually I had the thought of going out to Grace's. Maybe she or Gene had seen someone.

Her front door had drifted open. The faded doormat: YOU ARE WELCOME HERE.

"Hello," I called out. I turned on the light in the kitchen. A bowl of fruit had rotted on the counter—bananas shriveled into brown husks, apples gone soft and translucent. A cloud of fruit flies swirled above them, dancing merrily over the spoils. It was an alarming sight, the kind of thing I didn't think Grace would neglect, and for the first time I realized something might be really wrong.

The food in the fridge looked suspect, milk gone off in its plastic jug. I ate a few handfuls of crackers from the cupboard, then gulped some water straight from the sink. In the garage, Barry's plans lay out on the worktable, but it was otherwise empty. The floor was absolutely littered with sawdust. I saw a few left-behind scraps of willow, but otherwise all the materials we'd given him were gone.

❧

I thought I'd check Diane's house next. Her rosebushes looked awful, the pink petals browning and eaten through. When I knocked, nobody answered—which was odd, since her car was there. An old sedan with dated racing stripes, parked over a patch of lawn where the grass had died, tire tracks worn in the green.

It was just so eerily quiet.

I knocked again and waited too long, and when still no one

appeared I decided to go around back. Maybe I could get in somehow, see some kind of clue. I wandered in that direction, the windows too high-set for a good look. In the back, a chain-link fence marked off the yard, a flimsy barrier and not enough to stop me. I was just about to climb it when I saw something, a grayish scrap of fur.

It was her dog, I realized, remembering the frenzied yapping I'd heard through the door on the day we met her. It was lying there unmoving, its snout pushed through a diamond-shaped hole in the wire. I stepped closer and realized the animal was dead. The sight hit me all at once: the emaciated body, the cloudy eyes still open, the parched tongue black and lolling. Scuffs in the chain links from its teeth.

I stepped back, shaken. I covered my mouth to keep from screaming, but it was not enough and I screamed anyway, a cry muffled by the trap of my hand.

༄

I spent that night in the barn back at the compound. I had no idea where else to go, no sense of what to do. I paced back and forth across the floor, lit the stub-end of a candle, and cleaned up haphazardly, sweeping trash and dirt and wreckage into a corner of the room. A vision of Diane's dog kept coming back to me. It was clear what had happened: She'd just never come back. So the poor creature had starved, or died of thirst, its last hours squandered on a doomed attempt to escape through the backyard fence.

I lay down on the cot, but it smelled too much like Barry—his body's odor, a whiff of his blackening foot—and I rolled away immediately, repulsed. A sick feeling pinched in my gut. I was forced to admit that I'd come so, so close. Close to what? To dying. It had been possible, worse than possible, an outcome that had inched toward being inevitable.

What I didn't know, what I couldn't imagine, was what had become of everyone else. Had they been able to save themselves, like me? Had they found a better way to sustain their bodies? Or . . .

If I drove out to the dairy, someone might know more. But I wasn't sure I could ever face them again, not if I had my whole life to prepare. Because it was likely that they were just like me, left behind and forced to live with not knowing.

I felt dizzy. I sat down on the barren floor, steadying myself with my hands.

Barry, Barry, I asked the darkness, *what did we do?*

⁓

It rained that night. I lay on the floor listening as water drummed down on the roof, watching it pour from the eaves in strings of jewels. I could barely move. I felt heavy, inverted, as if I'd filled like an hourglass with sand, and with every passing moment it seemed harder to get up.

I just wanted to *do* something. But I felt completely loaded down—the old, sad sense that it was useless trying to act upon the world. It had found me again after all that time. Or maybe I'd never been free of it. Maybe it was only something I'd outrun for a little while, and now it had caught up again, as surely as thunder outlasts lightning.

What was it like to fly through the rain? It had never happened to me. I tried to imagine winging my way through a storm, battered by wind and water. But no, the weather would force you down, grounding you, the fabric too heavy to fly with. You could huddle under a tree, maybe. You could lie facedown in the mud, the wings an imperfect cover, rain dripping unevenly through the cloth. Maybe the rain was a good thing, in that way, the merciful imposition of a limit. Maybe it gave us another chance to come to our senses, before our strength ran out.

I hoped the storm would save anyone who was still out there. I wondered if it would have saved me.

When lightning flashed, the barn's windows flared briefly. An obliterating lilac glow.

⤲

Rain kept pouring in the morning, the skies gray and torrential, droplets whipping in ghostly ropes. The feeling hadn't lifted—I felt narcotized with shame and grief—but my body needed to be fed. At least there was that. Hunger shining keenly in my belly, the crack of light beneath a door.

I ran out to the garden, frantic and instantly soaked, and started to grab the first thing I saw: Ike's zucchini squash. The fruits hung from the vine, their leaves trembling, the whole world pelted with water. I gathered what I could. Drenched, I sat on the floor of the barn and ate, tearing at the spongy fruits with my teeth, relishing their springy, uncooked taste. I was grateful for Ike's efforts, the way his work and foresight let me fill my stomach.

I lay down again, pushing away my cluster of uneaten green stems. I felt many times heavier than I was, as if I'd been transported to another, larger planet—stunned by its gravitational pull, sick from its poison seas. I needed to think, but I only wanted to sleep.

I hoped someone would come. No one did.

⤲

Eventually the rain stopped. I woke up, not sure how much time had passed. The world was itself again, bright and resplendent with birdsong. I stood unsteadily and wobbled outside. The beginning of a rainbow had arched into the sky, vanishing where it plunged into the blue, a vivid and half-finished thing. It was hard not to feel cheered by that, the earth's perennial goodwill.

For the first time, I allowed myself to wonder if maybe everything just might turn out all right.

I swam in the river, the water's allure more powerful than my fear of the chemicals I'd seen evidence of. I washed and changed my clothes. I let myself be swept up in the beauty of the day, but then I would think about everyone and feel sick, my stomach squeezing into a nauseous twist. I just wanted whatever would bring them all back, but nothing could.

What I clung to was the fact that I'd saved myself. If I could, maybe they could, too. The body will do anything to survive.

When it hurt too much to think about, I tried to busy myself, letting my mind fill with the anti-thought of tasks. It took all my strength, but I got the Singer upright again. I pulled the ladder from the wall and returned the gliders that had been taken down, at least those that were still in any shape to hang, and carried the smashed ones out to the firepit for burning. Loose willow had been scattered everywhere, so I gathered it into bunches. I picked up the trash that lay around, chip bags and cracker wrappers. A crushed soda can, smashed by someone's heel. I piled all the wreckage by the door, unsure what to do from there, since there was no one else to come and pick it up.

It was a big job, and still I wanted more to do. That was how I ended up inspecting one of the sheds, the ramshackle little structures Barry and Ike stored stuff in. I'd forgotten that Ike had used one of them to store extra supplies—many bolts of his rough cloth folded like bedsheets, whole bushels of willow tied and stacked by the wall. I marveled at their industry. They'd had so long to prepare for everything, so many hours in which to generate excess.

I didn't mean to start building the wings again. It was just what happened. A thing that stemmed from my need to purge thought with work, with the restless energy of my hands.

At first it was just a way to pass time, toying with Barry's tools, freeing some wooden shapes from a log with a saw. But then I was shaving and sanding the wood again, perforating its sides with a drill. It was thrilling to know I remembered how to do it. I fit the willow rods into the holes, the familiar skeleton beginning to take shape. A night passed. I woke again and resumed work, barely realizing I had started to build in earnest.

I went out to the Saab and took a copy of the plans, letting them guide me, feeling close to Barry again. There were still plenty of supplies, thanks to the cache I'd found. But I wondered if I could fix the loom if I had to, if I could find a way to lift the massive Singer, if my creativity could overcome the damage.

I forgot everything except the rush toward completion, my palms rubbed raw from tools. I was starting to cut out slips of cloth to hold the struts when I heard something—a soft sound, like the swish of fur on wood.

I put the scissors down and turned around.

A shadow blocked the doorway. I knew that shadow. It was Ike.

❧

I stood up. There was so much to take in that I felt dizzy, each second stretching past what it could hold. I saw his face, only half visible, darkened by his silhouetted hair.

"Ike," I said. My voice broke at the sight.

Then I saw the strangest thing of all. A small girl was standing beside him, holding his hand. She stared at me silently with her big eyes. It was strange and overwhelming. I wanted to do so many things at once—hug him, thank him, beg for his forgiveness, cover my face in shame.

I became acutely aware of the tools surrounding me, my desperate and discrediting attempt to rebuild the wings. Instantly I wanted nothing more to do with it. I could change. I would do everything differently. I only wanted to be worthy.

"I'm so sorry," I said, the words just bursting out. "I don't even know what happened. I'm just so sorry, Ike—I—"

He stood there, watching me struggle, perfectly calm. But there was a new expression in his face, something I'd never seen before. This distance in his eyes, like he was gazing down at me from a high window.

It crushed me to see him look at me like that, because it showed what I'd become to him. It wasn't exactly gone, whatever had existed between us. It had just been changed forever, and not for the better.

He turned around and left, the girl trailing behind him.

❧

I followed them outside. Way off in the meadow, Friday, the feral horse, had come again, grazing with her head lowered in the plants that drew her back, tail whisking at the flies. It hurt to see her, to remember how full of hope we'd been that day we'd set off in the cart.

"Go get some sticks from the forest," Ike told the girl. "Just as many sticks and twigs as you can carry."

She ran off toward the tree line, bounding through the wildflowers. It was clear she already trusted and obeyed him, their bond surprisingly complete. Ike stood and watched her go. He didn't turn toward me as I approached. I struggled to think what to do, how to address him after so much time had passed.

"Ike," I said finally. "Who is she?"

He whirled around, his eyes stormy and accusing.

"They *abandoned* her," he said.

"Abandoned her?" I said, flinching, his words an unexpected barb. "Who did?"

"Grace. Gene," he said. "Her parents. They flew away and they didn't come back."

Something crumpled in me, collapsing under a sudden weight. It was so obscenely obvious. She was the foster child, the younger of the two. And then, a new shame: that I'd forgotten about them.

"They weren't her *parent* parents," I said, a horrible thing to say, and the wrong thing to focus on, but a shield I needed to deflect what I felt.

"Well, they're what she had," Ike said indignantly. "I heard her crying in the woods. She was scared. Alone. I couldn't—"

His face wrinkled up, then hardened again, a sorrow that swelled and passed through.

"She didn't trust me. Not for a long time. She was scared of me, too."

"What about the boy?"

"I don't know."

The horror slid into me, down a dark chute with no bottom. I couldn't even understand it. I knew Grace. She'd give her life for those kids; she already had. Leaving them was the last thing in the world that she would ever do.

"How?" I said, almost dizzy with it. "She wouldn't do that. I just don't see how—"

Ike squared his jaw and stayed silent. He only gave me a look, as if I should already know.

I wanted to ask him what he thought had happened to them, to everyone. I needed his reassurance, for him to tell me they were probably safe, the way he and I had found ways to be safe. But I knew he wouldn't know for sure, and sensed he had no comfort to give me. Whatever had happened, it was becoming clear: everyone who had flown had been changed, and probably not for the better.

"I've been trying to decide what to do with this place," Ike said.

In the distance, we could see the girl's bright clothes flitting through the trees as she crouched and bent to pick up sticks.

"Sometimes I think that I should burn it."

I looked at him, trying to sense how serious he was. He tucked his hair behind his ear.

"I mean, it's pretty trashed already. I don't know what happened. No one will talk to me at the dairy. I've tried. Some of them never came here, but there are people there who did. They won't tell me anything. They won't *speak* to me."

He hit the word with so much feeling, so much suffering contained in his emphasis.

"They just stare at me. These cold stares, so I just give up. And then they watch until I go, until they're sure I'm really gone."

"Ike," I said. My heart broke for him, the closing of another door. But it was worse to sense the anger of the people from the dairy, the way they'd hardened themselves against us with righteous judgment, and to know that we deserved it.

"Sometimes I think I should just leave it," he said. "All my dad's stuff, some kind of reminder. Everything ruined anyway, like it *should* be ruined."

He paused.

"But then, I wonder. What if someone comes back here, and tries—could they actually—I mean, is it enough—?"

We were facing each other then. His eyes searched mine. He was asking me something, a question on the tip of his tongue.

"And then I get back, and *you're* here," he said. "And *this* is what you're doing."

"I—"

"No," he said, shaking his head. "No. No."

I wanted to explain myself. That I hadn't meant to, that it was just something that had started to happen, never really a choice I made. Just something about being there immersed me in the old rhythms, my hands finding their way on their own. But I'd never have *chosen* it. I wanted him to know that. It was so subtle, the way the wings wore down your will.

In the end, I didn't have to explain. The girl was coming back from the woods, her T-shirt held out in an improvised sack, heading toward us with the fabric filled with twigs. She smiled at us, proud she'd finished. That was when Ike turned to me, in one last act of empathy. His final, gracious gift.

"I know," he said, his eyes troubled, his mouth all crooked with dismay. "I feel it, too."

❧

A fire builds slow, then quickly. Once they had a blaze going in the pit, Ike lit a tree limb and walked with it carefully toward the barn. He held the flames against the doorjamb until they spread to the wood. When he was satisfied, he threw the torch inside the open door. At first it seemed it wasn't catching. Then fire forked out of the old shingled roof. I knew the gliders would be blazing on their lines inside, twisting in the heat. We heard something fall, a crash of wood. Glass shattered somewhere, a musical splash of notes.

But Ike wasn't done. He lit a second torch and walked with it toward the house. He took it with him inside, through the screen door. For a minute, he was gone—it was just the girl and me waiting in the yard. *The horse is gone*, I thought randomly, scanning the meadow. No fool, she hadn't stuck around. Then the screen door banged, and Ike came running. The whole house was a nest of paper, every surface teeming with sketches of winged bodies. Already I could see a blaze starting behind the kitchen windows. Black smoke poured out of the wall.

Ike joined us in the field, breathing heavily, dropping into a crouch. It was surreal, those twin blazes going both at once. A sound like an endless rushing wave as the heat consumed the wood. The girl watched in awe. Fire, so alluring in its power, but she knew not to touch.

"Let's go," Ike told her gently. He scooped her up in one arm and kissed her quickly on the cheek, the gesture so tender and natural that my heart filled for them. I wonder where Ike had learned to be like that; I had never seen Barry be that way with him. He started to walk toward the woods with the girl still in his arms.

"Wait," I said, trying to catch up. "Where are you going?"

Ike didn't look back.

"Anywhere," he said over his shoulder. "Everywhere. Not here."

"Let me come with you," I said.

That was when he finally looked at me. I almost wish he hadn't, the kindness gone out of his face. There was none of it left for me. He watched me for a minute, the same high-window look in his eyes I'd noticed earlier. I knew I would never see him again. I knew even before he set the girl down, took her hand, and ran with her toward the woods. There was no point in following—they weren't mine to chase anymore. So I turned back to the meadow, toward the fire and the heat.

∽

By the time I reached my car, white smoke was pouring from the first-floor windows of the house. The stuff of Barry's life—his drawings, his journals, his books, his keepsakes, his wishes—a perfect recipe for a structure fire. The sound was growing frighteningly loud, like a million branches breaking. The windowpanes shook with orange light.

I ran to the Saab. Before driving off, I looked back one last time—I couldn't help it. The house was by then an inferno. No, there was no house. It was just a stone chimney inside a writhing cage of flame. In the distance, over the trees, black smoke rose where the barn was burning. It all made for so much brightness, a kind of second sun.

So that was how I left.

I drove down the dirt lane a final time, and took all the turns. I looked up into the sky and saw no one. I didn't know where I was going. I just knew it was over.

I drove around for a little while, looking for signs of people. But if anyone was left, they were outside my reach, beyond my capacity to help. The whole place seemed as empty as on the day I first arrived—when Lack, to me, was just a word on the side of an abandoned water tower.

I got off the state route, merged onto the highway. I was trying to imagine what would happen if I just showed up somewhere, my disappearance done with. How I'd talk about what happened. Who I'd tell. Or maybe I'd just never talk about it at all. I couldn't imagine ever finding the right words for it, or discovering how things could ever feel put-together again.

It would take me years to come to terms with what had happened, with my part in it. I sensed that even then. But there was one good thing: I wasn't in the grips of it anymore. I could learn to live again without the wings. Ike had given me that. Thank god, he had given all of us that.

I drove for a while, heading south. Maybe I would go to see my parents. Just show up, if my father's heart could take it. I was ready to come home, and I knew they'd take me—for better or for worse, they would always take me back.

Home—it was what you had. No matter what you did, you could never be from anywhere else.

I was almost back again, past the Connecticut state line, when I heard it. I'd finally turned the radio off, trying to summon all my spirit. There it was again: something had fallen over in the back. I turned around quickly, but there was nothing on the seat. And then I knew. I knew without looking. I'd forgotten Barry's plans in the trunk, so many stacks of them. Each step outlined with precision, the sketches annotated in his hand. I went cold with horror.

I scanned the roadside, trying to think. Maybe it wasn't too late. I could find a dumpster. I could run into the woods and burn them. There was still time, no one would know. Instead, I saw my future in that moment. I felt the end foretold. I would never get rid of them, I didn't have the strength. The wings, Barry's pages: I knew they'd go on haunting me forever, and they do.

LAST PART

Poor moth, I can't help you,
I can only turn out the light.

—RYSZARD KRYNICKI

TWENTY-SEVEN

I didn't go home to my parents, not at first. I couldn't make myself do it. Instead, I drove to the Hearth at Pine Gables to see Ian.

I signed in at the front desk and walked in as I always had, like nothing had happened. People stared. Of course they did: I'd been missing for months and had nearly starved, my too-big clothes were soiled and torn. It would be a few days before I'd feel ready to confront myself in the mirror, my face a skull with hair. But none of that mattered then. I walked toward Ian's room, the only place in the world I was certain I belonged.

Ian. I found him sitting alone by his bed, his hair dark and still wet from a bath. He looked up from his chair, saw me, and smiled. His radiant smile, the sun coming out. It saved me, that look of recognition. To know there was someone who remembered me for what I was, unspoiled by everything that had happened. I bent down and hugged him. Buried my face in the crease of his neck. Felt his arms fold around me in their gentle, wandering way.

Later, I took him to the dining room and fed him, grateful for the rhythm of it—hand to mouth, hand to mouth, a ritual I'd known most of my life, the universe stripped down again to its essentials. I could feel the horror of what I'd done eating at me, lurking at the edges. But for a little while, I fed my brother and let my shame dissolve in his force field, the mystery and power of love for its own sake. Had I forgotten so easily? So much of what I needed came from this.

⟆

Someone must have called my parents. I was wiping Ian's lip with a napkin, the meal almost finished, when I saw them coming toward us across the room—my mom still in jogging clothes and sweaty from a run, my dad's shirt tossed on hastily, the buttons misaligned. Later, they'd tell me how they sped there, way over the limit, afraid I'd dropped in only to see Ian and would disappear again. My father glaring flintily at the road as he drove, both hands on the wheel, the muscles pulsing in his jaw. But I didn't know any of that yet. I pushed my chair back and stood, steadying myself on Ian's headrest as I waited to receive them.

I should have run over to them, like a reunion in a movie. But I felt rooted to the spot, watching helplessly as they approached, and as they came closer I saw how much they'd changed. They still looked like themselves, but so much older. As if they'd been deprived of some essential vitamin for too long, a malnutrition that had wizened their faces subtly, altering the color of their hair. Their eyes slightly sunken, their gazes haunted and peering. And it was me—there was no denying it—me, Jane, I alone had done that to them.

I'd braced myself for a long, embarrassing scene, weeping and accusations. Instead, it was so quiet. My mom held me. My father held both of us. By then some of the residents were watching, one staffer whispering to another as they stood against the wall. My parents said nothing—there was nothing to say—and I was grateful for their silence. But for a long time, long after I stopped hugging back, they refused to let go.

I spent a few months living in their house, sleeping in my childhood bed. They'd left my room undisturbed, like a tomb or shrine. The walls still covered with faded magazine clippings, stale candy in my desk drawer. The closet musty with clothes I hadn't worn in years. I found a forgotten dime bag in one of my jacket pockets, an ancient clot of weed inside, shriveled and browning. Everything was just as I'd left it, smoke signals from a person I no longer was.

Those early days were strange for all of us. I wouldn't tell them anything, and they seemed to know not to push too hard, that having me back was all they could ask. But my silence was far from a blank slate. I'd come home again bodily, but emotionally I was still in Lack—constantly googling for news stories, standing at the window to stare at the sky. I was jumpy, brooding, evasive, a deer loose in the house. I'd jolt up from the couch as they entered, slamming my laptop shut and escaping with it to my room.

Any day, the networks might report a person flying over Lake Ontario. Or that others had surrendered themselves to hospitals half starved, some with broken limbs, raving about flight. Barry was probably dead. Even more unthinkable: What if someone else had succumbed to thirst and exhaustion, the way I almost had? I could imagine a pair of wings, pulled out of the forest by state troopers, with a body tied up inside. The thought was sickening, enough to make me tremble. And yet I knew it was possible. The stress of that—of sitting around and waiting, while trying to act naturally around my parents—threatened to tear me in two.

The first days went by, and there was nothing. No sign in the *Syracuse Post-Standard*, or on smaller local news sites, or in a North Country community forum, or in a few janky blogs I found. I passed the hours in disbelief. I could only assume that Barry was dead, that his revolution was dead. I just hoped the others had survived it, had found the strength to pull back from the brink. I found myself begging the universe to protect them. This state of fervent pleading, channeling my whole self into a wish, an attitude I came to understand as prayer.

～

I'd been home a week at most, the afternoon I heard my mother call my name. I ran down the hallway toward her voice and found her in the kitchen, a spooked look on her face. She was holding the wall phone with the curly, tangled cord. She'd cupped her hand over the receiver.

"Janey," she said quietly. "There's someone on the phone."

My hands went cold, the blood thinning out of them.

"A reporter," she said.

"What do they *want*?"

"They want to know what happened."

It all felt so sudden. I stood there, trying to think, a high, trailing sound in my ears like after a cymbal crash.

"Janey," she said. "What can we tell them?"

She was almost begging, this needy cadence in her voice. Because I'd told her nothing, after all—she had unanswered questions, too. I sensed how relieved she was that some higher authority had finally intervened, someone with the power to pry from me what she wanted for herself.

By then I knew some of what had happened. I'd imagined my disappearance as the quietest thing, a stone slipping away beneath the surface of a lake. But of course it hadn't been like that. When someone just vanishes, it scares people. My teachers and classmates at Partridge—who'd sensed something was wrong long before I left my chair empty—had taken up my cause. (Surprising to me, but they cared more than I knew.) They'd mounted a campaign, plastering phone poles with flyers. The cops got involved. Search-and-rescue teams combed the gorges. Reporters inevitably got wind of my disappearance, and then new information emerged. Details about my torched kitchen and erratic behavior, which the Stephens gamely played up for the press. A news crew drove to Connecticut to ambush my grief-stricken parents, cameras on the front steps. The prevailing theory was that I was alive but a danger to myself, and might at any moment cease to exist.

Ultimately, the police concluded that I was a "voluntary missing person," someone who chooses to go missing—which isn't a crime, no matter how heartbreaking it might be for the people in one's life. Things just kind of moved on. But my parents couldn't move on. They'd lost their daughter, without explanation. And not only that. My sudden absence was for them tied to a second, more specific fear: that they'd leave Ian stranded in this world one day, with no other family to count on when they died.

That's what they couldn't fathom, that I'd abandon Ian. So they believed something had gone very wrong, something no one else had thought of—which, in a way, was true. And then I showed up the way I did, looking like that, thirty pounds underweight and my nerves fried to hell. I'd lived through something unimaginable. And they wanted to know, the way parents do, even if that knowledge would destroy them.

I wanted to give them some peace, I really did. But what I wanted didn't change the situation we were in. Until I better understood what had happened in Lack, the secrets I kept had to stay secret.

I went to her. Slowly, firmly, I took the phone away. At first her fingers resisted mine, tightening their grip, trying briefly to hold on. But then she let go. I hung up in a tiny crash of plastic, the receiver back where it belonged. I pulled her close.

"Please," I said. "Never tell them anything. Not until I say."

She didn't give in right away, her spine stiff and unyielding. Our bodies hadn't touched since that day at the Hearth.

"Please," I said.

"Janey—" she said, and then the phone started to ring again.

Reporters get cold-shouldered all the time, and this one was undaunted. But I was stubborn, too. I stood there with my arms around my mother, letting her feel my insistent closeness, while phones rang in rooms across the house. An electric bleat in the kitchen, a tinny jangle down the hall. The sounds seemed to unlock something in her. She wanted to know everything, if only to close the gulf between us. But she'd come to accept that I couldn't tell her, whatever my reasons were. I felt that in the way she held me back.

⌇

A few news items came out. Thin ones that passed quickly, because we wouldn't comment, which meant there was nothing to report. *Someone was gone until she wasn't*, basically. I got a few texts and emails from people in my past. Even one from Bruce, which I deleted without reading—an act of spite I immediately regretted, though I wasn't sure I should. And then it all blew over, as if nothing had ever happened. This ambivalence was a relief, but also terrifying in its own way. Because lives had been changed. The very fabric of existence, ruptured. People *flew*. When I listened to the radio, or watched TV, I couldn't help it: their obliviousness to the central facts appalled me. They saw nothing, those who showed the way. They heard nothing, those who spoke.

Late one night, when I was sure my parents were asleep, I stole out of the house, padding in bare feet down the driveway to my car. Crickets and tree frogs called to each other across the suburban darkness and stars threw cold light between the trees, guttering in distant palaces of ice. I checked to see if anyone was coming, the neighbors on a late stroll with their dog. Then I unlocked the trunk, lifting the metal hatch for the first time since coming home.

They were still there, of course: hundreds of photocopies, the ones I'd made with Ike. I'd arranged them in neat, stacked rows, but those had long ago toppled over, their order unmade. The copies had been sliding around loose on my drives through town, a chaotic, papery spill.

For weeks I'd worried someone would discover them somehow, an irrational fear that tainted my days. It couldn't happen—the trunk was locked, and I had the only key. But I found myself going to the window now and then for reassurance, relieved to see the Saab still sitting there undisturbed. I resented the passing cars, seethed silently at my parents when they occasionally walked by the car. My muscles tensed up each time my dad went out to check the mail.

I took one of the copies out and examined it under the trunk's dim lights. The quality of Barry's drawings hit me with fresh astonishment—they were even more intricate than I'd remembered, more detailed than memory could hold. I turned the pages and the old desire welled in me again, water spilling over the walls of a tub and weeping out onto the floor. I found myself wondering how hard it would be to re-create them. My father's tools would almost do, plus a few extras from Home Depot. I could buy some bolts of fabric from the crafts store in town.

A sense-memory snapped across my brain like lightning—the strength I felt in my arms when I joined them to the wings. The rush that took away my breath. The intuition we all tapped into, helping us turn the right way in the wind.

After all that time, I wanted it again. I wanted it with a throttling, scary fierceness, my whole being bending to desire's will. But I found a way to put the pages down. So much depended on this fragile, precious fight: the ability we all have to say no.

My first instinct was to throw them out, to shovel all those pages into a black plastic sack and let them get carried with the week's trash to the dump. But I couldn't quite force myself to give them up forever. Instead, I took a few boxes from the recycling, rooting around in the bins like a raccoon. I filled four boxes with Barry's plans. Then I duct-taped them shut, looping the tape around again and again, until each one was mummified in silver. I didn't open them again for a very long time.

❧

During the days, I wandered into town and lurked around at the public library, losing myself in the stacks. Or I'd go visit Ian, pushing him around the gardens in his chair, or listening to music in his room. He loved it when I read out loud to him, and as we worked through *The Fellowship of the Ring* I felt a relief at being present, knowing we wouldn't always have this kind of unbroken time. I felt overwhelmed with gratitude toward the staff, the people entrusted with Ian's care, for how expertly they moved him to his bed, to his chair, to his bath, how they clothed him and changed him and fed him as the days passed. I leapt up to help them at every turn, inserting myself, trying to be useful, striving to be present. Eventually Donna, his assigned assistant, took me aside. In her blunt, kindly way she told me to relax. The staff could do their jobs without my help.

"I haven't been here," I said, suddenly blubbering. "I've missed out on so much."

"I'm his aide," she said. "So let me be his aide. You be his sister. You're the only one who can do that."

◦〰◦

The only thing my parents made me do was see a therapist. As long as I was talking to someone, they'd continue to tolerate my silence. So on Thursday afternoons I drove to an office park in Danbury and met with the shrink, a small fine-boned woman who scrutinized me from her chair with bird-like eyes. I was stubborn at first, committed to my secrets. For my own sake, for her sake, for everyone's sake, it was better if no one knew. So I kept my mouth shut. I talked about everything except what I wanted to talk about.

I told her about Ian. About Bruce. About Partridge and running away. But she knew I was withholding. Eventually I relented. I explained how I'd seen Ike at the water tower, how he'd led me to the compound in the woods. I told her about the wings, about Barry. It all unfolded over a number of sessions. How we finally flew, our first attempts at converting others. And then how things went wrong.

She listened, her eyes shining and fascinated. It was obvious—she thought I was making it up. An elaborate fantasy of some kind, one I'd invented to disguise a plainer, more intolerable truth.

This really *happened*, I insisted. Sure, she believed that I believed it. The mind returns to experiences that resist memory, drawing myths from the well of what can't otherwise be said. I could feel her poking around, trying to sniff out what it was all a metaphor for. She never did find out.

There was much I loved about that era, hard as it was. I spent hours with Ian. And I felt closer to my parents: we made peace with the silence at the center of everything, easing slowly into comfort. That was enough, in a way. To rediscover what loving one another meant—a worthy project of any life, even if our efforts would never quite be finished.

Still, I couldn't go on like that forever. Our reunion was doomed for reasons that were, in part, material: I didn't have any money, my loans were due, I had to get a job. Besides, part of caring for Ian meant being secure enough to support him forever, no matter what—in a painful, paradoxical way, showing up for him meant following a path that took me elsewhere. But financial considerations weren't everything, if I'm honest. I didn't feel comfortable retreating fully into family life. I was a person, too, and that meant finding my own way. That balance—caring for them, while also caring for myself—added up to a tricky calculus, one without any easy answers.

What life could I have, after all that had happened? At first I wasn't sure. It was easy to feel the central part of my narrative was behind me already: never again would my story be so big, so dramatic, so freighted with consequence, and—ultimately—so tragic. But I had all this time left, and I had to make decisions about what to do with it.

Getting older: it forces you to decide what you care about. What *did* I care about? The old dreams I'd nursed for so long felt vain, dim, and lifeless—this fantasy I'd had about getting to play in a big Borgesian library forever, with time on my hands. I didn't want the reality of that life, shilling *The Faerie Queene* to bored undergrads term after term. What I wanted was a better world, and I saw the best things about our world slipping away.

This was Barry's impulse, too: to save the world. But his vision had betrayed us all so badly. I still didn't understand *why* things had gone so wrong, or when exactly our cause became corrupted. But I no longer trusted my own instincts around what was good, or right, or just. My credentials as a world-saver had been revoked. Because—after all that had happened—who was I to try to help, to try to save? I could only imagine starting again, in a totally different place. This time, with questions about atonement. This time, with asking what I owed the people whose lives my actions had damaged.

∽

I got a job as an assistant to the executive director of Beyond Borders, a nonprofit that advocated for more humane immigration policy in the U.S. while also developing frontline tools for people living in the States without documentation. I had zero admin experience. I got the job, ironically, thanks to my time at Partridge: they wanted a person who could do some database work on the side, and my skills went well beyond what they'd hoped for. I moved back to New York.

My boss's name was Ricky Jurado. His mother had crossed the border six months pregnant, so he'd been born here—and they carried that circumstance everywhere with them, a family forever on two sides of an invisible line. His mother got work picking fruit at big farms in California, his infant body swaddled against her chest. By the time some kids start preschool, he was picking produce, too. Later, she worked as a housekeeper, then as an at-home aide to the elderly and infirm, living with her son in guest rooms and basements. It wasn't that she hated the work, so much. She hated that she had to do it in the shadows, for people who understood she needed to stay hidden. Some of them would punish her, or withhold pay, knowing she'd be too scared to fight back. Other bosses were decent people—but these random strokes of luck underscored her situation's cruelty. Because she was at the mercy of them either way. Good or bad, her employers owned the very bed she slept in, and they could give her dignity, or they could withhold it.

A lot of my job was fielding Ricky's emails. And booking his travel. And making sure he got everywhere on time—he was gregarious, and loved people, and couldn't be counted on to leave events when he was supposed to, which meant that he was always running late. It was basic and unglamorous stuff, but it felt like something. My work helped Ricky do more, and when Ricky did more, the organization made more money, and when the organization made more money, more people got the help they needed. And that was good.

What excited me more concretely was getting to work on Beyond Borders' suite of digital tools. It turned out I knew enough to be useful, and became a swing player on their tiny team of engineers. Part of what I hated about Partridge, I realized, was the assumption that we'd go work for huge software companies, digital middlemen who sucked the value out of everything else and only worshipped money. This was different. The tech we built connected people with immigration lawyers who did pro bono work. Or helped people chase down back pay. Or streamlined the application process for asylum status and visas, green cards and citizenship. In other words, it changed lives. I found myself wanting to do more. When Ricky reminded me about the education budget for staffers, I signed up for night school, picking up where I'd left off before I disappeared.

I thought about Barry, the way he'd toiled for years on this wildly original, infinitely complex thing. But who was he really working for? Nobody had asked for what he built, he'd consulted nothing but his own internal voice. I knew Barry would have scoffed at what I was doing, its nominally high-tech sheen. He was the one who had it wrong, though. Yes, there was code involved, but that wasn't the point. The tools people needed were simple. You just had to know how to listen.

～

Sometimes, on my lunch break, I walked to the New York Public Library, pacing up the steps between its patient concrete lions. Once, standing at a computer terminal, I typed in Barry's name. It felt subversive, even dangerous, to see those letters on the screen. I looked around the room. At long tables, unsuspecting people read by the light of green-glass lamps. I took a deep breath and hit return.

To my absolute shock, some hits came back.

I couldn't take in everything at once. I just read. The first article was about the logging industry in the Pacific Northwest, and its skirmishes with a militant group called Earth Force. Members of the group had been accused of hammering metal spikes into trees in the forests outside Bend, Oregon, and injuring an employee of a company called Western Lumber. It had happened at a local mill: while a tree was being carved up, the unseen spike inside hit the bandsaw, ripping out like a bullet and lodging itself into the man's shoulder.

I scanned until I saw his name.

"'Forests like the one on Hardesty Mountain are the lungs of the planet,' said Barry Haliban, 33, an Earth Force supporter who says he does not personally advocate for tree-spiking," the story read. "'You can see why some people would protect them at any cost. It's not only about all the animals that will die once the trees are gone, the ravaging of a whole biotic system. We depend on the trees, too. To log an old-growth forest for timber is a form of slow suicide for human beings. We should all want to prevent that.'"

I heard his voice across the miles, the years. His italicized cadence, all spiky with emphasis. The surprise was not so much that he'd been part of such a reckless campaign—which, knowing him, he clearly had been—but how linked the argument was to everything he'd told me. The wings had been another way to weaponize a tree. I only wondered how much he'd changed since then. Had he believed so deeply that death no longer scared him? The loss of limbs, of lives, a bargain in the greater cause?

～

I also found his father's obituary. Lawrence J. Haliban, a minor tycoon who'd started and scaled a regional grocery chain. Over time he'd realized there was more money in the buildings than in the stores themselves, and became a local baron of commercial real estate. He was survived by his wife, Linda, his son, Barry, and his daughters Wendy and Irma. This was the family Ike had talked about, and it seemed some money remained. There was still a Haliban Foundation headquartered in an office on Sixth Avenue, though it seemed shady and disreputable. (It might have been a tax dodge.) After Lawrence's death, there had been a lawsuit of some kind over a secretive four-million-dollar loan. It was unclear where the money had gone, or who was supposed to pay. The family had spent years suing their perceived enemies and attacking one another.

In an article about the bygone stores of old New York, I found a picture of one of their establishments: HALIBAN's, a huge sign read, cured meats dangling in the window. This was the life Barry had fled.

He'd gone to school upstate, double-majoring in architecture and mechanical engineering at Cornell. I found a reference to him in a *Daily Sun* piece about architecture students, who apparently designed a huge clockwork dragon every year, parading the thing around campus before incinerating it on the quad. There was a grainy picture of Barry posing with some others by their creation, a winged beast made from wood and cloth. The other men smiled at the camera, but Barry looked unhappy, squinting uncomfortably against the sun.

That was all I was ever able to learn. The rest was silence.

~

Through it all, I kept the blueprints in their sealed boxes under my bed. I tried to force myself to forget them. Horrified by what had happened in Lack, by what I myself had turned out to be capable of, I'd reluctantly cast my lot with civilization. Maybe I could fake my way into a normal life, I thought. Maybe the harrowing dreams would stop.

One summer, I went to see *An Inconvenient Truth* at the Union Square AMC with a friend. I knew nothing about the film except the poster—a view of smokestacks, smog swirling around them like snow. The impact on me was profound, a sense of encroaching dread that never left. Humanity was killing itself, just like Barry had said. But the hapless figure of Al Gore was almost more frightening. If our last, best hope was a failed politician in a baggy suit, jetting around with a Power-Point on his laptop, we were well and truly fucked.

It wasn't until the United Nations' fourth IPCC report came out that winter that something shifted in me. The words in the headlines—*catastrophic, irreversible, unthinkable*—contrasted so starkly with the general state of things. We would just sit around and do nothing, wouldn't we? A doomed race of thumb-twiddlers. Trapped inside the machinery we'd built, captives of its suicidal logic. And we were too venal and self-interested to care, though it meant the world we loved would vanish more with each season, to be replaced by hell.

All of it had been so stupidly foretold. We'd already been

driven from the garden. Next, we'd murder our brothers. I walked the city streets with this choking sensation in my throat, this feeling like I was drowning in a pool.

We won't stop, I thought. *We won't stop—just like Barry had said.*

I thought back to the question I'd asked Zena, a lifetime ago—what can we actually *do*?—and didn't have the faintest glimmer of an answer.

One night, I took one of the boxes out from underneath my bed.

I cut the tape away with a pair of scissors, gnawing at the sticky silver layer with the blades. The box opened into darkness, and a smell escaped—sunlight and honeysuckle, the meadow's smell. I lifted the blueprints out.

There they were again. The graceful arches, the sense of scale and tension, the measurements in Barry's hand. A skeleton assembled rib by rib and sewn up with tight-fitting cloth, strong enough to carry a body toward the sun. The old longing hit me, a sudden T-bone smashing, so much more than I thought I could feel. There was still a way out. Wasn't there? The labyrinth we were trapped in had no roof. We could still be lifted upward, a joyful escape. . . .

I knew with sudden clarity how easy it would be. No one to stop me, my memory still strong. All I needed was the right supplies and a few crude tools. There was a whole afternoon when I really thought I'd decided. My will hardened, my spirit settling, a bird's talons spreading as it comes down on a branch.

Only one thing held me back that time, and so many times since. It's the memory of the people I met in Lack. My nights were still haunted then, as they are now, by terrible dreams about them. I hope they're okay, that they survived like I survived. But when I sleep, they're dying, their faces shrunken, starving, suffering, the way I was the day I finally came home.

Jane, Jane, I'll warn myself, more out of habit than anything else. *Don't you ever do it.*

⌐∿

I'm still bound to this stack of blueprints, sealed boxes under my bed. I've tried so many times to burn them. The page edges are all singed from my trying, but I always pull my hands back from the flames. Once, I took a shoebox to the end of Manhattan, near where the river's mouth empties into a warming sea. Sunlight snaked bright across the water as I waited on the bench, fingering the string I'd knotted, trying to feel what it would mean to watch my burden drown. I couldn't do it, not that day. I walked home as night fell, the box still cradled like an infant in my arms.

It's been years now. The kind of time you measure in people. Three serious boyfriends. One father, gone. Friends with children and gray hair. I'm still at the nonprofit, on the tech team now. I still believe in the work, though I've also been there long enough to understand its limits. I struggle every day with what I remember. I gave up on having any life but this.

What's left for me? I *flew.* I know what the birds feel, how the heart throbs as you pull away from the earth's dead weight and dive upward into space, nothing holding you but sky. That feeling can't be written, though I've filled notebooks trying to find the sound. It was everything you've ever wanted, nothing less. It really was that good.

People walk down the street looking downward, hunched over handheld screens that didn't exist so long ago, then were suddenly everywhere, the kind of effortless replication Barry dreamed about. Sometimes, pushing through crowds on the way to the train, as the endless hordes amble on with the slow-witted gait of livestock, this pressure builds in my throat and I want to scream to them: *Stop, stop, we're so much more than this*—

I say nothing. But I can't help it: I still fantasize about flying over the city, soaring over a thousand-foot drop, a harbinger in the sun.

~

A second therapist. A man this time. He dresses well, but can't disguise something plain and menial about himself, the hard gaze of a gym teacher. He, too, hears me out, once the truth comes tumbling. I just want to know what to do. I want to know how to live with this.

He's patient, beyond patient. But his exasperation grows, and then he can't hide it anymore.

"You're asking me to believe something that's physically impossible," he said, his face flushing. "You have to understand that. If you told me that you turned green and grew a tail, should I believe that, too? Of course not. I wouldn't dispute the significance to *you* of what you're saying—I *don't* do that. But it would be counterproductive for me to wonder out loud with you if you should go to the government, explain to them how you grew a tail and swam to Canada with the mermaids."

"But this isn't like that," I said. "It's something that could actually happen. It *did* happen."

"So why aren't there any pictures?" he said. "Photographs? Someone else who knows about it? *Any* kind of proof?"

He let the accusation hang between us.

I wanted so badly to bring him Barry's sketches. To watch his eyes widen. They were my trump card, my everything, my last connection to the person I'd been. He might not trust me even then, of course—he'd probably think I copied them from a book or something. But I also knew the physical sight of the wings could change him, as they had changed me. And that might be the beginning of something, a sequence I couldn't control. So I stayed silent. It was better that way, hard as it was. That was the cruel part. It was better that I wasn't believed.

❧

The past fades, the way dreams fade. And as I feel more distance from it, sometimes I start wondering if I really did imagine it. Could that be possible? Did I simply invent a mythic self to reckon with the unexpressed self, the unbearably true self? Some days no other explanation feels possible. But then I'll kneel down to look again at the boxes under my bed. I know Barry's drawings wait inside, irrefutable, nothing my hands could ever make.

I went back to Lack once, only once, just to remember. The gas station had long since closed. I let the engine idle in the parking lot, staring up at the last remaining landmark: the water tower, that high steel canister looming over the tree line on its stilts. The painted blue that tries and fails to match the color of the sky. And it struck me how our human plight is captured in that color. This dissonant near-miss, part of our surroundings and yet nothing like them, and doomed to forever wonder why.

I drove around awhile, wanting so badly to see Ike. I would have done anything for a glimpse of him—the gaunt, familiar figure, ragged in homemade clothes. He'd be older, just as I was older. The girl, if she was still with him, would be tall.

It was harder than I expected to find where the house had been, the dirt-paved passageway overgrown by trees. There was no sign of anything from the road. I only knew the entrance from the telltale bend in the road.

There was nothing left. Just the meadow, its tufted grasses

high as my hips. What was left of the house was a jumble of charred boards. Only the stone chimney still stood, with weather-eaten holes in all the mortar, and the sky shone through them like a thousand eyes.

As I stood there, the old urge swallowed me again. And I knew that if I'd found the place the way I'd half expected to— the place I remembered that no longer existed, with the loom and the reams of cloth and Barry's handheld tools—I wouldn't have been able to resist. I wasn't *built* to resist. If I'd had the choice, I would have flown again—and, from there, anything might have happened.

The barn was an ashy heap. A smoke smell still lingered near its ruins. I thanked Ike, silently, for burning the place down. He'd saved me one last time, and he'd been right to do it.

 ⁓

That feeling doesn't last. I left Lack swearing I'd go home and tear up Barry's drawings, flush them, chuck them in a dumpster, sever them from me forever. Of course, I didn't. I couldn't. I didn't want to. I kept them hidden under my bed, never quite ready for the last goodbye.

It distances you from people, a thing like that. I go out with friends, the last few who've stayed single, and do my best to listen to their chatter. But at a certain point the loneliness gets overwhelming, and I vanish into the night. People expect it of me now. The Jexit, they say. Like Brexit.

There was a man, not long ago. Charming, and smart, a little bit vain. His eyesight poor, his glasses stylish. Cutting but basically kind. We'd failed in similar ways, our high-flown dreams delayed. I'd wanted to be a scholar, or writer, before I wanted a secret revolution; his goals were much more vague, if still intense, rooted in an ill-defined sense of personal greatness. We shared a sense of squandered potential, as different as we were. We'd both wanted to matter somehow, and no longer felt certain we did.

We dealt with our disappointment differently. He'd chosen money, the consolation of well-paid, meaningless work. And I'd chosen . . . what? To wait for something to happen. To sharpen a tiny ax against a system of vast injustice. To wrestle with a private life that had to stay private forever, a violent history that insisted on a quieter present.

I didn't know if we'd last, long-term. He had a kid in first grade, tuition owed to some posh Episcopal school, an expensive divorce in the not-so-distant past. Still, there was something foolish and easy about it. A carefree kind of goodness. It felt doable. Maybe getting older meant turning away from what could be and learning to love what was doable.

He thought I was a writer, because I'd published some poems in the college lit mag years ago, because my bookshelves impressed him. I liked the potential he saw, the way he took me for more than what I was. But, while he sensed a strange energy in me, he couldn't know its source. I could never tell him about Barry. Sometimes, in my dreams, I fought to stop him as he searched for something among the boxes under my bed.

Once, he stayed all Saturday, until I needed to go to an event for work. I'd gotten dressed and was ready to walk to the train. But he was still reading, naked, in my bed. He was always taking my books off the shelf and starting them in the middle, one eyebrow subtly raised, as if he'd never seen a book before and wanted to know what the big deal was.

"You have to go," I said. "I'm leaving."

"But I'm reading," he said.

"You're not reading," I said. "You're just looking."

"Can't I wait for you here?"

"No," I said.

"I don't pick up Manning until three tomorrow," he said. "I could stay. We'll do brunch."

Manning was the worst name I could think of for a boy. It sounded like a verb.

"Come on," I said, nodding toward the door. "Get dressed."

He sat up, suddenly interested, adjusting his glasses on his nose.

"It really bothers you," he said. "Doesn't it! You don't want me in your apartment when you're not here."

"That's not true," I said.

"It *is* true," he said. "You get antsy about it. It's not the first time. You don't want me here alone."

"That's ridiculous," I said, but he was right. I couldn't have him snooping through my notebooks, as he almost certainly would. I felt a dark presence in the shelves of my black Moleskines by the window, where I'd written so much down. The boxes stowed under my bed radiated with malignant force. These things were doors that needed to stay locked.

"Jane," he said. "What is it?"

"It's nothing," I said. "I just need you to go home."

He leaned forward, his eyes glinting with truthfulness.

"There's something you won't tell me," he said softly. "Why? What aren't you telling me about?"

I meant to deny it, defuse it, say anything. But there was only this sharp intake of breath, harsh in our ears, and in that half second of hesitation we both knew we were doomed.

⤺

A week into the pandemic, the Hearth at Pine Gables shut off access to visitors. This was to protect Ian and his fellow residents, but I was terrified. People were dying by the dozens in nursing homes outside the city, the papers said. If there was an outbreak in the Heroes Ward, I wouldn't be able to get to him. My brain kept supplying images of Ian, scared and choking in his bed. The thought of it was more than I could take.

Everything closed down. Work went remote. Sirens wailed all night, the parks were converted into morgues. I was frantic. My mom was frantic. It would only take one aide, bringing the virus in from outside, and the thing would start to spread. What would we do if the residents started getting sick? If Ian himself got sick? We talked through every scenario, which didn't change the fact that there was nothing we could do.

Those first few weeks upended everything, and at an unstable moment Ian's situation seemed especially precarious. But as time passed, as we counted the days by tallying the dead, I realized his circumstances weren't all that different. We were all at the mercy of the world, dependent on the care and goodness of others, a system held together by kindness and silver thread.

I found myself looking at apartments in Connecticut, places that were closer to Ian and my mom. Mercifully, I was near the end of my lease. I even had the fresh one on my desk, already signed—I just hadn't returned it yet, the way I put everything off. I tore into the envelope and threw the paper in the trash. I got my security deposit back, enough for a few months' rent somewhere else.

My mom said I could just come home, but I didn't want to risk infecting her. Besides, that wasn't a real solution—I needed my own place. Still, the chaos had changed something in me. Whatever it was, it felt permanent.

I found a spot not far from Ian's, a quaint little stand-alone house on a hill. A realtor showed me around by Zoom. Old wide floorboards. Steam radiators. Unfancy and—by Brooklyn standards—unthinkably cheap. I took it. I packed my apartment into boxes and rented an oversized U-Haul, the smallest one they offered bigger than what I needed. I drove away with Barry's blueprints in boxes on the front seat, all wrapped up in tape, the rest of my stuff sliding around in the back.

In those first days, the highways were clogged with people fleeing the city. A sea of brake lights pinked the sky. After all the warnings, it really did seem like the world could finally end.

The house was good enough. It was better than being squeezed into my little one-bedroom apartment, walking through empty streets to the bodega. At least, when I woke up, I could hear birds in the trees, the rustle of life—not just sirens rising against a huge, unnerving silence. I unpacked. I worried, paced, unpacked some more. No one knew when the Hearth would allow visitors again. No one could tell me anything. My mom and I didn't even dare to see each other. No one knew when the scourge would pass.

I bought some masks from a craft store in town, the only place I could find any—a double fold of paisley cloth, green ribbon to tie behind your head. The ones I'd ordered online never came, stuck somewhere in limbo, the mail a logjammed disaster. With my face protected, I finally went to the grocery store, buying way more than I needed. I came home again and cleaned everything off with Clorox wipes.

Days passed. I returned the U-Haul, got everything up on shelves. It still wasn't safe to go see Ian, and they still weren't letting anyone in. I couldn't do any work—I didn't have internet yet. I checked the news on my phone. Thousands were dying in my city, their lungs filling with fluid. In cities all over the world, trapped people stood on their balconies, banging pots and pans, cheering the nurses on when hospital shifts let out.

That was how I started writing this. There was nothing else to do, and it took my mind off things for a while, the new fears held at bay by the old fears. I just started at the beginning and kept going. In a way, it felt like what I'd been training for years to do. There were hours and hours to fill. I finally had my chance. And at least, if I die before I have the courage to burn Barry's drawings with my hands, some words will come parceled with them—these letters arranged into order, this warning to a future self.

∽

I am bound to Barry Haliban, the dreamer, the blue-eyed builder who tried and failed to save us. I helped him build his strange machine, and when he seemed crazy I stood by him. I so badly wanted what he wanted. To believe in the force of bright white wings. To believe we can set human genius against the world and win, a simple assault on an elaborate, depthless darkness.

In a way, I understand: Barry refused to lose the world. I, too, refuse to lose the world. Our world, the green and patient mother that has nursed us. The radiant, almost miraculous health of things in good relation. The pleasure of a river, to eat from and to bathe in. Of land that holds our stories, our laughter, and our singing. The animals we know—cousins, wellspring of our language, source of our metaphors. If we lose all that, it was never inevitable. We were warned, and we had time.

I would do anything not to lose the world. But Barry fought the wrong way. He spoke of liberty, but wanted an escape hatch. He promised freedom, then built new forms of domination. When he tore things down, he never asked who might be left behind, trapped in the rubble as the walls fell. He wanted to save what he didn't understand. And, while he claimed he could help us, that's not what I saw: it was all a way to circumvent us, to manipulate us, to *fix* us. Because, deep down, he believed people are the problem, and not the prize. So he looked for answers everywhere but in our hearts.

For Barry, hope came only in the shape of strange, sharp wings. No—hope is human hands, reaching for each other.

Why didn't I see it sooner? Ian had no place in Barry's dream. Which always should have meant there was no place for me.

I've started to feel the truth is simpler, and harder, than I realized. It starts with shutting the door on the hero I wanted to be. It starts with human care, with the love that survives losing everything we love.

I pray I'm finally ready. I think I will be, if Ian can only be okay. If Ian will be okay, I'll finally do it, I promise. Start a fire in the yard. Stick by stick, the way I learned from Ike. I'll hold Barry's pages into the flames, the corners eaten by the heat. My hand won't flinch. I'll let go once I'm sure they're burning, when there's no going back. I'll dump these pages in, too—I won't need them anymore. I'll watch the smoke rise into the filthy sky, its kingdom lost to me forever, and with hope in my heart, I'll go and see my brother.

Acknowledgments

This novel took an unusually long time to produce, and many people and entities helped sustain me emotionally, intellectually, and materially along the way. Thank you to the people who most directly and lastingly impacted *The Sky Was Ours*, especially, in chronological order:

My dad, Peter Jeffery, for Brooklyn, and my mom, Margot Fassler, for upstate New York. Thank you both for the enduring love of books—the first writers in my life, in addition to everything else.

My brother, Francis Jeffery, for seeing the world in ways that reshape how I see the world, for being integral to the emotional landscape of this novel, and for remembering absolutely everything.

Lan Samantha Chang, for a transformative phone call on a March afternoon. The Iowa Writers' Workshop made the life I wanted possible, full stop. All writers should be lucky enough to meet someone along the way like you.

Connie Brothers, Deb West, Jan Zanisek, and the Workshop's administrative staff, for all you did to support three years of artistic growth and development—you made everything feel seamless in a way that was a blessing for my work.

My writing mentors—especially Justin Tussing; Kenneth McClane and Debra Fried; Marilynne Robinson, James Alan McPherson, Ethan Canin, Peter Orner, Allan Gurganus, and Alexander Chee—for teaching me so much of what I know, helping to equip me with the hard skills that make all of this possible, and deepening my commitment to this path.

My extraordinary agent, Ellen Levine, who saw the potential in my work long before anyone else did, who had the patience to see me through, and whose unparalleled advocacy floods me with gratitude.

The many writers who participated in "By Heart" and *Light the Dark*. There were many times I would have abandoned this project without your stories, wisdom, and insights to draw on.

Jerry Pavlon-Blum and The Gateway School for a quiet place to work when I really needed it—for sanctuary in the middle of New York City.

Mary and Tony Fagnant, for a secluded forest cabin when sustained focus was otherwise hard to come by. Peace and quiet were always abundant there, aside from the incident with the meth dealers, and I learned so much in those important spells of time.

The many people who took time to read this book in all its various incarnations and share feedback. Andy Bates, Sarah Chihaya, Doug Bock Clark, Michael Fauver, Helen Jeffery, Claire Kelley, Chris Leslie-Hynan, Kyle McCarthy, Doug McLean, Caitlin Miner-Legrand, Thomas Fox Parry, Sean Reap, and Cutter Wood—your praise, criticism, and advice made the final product better.

My first editor, Sam Raim, for taking a chance on this novel when it was still in its infancy (even if I didn't know it then). At a time when I'd reached the limit of what I could do on my own, Sam, you threw me a lifeline. Your incisive notes and questions were a new beginning, and they served me so well until the end.

My second and final editor, Amy Sun, for somehow drawing out the novel I'd always hoped to write. Amy, I still don't understand quite how you did it—this book couldn't have found its way without you. Thank you for your unerring insight, for your willingness to advocate for the time we needed, for the care you took, draft after draft. I was always in the best possible hands.

The incredible team at Penguin, including Brian Tart, Andrea Schulz, Patrick Nolan, and Isabelle Alexander; Kate Stark, Lindsay Prevette, Mary Stone, Rebecca Marsh, Alex Cruz-Jimenez, and Becca Stevenson on the publicity and marketing side; Paul Buckley, Jason Ramirez, and Sabrina Bowers for making the book beautiful inside and out; and Dave Cole and Eric Wechter for taking so much care with the final text.

My son, Luke, for every day reminding me what love is, for challenging me always to be a better artist and a better man.

Finally, thank you to Rachel, who lived with this book as a daily reality for so many years, who fought for the space and time I needed even when it wasn't easy, and who always pushed me to expect more from myself, as a person and on the page. Rachel, only you know what this undertaking really required, the triumphs and setbacks and dark nights of the soul. Thank you for being my best friend, the reader I write for, my forever collaborator, the absolute love of my life.

A PENGUIN READING GROUP
DISCUSSION GUIDE TO

THE SKY WAS OURS

JOE FASSLER

1. As the book begins, Jane feels that modern American life under capitalism is dooming her to unhappiness—and yet she feels powerless to choose an alternate path. How powerless are we, really, in this moment? What kinds of positive change feel achievable, and when does progress feel beyond our reach?

2. In deciding to abandon the life she's chosen, Jane tries to realize a healthier, more authentic self. By doing so, though, she hurts some of the people who love her most. Is her disappearance justifiable? What's challenging about balancing one's own desires with the needs of others, and how does the novel explore that theme?

3. Jane becomes fascinated by Barry's plan to redeem humanity through flight. Why do you think she finds this idea so alluring? What do you find compelling or beautiful about Barry's vision, and where does it fall short?

4. Jane, Barry, and Ike all have different, sometimes competing values and priorities. How would you describe their diverging attitudes toward the world? Whose point of view do you most identify with and why?

5. Jane's brother, Ian, plays a supporting but central role in her life. To what extent does Ian serve as a foil for Barry? What has Jane learned through her sibling relationship, and how does that experience influence the choices she ultimately makes?

6. *The Sky Was Ours* borrows themes and mythic imagery from the famous story of Daedalus and Icarus, without being a direct retelling. To what extent does the myth inform the novel, and how does the book diverge from this original point of influence?

7. American culture is filled with stories about genius originators who change the world through the brilliance and sheer force of their vision—figures like Thomas Edison, Steve Jobs, and Elon Musk. What is the novel's relationship to the archetype of the disruptive genius? How does it critique or subvert it?

8. New technologies tend to be described in utopian terms. Air travel, radio, television, and the internet were all supposed to redeem humanity and bring us all closer; Barry uses this same rhetoric when he talks about his wings. Why do paradigm-shifting technologies tend to fall short of their world-saving potential? What kinds of problems does The Sky Was Ours suggest technology is ill-equipped to solve—and what approaches might be better?

9. For all her flaws, Jane genuinely does want to be a force for positive change. Or maybe she just wants to feel like a hero or savior. What do you make of the desire to "help the world" when you encounter it in Jane, in others, or in yourself? What kind of help does the book suggest is genuinely valuable, and when might "helping" be counterproductive?

10. Barry's vision for flight is focused on the individual, with wings that allow people to abandon their lives for a solitary kingdom of wind and sky. And yet the characters in the book inevitably continue to depend on one another in various ways. To what extent is Barry's vision of the free, totally unconstrained individual unrealistic? To what extent are we all dependent on others, no matter what cultural or technological changes we witness in life?

11. Though Barry is far from a perfect character, he's right about one thing: humanity is in need of a radical intervention. We've known since the 1980s that continued rates of fossil fuel consumption would go on to threaten life on earth as we know it—a frightening reality that's become more vividly evident now. And yet, collectively, we haven't done enough to avert this fate. What, in your view, needs to happen to overcome this inertia? And what, in the end, should we do?